"And are you now?" Avery asked, her
light blond eyebrows furrowed.

"Am I what?"

"You know," she said, as if he held the key to some
mystery she didn't quite dare talk about. "Happy."

He stopped walking and turned to face her, thinking
in silence for a moment, lost in the blue-gray storm
clouds in her eyes.

"That's a complicated question, isn't it?"

"Not particularly," she challenged, a twinge of
sorrow in her voice.

"Well, then, perhaps it's the answer that's
complicated."

"Yes, maybe so, but I still want to know—are you
happy, Isaac Meyer?"

In her question, Isaac sensed she was really
asking something else—something along the
lines of, was it possible that she'd ever be happy
again?—and he wanted, badly, for her to believe
that, yes, she could be. Yes, despite everything that
had happened to her, despite all the evil he could
assume she'd witnessed, she could indeed find
happiness again.

Rescued Hearts

Amy Woods & Pamela Britton

Previously published as *An Officer and Her Gentleman*
and *His Rodeo Sweetheart*

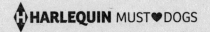

HARLEQUIN MUST♥DOGS

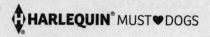

HARLEQUIN® MUST♥DOGS

ISBN-13: 978-1-335-00802-2

Recycling programs for this product may not exist in your area.

Rescued Hearts

Copyright © 2020 by Harlequin Books S.A.

An Officer and Her Gentleman
First published in 2016. This edition published in 2020.
Copyright © 2016 by Amy Woods

His Rodeo Sweetheart
First published in 2016. This edition published in 2020.
Copyright © 2016 by Pamela Britton

This edition published by arrangement with Harlequin Books S.A.

For questions and comments about the quality of this book, please contact us at CustomerService@Harlequin.com.

Harlequin Enterprises ULC
22 Adelaide St. West, 40th Floor
Toronto, Ontario M5H 4E3, Canada
www.Harlequin.com

Printed in U.S.A.

CONTENTS

Amy Woods took the scenic route to becoming an author. She's been a bookkeeper, a high school English teacher and a claims specialist, but now that she makes up stories for a living, she's never giving it up. She grew up in Austin, Texas, and lives there with her wonderfully goofy, supportive husband and a spoiled rescue dog. Amy can be reached on Facebook and Twitter.

Books by Amy Woods

Harlequin Special Edition

Peach Leaf, Texas

An Officer and Her Gentleman
His Pregnant Texas Sweetheart
Finding His Lone Star Love
His Texas Forever Family

Visit the Author Profile page
at Harlequin.com for more titles.

AN OFFICER
AND HER GENTLEMAN

Amy Woods

For Mason Dixon, US Navy, with love and respect. And to Renee Senn, LCSW, for her generous help with research. Any errors are mine.

Chapter 1

A blast rang out in the still night air, rattling windows and setting off the bark alarm of every canine within a mile radius.

In a small guest room of her younger brother's ranch-style home, Avery Abbott's eyes shot open as she was ripped suddenly from what had passed as sleep for the past few months—a shallow, daydream-like consciousness that really didn't qualify as true rest.

Pulse thumping against her temples, Avery kicked her legs free from tangled sheets and fumbled in the darkness for the baseball bat she kept nearby, cursing when her fingers didn't grasp it immediately. Her nerves had always been her biggest weakness during army basic training. Even the tiniest spark of fear or anxiety could transform her otherwise capable hands into jelly. The slightest hesitation or worry over a possible imperfection had the potential to eradicate months of training in an instant, leaving Avery, who was at the top of her class, one of only a handful of females in a company dominated by males, frozen and utterly useless. It hadn't happened often during her service, but the occasion it did stood out in her memory, far above her many accomplishments.

Seconds, Abbott—her sergeant's voice boomed through her brain as Avery finally gripped solid material and held it poised—*seconds mean the difference between the life and death of your comrades.*

As she made her way from her room into the hallway, through the house and out the front door into a thick darkness punctuated by only a thin sliver of light from the waning crescent moon, her nightmare blended seamlessly with reality.

Her brother's small farmhouse and the old red barn disappeared as Avery stalked the grounds, weapon firm and steady against her side, its material solid and reliable in her grip, searching for the source of the noise that had awoken her and threatened the safety of her fellow soldiers.

When the flashback gripped Avery, it was no longer cool, wheat-colored, late-autumn grass her bare feet plodded through, but the warm desert sand of a country in which she'd served three tours.

She wasn't safe at home in Peach Leaf, Texas, anymore, but a stranger in a foreign land, her vulnerability evident in every accented word she spoke, in her uniform, in the caution she knew flickered behind her eyes each time she faced a potential enemy.

She would be okay, she thought, pacing the too-quiet darkness, so long as she didn't run into any kids.

The women and children were the worst part of combat. You never knew whose thumb they were under, who controlled their futures…who'd robbed them of their innocence, threatened their families if met with anything but obedience, and turned them into soldiers to be sacrificed without a choice.

Regardless of where their loyalties were planted, they were children… It didn't make sense to hold them responsible for their misguided actions.

Avery wanted to bring the many homeless ones back with her when she returned to the US. She had something in common with them. She knew what it was like to be an orphan, to feel alone in the world, unprotected.

Once, before she'd been adopted by a loving couple, the birth parents of her brother, Tommy, Avery, too, had known firsthand what it was to be without a family.

But that was a long time ago, and now she needed to focus on the threat at hand. Still holding her weapon, she used her forearm to brush a strand of long blond hair out of her eyes. When she'd tumbled from bed, she hadn't time to twist her hair into its customary bun. There was only room in her brain for one objective: locate and—if necessary—eradicate the cause of the blast.

She paced silently through the muggy night air, the blanket of darkness hiding any detail so that all she could see were the shapes of unfamiliar objects.

In her mind, it was her first week in Afghanistan, and she was afraid.

Despite extensive predeployment training, nothing could have prepared her for what it would feel like to be hunted. She knew she shouldn't be outside of her bunker alone, but evidently no one else had heard the explosion, and for all she knew her team could be in danger at that very moment.

So First Lieutenant Avery Abbott pressed on through the black night, searching, searching, searching.

Isaac Meyer was humming along to the local country music station when a rear tire blew out just a quarter mile away from home, causing his truck to skid into a ditch on the side of the road.

Only seconds passed before he got it under control and pulled to a stop, but they felt like hours.

"You okay, girl?" he asked his backseat passenger, still trying to deep breathe his way back to a normal heart rate. His palms were shaking and slick with sweat despite feeling like ice, and his brain was still too rattled to discern whether or not he was okay. But he needed to know if his best friend was all right before he made a single move.

He turned and still couldn't see her. Then Jane gave an uncharacteristically high-pitched *woof* from the seat directly behind him, letting Isaac know she was startled, but the absence of any cries of pain settled his stomach a little, and a second later her sandpaper tongue swept along his elbow.

Isaac heaved a sigh of relief and unbuckled his seat belt before getting out of the truck to check on his companion.

As soon as he moved up his seat to let her out, Jane bounded straight into his arms and both dog and human crashed to the ground in a heap.

"I'm so sorry, sweetheart," Isaac said, stroking Janie's coat and feeling her limbs and ribs for any injuries. "I sure am glad you're not hurt."

His statement was conservative. They were *damn lucky* to be okay. After all, it was pitch dark on the gravel country road to his ranch house; even with his bright headlights on, they could have hit just about anything swerving into that ditch. Not to mention they'd have to walk home now, and Isaac was bone tired after a long day on his feet at work. All he wanted was a cold beer and his bed. He could only imagine that Jane, who'd worked just as hard as he had training a new puppy for a recently returned veteran, felt the same.

"All right, girl," Isaac said, attaching Jane's leash to her collar. "Let me just grab my stuff from the truck and we'll head home the old-fashioned way."

He'd only gotten as far as reaching into the cab before Jane erupted into a low growl, followed by loud, staccato warning barks.

A tingle of apprehension fluttered up Isaac's spine and the tiny hairs on the back of his neck stood at attention.

Jane wasn't the sort to cry wolf; she wouldn't give a warning unless she'd seen, heard or smelled something beyond the range of Isaac's senses.

"What is it, girl?" he whispered, turning to peer into the curtain of trees on the other side of the ditch while reaching under the driver's seat of his truck for the hunting knife he kept there. Jane would have to be his eyes and ears. He couldn't see squat with everything obscured by the thick darkness.

The dog let out another growl and raised her hackles.

Finally, Isaac caught sight of something moving in the blackness. He squinted, trying to see a little better, as a shadowy form emerged from along the tree line. His instinct was to simply shout out a greeting. This was Peach Leaf, after all. The idea of a prowler out on the lonely ranch road leading to his home was almost laughable. But until he got a better look at whatever or whoever was traipsing through the night, he'd be wise to assume the worst.

Suddenly, the figure—almost certainly human, he could now tell—crouched down low and crawled quickly toward the ditch. Jane barked furiously at this new development and tugged at her leash to be set free so she could investigate. But a threat to Isaac was a threat to her, so he called her to his side and patted the truck seat. Jane gave a whimper of protest but obeyed, jumping up into the cab. Isaac quickly rolled down the window an inch and locked the door, pocketing his keys and knife.

He expected more movement from the ditch, but all remained still. Part of him knew it wasn't too bright to follow up on whatever or whomever lay there in the dirt, but he didn't have much of a choice. If he and Jane headed off down the road toward home, whatever it was might follow, and he'd rather deal with it now than have to look over his shoulder on his way back to the house or potentially deal with a break-in later in the night. On the other hand, it could be some runaway kid, lost or potentially hurt, and he wouldn't be able to sleep wondering if he might have been able to help one of his community members.

He realized he'd been standing still while he thought this through, but that settled it, so he grabbed his cell phone from his back pocket and turned on the flashlight app. The low-battery warning flashed across the screen a second later and Isaac cursed under his breath.

He told Jane he'd be right back and climbed up out

of their place in the ditch so he could walk along the edge. That way, he'd have the upper hand once he made it to wherever *it* was, and if Jane started barking again, he could run right back to the truck.

He stepped slowly, holding the light out in front of him until he spotted a dark lump, stopping abruptly to get a better look.

"What the—" he murmured, powerless to make sense of what he saw until it moved, which didn't help at all as things only became less clear.

The *thing* was a woman, Isaac realized.

For a full minute, he simply stood there, unable to pick up his suddenly leaden feet. His heart might have kicked up its pace again at the sight of her, if it hadn't already tumbled down into his stomach.

Being the youngest child, and still single, despite the town's many ill-advised attempts to remedy that situation, Isaac had never had anyone to protect. He had Jane, of course, but the spitfire dog who'd landed on his doorstep a few years back, demanding a home, had always done a damn good job of looking out for herself—and now she lived in the lap of luxury, spoiled beyond belief by her human.

But he'd never really experienced that protective instinct, had never known the feeling that another person relied on him for safety.

Until now.

For some reason—as he stared down into that ditch at the pathetically thin, shaking woman curled into a ball there—a fierce burning sensation flooded his insides.

He didn't know who she was, or what in the hell she

was doing there, but somehow something outside of him pulled Isaac toward her.

Somehow, he knew she needed him.

When the flashback subsided and Avery finally came to, she had no earthly idea where she was.

This wasn't the first time it had happened.

It wouldn't be the last.

She closed her eyes and pulled in a deep breath, but, as usual, the terrible shaking wouldn't cease. The air around her was humid, and a warm spring breeze rustled through some nearby trees every now and then, but inside Avery was freezing, even as sweat rolled down her arms.

Too-skinny arms, Tommy would say. She was thankful every day that he'd let her live in his house when things had become…too much…but sometimes his constant concern for her—the endless checking up to see if she was okay—was another kind of too much.

"Ma'am?"

The male voice came from somewhere above her head and, within seconds, Avery had uncurled from her position and bolted upright to face its owner.

The last time she'd had an episode, her sister-in-law, Macy, had found Avery in Sylvia's room. That was plenty awkward, especially when the two women had to work out how to explain to Avery's five-year-old niece why her aunt was crouched, armed, in the child's bedroom closet.

That was when her brother insisted they clear the house of anything "dangerous" she might end up wielding in self-defense when one of the flashbacks hit. He didn't know about the baseball bat she kept hidden under her bed in case she needed to protect her family.

"It's not that we don't trust you," Tommy had said in the same sotto voce he used with his children, while refusing to meet her eyes. "We just can't risk anything happening. It's for the best."

Avery's stomach churned at the memory. The worst part was, her brother was absolutely correct. If she'd had anywhere else to go after that, she would have. But she did not. And, worse, she was completely dependent on the few remaining people in her life—the few that hadn't given up on her—for everything.

But that was the last time.

This time, from what little she could deduce in a quick survey of her surroundings, might just turn out to be downright humiliating.

He spoke again. "Is there anything I can do to help you?" he asked. "Are you lost?"

Avery almost grinned at that last part, because yes, indeed, she was very, very lost.

The only thing that stopped her was the tone of the man's voice. Glancing around, she could see that she was completely alone in some dirt hole on the side of a gravel country road, in—she looked down at her body—a thin white tank and army-issue workout shorts. Clearly she was at the mercy of this guy, who'd evidently stopped to check on her. Under other circumstances, her training would have kicked in and she'd have flipped him onto his back in mere seconds.

But something told her he wasn't a threat.

His voice.

It was deep and smooth, his words bathed in the local accent, and full of genuine concern. On top of that, he stood above the ditch staring down at her, hands at his sides, and hadn't made a single move to come closer. The man seemed...*safe*.

Having lost her bat somewhere along the way, she braced herself for an attack when he bent his knees, but instead of jumping into the ditch with her like she thought he might, the man simply knelt down.

The movement brought attention to long, muscled thighs beneath faded denim jeans, and when he leaned an elbow on his upright knee, Avery noticed the stretch of tendons in his sinewy forearms.

How ridiculous it was, she thought, for her to notice such a stupid thing when her life could be in danger for all she knew. Seeing as how the guy hadn't mauled her by now, it probably wasn't, but still—it could be.

Avery crossed her arms over her thinly clad chest. Not that there was much to see there. Not anymore.

"I'm fine, actually. Just...taking a walk. Enjoying the stars and all." She waved a hand above her, indicating the spread of twinkling lights above them. It was plausible.

But when she looked up into his eyes, she could tell he didn't agree. The man looked to be somewhere near her own age, maybe slightly older, and Avery was surprised she'd never seen him before. She'd grown up in Peach Leaf and knew just about everybody, so it was strange that she hadn't met this person.

Sure as hell would remember if she had.

Not only did he have the toned body of someone who either worked at it or had a very active job—he had a face to do it justice. Clear, dark chocolate eyes—eyes that had a certain glint in them, as though they saw more than most—a strong jaw and hair the color of a panther's coat.

Right now those brown eyes narrowed with what appeared to be strong suspicion, but after a few seconds, they filled with a certain kind of warmth Avery wasn't used to seeing anymore.

Pity—she was used to that—but not warmth.

"It is a beautiful night, isn't it?" he said, seeming to relax a little.

There was something easy about him that made Avery want to let her guard down a smidge. It was almost as if his mere presence lowered her blood pressure.

"That it is," she agreed, wanting the strange exchange to be over so she could figure out how far she'd gotten and how, for the love of all things holy, she was supposed to get back home.

"Name's Isaac," the man said, stretching out a large hand.

Even in the dark, Avery could see calluses and healed-over scratches. Must be some kind of laborer.

She just stared at him, not offering her name, willing him to take his leave. It would be futile to try to explain the complexities of her *condition*, as she'd come to think of it, to this handsome stranger. She didn't even completely understand it herself, even after almost a year of therapy. Besides, her knees were beginning to feel a little wobbly and a spot just above her left temple had started to ache…

"Well, if you're all set here—" he looked like he believed her to be anything but "—I've got a walk ahead of me."

Isaac hesitated for a long moment, then nodded and turned to leave.

Avery was about to do the same when everything went blacker than the night sky.

Isaac had just started back toward his truck—every nerve in his body telling him to stay behind—when he heard a thud.

He whipped back around and broke into a run when he saw that the woman had collapsed in a heap, dust billowing around her.

Crap.

He knew he should have stayed put and tried to talk her into letting him help. It didn't take a genius to see she was in some kind of trouble.

Walking even a few yards away from her had gone against his every instinct, but he hadn't planned to actually leave her alone in the middle of the night, not for a single moment. He just needed a second to regroup.

His legs made quick work of the distance that separated them and seconds later he plunged into the ditch and reached her side, lifting the woman's negligible weight into his arms and propping her up so she might draw in deeper breaths. Her skin was clammy and she seemed to flutter on the verge of consciousness as she pulled in shallow doses of air.

Isaac had no idea what steps to take from there; as a certified dog trainer, he was generally better prepared for canine emergencies than those of his own species. His heart beat frantically for several long minutes as he held her, waiting for her to come back so he could better help her. As slow seconds beat past, he studied the woman in his grasp, seeing for the first time how lovely she was.

Her long blond hair seemed to shimmer in the moonlight, its corn-silk strands tickling his arms where it fell. Creamy skin, just a shade or two lighter than her hair, lay like soft linen over sculpted cheekbones, creating a perfect canvas for full lips and large eyes, the color of which he suddenly longed to know.

She wore a white T-shirt and athletic shorts, and Isaac grimaced when he caught sight of the sharp ridge of collarbone peeking out the top of the threadbare cotton. She was so very thin. No wonder lifting her had felt no more difficult than picking up Jane. A glint of metal got his attention and he reached up to search for a pendant attached to a silver chain around her neck, adjusting her so he could remain supporting her with one arm.

Running his finger along the tiny links, Isaac finally touched an ID tag of some sort and pulled it closer to his face.

It was an army-issue dog tag; he'd recognize it anywhere because of his brother, Stephen, and working with so many veterans and their companions at his dog training facility. This one was engraved *A. Abbott*.

Somehow seeing her name made him even more impatient to wake her up. He knew nothing about the pretty woman, except that she looked like she could stand to eat a quarter pounder or two, but something about her pulled him in and wouldn't let go.

His buddies would've teased him relentlessly if they could have seen him then. *Meyer can't resist a damsel in distress*, he could almost hear them say, joshing at his tendency to offer assistance to every granny who chanced to cross a street in Peach Leaf or any single mom who needed the use of his truck for a move.

But this one was different.

Before she'd tumbled to the ground, Isaac had seen

enough to know that Abbott was no damsel in distress. Her voice had been tough—commanding, almost—and, despite her smallness, she'd stood tall and carried herself with authority and confidence. It was her body that had finally lost its resolve—no doubt, from the look of things, due to not eating enough—not her mind or her survival instinct.

Now that he'd seen the tag, he understood why.

Now that he'd seen the tag, he'd also begun to form an idea of what might have happened to her and, more important, how he might be able to help.

Chapter 2

Avery woke for the second time that night about an hour later.

For a moment, forgetting the strange dreamlike events of the night, she thought she might be back at home safe in her bed while Tommy and Macy cooked breakfast for her niece and nephew.

But when Avery sat up and opened her eyes, a rush of panic hit her like a bucket of ice water and she shot up from an unfamiliar couch, gasping for breath as she fully realized that she had no idea where she was.

Again.

A hand-knit afghan in alternating tones of light and dark blues tumbled to the floor, covering her feet, and as her eyes adjusted to the golden light coming from a nearby table lamp, Avery glanced briefly around the room. It was minimally decorated but cozy, and she wondered at the comfort it provided despite its newness to her.

"Easy there," a low voice came from behind the sofa and she nearly jumped out of her skin.

Avery put up her fists and turned around in one quick motion, ready to face whatever situation her unpredictable, unreliable mind had gotten her into now.

"Who are you, and where the hell am I?" she spat out, willing her voice to mask the fear that was quickly weaving its way from her gut to her chest.

The nightmares were bad enough, but the flashbacks, rarer though they were, absolutely terrified her. This wasn't the first time she'd found herself in a place from which she couldn't retrace her steps. If it happened on too many more occasions, she didn't even want to think about the action her family and therapist might agree on against her will. She'd already lost her job and her own place. The thought of being locked up somewhere…

The man in front of her gently placed the cell phone he'd been holding on a small end table, immediately holding up both of his hands. She vaguely recalled his handsome face as a tiny slice of memory slipped from the recesses of her mind, but it vanished before she could catch it, leaving her with nothing helpful.

"My name's Isaac. Isaac Meyer. I'm not gonna hurt you. And obviously you don't remember—you were pretty out of it—but we did meet earlier." A Southern accent similar to her own slid over the man's words like hot gravy, identifying him as a local.

"Avery," she murmured.

He stood completely still as Avery looked him up and down, her soldier's instincts and peripheral vision checking every inch of his person, even as her eyes remained steadily locked on to his. They were a rich brown, she noticed, instantly chastising herself for wasting time on such a silly thought when she faced a potential enemy.

When Avery didn't speak for a long moment, he continued.

"Look, I know this has been a strange night, at least for me, but—" He hesitated and seemed to be working through his thoughts before speaking. "I found you on the side of the road. In a ditch. Jane and I didn't know what to do and there wasn't a damn thing could be done to help you out there in the dark, so we brought you back here."

He lowered one hand, slowly and cautiously as if trying not to unsettle a rabid animal, and pointed toward the phone before putting his hand back up. "I was just about to call 9-1-1 and see about getting someone out here to check on you. Then you woke up and, well, here we are."

Avery had no recollection of meeting him earlier, only his word to go on and the vague, déjà vu–like inkling that she'd seen him before. The past few hours were as blank as a fresh sheet of paper. In all he'd said, only one insignificant thing stuck out to her. That seemed the way of it lately. If she couldn't focus on everything, she picked out the smallest bit and used that to ground her in reality. It was one of the few things her therapist had taught her that she'd actually practiced.

"Jane? Who's Jane?" she asked, wondering, of all things, why that particular piece of information mattered.

At the mention of the name, Isaac's features noticeably softened and Avery let her body do likewise, relaxing a little as she checked off facts in her head. One—if he'd a mind to, he could have murdered her already. Two—the man had placed a homemade blanket on her, for goodness' sake. What murderer did such a thing? And three—if he was to be believed, and there was no clear indication why he shouldn't at this point, as she was standing there unharmed in his comfortable home, he'd been about to call for help, something she absolutely did *not* want him to do. Thank goodness she'd woken up in time to prevent that from happening. The very last thing she needed right now was for Tommy or her parents to have another reason to worry about her. Of all the things she hated about her PTSD, perhaps the worst was the way it had turned a grown, successful woman into a child, or at least that's how her family saw her.

She had to get back home as soon as possible, but first, she needed to find out exactly how far her deceitful mind had dragged her this time.

She waited for an answer to her question but instead of providing one, Isaac gave a sharp whistle and a large dog of an unidentifiable breed, with an unruly coat consisting of about a hundred varying shades of brown, strolled into the room to sit beside him, looking up at its human with what could only be described as pure adoration. Man looked down at dog with open pride.

"Avery, meet Jane," he said, then gave the canine some sort of hand signal.

Before she could protest, the dog was standing in front of her. She watched, unmoving, as Jane reached out a large, fuzzy paw and stared expectantly up at her with huge brown eyes. The whole thing was so absurdly cute that Avery couldn't keep a smile from curving at the edge of her lips. Noticing for the first time that she still held her fists defensively in front of her, Avery lowered both hands and reached one out to grasp the offered paw. The warm, soft fur was instantly soothing, but when Jane took back her paw and pressed her large, heavy head against Avery's thighs, her tail breaking into a slow wag as she waited for her doggie hug to be reciprocated, Avery's heart caught in her throat.

A wave of emotion swept over her like an evening tide and her knees nearly buckled beneath her. She was suddenly, desperately sad. And oh-so-tired. Tired of being dependent on others to keep her safe when she'd once been so self-reliant. Tired of being locked inside her own head. Tired of being afraid to go to sleep, knowing the nightmares would meet her there like a mugger waiting in the shade of night for his next victim, and tired of feeling crazy when she knew—even if everyone else believed otherwise—that she was not.

She gently pushed the dog away and sat down on the sofa. Jane jumped up, too, but sat a few feet away, as if giving Avery her space. Isaac moved across the room to sit in a chair on the other side of a mahogany coffee table. He folded his hands in his lap and looked at the floor. Avery knew she should keep an eye on him until she could get out of there but her lids felt weighted and she let them slip closed for just a second as she gathered her thoughts.

"How long was I out?" she asked, swallowing, not really wanting to know the answer. Her flashbacks, blackouts, whatever the hell they were, sometimes lasted for hours before she came back around. She hated the loss of control and the resulting feeling of irresponsibility, as though she'd had too much to drink and passed out at the wheel.

She looked up at Isaac, meeting his eyes. In them, she found none of the things she'd expected: pity, irritation, confusion. Instead, they were like deep woods in the middle of the night—quiet, dark, mysterious—but for some reason, she felt safe there. She knew enough to sense menace when it lurked, and so she knew then as sure as she knew her own name and rank that this man was not dangerous.

"About an hour," he said, his voice smooth like strong coffee. "Took me half of that to get you here. My truck broke down just up the road and my cell had almost no charge left. You were pretty cold when Jane and I got you inside the house, so I covered you with a blanket and plugged in the phone for ten minutes or so. You didn't seem wounded or anything, but it's not every day I find people prowling around in the dark, so I figured best thing to do was call the authorities and let them make sure you're okay and sort you out."

Isaac paused, brow furrowed, and it seemed he might say more, but then he closed his mouth and looked at her expectantly.

She sifted through his comments, appreciating his effort and the fact that, other than to carry her, he hadn't handled her any more than necessary; in fact, he seemed wary of being anywhere near her—a thought that touched her heart with the gentlemanliness it bespoke. His simple, strong kindness reminded her of some of the men she'd served alongside, and for a fleeting moment, she missed her comrades.

There had been a time, not that long after returning home, when she would have done anything to forget her tours overseas if it would have helped her blend back in to civilian society. But after being back in Peach Leaf for a few months, newly burdened with the knowledge that such a wish might never come true, she'd begun to long for another deployment, if only for the fact that she didn't know how to be "normal" anymore, whatever that meant. She didn't belong in her own world, and she hadn't truly belonged in that barren, violence-riddled land, so the question was, as always: Where, if anywhere, did she belong?

"You could have left me there, you know," Avery said. "I didn't need any help." The words sounded hollow and impractical even as she spoke them.

"We both know that's not true," he answered, his tone thankfully free of judgment.

She didn't want to have to explain herself to a complete stranger. Even a kind, gentle, admittedly handsome stranger.

"All the same, though," he continued, "I don't think it's safe for you to walk home on your own and, as I said, my truck's out of commission for the night. Is there anyone you can call to—"

"No!" she shouted as her body simultaneously lurched forward a few feet, startling them both. She covered her mouth with her hand, the skin icy against her warm lips.

"Look, if you're in some kind of dicey situation, it ain't any of my business, but I can't let you stay out here alone in the dark, either.

She shook her head and lowered her hand, clasping it between her knees. "No, no, it's not like that. I'm not… I mean… I just have these episodes sometimes, and occasionally I lose track of where I am." She stopped abruptly, not really knowing what else to say but thankfully, he didn't seem to expect much more. Trying to put her problems into words was always a fragile balancing act of saying too little or too much. Even though they appreciated her service, she'd quickly discovered that most people would rather not think or talk about the things that Avery had experienced, and it was hard to describe something she herself didn't fully understand.

Isaac swallowed and held out his hands, palms up. His face was difficult to read but not hardened, and his expression gave her the idea that he was genuinely waiting to hear what she had to say, who she was, before making his mind up about her. It was refreshing. In her small town, Avery was used to people thinking they knew everything about each other just because they'd racked up some years together in the same place. They made the frequent mistake of assuming that you'd always be who you once were.

"Speaking of," she went on, struggling to hide her sudden embarrassment at having to ask, "would you mind telling me where we are?"

Isaac's lids lowered and his mouth relaxed into an easy grin, as if he'd been waiting for her to ask so he could have something helpful to offer. "Sure thing. We're about two miles outside of Peach Leaf proper, and my house is about half a mile from Ranch Road 64. Closest landmark is Dewberry Farms, my neighbor."

His neighbor. Her brother.

Avery released an audible sigh of relief that she hadn't wandered too far from home in her—she looked down, suddenly aware of the goose bumps that had formed a tiny mountain range along her arms—*very* thin pajamas. Thank goodness she'd been unable to shed the habit of sleeping in her sports bra or she'd have been sitting in a stranger's living room without a shred of modesty.

"Dewberry is my home, at least for now," she said, and Isaac nodded, seeming unsurprised. He probably knew her recent history as well as any of the other locals. It said a lot about his character that he wasn't acting as though that meant he knew *her*.

"Well, as you know, it's not far from here. I think I feel well enough to walk back now. If I don't make it home before everyone wakes up, they'll be worried, so—" she pointed a thumb in the general direction of the front door "—I should probably get going."

Isaac held out a hand as she stood. "I don't think that's such a good idea."

"Why not?" She rolled her eyes almost immediately, sitting back down as the inside of her head did another dizzy spin. "I mean, I know why not, but how is it any of your business? I appreciate you helping me, but I'm okay now."

Isaac shook his head. "For one thing, you're pale as a ghost, and let's not forget you were passed out for a solid hour. Plus, pardon my saying so, but you look like you could use some energy if you're going to walk a half mile, which, for the record, I'd recommend putting off until the sun comes up."

Avery bit her lip, considering. Everything he said was absolutely right, but she couldn't risk letting Tommy or Macy find her bed empty again. She wouldn't put them through that worry another time.

Her brother and sister-in-law had already given her a place to stay and a hell of a lot of support through the lowest point in her life so far, for which she'd never be able to repay them. They said they were glad to do it and they meant well, but Avery wasn't naive, and she wasn't blind; she could see the way they looked at her when they insisted she was no imposition, as if they weren't sure what she might do next, or worse, how her involuntary actions might affect their kids. She could see the way they walked on eggshells around her. The familiar guilt made her empty stomach clench in pain.

She sat back down on the sofa and Jane thumped her tail against the worn fabric. Avery reached over to pet the dog's soft fur, surprised once again at how comforting it was just to stroke Jane's broad back. When she gave Jane a few scratches behind her enormous, fuzzy ears and the scruffy mutt closed her eyes in bliss, Avery was pretty sure she'd made a friend for life.

"It makes me feel so calm, petting her." Avery was surprised to hear herself state the thought out loud, but the combination of the kind stranger's presence and the silky sensation of the dog's warm coat made her feel more at ease than she had since she'd been home.

"She tends to have that effect on people. Lots of dogs do," he said.

Avery looked up to find Isaac beaming with pride, and she noticed again how good-looking he was, in such a different way than the men she'd been attracted to before. His features were less sharp than the square-jawed, light-featured military types she usually preferred. His hair was collar length, wavy and dark, almost black, in the soft glow of lamplight flooding the living room, and his eyes were nearly the same shade of brown. He reminded her of a rakish lord from one of the historical romances she devoured at an incredible pace, one of the few pastimes that allowed her to completely escape the bleak hollows of her own thoughts.

It wouldn't be inaccurate to describe him as *devilishly handsome*, she thought, a smile blossoming over her lips before she caught herself and bit the bottom one.

He caught her smiling and she pretended to study Jane's fur, the heat of a blush rushing to her cheeks. She couldn't remember the last time she'd felt drawn to someone that way, much less *blushed* over a man, for goodness' sake. She'd had a few boyfriends before her first deployment, but it always seemed sort of futile to get into something serious when she'd been on active duty, never knowing when she might have to pack up and leave at last-minute notice. Sure, lots of people made it work, as her mother constantly reminded her, probably with visions of more grandbabies dancing through her head, but Avery had seen enough hurt in that area to last a lifetime.

She swallowed against the dull ache that rose in her heart every time the memory of her best friend crossed her mind, at least a thousand times per day—her punishment for being alive when Sophie was not. Sophie, who'd left behind a husband and child who blamed Avery for Sophie's absence in their lives. It didn't matter whether it had been Avery's fault or not—the center of their world was gone, and Avery had been the last one to see her.

It was Avery who'd promised them she'd watch over their wife and mother, and it was Avery who failed to keep that promise.

She felt Isaac's eyes on her and looked up to meet them.

"You're right about it not being a good idea to walk

back in the dark," she admitted. "If it's not too much trouble, I'd like to stick around until the sun comes up, then I'll head back that way."

If Isaac's house was as close to Tommy's as he'd said, it would take her less than ten minutes to jog back at daybreak, and she could slip in the back door and make it into her bed before anyone tried to wake her. Tommy would be making coffee and Macy would be busy with the kids.

He nodded. "Not a problem. If you passed Jane's character test, then you're welcome to stick around as long as you need to," he said, his tone lighter now. "On one condition."

Avery stopped petting Jane and raised an eyebrow in question.

"Let me cook something for you."

Chapter 3

As he waited for her answer, Isaac glanced at the grandfather clock near the hallway, one of the many things he'd been unable to part with when Nana had willed the old ranch-style home to him a couple of years ago. Its iron hands indicated the hour was near two o'clock in the morning.

They had plenty of time for a bite before daylight when Avery would leave and go back to Dewberry—a thought that, had he more time to entertain, he might have admitted he didn't much care for. He liked the quiet comfort and surrounding memories of the house he'd spent so many happy summers in as a child, and most of the time he was okay with the fact that he lived in the country and didn't entertain a lot of visitors, but there were times when he got lonely. Even though Jane was one hell of a listener, she didn't do much in the way of talking.

It was nice to have a woman in his home. He liked the way Avery's presence added a certain softness to the atmosphere, and he found himself caring whether or not she liked the place.

"I'm not really very hungry," she answered, earning a pointed look from him.

"Come on, now. I'm a very good cook. I'm famous for my barbecue, but I can make a mean sandwich in a pinch. Seriously, call your brother and ask him," Isaac joked, regretting the words when he saw they'd caused her to wince. Tommy had mentioned, of course, that he had a sister who'd recently come home after a few tours in Afghanistan, but since they'd never been introduced or run into each other anywhere in town—which was odd in itself—Isaac hadn't given much thought to the mysterious female Abbott. He and Tommy crossed paths frequently, as the farm always provided food for the events Isaac hosted on behalf of his dog training center, Friends with Fur, but he'd never once seen Avery.

He wouldn't have forgotten her if he had.

The locals talked about her enough; they all had theories about how she might be doing now that she was back, what kind of girl she'd been growing up and—these comments were always in hushed tones accented with the sympathetic clicking of tongues—how she wasn't quite *right* anymore, *bless her heart*. But in Isaac's line of work, he'd learned to withhold judgment until he got to know someone.

And he knew that when broken people kept to themselves, holed up behind walls built to keep out hurt, eventually their family and friends, even the closest ones, stopped asking the hard questions and accepted the new, hollow versions, forgetting that at one time those wounded people were whole.

He got up from his chair and moved toward the couch to scratch Janie's pink tummy, which she'd shamelessly turned over and exposed so that Avery could have the esteemed privilege of rubbing it.

He raised his eyes and watched as Avery pet Jane, admiring the way the dog's gentle serenity seemed to seep into the woman's weary bones.

"Tell you what—I had a long day and I'm hungry, so I'm going to start up a grilled cheese sandwich." He watched Avery for any change in her expression, but her features remained still. "You're welcome to join me if you want to, and I'd be happy to make two."

She raised her eyes then and he was reminded of how blue they were, like shadowy mountaintops at dusk.

"I wasn't always like this, you know," Avery said, her voice so quiet he wasn't sure the words were meant for him to hear.

Even though her gaze was on his, Isaac could tell her thoughts were far off somewhere he couldn't reach. He'd seen the same look on many of the veterans he worked with at the training facility, and he'd learned not to push too hard. Sometimes it was best to stay silent and let the person decide how much he or she wanted to say or not say.

"I used to be strong. Independent." She glanced away. "I can't tell you how humiliating it is to be sitting here in your house, having to trust your word on how I got here."

Isaac's insides ached at her admission and he had the sudden urge to reach out and hold her hand. He wouldn't, but he wanted to.

He'd always had an easier time relating to canines than to his own kind, a product of being homeschooled by a widowed young mom who'd been overwhelmed by the world outside their door, with only his older brother and a series of family pets to keep him company. He would never complain about his childhood. After all, it had been safer and saner than many of his friends' and colleagues', but it had also been lonely.

Ever since he'd moved away briefly for college and then come home to start a business, Isaac had longed for a family of his own. He wanted life to be much different from the way he'd been raised; he wanted kiddos running around shouting happily, dogs barking joyfully and, above all, lots and lots of laughter.

Most people wanted quiet when they came home at the end of a long workday, he thought with a chuckle, but Isaac craved noise.

He wasn't sure what he could say, but he gave it a try anyway. "I know I don't know you, so my saying so doesn't mean much, but you have nothing to be embarrassed by."

He looked up in time to see Avery shaking her head, but he went on, sharing things he rarely got a chance to. "You served your country with honor, and I can bet you dealt with a lot of things no one should ever have to, but that doesn't mean you're different than any other human being. People aren't meant to be around the things I'm sure you were, and come out the same on the other side. War is bound to do some damage to a person's soul. I don't think anyone expects you to come back and pick up where you left off without a few hurdles to jump."

Avery closed her eyes and then opened them slowly, regarding him with an expression he couldn't read.

"Sometimes it feels like that's exactly what they expect."

"Well, they shouldn't," he responded. "And I think that's just a product of not really being able to understand what you went through over there."

Not wanting to say anything that would make Avery uncomfortable, that would make her retreat back into her shell, Isaac gave Jane one final pat and then headed off to the kitchen.

He'd pulled cheese and butter out of the fridge and was opening a wooden bread box when he heard her soft footsteps behind him. He tossed a welcome grin over his shoulder, pleased when he noticed that she wasn't alone. Jane, his big, goofy sweetheart, had followed Avery and was glued to her side. It was one of the characteristics he loved most about dogs. They were quick to make friends.

"How are you so wise about this stuff?" Avery asked, giving him a sad little smile. "Did you serve, as well?"

He shook his head. "No, but in my work, I meet a lot of people who did, and I've learned a few things along the way." He bit back the urge to mention the brother he'd lost; talking about what happened to Stephen would likely be unhelpful at that particular moment.

Her eyes, huge and dark blue in a small, lovely, heart-shaped face, were full of questions and she seemed almost eager, for the first time that evening, to talk with him.

"What kind of work do you do?" she asked, not meeting his eyes as she ran a finger along the glossy edge of the oak table in the adjoining breakfast nook.

"I own a dog-training facility. I opened it a couple of years ago and I have a few assistants now, other trainers. We do all kinds of work—basic obedience, scent, search and rescue—but my most recent project is working with veterans."

"Do you mind if I ask, I mean, how well does that usually work? The vet-and-dog combination?"

Out of the corner of his eye, he watched her sit down at the table and he began cutting squares of cheese off a block of cheddar.

Isaac gave a rough little laugh. "You're not the only one who wants to know that," he said. A lot of people—influential people—wondered the same thing, and soon Isaac hoped to have a way of answering that with his own research, so that he could raise the necessary funding to expand his project. A project that, thanks to great dogs and veterans willing to work hard to overcome their pain, had already changed several lives for the better. He enjoyed all kinds of training, but this particular sort had become his passion over the past couple of years.

"Quite well, actually."

Avery's forehead wrinkled in curiosity, which he took as an invitation to keep talking. Normally, he was a pretty quiet guy, even a little on the shy side, one might say, but when it came to his career, he could go on all day.

"Service animals make some of the best companions to soldiers who've returned from war carrying more than physical baggage. With the right training, they can be a huge asset to people dealing with past trauma or symptoms of PTSD, and they can be even better than medication at calming soldiers in the midst of panic attacks, or…even flashbacks."

He wasn't going to put a label on what had happened with Avery that night. He wasn't a doctor and he didn't have all the details, but his gut told him that's what had occurred to her prior to him stumbling upon her in that ditch.

"Sorry if I sound like a public service announcement. I just care a lot about this stuff. It's affected a lot of people I care about."

Her shoulders let go of some of their tension as he spoke, and there was even a hint of hope in her eyes as he explained the process of rescuing dogs from the local shelter and giving them homes, purpose and new, full lives.

"So basically you're saving two people at once," she said, her eyes brighter than they had been since he'd met her. "Or, well, one person and one dog—you know what I meant," she said, her cheeks turning a pretty, soft pink.

He bent to pull a skillet from a low cabinet, partly so he could warm up a pat of butter and start the sandwich, and partly so she wouldn't see the way her sweet expression had affected him.

He didn't mind helping her out—any decent guy would have done the same—and he was glad to let her stay awhile until the sun came up. He was even happy to make her a much-needed meal. He told himself it was harmless to feel attracted to a too-thin but still gorgeous woman he'd happened upon by some stroke of fate, but what he could not allow was for that attraction to go any further.

From the looks of things, Avery Abbott needed a lot of help, some of which he might even be able to offer, but it was highly unlikely she was looking for a relationship. Not with what she was obviously going through right now.

And Isaac, truth be told, very much wanted one.

He lit the stove and waited for it to heat, finally placing the butter in to melt.

"I haven't saved anyone," he said. "They save each other."

While the butter changed from solid to a sizzling little pool, he put cheese between bread slices and arranged two plates to hold the finished food. Once he'd set the first sandwich in the pan, he chanced another look at her, surprised to see unshed tears shimmering in Avery's eyes. She rubbed at her lids and he looked away, kicking himself for saying something that might have added any more pain to her already awful night. He wanted to apologize, but wasn't sure what to say; words had never been his strong suit. He much preferred movement and action, but those weren't always what were required.

Five minutes later, he plated the sandwiches and brought them, along with two glasses of water, over to the table to join Avery, who smiled up at him as he sat, all traces of moisture gone from those sapphire eyes.

"Thank you for this," she said softly, "and for everything. I owe you one."

"You don't owe me anything," he said. "What was I supposed to do, leave you out there alone on the side of the road? What kind of man would that make me?" He winked and picked up his sandwich.

That coaxed a little grin out of her, which gave him more satisfaction than it should have.

"I have to say, Mr. Meyer, you do seem like a stand-up guy. Do you make a habit of rescuing lost women in the middle of the night?" she asked, and he had the distinct feeling she was flirting with him a little.

Something fluttered in his belly, and he didn't think it was hunger.

"I haven't before," he answered, "but after tonight, who knows? Maybe I will."

Avery laughed so hard at that cheesiness that the sip of water she'd just taken almost came out of her nose. Within minutes, they were both laughing like idiots, at what he really couldn't say.

But it felt good.

After the weirdest night of his life, and after the too-strong sense of relief he now felt seeing that this woman, this soldier, could still laugh despite the things life had thrown her way, it felt good to join her in a moment of ridiculousness. It was almost as if something in his heart had come unknotted.

Even though he knew it was completely irrational, he realized suddenly, with as much certainty and force as one might realize it's raining as drops hit the ground, that he would do absolutely everything he could to help her get better.

Chapter 4

Avery's heart hammered out a quick rhythm as she opened the back door slowly and with measured care—then winced as it squeaked loudly in protest, as if its intention was to inform the entire house of her...adventures.

She resented feeling like a teenager, sneaking into her brother's home. Just another reminder that her life as of late was anything but normal. And, oh, how she craved normal.

"Morning, sweetheart."

Despite its softness, Macy's greeting caused Avery to gasp and turn around so fast that whiplash wouldn't have been an implausible outcome.

"Holy goodness, Mace. You scared the living daylights out of me," Avery said, shoving a hand against her heart. As she leaned back and let her spine rest against the closed door, fighting to catch her breath, she studied her sister-in-law. Macy was, as always, as pretty at the crack of dawn—with her golden hair all messy and the imprint of a pillow seam etched into her cheek—as she had been on her and Tommy's wedding day. Avery indulged in the memory—a time when everything was simpler, purer—before she'd brought home a personal hell that had begun to seep into all their lives.

"Speaking of daylights," Macy said quietly, tugging her frayed, pink terry-cloth robe tighter around her waist, "the sun hasn't even risen and here you are looking like you've had quite a night."

Avery's lips formed a thin line, but she held Macy's gaze, despite the temptation to look away from what she saw in the sweet, open face.

"What do you want me to say?"

Macy closed her eyes and then opened them again, sympathy etched into her features. "I just want you to be okay, honey, that's all. We all do." She looked as though she might want to touch or hold Avery, but knew better from experience.

Even though the conversation wasn't anything new, something tugged at Avery's heartstrings and for a second she longed to just collapse and let it all out—to tell someone how desperately scared she was, how the nightmares kept getting worse, and how she couldn't always tell the difference between those and the flashbacks. How sometimes she wasn't sure whether she was awake or asleep.

But something else, something strange and new, told her this wasn't the time or place…but that maybe she was getting close to being able to do just that…and that maybe Isaac was that place. As Macy waited for an answer to the questions she hadn't voiced out loud but were always there, Avery thought back to the man she'd met that morning.

Even under the strange circumstances that brought them together last night, he had been so calm, so sturdy and safe, like a lighthouse in a raging storm. He'd taken care of her without hesitation, and for some reason she knew he would have done the same for any wayward creature.

He was the embodiment of that most rare and beautiful thing, something Avery had seen precious little of over the past few years: basic human kindness.

"Well, now, there's something you don't see every day," Macy said, a giggle bubbling up around her words. "You want to tell me what has you smiling like that, or is it a secret?"

Avery, disbelieving, reached up and touched a finger to her lips, realizing only upon feeling their upward curve to what her sister-in-law referred. Before she could form a response, Macy's eyes lit up and her mouth opened wide.

"Oh, my gosh, Avery," she blurted. "Were you—" she crossed her arms over her chest and leaned forward "—were you...with a guy?"

"No!" Avery spat, but she wasn't fooling anyone. She winced. "Well, technically, yes, but it's not what it seems." She held her palms out, hoping for emphasis.

Macy eyed her with blatant skepticism. "Yeah," she said, grinning, "usually when people say that, it's exactly what it seems."

A little unexpected laugh escaped from Avery's throat. She peered at her sister, her friend, with narrow eyes. "You've been watching too many romantic comedies," she said, hoping to divert attention away from herself, blushing a little at the mere thought that Macy's suggestion put into her head.

She had a feeling it wouldn't go away as easily or as quickly as it had arrived. Isaac's dark, unruly hair twisted around her fingers, those deep brown eyes gazing at her with...with what, exactly? Lust? Over *her*?

Not likely, at least not in her current state of skin and bones. She'd need to put on a good ten pounds before anything like that happened, or someone might get hurt. Before she could stop them, more thoughts tumbled in, unbidden. Suddenly, she remembered being carried in those arms—strong arms, brandished a deep gold by the Texas sun—and, for once, the thought of being held didn't seem quite so scary. It was nice to feel attraction to a man, a welcome distraction from her usual preoccupations.

"Something tells me I'm not too far off," Macy said, interrupting Avery's ridiculous reverie.

It would be great if her dreams were more like that than the terrifying things they actually were. She met her sister-in-law's curious gaze. "No," she answered truthfully. "I did run into your neighbor Isaac Meyer, but it's not like what you're thinking."

Macy's shoulders sagged and Avery's heart bruised. How desperately she longed to bring smiles to her loved ones' faces—not pain or disappointment.

Macy reached out a hand, tentatively, and after a second's hesitation, Avery grabbed it, anxiety and a desire for comfort raging a familiar battle at the sensation of human contact. Macy's expression registered the wound, but there wasn't much to say on the subject that hadn't already been rehashed a hundred times.

Her family knew she'd suffered plenty of emotional

trauma during her last tour; she spared them the details of what happened in that place. She knew that these people who loved her were not the enemy. She knew they meant her no harm, but her body, and parts of her mind, still struggled with the difference between a friendly touch and a hostile one.

"I'd be lying if I said it wouldn't be nice to see you spending some time with a sweet fella," Macy answered. "Isaac Meyer definitely fits the bill, and that boy has been single for way too long." She gently squeezed Avery's hand before tugging her in the direction of the kitchen. "Come on. Let's get some caffeine in you and you can tell me what exactly did happen."

She winked and Avery rolled her eyes, but allowed herself to be led toward the energizing scent of fresh coffee.

Maybe it wouldn't hurt for her to talk to Macy about the strange past few hours. Maybe it would be nice to share breakfast and silly, carefree chatter about a man, like the old days.

Or at least she could pretend to, for her family's sake.

"All set?" Macy asked later that morning as Avery stepped into the lobby following her weekly appointment with Dr. Santiago, her therapist.

Avery nodded and Macy smiled warmly as she put down a magazine she'd been reading, grabbed her purse and stood to leave. They walked quietly to the elevator, Avery reviewing her session with Dr. Santiago. Though she saw the doctor regularly, most of her previous appointments ran together, characterized only by the strong feeling that nothing ever really changed; some days were better than others, but overall, she felt she'd made no true progress over the past several months, a thought that only served to decrease her confidence that she would someday get past it all.

But today—something felt different. Something felt…better. She couldn't quite put her finger on it. Was it that she had tried harder to talk about her struggles? Had she simply opened up more? Yes, and no. She shook her head as she reached out to punch the down button on the panel between two elevators. Perhaps she'd made a little more effort than usual to speak frankly with the doctor, but it wasn't just that. She always did her best during her sessions, always pushed as far as she could go, working to excavate that deep abyss of painful war memories. No. This time, it was something else. Something to do with her night with Isaac.

"So, I was thinking," Macy said, her words tentative, almost as though she knew before she spoke them that whatever idea she had would be shot down. Avery winced, fully aware that she had a large part in making her sister-in-law feel that way around her.

Avery looked over to see Macy fiddling with her purse strap, her forehead creased. "What is it?"

"Well, you know that new nail salon they just opened up the street from here?"

"Uh-huh," Avery answered, her thoughts still partly focused on her session with Dr. Santiago. She heard Macy swallow.

"I was thinking we could stop on the way to the grocery and maybe get pedicures or something." She looked over at Avery, cautious hope in her eyes. "My treat."

A sharp *ding* sound rang out and the elevator doors slid open. Once they'd stepped inside and chosen the ground floor as their destination, Avery glanced over at Macy, who was biting her lower lip now, her features giving away her trepidation.

Avery's heart sank. How many times had she said no to such a simple request, to things that Macy offered as a way to reach out to her, in constant effort to help her through her tough times? How many times had she denied those offers, yet they kept coming? She smiled softly at Macy, realizing for the first time how lucky she was to have this persistent, positive woman in her life. How many others had she hurt and pushed away because she was too afraid they wouldn't be able to handle the new, dark parts of her soul?

"I'd like that," she said, and Macy's face lit up. Macy squeezed her palms and raised her forearms, then lowered them quickly so as not to appear too excited.

"It's okay," Avery said, giggling. "You can be happy about it."

"Yay!" Macy cried out as she did a little bounce, causing them both to laugh.

The elevator stopped and both women stepped out into the parking garage.

"Look, Macy, I know it must be hard for you to keep...trying...with me, and—" Avery swallowed over the lump developing in her throat, startled by the sudden onslaught of emotion "—I want you to know I notice how hard you've been trying to make me feel better." She closed her eyes, working to organize her thoughts around the most important thing she needed to get across. "I mean to say that I'm thankful for you. For all that you and Tommy do for me, really. But especially you."

Macy stopped and turned toward Avery, her eyes filling as she reached out and wrapped her sister-in-law in a hug, squeezing hard.

When she let go, they walked to the car in silence, both smiling. It felt good to say yes to something, even something as small as a pedicure with a special family member—and friend—who'd remained close, no matter how hard Avery unintentionally pushed her away. She thought of that night with Isaac, how she'd allowed him to feed and care for her, despite feeling afraid of what conclusions he might draw about the state of her mental health. It was almost as though that choice—the choice to let someone new in, despite the difficulty it took to do so—was an opening for other opportunities that she'd been missing out on for so long.

Besides, she thought, grinning to herself, she could use some color on her toes. She decided then that she would pick something bright, something that would make her feel uplifted when she looked down at her feet. Something that maybe Isaac might notice and like.

As Macy pulled her car out into the sunshine, a small spark of life lit up somewhere deep inside the darkest place in Avery's heart.

Chapter 5

What had seemed like a good idea earlier that morning was really just a sack of zucchini in the light of day.

Isaac could have kicked his own ass for not coming up with a better ruse for stopping by to check on Avery Abbott after the night they'd spent in each other's company. A week had passed since that strange night—the slowest week of his life. He'd only been able to go through the motions during that time, each task permeated with thoughts of a woman unlike any other he'd ever met.

But still…zucchini? Anyone would be able to see through his excuse. The vegetable was insanely easy to grow, even in a dry-as-a-bone Texas summer like the one they were having—they were so good at growing that anyone within a hundred miles of Peach Leaf who wanted the vegetables already had enough to feed an army. People could only stand so many salads and breads and desserts with the stuff snuck in. But, for some knuckleheaded reason, Isaac had decided that bringing a bag of the green things would pass as a decent excuse to visit his neighbor's farm.

Yes, that's correct, he thought. *I'm bringing a crap ton of zucchini...to a farm.* He shook his head. Hell, it might have *come* from that very farm, he noted with a sinking sensation in his belly.

With so many well-meaning locals—overwhelmingly widows and grannies...and widowed grannies—dropping off food at his place on a regular basis, he lost track of its origins. He didn't hold it against all the sweet gals, but once in a while, it was enough to make him consider moving to Austin, where a thirtysomething bachelor wasn't likely to turn so many heads.

He pulled his four-wheeler into Tommy and Macy's drive, careful to watch out for free-range chickens and goats. He got out and Jane jumped down from her perch on the seat in front of him, hightailing it up the porch steps. As the front door swung open, the scent of something sweet cooking wafted out into the already warm air.

"Hey, Janie girl," Tommy said, scratching the dog between her ears before she invited herself into the house. "Hey, bud," he said, turning to Isaac and heading down the steps, cup of coffee in hand.

"Mornin', Tom," Isaac said, returning the greeting as he reached into the seat compartment to pull out the embarrassing sack of vegetables.

Tommy's eyebrows rose up so far they almost met the brim of his straw Stetson. When Isaac just stood there, holding the offending sack away from him like a baby with a dirty diaper, realization crossed Tommy's features and he started to slowly back away, holding up a hand. "Aw, no way, man. Macy's got so many of those damn things. If she strung all the little bastards together, they'd reach the moon and back."

Isaac cursed and swung the bag over his shoulder, feeling more and more like a complete idiot.

"What in the world were you thinking bringing those things here?" Tommy continued, keeping his distance. "You lost your ever-lovin' mind, my friend?" He took a long sip of his coffee, clearly waiting for a response.

The two men had been good friends ever since Isaac inherited his grandma's property and moved in to the old ranch house. They were living proof that opposites really do attract. Isaac, who wasn't usually keen on too much chatter, had taken an instant liking to his neighbor, despite the fact that the man never shut his mouth and could carry on a conversation with just about anybody or anything. His easygoing habit of yakking made Isaac comfortable, mostly because he didn't have to say much for them to get along just fine, and, well, Tommy was just so damn nice. Also, it was obvious that the man doted on his family, as if Macy had hung the moon, and their two little ones, all the stars in the sky.

It was exactly the kind of family Isaac had always pictured having himself one day. If only he could find the right girl. Someone who wouldn't mind his quiet nature and his shyness around new people. Someone, maybe, kind of like Avery Abbott—his true reason for dropping by.

"Oh, just forget about those things and come on in. Macy's got breakfast on. But, if you think it's just flour, milk and sugar in those waffles, guess again. It's like I said before, that girl has stuffed those green devils into everything we've eaten in the past month because she hates to waste them, and, I'm telling you, at least fifty more popped up in her garden overnight."

Isaac smiled at his friend's happy chatter.

"Don't be surprised if next time you stop by, I've turned into one of 'em." Tommy stopped suddenly at the top of the steps. "What'd you say you dropped by for, again?" He lifted up his white hat and scratched his forehead. "Not that you need a reason. Just want to make sure you don't leave here empty-handed if you were needing something—"

"Tom?" Isaac said quietly, seeking a brief break in his friend's out-loud thinking.

"—Macy would never let me hear the end of it if—"

"Tom!"

He finally turned around, a sleepy smile on his face. Isaac had never known his friend to wear any other expression.

"What's on your mind, bud?"

Now that he had Tom's attention, Isaac hesitated, unsure what can of worms he might risk opening if he answered the question truthfully.

He knew Tom was protective of Avery beyond what would be expected of a brother, and he could understand why. From what he'd seen the other night, what folks said about her time in service, and from the way she seemed to socialize far less than other locals, he could guess that she'd come back from war bearing a few scars—the kind you couldn't see with a good pair of eyes.

The jumpiness he'd witnessed in her that night and her disorientation in an area she was familiar with were textbook post-trauma symptoms. He recognized them

from the vets he trained service dogs for, and from—
the memory still ached in a part of Isaac's heart that he
knew would never heal—from his brother. Which was
why he'd avoided visiting the farm and his friends the
past few months since he'd heard that Avery moved in.
Working with PTSD victims in his job was one thing—
watching his friend's sister struggle through it was entirely another.

She needed help. More help than whatever Veteran
Affairs currently provided, more help than her family
would know how to give her, regardless of how much
they loved and supported her.

Isaac knew, better than most, that love wasn't always enough.

Love couldn't always save someone.

So, as much as it might cost him in the long run,
Isaac decided it was best to be open with Tom, for Avery's sake. He'd just have to make sure Macy didn't read
too much into his visit, or she'd be on his case, and he'd
find himself being set up again, only to turn up disappointed if it didn't work out.

The other night, despite her condition, he could feel
the electric hint of possibility between them, and he
couldn't deny that she was the prettiest woman he'd ever
laid eyes on—but for now, all he wanted to do was help.

He set his shoulders back and held up a hand to shade
his brow against the first rays of the rising sun. The day
was already plenty warm, and he could tell it would be
a hot one.

"Actually, yeah. There is something on my mind.
Two things, actually. I'm so sorry I haven't stopped by
to see you guys lately, and, well, I'm not here to see you
now, to be honest."

Isaac ignored the goofy grin on Tommy's face, not really caring that he wasn't making any sense.

"I'm here to check on Avery."

Avery accepted the mug Macy handed her and took a long sip of the rich, strong coffee it contained, closing her eyes as the taste of good beans, a little sugar and a splash of fresh cream washed over her taste buds.

Macy was grinning from across the table when she opened her eyes.

"Good?"

"The best. I've always loved your coffee. Not like the coffee-flavored water Tommy always made before you came along," Avery said, laughing.

Macy beamed with pride. "Well, I'm glad you like it, and it's here every morning, but it's not enough to put meat on your bones, girl. You can't keep going on caffeine and the occasional bowl of cereal. You need to eat. You've barely had a real meal since you moved in here."

Avery took another sip and nodded in agreement. "I know I do."

"So, tell me what it is. Is there something I can make that you'd wolf down? When I first met Tommy, you were a nachos-and-beer kind of girl. Maybe we just need to get you to a Tex-Mex place, stat." Macy's voice was light, but Avery didn't miss the hint of seriousness in the woman's words.

"It's hard to explain, Mace. It's almost like…like everything tastes stale or cardboard-y. I couldn't tell you why. Ever since… I just can't seem to eat like I used to. But I'll try harder. Really, I will. And last week, I did eat a pretty mean sandwich at Isaac's—"

At the sound of the front door swinging open, both

women exchanged glances and then turned their heads to the kitchen entryway.

"Honey, is that you?" Macy called out.

"Me and company," Tommy bellowed from the hallway.

A racket started at the front door and thundered down the hall, and suddenly Isaac's dog, Jane, was rushing through the kitchen entrance, headed straight toward the table. Macy's eyes widened in surprise but Avery's heart swelled at the sight of the dog.

"Janie!" Avery said as the giant mutt bounded over to her chair. She stopped short and sat in front of Avery, her behind wiggling with the effort of not jumping into Avery's lap. She reached up a paw and Avery touched it, laughing. "High-five!"

"Goodness," Macy said. "Someone's in love."

"Who's in love?" Tommy asked, entering the kitchen and heading over to kiss the top of his wife's head, then on to the coffeepot. "Mornin', sweetie. Mornin', Ave," he said as Isaac sidled up behind him to prop a shoulder against the doorway, arms crossed over his broad chest.

Avery's breath caught at the sight of him. Good Lord, he was even better looking in the morning light: shoulder-length hair still unruly but obviously moist and gleaming from a shower, dark eyes glittering as they met hers. He was dressed in faded jeans and a cobalt-blue T-shirt that brought out the olive tones in his sun-kissed skin.

"Avery," he said, his voice velvety-soft. He nodded at her, his lips offering just a hint of a grin, and, if she hadn't been sitting in a chair, she was fairly certain she'd have melted into a puddle right there on the kitchen floor.

Thankfully, he turned from her to say good morning to his hostess, who jumped up from the table to give him a big hug. "Isaac," Macy said, squeezing his midsection before turning to get him a cup of coffee. "It's so good to see you. You've been such a stranger lately." She held him at arm's length so she could get a good look at him. "I've told Tom to head on over and check on you and Jane, but he insisted you've been fine, just busy.

"And he's right," Isaac reassured her. "But I do appreciate you thinking of me."

Macy let go of him and picked up the carafe to pour him a mug, and, without asking how he took it, left it black and set it at the place next to Avery on the round, antique oak table. She winked and Avery felt her cheeks warm.

They'd been talking about him just before.

He walked in. As he drew near and pulled out the chair only inches away from hers, Avery had to remind herself that he wasn't aware of that fact.

It was true that her family had spent a lot of energy worrying about her lately. She'd been back home for almost six months and dutifully kept her appointments with her therapist at the VA clinic in downtown Peach Leaf, but her symptoms weren't going away; in fact, they hadn't even gotten better. Sometimes, she thought, they seemed to be getting worse.

And with each flashback, each nightmare, each— her favorite—panic attack, Avery lost more and more of her self-esteem.

Where was the strong woman who'd enlisted after nursing school, hoping to see the world and serve her country as a medical professional? Where was the girl who'd always been drawn to the needs of others, to healing broken bodies?

She couldn't help anyone in her current state—least of all, herself—and it killed her a little more each day.

Avery hadn't realized it, as lost as she'd been in her own thoughts, but when she looked up, she met Jane's brown eyes, and noticed that her hand was buried in the dog's fur, stroking it. The repetitive movement and the feel of the satiny coat soothed her. If she focused on that motion instead of the turbulence inside her mind, things began to settle down.

She turned to Isaac and he met her eyes. There was a gentle smile in them that made her think maybe it wouldn't be so hard to try, just a little.

"I've always liked dogs so much," she said, still petting Jane, who promptly rolled over to expose her pink belly.

Avery and Isaac both laughed.

"She's a big, spoiled-rotten ham," he said. "A very good girl, don't get me wrong. But spoiled nonetheless."

"No way," Avery said, defending her new best friend from Isaac's good-humored chiding. "She's a sweetheart."

"Ha! She's got you wrapped around her paw there, I see," Isaac answered, shaking his head.

Macy informed him he'd be staying on for breakfast and it didn't take too long for him to give up his protest that he had work to do and didn't want to be in their hair all morning. Finally, he agreed to stay for waffles. Avery's niece and nephew joined the adults, rubbing their eyes from sleep. She snuck kisses on their matching strawberry-smelling, soft, flyaway blond hair before they saw Jane and ran over excitedly to pet the dog, completely ignoring everyone else in the room until Macy gently scolded them to say hello to Mr. Isaac. They did, before promptly returning their attention to Jane.

Avery chuckled. The dog *was* indeed spoiled, but she deserved it.

Tommy headed off to wash up from the morning's milking, which he always did alongside his six hired hands, and Macy busied herself with the waffle batter.

"You're a natural with Jane," Isaac said as she set places with plates and utensils, then sat back down at the table, having been shooed away from her offers to help Macy prepare breakfast. "Mind if I ask why you don't have one of your own?"

Avery fingered the yellow stars that decorated her favorite black coffee mug. "Well, I haven't really given it much thought," she answered, noticing that Isaac's eyes traveled over her face with intensity that made her both extremely flattered and disconcerted. As one of just a couple of females among the majority of males that had made up her team, she wasn't used to such attention. She was used to being just one of the guys. Part of her thoroughly enjoyed the way those brown eyes studied her features with obvious interest; another part warned her to turn and run. She wasn't relationship material—now or possibly ever. Too much baggage. Too much damage.

"Before I went into the army, I was a nurse, and my shifts didn't allow time for me to be a good pet owner." Nervous, she tucked a strand of hair behind her ear, wondering, for the first time in a long time, how it looked and when was the last time she'd brushed it or had a proper trim. It occurred to her that it wouldn't hurt to ask her stylist friend Jessica if she could squeeze in an appointment during the upcoming week.

A little change might make her feel better.

Isaac nodded, so she continued. "Then, when I joined, well…that's no mystery." She offered a soft smile. "I wouldn't have wanted to leave a pet behind for my family to care for in my absence, and I'm enough of a burden on them as it is for me to bring someone else into their home."

Wow. Her mother would turn over in her grave if she'd heard Avery sharing something so private with a relative stranger. The thing was, though, he didn't feel much like a stranger.

She turned quickly away and stared into her coffee mug. But before her eyes had left his, she'd seen the flash of sadness on Isaac's features and chided herself to be more careful; she didn't want him feeling sorry for her. Him or anyone else.

"Sounds to me like you'd make a wonderful pet owner," he said, surprising her. "You've obviously thought through these things, which is more than I can say for a lot of people."

"What do you mean?" she asked, unable to keep her eyes from him. Something about the man drew her in, and the more time she spent around him, the more she realized his company was like a balm to her frayed nerves. He was like a dip in cool spring water on a hot summer day, and she'd have to be very, very cautious to avoid getting pulled under.

"Just that a lot of people get pets, especially dogs, thinking that the animals will just be happy to have a home and food, but they need so much more than that. They need love and attention and medical care and training. They're incredibly wonderful, but a big responsibility. Most people don't think about all of those things, but it's obvious that you have, and I just think you'd be a wonderful dog mom if you ever decided that you wanted to be."

He gave her another one of those sweet but sexy grins—the kind that made her forget she was in a room full of other people, full of her family and full of the morning chaos of another busy day. Though she was apparently the only Abbott born with a black thumb, Avery did her best to help out around the farm—watching the kids so Macy could bake or have some time to herself, riding one of the horses out to check fences and crops with one or two of the hands, or helping Tommy with the milking.

Six months ago, when she'd come to live with her brother and his family, she'd thought that kind of work would save her from the persistent, dark memories she'd brought home from war. But now, after living through several months of hard, manual labor–filled days, she knew it wasn't enough. It was just another kind of running. She could cover a thousand miles, and those same memories would always be one step ahead of her, ready to knock her back down into the pit.

But something about Isaac's compliment, about the idea of a dog, sparked her interest. Something about the thought of having a living thing to take care of—one that was all her own—offered an inkling of hope. But with hope came the risk of opening up, of putting her heart out there, and she wasn't quite sure she could do it just yet. Still, maybe if she took the tiniest of steps in that direction…

She cleared her throat and looked back to Isaac, who

was draining the last of his coffee. "Tommy tells me you've helped a lot of vets with your training," she said, her voice sounding uncertain even to her own ears. "I'd love to hear more about it."

"Well, I'm certified in general canine training, and I do all kinds of basic and advanced behavioral training, plus some search and rescue and drug-finding stuff for the local sheriff's department, and I do work with vets sometimes, mostly pairing them with companion animals that we all feel are a good fit. Then I tailor the training to whatever a client's particular needs are. I've taken several courses in training therapy dogs, but I'm always learning more, especially from working directly with veterans."

He stopped there and she could tell he was trying not to bore or overwhelm her, which shouldn't surprise her after the other night. Most people would have labeled her crazy and gone on about their business. Isaac was different. He was testing the waters and giving her room to go at her own pace, to seek information rather than being force-fed facts. It was a relief after all of the VA appointments and therapy sessions.

"What happens then?"

Isaac's brow furrowed. "Well, as you've seen with Jane, dogs can be very calming. They can relax us when we're getting to that breaking point where nothing's helping and we just need a lifeline—someone to pull us back from the edge. All dogs, all breeds, have the potential to be amazing with humans, given a chance. But they're just like people in that they don't all get along. Not every dog likes every other dog, and not every dog is right for every person. It's a matter of finding the right dog for the right vet. When that happens, it's incredible what they can do for each other."

Okay, now she was really interested.

As a waffle-filled plate appeared in front of her, Avery looked up to find Macy smiling. She rolled her eyes but the truth was, she was glad to have someone to talk to who didn't seem to judge her. Someone who had seen one of her worst episodes and hadn't overreacted or, well, freaked out the way most people did. She was lucky Isaac was the one who'd found her wandering around in the darkness. It could have been anyone—but it was him. He'd taken care of her as though she belonged to him, as though she was his to keep safe and protect. And, because of his work, which she'd grilled Macy about the week before—something she'd made her sister-in-law swear to secrecy—he had the knowledge and experience to maybe help her, or to at least be her friend.

After what they'd been through in just a short amount of time, Avery knew he wouldn't scare easy the way most people did. She didn't blame them, really. It usually was just a matter of not knowing what to say, not knowing how to talk to her about her experiences in a combat zone most had only seen on edited television. Still, it hurt that her old friends seemed almost…afraid of her, as though she might break at any moment. And, to be fair, she could.

But Isaac wasn't like that. He was gentle and careful with her, but at the same time, he didn't treat her with kid gloves. He'd gotten her to talk more about her problems last week than her therapist had in months of trying different approaches. Plus, the idea that he could somehow even help her to get better—could maybe even work with a dog to help her—brought her more optimism than she'd felt since coming home, and she was smart enough not to resist a good thing when she saw it.

Also, it didn't hurt the situation that he was the most ruggedly beautiful man she'd ever seen.

"I want to know more," she said, pushing her shoulders back and meeting his eyes, a dose of bravery coursing through her veins. "How do I do that?"

Isaac's eyes flashed with interest and pride as he swallowed the bite of waffles he'd taken and set down his fork. Avery noticed that he'd finished over half of the food on his plate while she hadn't eaten a single morsel. "First, you eat."

"Oh," she said, looking down at her food. It did look good, but she knew that when she put a forkful into her mouth, it would taste like nothing. "I'm not really hungry."

He pulled a face that told her he wasn't buying the excuse. "All right, Abbott. Let's make a deal."

The twinkle in his eyes sent an arrow through that surge of bravery she'd felt only a moment before, but she wouldn't let him see. Over three tours, she'd had plenty of practice pretending to possess courage when in fact she did not. "Fine."

"Good," Isaac said, folding his hands in his lap. "Eat at least half of those waffles, and instead of telling you more about my training, I'll do you one better."

"How's that?" she asked, eyeing her food, deciding if she was really up for the challenge.

"You can come in to the office with me tomorrow."

"You've got work tomorrow?" she asked, and he nodded. "It's Saturday. I thought only us farm folks and emergency professionals had to report for duty so early on the weekend."

Isaac smiled and his eyes crinkled at the corners, lending sweetness to his sharp features.

"Yes, well, running a small business means there's always work to be done, and even when I do take a day off, it's hard not to think about all the things I could be doing."

"Sounds like a lot to handle," said Avery.

He nodded but his eyes held only satisfied joy, and she found she wanted to learn more about something that brought such contentment to his life.

"It is that, but I absolutely love the work. I opened the training center a couple of years back when my grandmother left me her house and land here. And, after having worked a corporate desk job since college, I'll never go back. Being my own boss and setting my own schedule is the best thing in the world."

"Even when you have to work weekends?" Avery asked, grinning.

"Even then," he said, returning her grin.

Isaac's eyes lit up when he talked about his work, and his enthusiasm got her excited about the opportunity to see where he spent his days. But, behind all of that, a little bit of sadness stung inside her chest. She missed her own work. She missed her patients at the hospital, her daily rounds and having the chance to give back to her community by caring for people. For Avery, being a nurse was more than just a job—it was a calling, something that filled her soul. And, even more simply, she felt lost without the daily routine of getting up and driving into town.

She'd tried to build a new life for herself on the farm

after the incident she'd had at work. It still made her face burn to remember her boss finding her huddled up in the corner of a patient's room, having mistaken the sound of a dropped food tray for an explosion. The resulting mandatory vacation leave her boss had ordered was justified, but it wasn't easy adjusting to time away from work. Despite pushing herself for long hours in the Texas sun to help her brother, she felt useless there. It would never be enough to replace nursing.

"Did I say something wrong?" Isaac asked, worry lines etching the dark skin of his forehead.

"No, no," she answered, surprising them both when she reached out and gently lay a hand across one of his. Even more startling was the absence of need to pull it away.

Isaac looked at their hands, then back at Avery, before winding his fingers through hers. The motion pulled all of the air from her lungs for just a second, but she didn't flinch.

Be brave, she told herself. *It's just a friendly gesture. It's just ordinary human contact.*

And, much to her pleased relief, it worked. As she allowed him to hold her hand, ignoring everything else in the room, her fear trickled away drop by drop. It was, after all, just a hand—but it belonged to Isaac, which made it okay somehow. Safe, steady Isaac.

She thought suddenly of the towering stack of historical romance paperbacks on her night table, of all the ways the authors described the heroes therein. In those books that she loved so much, the rakes and Vikings were always full of adventure and the promise of pulse-pounding, high-stakes danger, and though Avery could lose herself in those stories for hours, she'd always had difficulty relating to heroines who would want all of those things, when she herself craved just the opposite.

To Avery, the most romantic thing in the world was also the simplest: a partner who provided a safe home, gentle hands, stability and unconditional love.

She'd had enough adventure to last a lifetime, and all she really wanted now was a soft place to land.

She hadn't spent much time before, considering what that might look like in her own life, but seeing Isaac's hand wrapped around her own and the warm affection swimming in his dark eyes, she was starting to get a pretty good idea.

Avery cleared her throat and shook her head. "No, you didn't say anything wrong." She gave his hand a little squeeze. "I was just thinking about my own job, hearing you talk about how much you enjoy yours."

He was silent for a moment, just looking at her, no judgment discernible in his expression. When he spoke, his voice was kind but determined. "Listen, Abbott," he said, "whatever happened to you over there, whatever made you stop doing something you love, you can't let that make you quit for good. If you want to go back to nursing, or even train for a different career, you absolutely can. And I think I can help."

No hesitation, no "Let's take things slow," no "Maybe someday in the future"—none of the platitudes she was so used to hearing—just pure confidence in her ability to help herself get better.

It must have been exactly what she needed to hear, because in just a short time with Isaac Meyer, she felt better than she had in months. And to think he'd been there all along, just a short walk up the road.

She was tired of taking baby steps and getting nowhere, tired of carefully stepping on stones across a deep abyss only to fall over and over again, then to face the challenge of climbing back out over slippery walls. Her therapists at the VA were wonderful, and she knew she needed their help to find balance again. But it wasn't enough to commit to doing the mental work; she needed some actionable steps to take in order to feel more than passive in her own journey.

She'd read about service dogs for vets with PTSD, and most of the research was positive. Besides, she had nothing to lose. Everything she'd known before—the life she'd left with when she joined the military—was gone, and she knew it would probably never return. So, if Isaac wanted to help her with this new one, and if the way to do so was by working with a dog, it was worth one hell of a try. She wanted to be whole again, whatever that meant, and she was willing to try something innovative to get there, even if being whole now wouldn't look the same as it had before she'd left.

In fact, she was beginning to hope it didn't, because before, Isaac hadn't been a part of her world, and she'd decided this morning that she very much liked him in it.

Chapter 6

Friends with Fur had started out as just a business for Isaac—a way to earn a living and to get out from behind the desk that he'd sworn at the time would eventually kill him—but in the years since its opening, it had become so much more.

Even looking back on those *before* days from a safe distance made him cringe, and caused a trapped feeling to rise up like a scream from his chest to his throat. He'd been thirty when Nana passed and surprised the hell out of Isaac by leaving him her farm and savings. Inheriting Nana's property shouldn't have come as a shock because his mom hadn't survived her last heart failure, and of course his brother, Stephen, was gone long before that, but it had nonetheless. Suddenly, he'd been given a chance at a new life, and he didn't take that lightly.

After years of working his way up from mail clerk

to a corner office at an investment firm in Austin—a relatively reliable job with a steady, respectable paycheck—Isaac had begun to feel the claws of suffocation wrapping around him, longing for days that didn't all look exactly the same as the ones that came before and after. He'd gone to college mostly to please his mother and to get a taste of city life, but everything that followed seemed to rush in as smoothly as though he'd been on autopilot, just following a predetermined set of steps. Internships, job offers and a ladder to climb.

He'd gotten very near the top, but it wasn't enough. When he'd confided in his friends about his increasing longing to do something else, most had responded in the same way his mom had: they'd told him he was lucky to have a high-paying job, and he could do what he pleased as soon as he retired. He knew there was an element of truth in their statements, but there was also fear. Something inside him burned for change, and he didn't want to wait thirty more years to feel that his days had real purpose. Surely, he'd begun to dream, there had to be some way to earn a living doing something he loved. And just when he'd worked up the courage to take a leave of absence to try and figure out what to do about his future, Nana had gotten sick.

He'd come back to Peach Leaf to take care of her and to make certain she lived her final days in peaceful comfort. When she breathed her last, she gave him a new beginning. The farmhouse where he'd spent his summers was old, but in decent shape, and with Nana's life savings, he'd fixed it up and studied to become a certified animal trainer. Then, along the way, he'd bought the building that now housed his facility.

Often, he thought of the irony. Animals—dogs in

particular—were his greatest love as a little boy. Had he listened to and followed his passion earlier in life, well… It didn't do much good to dwell on the past. He was happy in his job now and absolutely loved getting up for work every morning. He had what so many people wished for but never obtained: a beloved career that brought satisfaction and joy, and that also made it possible to pay the bills.

Isaac had started small, with just a website and cheap business cards, training pets in clients' homes, and eventually word of mouth spread and he'd hired on Hannah and Mike. Now they offered training at all levels from basic to specialized service, along with pet sitting and customized curricula for owners with individual needs.

At first he'd been reluctant to train dogs as companions for veterans with psychological struggles. The pain of Stephen's death was still too raw. But when a friend of his had returned home from war and requested Isaac's help to keep from drowning at the bottom of a bottle, he couldn't say no, and that aspect of his training programs had grown. Now, vets from all over Texas came to Friends with Fur to meet and train with dogs to take home and make their lives infinitely better.

Isaac's heart lifted each morning when he drove into the parking lot, but it rose a little higher as he did that Saturday with the beautiful Avery Abbott by his side.

He hadn't specifically planned on convincing her to spend the day with him when he'd visited her home the morning before. But when he'd walked into Macy Abbott's kitchen, he was a goner. Avery's blond hair was wet from a shower and her skin glowed dewy fresh. He loved that she didn't need to fuss or put on a bunch of makeup; she was naturally beautiful, dressed in a fitted blue T-shirt, faded jeans and bright green flip-flops. When he'd sat down next to her at the table, the scent of apple shampoo from her freshly washed hair had filled his nostrils and made it damn hard not to draw closer to her as he'd focused on getting her to eat her breakfast.

He wasn't one to fall quick. Hell, he wasn't one to fall at all if the past was any indication. Aside from a couple of short-term college girlfriends and the nice-but-not-for-him dates the women in town set him up with, Isaac didn't have much of a romantic past to speak of. It wasn't that he didn't want love, no, it was more that he wasn't sure it was even possible to find what he wanted.

His mom and dad had been the perfect bad example of the kind of relationship he was looking for. He had to thank them for that. They'd taught him exactly what he did not want. What he did want was something simple, but right. Someone he could trust with every fiber of his being, someone who wasn't intimidated by the fact that he loved his work and that it was more than just a job and he'd have to put in long hours sometimes to make sure he got things done well. Someone who wanted to be a mom to his kids, and to help him raise them with good old-fashioned manners and sense.

Yet again, he thought, Avery brought all of this to the surface when he usually just ignored it and plugged along, happy to be single, but wishing for more. But what did he know about her, really? How could he even think of her that way when clearly all she wanted or needed was his help? It would be wrong to hope for more from her, wrong to show interest at a time when she was at her most vulnerable…wouldn't it?

"I've been by this place so many times," she said softly as he stopped the truck they'd borrowed from

Tommy for the day, "but I always thought it was just a doggy day care or something. I didn't realize you were doing such important work in there."

Isaac smiled at the sound of her voice. As she unbuckled her seat belt, he snuck another good look at Avery over Jane's furry head between them. She looked refreshed after eating the blueberry muffin Macy had pushed on her as she'd left the house that morning, which he'd then insisted she finish, but he knew she'd probably done so more to prove that she could meet his challenge than to add weight to her thin figure. Oh well, he would take it, and if he had to spend every meal by her side that day to get her to eat, then so be it. She was his to take care of, at least for the day, and he meant to do just that.

He let Jane out and then opened Avery's door for her. She took his offered hand and he found great pleasure in the pink clouds that floated across her cheeks when their palms touched. Her beauty was quiet, like a landscape painting of a bright summer day. Makeup-free, it didn't demand attention, but once he'd laid eyes on her, he'd known he would miss her face if a day passed when he couldn't see it.

Isaac didn't want to think about what that meant.

For now, all he wanted was to spend time getting to know her better, helping her if he could.

"Oh, wow," Avery said as he unlocked the back door and led her into the building, Jane trotting happily along at their feet. "It's like doggy heaven."

She faced him with sparkling eyes and he laughed.

"Well, I'm glad you think so," he said. "That's exactly what it's supposed to be."

Showing the training facility to Avery gave Isaac the opportunity to view it with new eyes. He led her down a long hallway, showing her inside each of the different classrooms, stocked with supplies for all sorts of training exercises. There was a puppy room featuring long leads for recall training, toys and, of course, paper pads in case tiny bladders needed sudden relief, a large arena floored in Astroturf for agility training, and—Avery's favorite—the search-and-rescue classroom with its boxes labeled for different scents that would be filled and closed for dogs to identify. Finally, he took her past his office and up to the storefront, where his staff sold good pet supplies at discount prices, so clients could pick up what they needed on their way out after classes.

Seeing Avery's enjoyment of her personal tour gave him a burst of pride in the business he'd started.

"I love it," she said. "Very cool." She reached down to pet Jane who, Isaac noticed with a grin, had helped herself to a tennis ball from one of the classroom bins along the way.

"She has a mild rebellious streak in her, doesn't she?" Avery asked, teasing.

"Doesn't get it from me," Isaac said, thrilled when Avery let go a small rush of musical laughter. "But it's one of the things I love about Janie. She's loyal and reliable and obedient about ninety-nine percent of the time, so it just adds to her charm."

Avery stroked Jane while she listened to him talk.

"But damn, was she ever a mess when she found me. I suppose it was mutual, though," he said, his tone more serious than he'd planned. "I wasn't a very happy man at the time, and she'd just come from being a homeless puppy, so we both had some fixing to do before we were on good terms."

"And are you now?" Avery asked, her light blond eyebrows furrowed.

"Am I what?"

"You know," she said, as if he held the key to some mystery she didn't quite dare talk about. "Happy."

He stopped walking and turned to face her, thinking in silence for a moment, lost in the blue-gray storm clouds in her eyes.

"That's a complicated question, isn't it?"

"Not particularly," she challenged, a twinge of sorrow in her voice.

"Well, then, perhaps it's the answer that's complicated."

"Yes, maybe so, but I still want to know—are you happy, Isaac Meyer?"

In her question, Isaac sensed she was really asking something else—something along the lines of *Is it possible that I will ever be happy again?*—and he wanted, badly, for her to believe that, yes, she could be. Yes, despite everything that had happened to her, despite all the evil he could assume she'd witnessed, she could indeed find happiness again.

And, more important, she deserved to.

So he thought very carefully before responding, "Yes, most of the time, I am."

"And the others?"

He nodded. "Other times, I cling to the times that I am, and trust that if I'm patient, I'll find my way back to that place."

He looked down at Jane's happy dog face, remembering the days just after Stephen's death when he could barely breathe, let alone find the strength to drag his body out of bed to help his mother with her own grief.

"Sometimes happiness takes work," he said, ignoring the tension that came over Avery's body at his words. "Hear me out," he said, his voice firm. "We don't always want to do the work, the hard stuff, to put ourselves back together after something awful knocks us to pieces. But that's when it's most important to try, to keep doing the things we love and being with the people we love, until it meets us halfway. Some days, Avery, showing up and doing the work is enough."

He hadn't meant to say so much about how he'd handled his own pain after he lost his brother, and the liquid shimmering in her eyes hit him like a punch to the gut, but if his own experience could make hers even a fraction easier to bear, then it was worth pulling the stitches out of those wounds.

For her.

There was a great deal he would do to see this woman smile—this new, complex, damaged-but-not-destroyed woman who'd quite literally walked into his life.

He reached out and took her hand, glad when she only twitched a tiny bit at his touch before letting their palms fold together.

"There's someone I want you to meet."

Avery's shoulders rose a little and tension tightened her fingers around his; she didn't seem to realize how hard she was gripping him until he asked what was bothering her.

"I'm not... I don't really..."

"It's okay," Isaac said, running his thumb softly over the tips of Avery's fingers. Her eyes were huge, and even as he focused on how to calm her, he couldn't help but notice how their clear blue shade resembled the beautiful cloudless Texas sky above as they'd driven into town earlier. "It's just one of my trainers, Hannah, and a puppy we've been working with."

A smile spread across his lips involuntarily. "I think you'll really like him. He's a little fireball, but he's got all the makings of a great service dog, if we can match him to the right person."

She swallowed and some of the tension eased out of her grip.

"I think that person might be you, Avery."

"I'm just not sure if I'm up for meeting someone right now. It's been a few weeks since I've even—" unmistakable embarrassment crossed her features "—well, since I've even left the farm, aside from wandering onto your land, of course. I'm just not sure if I can handle meeting a new person yet."

Though Avery's jaw was set with stubborn resolve, Isaac wanted to wrap his arms around her and tell her she had absolutely nothing to be ashamed of. He could see the scared girl behind the strong woman's facade, and his instinct was to protect her from any harm or pain, but he also knew from experience that she wouldn't get better by isolating herself from other people.

"Listen, Hannah works with combat veterans all the time, and she is one of the kindest, gentlest people I know. And I'll be right here, right by your side," he offered. "But if you want me to take you home, say the word and it's done. You don't have to do anything you're not comfortable with, Avery."

As he continued to hold her hand, Avery bit her lip, considering. Isaac gave her all the time in the world to decide if she was up for it and eventually, she pulled her hand from his and shook out her shoulders. "All right," she said, tossing him a confident grin as she rubbed her palms together. "Let's do this."

"Okay, then. That's my girl."

The words were out of his mouth before he could even think, and, slightly overwhelmed with what they implied, Isaac simply turned to lead the way back to Hannah's office near his own at the rear of the building.

But when he glanced over at Avery, he caught the smile in her eyes and the way her lips curved slightly at their corners.

Just one of those smiles, he knew, could keep him going for a week.

Avery was out of practice.

It had been over a month since she'd met someone new, before she'd stumbled into Isaac, of course.

In her job as a nurse, she'd encountered new patients every single day, and for a time after returning from war, she'd managed not to let that intimidate her. But, as she had come to realize over the past few weeks, there were some things she didn't yet understand about her PTSD diagnosis, some things that reared their ugly heads when she least expected. Somehow, difficulty being around people she didn't know—and, more important, didn't know if she could trust—was one of those things. It didn't matter that logic wasn't involved; most citizens of sleepy, friendly Peach Leaf weren't out to ambush her in broad daylight. It was easy to rationalize, far more difficult to put into practice.

But, like Macy always said, she could fake it till she made it.

For some reason, she wanted Isaac to be proud of her, to feel comfortable introducing her to his staff and friends, so she would put on a brave face and try to keep her trepidation from reaching the surface.

He'd looked so happy when she agreed to meet Hannah and the puppy. It was adorable, really. How long had it been since someone had been so interested in her reaction to a new situation? How long had it been since someone had dared take her out in public and have her meet new people without worrying how she might behave? She couldn't tell if he just wasn't aware of how big a deal it was for her, or if he was doing this intentionally, to give her a chance to feel like a real person again, a person who could be okay in normal social situations. Either way, his thoughtfulness touched a place deep within her heart and somehow lent her courage.

Plus, if she were honest, she was absolutely dying to see the pup Isaac was so excited about. It was adorable the way his face lit up over a little furry guy. As far as Avery was concerned, a guy who loved animals already had a lot going for him. Maybe that was one of the reasons she found she could trust him so easily, even though they'd known each other for less time than it took her to binge-read a new historical romance series.

And goodness, how she loved the way her hand felt in his, and the way he'd grabbed it without making a big deal out of anything. He seemed to have an intuition for what would push her just beyond her comfort zone without making her feel pressure.

He was…wonderful.

They reached a door at the end of the hallway and Isaac knocked gently before slowly pushing it open. Jane rushed forward into what Avery assumed was Hannah's cozy office, stopping only when she reached a red-and-blue-plaid dog bed tucked into a corner. Avery yearned to see the little guy immediately, but she knew she needed to focus first on being polite to the woman who stood up from a desk and came forward to greet them, reaching out a hand.

"Hi, I'm Hannah. You must be Avery."

Avery shook Hannah's warm hand and, even though her heart raced a little, she was able to force herself to relax, knowing that Isaac was nearby and had her back.

"I am. It's nice to meet you, Hannah."

Hannah was petite with short brown hair, wide, lovely green eyes and an open smile that filled her heart-shaped face. If she was half as sweet as she looked, Avery could see why she'd be good at working with war-scarred veterans and dogs, and she could even imagine making a new friend.

"When Isaac texted to let me know you two were coming in this morning, I got so excited." Hannah squeezed her hands into fists at her sides and her enthusiasm for her work was palpable. "We've been working with Foggy for a few months now, and we know he'll be wonderful, but we just haven't found the right person to take him home yet."

Hannah and Isaac exchanged looks, but Avery was too interested in meeting the puppy to pay much attention.

"Can I meet him?" Avery asked.

"Of course!"

Hannah led the way over to where Jane had high-tailed it upon entering the room. She stopped a few feet away from the doggie bed and called, "Foggy, come."

Seconds later, the cutest little thing Avery had ever seen came trotting out from behind Jane and plopped his bottom down right in front of Hannah, and Avery fell instantly in love.

Chapter 7

When she thought of service dogs, a very specific picture came to mind for Avery, and that image was about as far-flung from the little furry bundle that trotted forward at Hannah's command as it could be. This was no regal Labrador retriever or German shepherd dog; no, this fuzzy creature looked more like he belonged on a greeting card or a bag of dog food than in a serious working situation. Granted, he wore a little blue vest that said SERVICE DOG in bold white lettering, but other than that, he could have passed as anyone's beloved family pet.

Avery's hand flew to her mouth to hold off the baby talk and cooing noises that threatened to escape against her will. She was an army medic, trained to keep a clear mind and to control her emotions even under the most extreme duress. So how could one little dog turn her insides to complete mush?

Unbelievable.

She had to touch him. The urge was fierce, automatic and impossible to resist.

Avery began to reach out her arms, but Hannah gently held up a hand to prevent her from doing so. The young dog halted immediately. Hannah turned up her palm, lifted it a few inches, and the dog sat quickly and quietly in front of the two women, waiting for his next move.

Avery's face must have registered her confusion because Hannah turned and gave her a reassuring smile. "We're just reinforcing how to politely greet humans. Foggy's doing wonderfully with all of the basics, and we've recently moved on to some more advanced commands. He'll make someone an excellent companion and helper."

Hannah beamed with pride at her little charge, whose tail slowly began to swish back and forth.

"Foggy?" Avery asked, and Hannah nodded.

"Because of his coloring."

"It suits him."

And it did. He was the cutest, scruffiest little mess she'd ever seen, with a coat of wiry fur in all possible shades of gray. Avery hadn't known there could be so many. His paws and forearms were snowy white, resulting in what looked for all the world like four little boots, and his tail appeared to have been pinned on as an afterthought, for it was long, thick and black as coal, mismatched from the rest of his little body. And his face—oh, that face—a large black nose surrounded by smoky whiskers, mustache and beard, dark-rimmed, huge brown eyes with long midnight lashes, and triangle-shaped ears that bent forward at their tips like little question marks. And her favorite part of all—bushy gray eyebrows that curved over and down into his eyes. It was a wonder he could see at all, but they were too cute to trim.

That face could thaw the iciest of hearts, Avery mused. This little bundle of innocent happiness was in stark contrast to all of the dark things she'd seen; it didn't make sense to her, in that moment, that humans could be so evil in a world that was home to creatures such as Foggy the dog. Her chest swelled and tightened and moisture poised behind her eyes.

"Yeah," Hannah whispered at her side. "I know, right?"

Avery couldn't speak without blubbering cutesy nonsense, so she simply nodded and stood staring for another long moment. When Hannah's tentative touch grazed her forearm, she jumped a little, then apologized.

"No, no—don't you do that," Hannah said, her voice laden with tenderness.

"Can I pet him?"

"Of course, darling. Go right ahead. Just hold your hand out like this—" Hannah squatted down and held out her hand, low, palm up, demonstrating "—so he can meet you."

Avery followed Hannah's lead and Foggy sniffed at her hand, his cold wet nose tickling her skin. Satisfied that they were now friends, he looked up at her with his giant eyes and wagged his tail at top speed. He spun in two quick circles and then showed her his good-boy sit again, offering up a paw.

Avery shook it and then laughed, covering her heart with a hand, feeling lighter than she had in ages. This happy little dog made joy surge inside her like a wave, and the foreignness of all that raw emotion—the sort she'd come in contact with so frequently since meeting Isaac—was almost too much to bear. She reached down and stroked Foggy's ears, slowly calming as she ran her fingers over their velvety fur. It was the same effect she'd experienced when she had pet Jane for the first time the week before, except, it seemed, even more special.

It occurred to her that this little guy could be her dog, and she could be his person, if he liked her as much as she already liked him, and if Isaac and Hannah agreed it was a good match. She might actually get the honor of being his dog mom, and, if Isaac was right, Foggy could help her with some of her PTSD symptoms; he could help her take care of herself a bit better.

They could take care of each other.

On top of that, she would have someone to look after, someone to love—someone who saw only Avery, not the bad stuff that had happened to her, not the mistakes she'd made or her bad calls, or the fact that it was her fault she had lost her best friend. Foggy wouldn't judge her the way people did, and he wasn't scared to be near her.

As she looked into his eyes and ran her hands along his sweet muzzle, she felt an instant bond that surpassed all logic, reason and science. It was like she knew they belonged together.

She ruffled the fur on Foggy's head and it stuck out in a thousand directions, making Avery and Hannah laugh. Then she tilted back on her heels and stood up, catching Isaac's gaze from a few feet away. What she found there nearly overwhelmed her. He looked so selflessly pleased to see Avery getting along with the dog, it was as if his happiness and hopes for her were even bigger than her own.

He cared for her—it was written all over his face— and that scared the living daylights out of her.

The last non-family member Avery had cared for, had loved, was laid to rest in the Peach Leaf Cemetery.

She tore her eyes from Isaac and pushed aside Sophie's memory. Nothing she did could bring back her best friend; Avery would have to live with that for the rest of her days, but what she could do, what was in her power now, was to make sure something like that never happened again. And the best way to prevent someone she cared about from getting hurt was to keep her distance.

She decided then and there that she would let Isaac help her, and she would let herself spend time with him so that she could get better, so that she could be trusted again by her own family, so that she could get her life back together. And she would even allow herself to love this little dog. It was healthy to love, her therapist said, it was good for Avery to have reasons to get out of bed every day, but she would exercise extreme caution when it came to Isaac Meyer. She couldn't let him get too close. She'd already proven that she was dangerous, that for someone to risk loving her was potentially lethal, and she wouldn't let it happen again if she could help it.

What Isaac felt when he watched Avery meet Foggy was unlike anything he'd ever experienced before. In all of his years matching veterans with dogs, he'd seen plenty of compatibility and plenty of love grow from just a tiny mutual need for someone to care for. But this…this was something special. He could tell instantly that dog and woman were perfect for each other. Inside he breathed a sigh of relief, and when he exchanged glances with Hannah, he knew she was doing the same thing.

They had taken a chance on Foggy. Instead of the usual routine where they chose a puppy from a reputable breeder with a line of dogs of appropriate temperament, Foggy was an experiment, one that Isaac hoped with every ounce of his being would work out.

He caught Avery watching him out of the corner of his eye.

"Where did you find this little dude?" she asked, almost as if she'd picked up on his line of thought.

Isaac cleared his throat. "Foggy's from the local shelter."

"Oh," Avery said, not sounding surprised.

"Up until now, we've only worked with dogs raised specifically for therapy and service, but Hannah and I happened to visit the veterinarian a few months back to check on an injured cat she had found and taken in—she adopted him when he was free to go after surgery—and we met Foggy."

Isaac watched Avery, trying to decide how much to tell her. Working with animals wasn't always easy; heartbreaks happened now and then, and he didn't want to cause her undue pain. At the same time, though, Avery was tough, and if she was going to adopt Foggy, she deserved to know as much about him as she could.

"He was unwanted and abused by his owner, whose dog apparently wasn't spayed and had puppies with a stray. The doctor found Foggy on his clinic doorstep one morning along with his brothers and sisters, and he fixed them all up. Luckily they all found good homes, but Fogs was the last one and he was on his way to the shelter that morning when Hannah and I showed up."

Avery listened intently, her beautiful face full of emotion as she hung on to his every word, hungry for knowledge about the dog, just like a new parent learning to take care of a baby. She would make an amazing dog mom, Isaac thought again.

"It took him a little while to warm up to us, and then we had to get him to trust us, which took even longer, but from day one, he's been calm and easy, and, miracle of miracles, he doesn't overreact to stimuli. He's got all the makings of an awesome service companion. He's just special, I guess, despite what's happened to him, and we just couldn't bring ourselves to pass him up."

If Isaac could, he would take every animal home with him from the shelter. They all deserved far better than the cards life had dealt them. And now that he'd realized how much he could help them, he knew it would be the very hardest part of his job to visit that place and have to select which ones to take with him.

Avery nodded.

"After we found him, Hannah and I decided that we only want to work with shelter dogs from now on. It'll take some extra legwork to make sure that we find dogs with the characteristics needed to do this job."

"What kinds of things do you look for?" she asked, bending back down to rub Foggy's back as the dog reveled in her undivided attention.

"Friendliness, confidence in lots of different situations and with different types of people, predictable, steady behavior, and—most important—temperament. Dogs, even ones who have been severely mistreated, can almost always be rehabilitated if people spend the time and effort necessary to do so, but they're not always good candidates to be service animals. For that, we need to make sure that we're choosing dogs who have never, and aren't likely to, display any kind of aggression."

"Makes sense," Avery said, standing up. "I think it's awesome that you're choosing to work with rescue dogs."

Isaac smiled, warmed by her encouragement. "It's not been easy to convince new clients that this is the right thing to do, but we're working on it. Every dog that we pull from the shelter that ends up being a good fit is more proof that this can work. We loved doing this before, but if we can save homeless dogs instead of creating a demand for new puppies, then it's better for everyone. We save them, and they save people. Everyone wins."

"And they do deserve a chance, don't they," Avery said. It wasn't a question, and she was so right.

"They absolutely do. Dogs don't ask too much of us. They want to be fed, sheltered, healthy and loved. It's not a lot. And so many of them love having a job to do. I'm not sure they understand it, but it gives them purpose, and if they're anything like me, that means the world."

Color drained from Avery's face and Isaac caught his mistake too late.

"Oh, Avery. I'm sorry. I didn't mean—"

"I know you didn't. It's okay. I don't want you walking on eggshells around me, Isaac. I need for you to tell me the truth and to speak openly and plainly to me always, even if no one else in my life will." She walked over and set her hand on his arm. "I'll find my purpose again, even if it's different than my nursing job."

"Yes," he agreed. "I have no doubt that you will, and Foggy and I will do everything we can to make sure that happens sooner rather than later."

A flush of color returned to her cheeks and Isaac felt a thousand times better. He clapped his hands against his thighs. "Ready to get to work?"

"Definitely. Where do we start?"

Hannah shoved closed a file-cabinet door and joined them, a manila folder in her hand with Foggy's name scrawled along the tab in thick blue marker. She looked back and forth at both of them, grinning, and for the very first time since he'd hired her, Isaac wished she wasn't so damn observant. Hannah was a very intelligent woman, but she also had a gift for reading people down to their very depths. It was a little eerie sometimes. And right now she had that look on her face—the one that told Isaac she knew exactly what he was thinking about Avery Abbott.

He was in trouble.

A little involuntary cough escaped and he purposefully averted his eyes from his very astute assistant, which only made her chuckle.

"I've got all of Foggy's records here," she said, coming shoulder to shoulder with Avery so she could share the papers. "I've been keeping a journal of our training sessions, and since he's been bunking with me at night, I've also got all of his basic care info, down to the last poop."

A totally ungraceful and absolutely adorable laugh burst out of Avery.

"You keep a…a *poop* schedule for him?"

Hannah, so accustomed to working with new pups, didn't get the humor. "Well, yeah, why wouldn't I?"

Avery giggled and Isaac couldn't help but join her.

"Hannah's very thorough," he said. "It's one of the many reasons I need her around here."

Understanding crossed her features. "Oh, yes. I keep meticulous records whenever we get someone new. Dogs need structure to be productive, just like folks do, so as soon as a little one arrives, I get him or her all set up on a food schedule and, well, you know, so we can make sure potty training goes…ahem…as smoothly as possible."

"Ha!" Isaac and Avery both chimed, and even Hannah had to laugh at that one.

"All right, all right." She poked Avery playfully. "You'll get used to it soon enough if you decide to join forces with this little ball of love."

She reached down and gave Foggy a treat from her pocket, which he gobbled up immediately.

Hannah caught Isaac's attention and got down to business, going over each task she and Foggy had practiced enough that the dog performed them consistently. The two had mastered *sit*, *down*, *come*, *stay*, dropping and leaving items alone, waiting patiently at doorways, walking on a leash, exits and entrances into vehicles and buildings, settling down on mats and crates, and—as Foggy had so awesomely demonstrated with Avery—greeting people with excellent canine manners.

Isaac could see that Hannah was as proud of the dog as she would be of her own child. He couldn't wait to get to work with Avery and Foggy.

Once he and Hannah had finished going over Foggy's training log, Hannah reminded Isaac that she had other things to do.

"I'll leave you to it," she said aloud, then, leaning in to Isaac's ear, she whispered, "Alone."

She winked at Isaac and it took all his resolve not to roll his eyes. Of course Hannah would know he didn't mean it and that her intuition about his budding feelings for Avery was spot-on, which would only make things worse. She knew him well and obviously loathed the fact that she herself had been happily wed to her high school sweetheart since graduation, yet couldn't inflict her own marital bliss on everyone around her.

He knew. She'd been trying for years.

"All right, Hannah Banana. That's enough from you now. I won't be requiring any further assistance."

He'd used his most serious voice, but Hannah only laughed and hit him in the arm with Foggy's file before holding it out so he could take it. She glared at him playfully before pulling her giant sunglasses down from their nest in her poofy curls and over her eyes.

"I'm off to check on the play area fence out back. Let me know if you guys need anything, you hear?"

"Will do," Avery called from where she'd been practicing high fives with a delighted Foggy.

Isaac waved to Hannah and went over to join them. He was a pretty content man before he'd met this woman, but seeing Avery having so much fun with her new friend pushed him right over the edge into full-blown happy.

She was beautiful when she let go of her shield and put on that radiant smile that brought light into her entire face. For a moment, all of the shadows were gone, and there was only sun. What made him even happier was that she looked at him that way, too. It was often easier, of course, for someone with her past to befriend an animal than a human. Humans weren't as simple or as pure. They came with baggage and history and a thousand secrets upon that first meeting.

Nevertheless, she'd let him come near her, physically and emotionally, the other night and that morning. He was so lucky, he knew, to have the privilege of getting to know her. He got the distinct feeling that she didn't let many people get even that close, so it made him feel special that she'd chosen him; he wouldn't take that lightly.

He looked forward to every second of their time together that day and dared to hope that there would be countless more to come.

Avery practically bounced back over to join him, Foggy at her heels.

"So, where do we start?" she asked, optimism lilting in her voice.

"At the top, of course," Isaac said, tucking a finger under her chin. He was rewarded with a sweet smile that reached all the way into those blue eyes he'd begun to like so much that his need for them bordered on becoming a craving. It struck him instantly and with great force that what he wanted to do in that moment was kiss her nose.

Chapter 8

How ridiculous that his impulse was so sweet, so innocent, almost childlike in its purity and simplicity.

Most of his relationships with women—if they could be called that—up until that point had been casual dates that occasionally culminated in physical intimacy. Nothing serious, nothing complicated. He just hadn't met the right woman yet, to want more. He'd never felt a strong pull to get inside a woman's head, to know what made her heart set fire, what made her happy.

With Avery, already it was different. He wanted, no, needed, to know everything about her. He wanted to hear all the silly small stuff, like what her favorite movies were and what she liked to read. Was there something she loved to eat or drink? What were her thoughts on current events? What had she been like as a child? What did she want more than anything else in the world?

It was strange that he'd been so physically close to women before and yet had felt nothing like what he did when Avery was simply standing in the same room as he, breathing the same air. It scared him a little, yes, but he'd wanted to feel that way for so long that the fear did nothing to deter him from moving forward. It was too soon, he knew, to figure out whether or not this was what love felt like, but that didn't stop him from wondering.

It was certainly possible, wasn't it? It didn't matter that they'd only known each other for little more than a week, did it?

Isaac didn't think so. Life was short, and if something awesome came along and bit a man in the ass, it would be stupid to ignore it, to waste it. He had no intention of making that mistake.

"Everything okay?" Avery asked, and Isaac realized he'd been staring at her without blinking or breathing or doing any other normal thing to make him seem not kooky.

"Everything's great," he said, pulling in a breath.

Surely she couldn't read all the thoughts he'd just been having about her, about him, about the two of them. Surely she couldn't tell that he wanted to pull her close and bury his face in her golden hair, and much, much more. He studied her eyes, but they gave nothing away except obvious amusement.

"You sure?" she asked, tilting her head to the side, looking insanely cute.

"Absolutely." He cleared his throat.

Best get to work so his mind would have something to concentrate on other than Avery's lovely face.

"So, just a little info first. For dogs, trust is as important as it is for humans, although they're a lot quicker to give it away. For them, at least if they're raised from puppies, it's not so much that it has to be earned—although it did with Foggy at first, on account of his unfortunate past—as that you don't want to break it. If you show him that you'll reward good behavior, he'll give it to you consistently."

Avery nodded, her features registering discomfort at the subject of trust. Isaac knew it was something difficult for her, as it was for many people with PTSD. He knew it would always be something he'd have to work hard to show her if they were to build a relationship. That would bother a lot of men, he knew, but it didn't bother him. He was willing to work to earn Avery's trust. He would never break it if she offered it to him.

"And all dogs have something that motivates them."

"Like what?"

"Like toys, or affection, or food. You'll want to give all three of those things, but it's helpful to figure out what drives each specific pup. Foggy, for example—" the little guy's ears perked up at his name and he tilted his head to the left "—happens to love treats, so he's pretty easily motivated by food. Don't you, boy?"

Isaac dug a piece of dried chicken jerky out of his pocket and said, "Sit."

Foggy obeyed instantly, earning the bite.

"Very good boy," Isaac praised. He pulled more food from his pocket and gestured for Avery to open her palm, then dropped it in. "Now you try."

Avery set her shoulders back and stood stiffly, almost as if she were at attention. Isaac smiled at her seriousness, but regarded her with great respect. She understood how important her relationship with Foggy could be, and he loved that about her.

"Sit," she said, then laughed immediately as Foggy just grinned at her. "Oh, geez," she said, turning pink. "He's already doing that, isn't he?"

Isaac burst out laughing. "I'm sorry, Ave. My fault. Let's get him to stand up first." Isaac winked at Avery before asking Foggy to stand. "Up," he said, satisfied when the dog promptly stood to face them, earning another treat.

Avery watched Isaac carefully as he showed her one more time how to request that Foggy sit down, holding out his palm the way Hannah had earlier, then lifting it slightly.

"You can either just say the word *sit* to get him to do so, or you can give him the hand signal. That way, you've got both a verbal command in case you're too far away for him to see, like in another room, for example, or, if you're in a place where you need to be quiet, you can give him the visual cue."

Avery smiled, obviously enjoying the lessons as much as Foggy clearly did. Isaac hadn't spent as much time around him as Hannah had, but he could tell already that the dog was alert, responsive and extremely calm. It didn't even seem to faze him at all that Jane was amusing herself by tossing a tennis ball up in the air and chasing it around the room as they worked. He would be an excellent companion for Avery, Isaac was certain.

"So, I can take him with me…anywhere?" Avery asked, obviously pleased at the idea.

"Oh, yeah, that's the whole point," Isaac reassured her. "He's got his practice vest now, which should let store owners and restaurants and such know that he's allowed to be there, and then he'll get his official vest when he takes his exam."

"Awesome," Avery said, her face lighting up. "I can't wait to see what my niece and nephew think of him."

For the next few hours, they practiced through several basic commands until Avery was completely at ease asking Foggy to do all sorts of things he'd need to know in order to move around comfortably in public. Isaac showed Avery how to let Foggy know that he was off duty by removing his vest, and he and Jane chased each other around the room, stopping at intervals to show their play bows and wrestle, while Isaac and Avery laughed themselves to tears.

Foggy and Avery were a natural fit, Isaac could plainly see, and they were already becoming fast friends. Plus, he couldn't help but notice how well Foggy and Jane got along, which was wonderful on the chance that, someday in the future…

He couldn't let that thought stretch too far. Avery was already warming up, even after only a couple of hours with her new bud, but he had to remind himself that he didn't know what she wanted. There was something between them that couldn't be denied, something palpable and solid, but he wouldn't push her.

Even if she was beginning to have feelings for him the way he most definitely was for her, she would need time to come to terms with what that meant. She'd been on her own for a long time now. She was a trained servicewoman and she hadn't depended on anyone except her fellow soldiers throughout her time in the military, and it was probably difficult for her to depend on her family now, so Isaac couldn't ask her to lean into him.

And yet…

What he could do was give her a safe place to be

herself, to open up and start letting those deep, invisible wounds begin to heal.

The office door opened and Hannah poked her head through the door as Isaac turned.

"Hey, guys!" she called, pushing the door and walking into the room. "How's it going?"

"Going great," Avery answered, giving Hannah an easy smile. "Foggy is just…"

Avery looked up at the ceiling as if it might offer a word big enough to describe her feelings for her new sidekick, but then just shook her head and raised her hands in surrender.

"He's wonderful, isn't he?" Hannah offered.

"I can't get enough of him."

Hannah put her hands on her hips. "Has he been doing okay with all the basics?"

"Better than okay," Isaac said. "He's one hundred percent on everything. You did good, Hannah Banana."

Hannah shrugged. "It's my job."

"He's probably ready to take his test, but it'll be a couple of weeks before I can get our usual guy out here to run the exam. I have no doubt he'll do great. And, if Avery's ready then, too, she can take it with him as his handler."

Avery bit her lip—a sign that she was a little nervous, Isaac had learned by making a study of her pretty face.

"We've got plenty of time," he said. "And there's absolutely no pressure on you at all."

Hannah sent him a look but he shook his head. He would bring up the subject of the local animal shelter's upcoming 5K walk/run fund-raiser when the time was right and ask her if she'd like to attend.

There were a couple of sponsors coming that word

of mouth told him were interested in Isaac's new veterans program, and he'd hoped to run into, and if possible speak to, one in particular at the end of the walk that day. Having the owner of Palmer Motors offer to fund the program would be a dream come true—the money would make it possible to pull more dogs from the shelter to match up with veterans who couldn't afford to go through the training out of their own pockets.

Plus, it would be an excellent place for Avery to test things out with Foggy—all kinds of distractions would be present. But for now, she had had a long morning and was probably getting tired.

What they both needed was lunch. He wouldn't even pretend it wasn't an excuse for him to spend more time with her, to get to know her better, and he knew just the place.

"Well, guys," Hannah said, looking at her watch. "I've got to run." She pointed over her shoulder to the back of the building. "Isaac, the fence out back is fine. One of our new clients and his puppy are coming in later today to practice commands outside—" she raised her eyebrows at Avery "—and this little dude has a bit of a squirrel-chasing fetish. Had to make sure he won't get out of the play area and into the street. I'm determined to get him to focus, even with the little furry things jumping through the trees to tease him."

She winked and grabbed her purse from the file cabinet by her desk, then called to Foggy. "Are you coming, Fogs?"

Foggy stopped pawing at Jane and looked from Hannah to Isaac, then to Avery. He came to a decision and trotted confidently over to Avery's side, where he apparently intended to stay indefinitely.

"All right, then," Hannah said, feigning a bruised

ego. "Point taken. Avery?" she asked. "Would it be okay if this little guy spent the night with you?"

Avery looked surprised, but then childlike pleasure took over. "Um, yeah, that would definitely be okay." She clasped her hands together in front of her chest, elated.

"Okay, it's settled," Hannah said, grinning at Isaac. "Let me grab his supplies. Next time you come in to train, I'll pull all of his veterinary records from the computer and print them out for you. He's been neutered and is up to date on all of his shots, of course, and he's had regular treatment for fleas and parasites. We use organic stuff as much as we can, and I'll be sure to give you a supply, you know—if things work out." She winked, obviously confident that they would.

Hannah set about piling up Foggy's leash, food and toys, then wished them both a good day and headed out.

Immediately, Avery rushed over and wrapped her arms around Isaac's waist, taking the breath straight from his body.

"Thank you," she said. "Thank you, thank you, thank you."

For a second, all he could do was stand there, speechless and unable to move. But then, when the woman didn't let go, he decided he would. Isaac put his hands on Avery's back slowly, tentatively, in case she decided she didn't want to be touched in return, but she didn't even flinch.

Finally, he wrapped her small form in his embrace and tucked his chin into her hair, feeling, for the first time, that he'd found his perfect fit.

"Well, hey there, stranger! I haven't seen you in years, honey, how have you been?" Barb's voice carried all the way across her popular diner as Avery, Isaac and Foggy—looking adorable in his service dog vest—stepped inside. Avery's stomach did a little nervous flip, but she took a deep breath and grasped Foggy's leash tighter as she steadied herself for what she knew would be a big hug and lots of chatter.

"Come here right now and give me a big hug, honey," Barb said, coming out from behind the front counter. Avery did her best to smile as Isaac tossed her a concerned look. On the way to grab lunch, they'd had a chance to talk about some of the things that Avery felt she struggled with the most, and she'd shared how her heart beat faster and her palms became sweaty whenever someone came too close to her. It wasn't so bad with people she knew well, but strangers were another thing altogether. She'd had plenty of panic attacks by now to know the signs, and he'd promised to spend the rest of the afternoon teaching Foggy how to block people from getting too near.

As Barb hurried over, Avery concentrated on the red vinyl bar stools and the black-and-white-checkered tiles that she'd seen so often when she'd waitressed for Barb part-time in high school. Focusing on the familiar setting soothed her, and as Barb wrapped her in a mama bear hug, Avery's pulse finally slowed back to normal.

"I'm so glad to see you, Avery," Barb said before turning to Isaac. "She was my best waitress of all time."

"You say that about all your waitresses," Avery teased, making both Barb and Isaac laugh. "You look fabulous, by the way—haven't aged a day." She meant every word. Her former boss's curly hair had a little more salt to balance out the pepper beautifully, and her blue eyes were as bright as they always had been.

Barb's cheeks took on a rosy hue even as she playfully swatted Avery with a kitchen towel.

"I'll let you girls catch up," Isaac said, squeezing Avery's shoulder before heading off to put in their order.

Barb and Avery sat at a table and caught up while Isaac waited for their food, and Barb gave Foggy plenty of compliments on his excellent behavior. When their order was up, Barb disappeared into the kitchen and returned with a baggie full of chicken scraps. "For Foggy," she said. "Don't worry, it's nothing fatty."

"Why don't you take a break and join us for lunch?" Avery suggested, thrilled at how pleased Barb seemed with the suggestion. "Macy and Tommy and the kids are coming by, too." She glanced at her watch. "They should be here to meet us any minute now."

Barb's eyes sparkled. "I'd love to."

Warmth spread through Avery's veins. Normally she wouldn't have asked anyone to join her for a meal, preferring the company of her family, the only people who wouldn't judge her, who were accustomed to her edginess. Then again, nothing about that day was normal, was it? She had a dog now, she thought, smiling as she looked down at Foggy, whose paws spread across her feet where he lay, and she had a new friend.

Perhaps more.

There had been a moment back at the training center with Isaac… She was certain he'd almost kissed her, or at least had wanted to, and the thought surprisingly didn't scare her. She would have let him. She would have loved it.

"There they are!"

Her niece's high-pitched squeal at the sight of Foggy pulled her from her thoughts and Avery looked up to see Macy, Tommy and the kids crowding through the front door, bringing happy noise with them to the table. She and Barb stood for hugs all around, and Tommy went to help Isaac carry over several trays of food. After Avery introduced everyone to Foggy, whom the kids adored, of course, it was quiet for a bit while they dug into Barb's amazing fried chicken, the only sound a moan of happiness here and there. And it didn't take long for the hungry kiddos to finish up and run off to the playscape out back.

"Hang on, wait for Mommy," Macy called after them. "I better follow those guys," she said, getting up from the table, but Barb put a hand on her shoulder and gently pushed her back into her chair.

"You stay here and spend time with your family. My staff's got everything taken care of, the lunch rush is winding down, and I need more time with those little ones. It's been a while since I got my kid fix." She smiled around the table before hurrying off behind Sylvia and Ben.

"What'd you two work on this morning?" Tommy asked before taking a sip of his iced tea. Only moments before, his plate had been piled so high Avery could barely see around it, yet Tommy was as thin and solid as a post from all the farm work. It was a tender reminder that he'd taken a rare afternoon off to spend time with her.

"Mostly basic commands," Avery said, smiling at Isaac.

"These two get along like peanut butter and jelly," Isaac chimed in. "I think they're going to be perfect for each other."

"Anything we can do to help?" Macy asked, setting down her fork to wipe her hands.

Isaac nodded to Avery so she could answer. "Actually, maybe so," she said, looking back to him for reassurance.

"We do need a third person for an exercise we talked about earlier," he said. "The idea is to teach Foggy how to act as a sort of barrier between Avery and anyone that might get too close for comfort, like a stranger in a store aisle or out in public, that sort of thing."

Macy and Tommy nodded, eager to help. Isaac stood and they all followed to an open space near their table. "You remember the sit and stay commands from earlier?" he asked.

"Sure do."

He smiled at her, his expression proud.

"It's just a step beyond that. So what you'll want to do is tell Foggy to sit and stay in front of you, but facing away from you. It's a little tricky at first, but you'll get it."

He showed Avery how to circle a treat around in her hand until Foggy was facing out from her front. It took a few tries, but Foggy was a great sport, and eventually they got it down and practiced several times to reinforce the move.

"All right, so now what we need to do is have one of you—" he waved at her brother "—Tommy, you'd be good since you're larger. Come up to Avery and stand a bit too close like you're in a crowded spot."

Tommy moved in, holding his arms out like a zombie, and they all burst into laughter when Foggy began barking at him.

"Thank you, Foggy, but that's enough," Isaac said, and Foggy quieted down, keeping a side eye on her oh-so-threatening, goofy brother. "See, he's already got the right idea," Isaac said, chuckling, "but we need to redirect it a little."

They spent the next several minutes practicing having Foggy stand in front of her to prevent Tommy from getting too near, applying the "block" command when he performed the move correctly, so the dog would have a clear indicator of what to do if a similar situation arose, like in a grocery store line or on a bus or plane. Isaac also showed her that she could just have her pup sit in front of her, facing her, so that she could focus on him as a barrier between her and anybody else while she did some grounding and breathing exercises to calm down. It wasn't long before they had it down pat, and Tommy and Macy had fallen in love with her new furry friend.

As they chatted happily, Avery took a moment to enjoy the sweet little family surrounding her, as well as Isaac and Foggy, and her heart swelled.

She'd missed so much, had spent so long in darkness that she hadn't been sure she would ever again see light. But this…this was a glimmer. It was like waking up from a long, fitful sleep.

She knew she still had such a long, long way to go. But she had to start somewhere, and, as she let herself soak in the enormity of the blessings surrounding her, she realized a simple afternoon spending time with the people she cared about the most was as good a place as any.

Chapter 9

When they visited the park a week later, Avery had the strong sense that if Isaac and Foggy were not at her sides like two guards, she couldn't be sure that she wouldn't have just run away. The noises, colors, smells and all the chaotic stuff of life surrounded her as if she'd walked into a theme park on spring break opening day.

Gripping Isaac's large, steady hand in one of hers and Foggy's leash in the other, she closed her eyes and then opened them again, this time forcing herself to focus on one thing at a time.

There, beneath her feet, was the vibrant, soft Bermuda grass, a hardy green carpet formed from millions of thin, silky blades. She lifted her eyes and, straight ahead, they landed on the long, oval duck pond in the center of the park, gravel paths surrounding it like wagon wheel spokes. Above, the sky was the cobalt color of a robin's feathers, accented here and there with cottony clouds and glints of golden sunbeams. Several yards to her right, on the crest of a small hill, a young family enjoyed a picnic lunch consisting of what looked like chicken-salad sandwiches, dill-potato salad and spongy slices of pink strawberry cake adorning plates strewn across a red-and-white-gingham blanket.

The woman fed grapes to the small boy, who released peals of magic laughter each time she circled a plump purple orb round and round before popping it into his little round mouth, and a handsome man sat behind them, one hand at the small of the woman's back, the other capturing mother and child with his cell phone camera.

Down the path, an elderly couple strolled hand in hand, their papery fine skin linking them together as their matching silver hair reflected light from the sun's rays. College-aged men and women played a loud and happy game down at the tennis courts.

When she could pause and grant herself the patience required to take things in, one at a time, the barrage of anxiety that resulted from overstimulation subsided and the park was just a park, not a combat zone loaded with hidden dangers.

It was home.

This wasn't the place that had damaged her and turned her into a hypervigilant, fearful version of her former self. Instead, it was the one she'd fought for— imperfect, but full of hope and beauty—and freedom.

And, if she could only relearn to embrace it as her own, retrain herself to know that it belonged to her, she could keep going.

She understood now, after months of therapy, that

her PTSD would never go away; there was no cure for it. It would always be her silent enemy, lurking in the corners of her life like a predator, waiting for a weak moment to pounce and bring her down again. It would simply be a part of her forever. But hope wasn't lost, and she refused to focus on it, to give it strength. And she could develop the skills necessary for coping with the symptoms; she would survive. If she were lucky, she could even prevail.

Isaac's hand was on her shoulder then, its warmth reaching the skin through her T-shirt like a rich balm. "Okay there, sweetheart?" he asked, squeezing slightly.

Her lips curved upward at the buttery-smoothness of his voice and the term of endearment he'd used so casually.

"Yes, I am," she answered simply, not needing to say more.

Since they'd met, she and he had exchanged plenty of words, and talking and listening to him was, she found, a surprisingly welcome pleasure. But even more than that, she enjoyed their silences, those quiet moments of peaceful company, of just being together, that stretched out between them and required no dressing.

Now, though, she wanted to talk.

There was an itch in her chest and throat that she needed to scratch with words, with truth about the pain she'd suffered and had not, until now, had the courage to share with anyone—not even, if she were honest, herself.

It was time to open up.

She didn't care that the person she felt most comfortable with was someone she'd met only recently. If war had taught her anything good, it was that time was not the most valuable or the most important factor in a bond forged between two people. Rather, Avery thought, it was trust, which sometimes took years to build, yes, but could also be earned in mere moments, in small or large actions that communicated: *I am here for you; I will not abandon you.*

Isaac had given her that when he'd taken her into his home, fed her and offered sanctuary from her living nightmare. He'd done it by introducing her to Foggy, by intuiting that the dog would be a good companion for her and a protective layer between her and the world.

She could open her heart to this man, and if it bled, he would not startle at the droplets; he wouldn't run from her darkness. She didn't need months to know that much was true. She'd been given a gift in his kindness, in his generosity, and she was thankful.

Avery turned to face him and as she did, he cupped her face in the hand that had been resting on her shoulder. She closed her eyes, letting the heat of his skin seep into her cool cheek.

Wanting him to kiss her, to have him pull her near and cover her lips with his own, but knowing it wasn't yet time for that, Avery smiled and took his hand in her own, then led him across the grass to the duck pond. They sat together on the limestone wall that surrounded the pool of water. Foggy and Jane sat, too, at their feet, but their little doggie bottoms wriggled impatiently as they suppressed their urge to bark and chase the blue and green birds floating along the liquid surface.

"I never killed anyone over there," Avery said, her voice gravelly and so low she thought perhaps Isaac hadn't heard her.

He was silent for a full minute before responding, "You didn't have to tell me that."

Avery shook her head. "I did. I did have to tell you that." She turned and met his eyes. "It's what everyone wants to know, what everyone's thinking when they see me in town or talk about me behind my back, trying to figure out what happened to me over there. Sometimes, I wish they would just ask."

Isaac nodded. "Well, if it helps you to tell me, then I'm so glad you did. I'm glad you can trust me enough for that, though we haven't known each other long enough for me to expect it of you, and you never have to tell me any more than you feel comfortable with."

"I know that," she said. "It was my choice to tell you, and yes, it does help me to get that off my chest."

She looked out at the water and ran a finger over a long crack in the stone underneath her thigh. "I think people might believe I'm still human if they knew that about me. They might be less afraid to speak to me and say hello when they pass me on the street the way they used to, before I left and became someone else."

Avery could feel his gaze on her as she kept her eyes down, not sure if she wanted to look into his just then.

"You don't owe anyone any explanation, Avery. You have the right to say or not say what you choose. And you did not become someone else. You may have added some terrible experiences to your résumé, but you are still Avery Abbott, and the people who love you know that."

"I'm not so sure sometimes, but I don't blame them, either."

"What makes you say that?"

"Just certain things have changed. At my job—my

old job, I guess—for example. I was a great employee for years before I left, and I was thrilled when they wanted me back at the hospital after I came home. I was always at my best, always one hundred percent accurate in my diagnoses and medication calculations, often even more than the doctors I worked under. I never missed a day, I won awards and patients seemed to like me. Then, one day, something—I still have no idea what—triggered a flashback, and, well, you know how that looks. Anyway, after all of that time, I made one mistake and I lost everything. And I know that I scared the patient who was there when it happened. I can understand why they thought it best to put me on leave, but it still hurt."

She closed her eyes, remembering that tense, painful conversation with her boss. Avery couldn't help but feel betrayed.

"And with Tommy. The last time I had an episode like I did recently, he made it clear that if I couldn't get better, I couldn't stay in his home." The words caught in her throat and she struggled with the effort it took to say more.

"And the thing is, I don't blame him one bit—him or Macy. They have little ones to take care of, and if one of them had been awake, had come across my path when I was lost to reality, well—"

"Hey, hey," Isaac soothed, putting a hand over hers. Her fingers ceased their repetitive motion over the rock. "It's no good talking about what might have happened. The important thing is that your niece and nephew are fine, and what Tommy did was to protect them, yes, but it was also to protect you. Besides that, you are doing the work you have to do to get better. You're going to your therapy appointments, and now you've got Foggy and me to help."

She smiled at his sweetness, at his unfailing optimism. How wonderful it would be to have Isaac with her always, to lift her spirits each time they fell. But no matter how great he was, he couldn't fix her heart. She would have to do that herself.

"If Tommy really wanted to protect them, he should have tossed me out a long time ago."

"I disagree, and he and Macy would, too. They love you. They wanted you to realize how much pain you were truly in, and to help you find a way out. I just think they may not know the best way to do that. By giving you an ultimatum—a wake-up call, so to speak—they forced you to look for other options besides therapy. My brother was in therapy for a few years, and he still couldn't handle the symptoms. There is only so much doctors and medicine can do in certain cases. Sometimes you need a little something more, a little something off the beaten path."

It was Avery's turn to comfort Isaac. Lines creased his usually smooth forehead and his eyes were suddenly full of darkness she hadn't seen before.

"I didn't know you had a brother," she said carefully, not missing the past tense Isaac had used. "What was his name?"

Her statement seemed to pull him out of the depths of thought he'd been falling into, but the storminess remained in his face.

"His name was Stephen. He died when I was just out of college."

"Oh, Isaac," she said, resting her head on his shoulder. The gesture was meant to calm him, but it was possible that she'd benefitted the most from it. "I'm so very sorry for your loss."

"It was a very long time ago," he said.

"I'm not sure that matters, though, does it?"

"No, you're right. It doesn't. It still feels like he's going to walk back into the house and ask what's for dinner. And expect me to cook, of course. Stephen always was great at eating, terrible at preparing food."

He chuckled at the memory and Avery's heart picked up speed at the sound, glad he hadn't been pulled completely down into his sorrow.

"Do you mind my asking what happened to him?"

Isaac swallowed and tilted his head to the side, and for a second, Avery thought he might say that yes, he did mind.

"No, not at all. He took his own life when he was about the age I am now."

There was nothing she could say or do to express how acutely she felt his pain, and she wished for all the world that she could take it away, that she could bring his brother back for him.

Isaac was the closest person she had to a friend since she'd returned from war, battered and bruised in invisible ways, and if she were honest with herself, she wanted more from him than just friendship. So it hurt that she had nothing to offer in the way of consolation. The only thing she could do was to be there, and be open, the way he was for her.

Isaac spoke, softly. "He was very sick, and I can't say that I was…surprised…but that didn't make it any easier on me, or on Mom. I did the best I could for her, afterward, but she was never the same. I think she lost a lot of herself when her first child passed, and even though I knew, always, that she loved me just as much, I couldn't replace him."

Isaac's jaw set hard and Avery could see the extent of his hurt, despite his attempt to rein it in.

"He fought hard, he really did, but it wasn't enough. His death is what spurred me on when I left my old job and started to look for something more important to do with my life. I wanted out of the office, big-time, but a lot of my motivation to do something more was my need to live life to its fullest—for Stephen. It was almost like I had a duty to live enough for both of us, since he didn't have the chance.

"He's what led me into working with service dogs. I knew there had to be something different for people who weren't making it with the usual medication and psychiatric help. It wasn't until Stephen that I came across research that supported what I always felt to be true about animals—that they can feel strong emotion and can even help us when we are overwhelmed with our own. They love us without judgment, even when we can't love ourselves and when we think no one around us can, either. They don't care where we've been or what we've done. They care only about the present, about living in the moment the best way possible. It's a beautiful thing and humans could certainly stand to take a cue from our animal friends sometimes."

"Was he—" Avery chose her words carefully, not wanting to press on any nerve endings or cause any more hurt than he already felt, but wanting to know more, because she cared deeply about the man next to her. "Did he serve in the military? In combat?"

"Yes, he did." Isaac looked up at her, and even though his eyes held sadness, they were also full of optimism, and she wondered how someone who'd been through something so difficult could maintain his humble generosity, his pure but somehow not naive, outlook on life.

"Is that why you help people like me?"

Isaac grinned and Avery's heart lifted, relieved to see that wonderful sight again.

"To answer your question—yes, Stephen is the big reason why I got into training dogs for vets. I don't want to see anyone in my community go through the same stuff that he did and believe that there is no way out, that there can't be life on the other side—full life."

After a long moment, he raised both palms to her face and stared straight into her eyes with more intensity than she'd seen up to that point. Flecks of gold danced around his irises as he gave her a crooked, perfect smile, and Avery noticed for the first time that he had adorable dimples in both cheeks.

Sparks of electric joy shot through her entire body.

"But I have to correct you," he said, suddenly quite serious.

She knew that this…this was the moment she'd wanted so badly only minutes before. Instinctively, she could feel that this was one of those times she would look back on someday with great happiness.

The moment she started to think she might be able to find it again, to find love.

Take a chance, a little voice inside her prodded.

"Why's that?" She bit her lip, nervous and elated, sad and hopeful, vulnerable and brave, all at once.

He smiled, his brown eyes glittering in the sunshine. "Because, Avery, you asked if I help people *like you* because of Stephen, when, in fact—there is no one like you."

He caught her smile in his lips as he gently pressed them into hers, kissing her with a delicious combination of tenderness and passion. She closed her eyes and let herself drop over the edge into something new, losing herself in the moment, enjoying the sensation of falling, falling, falling, with the knowledge that she was safer than ever before in Isaac Meyer's strong hands.

It was incredibly liberating to forget everything that had happened to her before that moment, every cut, every scar, every bruise that had pulled her further and further away from her true self, from the strong woman she knew was still inside somewhere, waiting to be set free. And she knew he couldn't do that for her. Only *she* could fight her demons, only she could push until she reached the other side of the horrors that she feared would always return in her nightmares.

She knew all of those things as she kissed him back, wrapping her arms around his firm torso. But she had to admit, it was mighty damn nice to have someone at her side while she did the hard work.

Kissing Avery was far more than everything Isaac thought it would be. He supposed they were still there in the park near the pond, with the dogs at their feet and sunshine soaking through their shirts, but at the moment, he wouldn't have been able to tell if his life depended on it.

Wrapped up in the sweet, honey taste of her lips, the ones that were definitely, incredibly, kissing him back, he lost all sense of reality, all sense of time, all sense of anything except *her*.

He didn't care that this was probably too soon, that it

would mean things might change for them more quickly than either was prepared to handle.

It didn't matter.

This wasn't an ordinary girl, and this wasn't an ordinary relationship.

But there would be time for all of that later. Right now, all he wanted was to memorize the summery scent of her hair as its strands danced around her face in the gentle breeze, and the way her soft cheeks warmed under the touch of his fingers as they trailed along her jawline.

The way, when he'd finished kissing her, for now— he'd already decided that there would be so much more—Avery's blue eyes fluttered open as if coming out of a dream. A very good dream.

As she covered his hands with her own and pulled them gently away from her face, Isaac remained still, mesmerized by her beauty.

"Kisses look so good on you," he said, not caring that the words might be cheesy. Hadn't she told him that she always wanted the truth from him, no matter what? And it was the absolute truth. Her cheeks were rosy, which only made her blue eyes shine a shade brighter, and her lips were the color of strawberry jam, plump from their collision with his.

She smiled and gazed down at their joined hands. It didn't bother him that she didn't say anything. There was no need to. Everything they needed to say had already been stated in that kiss. The air buzzed between them with excitement and possibility, but they had plenty of time to figure things out.

A loud growl interrupted the quiet and for a second, Isaac thought it had come from one of the dogs.

"Someone's hungry," Avery said, laughing. She reached over and poked Isaac in his abs. Not a vain man, he was nonetheless glad he kept in shape, and her touch so near his groin set his mind off on a path that would be hard to come back from.

"Starved," he said, glad for the distraction.

He'd brought her to the park after their training session to relax and let the dogs out into the fresh air, but the park also happened to be the home of a food truck that served excellent burritos. The thought of lunch set Isaac's stomach to grumbling again.

"Let's do something about that, shall we?" Avery suggested, grabbing Foggy's leash and standing up.

Isaac did the same with Jane, but his girl wasn't a service dog, so it took a bit more work than just the "let's go" command to get Jane's mind off the ducks.

He'd kept an eye on Jane as they'd sat admiring the water. She had some hound in her, he was pretty sure, along with a thousand other things, and whenever she came across small animals her ears perked up and she fancied herself a hunting dog. Not that she was any threat. Whenever Jane got anywhere near a cat or a squirrel after a chase, she simply stood staring down her opponent, waiting to see if it would run off and start up their game again. She was completely harmless and a big doofus, but still, he always tried to make sure she was on her best behavior in public places.

"Come on, Jane," he said. "I promise I'll share some of my lunch with you if you'll promise me you won't run off after those ducks," he said, joking, but gripping her leash a little tighter all the same. At the mention of lunch, Jane's thoughts switched over to food and she finally decided that it was okay to leave the pond.

Isaac grabbed Avery's hand and they walked the hundred yards to where the food trucks parked. A row of shiny Airstream trailers, promising every variety of Texas cuisine, beckoned as they arrived at the gravel parking lot. Picnic benches painted in primary colors were scattered about, and kids ate rapidly melting ice-cream cones while their moms and dads munched on burgers and quesadillas.

"Wow," Avery said, her eyes wide at the sight. "I hadn't realized how much I missed this place until now."

Isaac shielded his eyes from the sun and smiled at her, glad that he'd picked a good place for their first date. Jane sniffed the ground, searching for dropped crumbs, and Foggy's nose twitched at the savory scents filling the air.

"We used to come here in high school," she said, her expression gone soft at the memories.

"Yeah, you were lucky to have it," he said.

"What? It wasn't here when you were at Peach Leaf High?"

"Nope. I'm a couple years ahead of you, according to Tommy. They built this right after I graduated."

She squinted, thinking about the timeline. "Oh yeah, you're right. It was my junior year when this all went up." She grinned. "I just remember sneaking over here on lunch break to grab hot dogs. We weren't supposed to go off campus until senior year," she said, giggling. "But you know, teenagers always follow the rules."

Isaac chuckled with her.

"So…you've asked Tommy about me, huh?"

Her voice was lighter than it had been before, and Isaac was almost certain it was more playful. His grin stretched from ear to ear when he realized suddenly that she was flirting with him.

"I have," he said, meeting her tone. Then he switched his voice to sound gruffer. "But, you know, I'm a professional and you're technically my client now."

He stopped walking and turned to face Avery, slipping a strand of hair behind her ear, enjoying the fact that he could touch her now without causing her to jump. "I make it a practice to know what I need to know about the people I'm working for."

"I see," she said, tucking a finger under her chin. "And what is it that you need to know about me, Mr. Meyer?"

There was genuine curiosity in her voice alongside the flirtatiousness. She wanted him to ask about her. This was the invitation he'd been waiting for.

"Everything," he said truthfully.

Chapter 10

"I want to know everything about you, Avery Abbott," he said, staring into her eyes in the hope that she could fully recognize his sincerity.

She swallowed, appearing suddenly nervous.

Had he been too honest? Said too much? He retraced his steps, wishing he could put that carefree look back on her face.

"But first—lunch."

She relaxed, giving him a smile, and he reminded himself to take things slow. He hated the thought of going anything but full speed ahead now that he'd been around this woman enough to know he wanted more, more, more, but if he pushed too hard, he could lose her altogether, and that simply was not an option.

"Anything you want, sweetheart. Take your pick."

Avery crossed her arms over her chest and surveyed

the selection. Isaac's favorite were the massive, over-stuffed delicacies from Freddy's Fajitas, but if pressed he'd have to admit that anything from any of the food trucks was guaranteed to be fantastic.

"I'm actually pretty darn hungry," Avery said, sounding surprised at herself.

"That's great news, and something we can definitely fix."

They must have been on the same wavelength because Avery's eyes wandered over to Freddy's and she headed in that direction. They ordered and walked away carrying giant tortillas stuffed to the gills with chicken, avocado, onion, sour cream and enough jalapeños to light the town on fire.

"A girl after my own heart," Isaac said, nodding at the spicy fillings spilling out of Avery's meal.

"Oh, don't get me started. I can't get enough. Macy is the only one who can make salsa that's hot enough for me, and I could beat the guys right out of my unit in pepper-eating contests. Every time."

She winked at him, proud, and he was thrilled to hear her sharing fun memories of her time in service.

"Man, I missed Tex-Mex while I was gone," she said, reminiscing and pulling her food a little closer to her as they walked over to a butter-yellow table and set down their cardboard boats of food, their drinks and a few paper napkins. Isaac excused himself and headed to the food truck to grab a plastic bowl, then took it over to a water fountain and brought it back to the table, placing it underneath for Jane and Foggy to share.

"How long were you over there? Afghanistan, right?" Isaac asked, watching her closely.

"Yep, that's right. Three tours, six months each."

"Wow. That's…a lot."

"It was," she said, nodding as she sat across from him and spread a napkin over her lap. "The time went by fast, in a way, but there were nights when I really, really wanted to be back in my bed, when I just wanted to be home again."

"I can only imagine."

"A lot of bad things happened, but…there were good times, too. At first it's hard, especially in Basic, because you don't know anyone and you miss home and everything is physically demanding and weird and it makes you all emotional."

She took a sip of her iced tea and peered into the distance, a trace of a smile crossing her lips as she watched a mom feeding a toddler little cut-up bites of pizza.

"And then, of course, you don't want to show everyone that you're emotional, so you try to hold it in and it just sort of comes out of you at random times."

Avery laughed at a memory. "Once, my friend Sophie and I were just chilling out after a drill, listening to the radio, and an old stupid song from the eighties came on. You know, one of those ridiculous, drama-queen hair band ballads, and I just completely lost it. I'm pretty sure Sophie thought I'd lost my marbles."

Isaac's chest tightened at the bittersweet picture she'd painted.

"Thank God I had Sophie with me over there. I don't know what I would have done without her." Avery's words came out a little squeaky and she hurried to tuck into her food.

They ate quietly for a while and Isaac relaxed into the silence. Jane and Foggy were lying under the table next to each other, their tongues hanging out.

They both took big bites of their fajitas and giggled as juice inevitably escaped to roll down their chins. Isaac pulled out a piece of chicken, wiped off the sauce and pretended to drop it under the table so that Jane could pick it up.

"Can you feed them people food?" Avery asked.

"Yeah, you can give them plain meat, particular veggies and fruit, eggs, stuff like that. Remind me later and I'll print you out a list of doggie no-nos. Certain things, like grapes and chocolate, are dangerous and potentially deadly to their systems, but there are quite a few things they can share with us."

He shook his head and gave Jane a look.

"I would not recommend feeding them from the table most of the time, though," he said. "It's hard to get them out of the habit of asking for scraps once you start. I've already ruined Jane for that. Foggy's so well-trained that you might be able to get away with it on occasion."

He pointed as Jane put on her very best sad face and rested her furry chin on his knee. "See what I mean?"

"Oh, goodness," Avery said, cooing. "She's too cute. How can you possibly resist her?"

"That's just it," he said, shrugging his shoulders. "I can't."

"I miss Sophie so much, sometimes," Avery said, so softly Isaac wasn't sure he'd heard her correctly.

"You were close, huh?" he asked.

Avery nodded, her lips forming a thin line.

"We grew up together and hung out all the time, but we weren't that close until we decided to join the army. I'd finished getting my RN at community college and was ready for a change, and, well, Sophie was tired of working low-paying jobs to get by. You know how

Peach Leaf is," she said, glancing up at him. "Not a lot of work to go around."

He nodded in agreement. It was true. Lots of folks who were raised in their small town couldn't find well-paying jobs. The options were simple: go off and get a degree or other vocational training, or work for peanuts. Most people who left didn't come back, finding that they'd outgrown their hometown. Isaac could totally understand and had grown up telling himself he'd never come back except to visit Mom and Nana, but after he'd been gone a few years, he'd begun to miss something about this place. Even if it wasn't perfect, and hell, nowhere was, at least there were people in Peach Leaf who knew his past, who knew who he was down to his bones and knew what he'd come from and where he'd been. There was something solid, something important about a person's home. You might not always love it, and you sure as hell might not always like it, but home was home. He imagined Avery knew that very sentiment well.

"I do know," he said, giving her a soft smile.

"So Sophie and I decided to go big or…well…stay home." Avery grinned. "So that's what we picked. She didn't meet her husband until later, on one of our visits home, and then they had Connor a ways down the road."

"It must have been hard, being so young and leaving your family."

Avery shook her head. "Well, I don't know if Tommy's ever told you, but our parents were killed in a car crash when I was twenty-two and Tom was a bit older."

"God, I'm so sorry," Isaac said, putting down his fajita. He touched Avery's hand and she closed her eyes, evidently enjoying the touch he'd offered to soothe her. "You've been through so much for someone your age."

"That might be true, but you know, things could always be worse. I'm lucky to have Tommy and Macy and the kiddos, and this town, and I was lucky to have Sophie and to make it home in one piece. Or, you know, mostly."

Avery choked up a little.

"I just wish, sometimes—" she looked up at him under hooded eyes, as if choosing her words with caution "—sometimes I wish that Sophie had been the lucky one. That it had been she who made it home alive."

Isaac winced at her words and at the similarity they held to some of Stephen's later statements. He put down his food, suddenly not hungry anymore.

"Avery, please don't say things like that."

"I'm sorry, Isaac. I don't mean to be morbid, and I don't mean to sound like I'm not thankful to be here, but there are times when I think… I mean, I can't understand why it was me and not her."

She poked at her fajita with a fork, pushing around the contents that had escaped the flour tortilla.

"It's my fault, you know," she said. "It's my fault she's gone."

Avery's eyes glistened with moisture and Isaac reached over to stop her anxious fidgeting, covering her hands with his own.

"How can you think something like that?" he asked.

She looked up at him, her eyes huge and shiny and full of sorrow.

"Because it's true."

"Look, Avery. Whatever happened, whatever you

think was your fault, please believe me that it wasn't. I know you."

Her brow furrowed and he could sense her skepticism.

"I know, we've only known each other for less than a month, but don't tell me that I can't feel your heart after that amount of time. You know there's something… something going on between us. Something special. And I don't need much time to be a good judge of character. And your character, Avery, it's the best."

She smiled sadly and he wondered if she didn't believe him. It would take more than words to convince her that what he felt was real and true.

"You wouldn't say that if you knew the whole story," she said, pulling her hands away from his to rub at her eyes.

"Then tell me. Tell me the whole story."

She closed her eyes and Isaac gave her the time she needed, taking a moment to check on Foggy and Jane under the table. The two dogs were snoozing side by side, their limbs and tails curled up, as though they knew they were meant to be together.

If only it were that simple with people.

If only he could convince Avery that he would be here for her, that he would support her as long as she would let him. That he wouldn't let what happened to Stephen, happen to her. He'd dedicated his life's work to ensuring that for as many men and women as he could help, but he hadn't known until Avery how much it really mattered that his program worked. It really could mean life or death for certain veterans. And those lives—lives that had been offered up in the most dangerous situations imaginable in an attempt to stand for the freedom of humanity—mattered. So much.

He looked up from under the table to check on Avery and noticed instantly that her expression was one of terror.

"Avery, what's wrong?" he asked.

The color had drained from her face and her skin was white as a ghost despite the afternoon heat, and her eyes were huge as she focused on something in the distance. Isaac followed her line of vision, but all he could see at the end was a man about his age, and a cute little boy who looked to be three or four years old.

Avery got up from the table as if in a trance, heading toward what he assumed were the dad and son.

"Avery. Avery?" he called after her, but she either ignored him or couldn't hear.

Isaac checked on the dogs again to make sure they were still asleep and hurried after her.

As soon as she'd seen them in the distance, Avery was pulled in their direction as if an invisible fishing line had begun to reel her in.

Nathan and Connor Harris.

Sophie's Nathan and Connor.

Her best friend's husband and son were sitting at a table enjoying a meal of their own, not too far from where she and Isaac had sat down to eat. Even from a distance, Avery could see lines on Nathan's young face that shouldn't have been there yet. He looked way too old for a man in his midthirties.

And it was Avery's fault.

She didn't know what she would say when she arrived at their table, which now seemed miles away as she trudged forward as if through mud. She just knew she had to see them, had to get close. She needed to make sure that they were okay.

Nathan had refused to speak to Avery at Sophie's funeral, and she couldn't blame him. She had decided that he agreed with her that it was her fault his wife, her best friend, was gone.

Nothing could convince her otherwise. It was her idea to trade shifts that day. It didn't matter why. It was her decision that had cost them all an amazing woman. How could Nathan—and even Connor, one day, when he became old enough to learn what happened to his beautiful mother—ever forgive her?

How could she ever forgive herself?

She neared the table and Nathan looked up, the smile that had covered his face as he watched Connor play with a fire truck evaporating when he saw who approached. He wiped his hands on his jeans and stood, covering the distance between them to meet Avery before she made it to where they sat.

"Avery," he greeted awkwardly, placing nervous hands in his pockets. She couldn't read his tone; it was absent of any emotion that might give her some clue as to how he felt upon seeing her.

Suddenly, she regretted coming over, wishing she'd opted to grab Isaac and run instead.

What had she been thinking?

They weren't exactly on decent terms. She had no right to just waltz up to Nathan like this and remind him of something he probably tried every minute of every day to forget. Just glimpsing her face probably brought back a million painful memories.

Suddenly, Isaac was at her side. She could feel him

there as if he were a part of her own body, but for some reason she wasn't able to pull her attention from Nathan.

"It's been so long. I haven't seen you around town," Nathan said, his words shaky but not unkind. What had she thought he would do? Yell at her in a public place? It would be what she deserved.

"It's...good to see you, Nathan. How are you holding up?" The words burned her throat as they came out.

"I'm actually doing okay," he said. "Despite...everything." He tried to smile but it wouldn't quite take. "How about you, Avery?"

"The same," she said.

"How's your family? Tommy and Macy and the kids?"

Images flashed before her eyes of all of them gathered together, the Thanksgiving before her and Sophie's last tour. It was the last time she'd seen Sophie with her boys, and her heart ached at the memory; she was suddenly quite certain that her chest was going to explode.

"Nathan, I'm so sorry."

He held out his hands. "Don't say that, Avery. You know it won't help."

"But I am," she said, taking a step toward him.

Warmth spread through her lower back. Isaac's hand was there, holding her steady, but she couldn't look at him, afraid that she might cry if she did.

And she couldn't cry. Soldiers didn't cry. Tears were for release, to make people feel better. Avery wouldn't allow them.

She remembered when she and Sophie had first gone into that home to speak with a few of the local women who had gathered for tea. Avery's job was to check on them, to see if they needed any medical care or advice, to build trust so that they could later ask questions, draw information. Sophie, a fellow medic, was her partner.

They'd been surprised that day at how much they enjoyed spending time with those women—sweet, shy ladies who were apprehensive at first, but opened up over several weeks, eventually inviting Sophie and Avery to come by weekly. She and her best friend, using what little they'd learned of the local language and a lot of smiles, had established a repertoire with them, had almost come to trust them, though they both knew that was a very dangerous place to tread.

Avery felt the desert heat again, the dry, sandy air surrounding her as she cared for an injured patient that morning, a soldier who had lost a leg to a daisy-chain IED only an hour before. She'd stayed late to prep him for emergency surgery and, when Sophie showed up to relieve her, had offered to extend her own shift so she could check on the progress of her patient.

Avery found out later that Sophie had decided to use the extra time to meet with the women, eager to get back early enough to take a Skype call from Nathan and Connor before picking up Avery's later shift. Sophie had taken another soldier with her, and they had both lost their lives when a bomb exploded inside the house where they met.

If Avery hadn't been so invested in working on that soldier that morning, if she'd just checked out and let Sophie work her regular shift, her best friend would be there now, sitting in the park with her husband and son, just as she should have been.

"Nathan, please. You have to know how sorry I am," she said, careful not to let her voice break.

"I can't do this, Avery. Not here, not with Connor."

She looked over Nathan's shoulder at the little boy. With his auburn hair, bright emerald eyes and a sprinkling of freckles like cinnamon across his button nose, he was the spitting image of his mother. Nathan must have seen her every day in their child.

"Can…can I see him? Can I talk to him?" she asked, folding her hands together at her waist.

Nathan's eyes narrowed and he averted his gaze from hers, his jaw clenched.

"I don't think that's a good idea, Avery. I'm sorry. I just don't think I can handle it right now."

She closed her eyes, willing the tears to stay put behind her eyes.

Isaac's voice came, low and soft. "Is everything all right, Avery?" He didn't bother introducing himself to Nathan. As it had been for the past couple of weeks, all of his attention and concern was focused on her. He was an amazing man, better than she deserved.

How could she let herself be so happy in his presence when her best friend was dead and it was all her fault? How could she allow herself joy when Sophie would never breathe again, would never again hold her little boy or see him graduate, get married?

Her stomach clenched. She couldn't.

Everything went blurry and she had to get out of there before she got lost again in the past.

"I'm so sorry, Nathan," she said, then turned and began to run.

She ran until she got to the duck pond and stopped, her breath coming in fits and starts as the panic threatened to return. She would never outrun it, could never escape it. It would always be there, lurking in the corners, ready to attack her at any second. She would never be safe again.

Her knees buckled beneath her at the reminder and she sat on the ground with a thud, curling her arms over her head as the tears broke free and spilled forth, dropping like rain into the dirt beneath her.

"Avery, sweetheart, it's okay. It's okay."

Isaac's arms were around her and he was rocking her back and forth like a child. He sat next to her and pulled her into his lap, wrapping her up and soothing her, stroking and kissing her hair.

Safe in his embrace, she let the tears come again.

Foggy forced himself into her lap and curled into a ball, raising his head to lick away the moisture from her face and all of a sudden, Avery started laughing. And then she couldn't stop.

We must look ridiculous, she thought, *like a crazy, mismatched set of Russian nesting dolls.*

She laughed and laughed until her stomach hurt, knowing it was her body's weird way of reacting to all the pain that had surfaced when she'd seen Nathan. She wished he'd let her near Connor. All she wanted was to look into his little face and see Sophie again, just one more time.

But she understood. She didn't have the right to ask such a thing. Nathan had already suffered enough at Avery's hands.

Isaac's arms loosened and she felt his chin nestled between her shoulder and neck. She leaned back into his chest, savoring the feel of his strength against her back for just a moment. He didn't speak for a long time, just held her and let her cry softly.

"I'm a hot mess," she said finally, earning a little laugh from him.

"Everyone is, Avery. Everyone's a hot mess at some point in life. I don't think there are too many who make it out of here without some crap happening that breaks them apart for a while."

"Yes, but I'm the worst."

"No," he said, "you're not."

"How do you know?" she asked, turning so she could see his face just above her shoulder. She scratched behind Foggy's ears.

"I just do," he said. "But, Avery, you scared me back there."

"I'm sorry. That was Nathan. He's…"

"I know, I guessed. It's okay. You don't need to apologize. I just got worried. I thought he might be upsetting you and I didn't want you to be afraid."

She shook her head. "It's not that. I just misjudged the situation. I thought maybe enough time had passed that he would let me see Connor again. We all used to be so close and I miss that kid. He doesn't understand that his mom is gone, and to tell you the truth, I don't really, either, sometimes. I just thought if I could see him… I know it's crazy, but I thought… I thought for some reason that it might make me miss Sophie less. He looks so much like her."

Isaac nodded, his stubbly chin tickling her cheek.

"But Nathan's right not to let me near him. I've already done enough damage as it is."

"I don't think that's the case, Avery, but we don't have to talk about that right now if you don't want to."

She rested her head under his chin.

"What is it that you'd like to do? Right now?"

"I think I'd like to go home, if that's okay with you."

"Absolutely," Isaac said, standing up slowly and offering his hands to help her up. Foggy stood as well, waiting for one of the crazy humans to tell him what to do, while Jane bounced on the end of her leash, eyeing the duck pond in vain once again.

How strange, how incredible it was that she was now part of this little crew. How odd that she'd somehow taken up with a gorgeous, sweet man and two fuzzy mutts in a matter of less than a month.

And how beautiful, too.

Chapter 11

The sun was sinking lower into the western sky as Isaac pulled into his driveway in Tommy's old spare truck; his own had been towed to the shop and would be fixed within the next couple of days. Tommy had offered to accompany Isaac to pick it up when it was ready, but he'd already decided that, if it was safe for her to drive the short distance into town with him, he would rather have Avery's company.

She was asleep on the seat next to him and didn't wake even when he pulled to a stop. He let the dogs out but left Foggy's things in the truck so they wouldn't forget them whenever he dropped Avery off at her brother's house. When she'd said she wanted to go home, Isaac had assumed she meant Tommy's, but when he'd started to drive away from the park, she'd shyly asked if it was okay if they go to his house for a few hours instead. He hadn't asked why, glad that she'd wanted to spend more time with him, but he could guess that maybe she needed some time away from family, some peace and quiet to put herself back together after what had amounted to a long, tough day.

He'd texted Tommy and let him know he'd bring Avery by when she was ready, and to confirm that Foggy would have a permanent home with their family, something he and Avery had forgotten to discuss thus far. The kids would be thrilled to have him stay, Tommy had texted back, and he was happy that Avery would have a companion. She'd been lonely, he had said, and he was glad she and Isaac had happened upon each other.

Isaac didn't need Tommy's permission to hang around Avery; she was a grown woman and could make her own decisions, but it was great to have all the same. The two men were neighbors, and Isaac valued Tommy's friendship and opinion. Plus, he'd really enjoyed their fried chicken lunch the other day and liked the idea of becoming closer with the whole Abbott clan.

After unloading the truck, when the dogs were safe inside the house, Isaac headed back outside to gather Avery. When he opened the door, she was still sound asleep, her blond hair strewn across her shoulder like a scarf, eyes fluttering with dreams he hoped were happy ones. He pulled her arm over his shoulder and placed his hands beneath her back and knees, lifting her out of the passenger seat with minimal effort. Her head tilted in against his shoulder and her soft breath brushed against his chin as he carried her into the house and laid her on the couch.

The similarity to that first night didn't escape him, and he realized with a jolt how different things were now, how much more he knew about this woman who'd stumbled into his life.

How, even in such a short time, he couldn't imagine a day without her.

Nor did he want to.

He wanted her to be his—his to protect, his to take care of, his to...

Well, maybe it was too soon for that. It was crazy to be thinking about that already—or was it?

Of course it was. Avery was different from anyone he'd been with before. She needed more from him. Isaac didn't want to push things so far, too fast.

But then again, what if?

She was a powerfully sexy woman, after all, whether she knew it or not, and he wanted her more than he could stand to think about without sending his body into overdrive. With all of his strength, he pushed the thought aside, for now.

While Avery snoozed, Isaac took the dogs out back to do their business before setting up Foggy's bowl next to Jane's in the kitchen and filling them both with food. He checked that there was fresh water in the large bowl and, when the dogs were crunching away at their kibble, he grabbed a beer on his way out of the kitchen.

He'd expected to find Avery still sleeping, but when he got back to the living room, she was on the far side, staring at a collection of photos on the wall.

She turned to face him, hair falling onto the afghan she'd wrapped around her shoulders. "Is this your family?"

He nodded, holding the beer bottle out to Avery. She took a sip and handed it back to him. "Would you like one?" he asked.

"No, thanks. I'm careful with alcohol…with my meds and all. And I've seen too many of my friends spiral down with it, trying to medicate themselves." She shook the thought away. "I love a good brew now and then, but I don't want to take chances."

Isaac admired her. Like Avery, he knew many veterans—many people, really—who tried to find peace at the bottom of a bottle, but the end result was the same as if they'd been searching for a pot of gold at the end of a rainbow, and it would kill him to see something like that happen to Avery.

"That's just another thing that makes you strong, Avery," he said, reaching up to touch her hair. She closed her eyes as he ran his hand over her back and he pulled away, very much aware of the impulses coursing through his veins.

She was vulnerable, and he would not let anything happen that she might regret, just because her wounds were open and she'd had a trying day. If she wanted him as much as he wanted her—and God, he hoped she did—there would be plenty of time for that when she was ready.

"So," she said, opening her eyes and tilting her chin toward him. "Introduce me."

Isaac smiled and set his beer down on an end table. "All right, but most of these are my nana's photos, so I take no responsibility for any stupid ones of me."

She laughed, the sound like a balm to his soul.

"So, this is Nana herself, as you might have guessed. She was an amazing woman—strong, smart, kind— like you." He touched Avery's cheek briefly, the gesture softening her blue eyes. "And this is me when I was a teenager."

"Very, very handsome," she said, winking at him over her shoulder. "Too bad we never had a chance to meet back then. I would have definitely been interested."

The breath disappeared from his lungs and Isaac sucked it back in, willing himself to calm down, to focus on something other than the beautiful woman standing right beside him, telling him she would have dated him if only they'd met years before, hoping that what he read between the lines was accurate.

He went on, desperate for a distraction from the sweet scent of her skin, from those berry lips he'd gotten to taste only hours ago, an action that had only served to make him want so, so much more. She was in his system now, he realized, and he needed another dose of her to keep him going.

"This is Mom," he said, pulling his eyes away to point at a faded snapshot of his mother holding a baby version of himself in her arms, three-year-old Stephen by her side, just after his father had left the three of them alone, choosing to start over and make another family instead.

Those had been hard times, with little money for a woman with two growing boys to feed. It wasn't until high school that Stephen had been able to get a part-time summer job and help out; Mom hadn't allowed him to work during the school year, concerned that his studies would be neglected. He had then gone on to train as an electrician—work that seemed to make him happy.

Then 9/11 happened; Stephen was twenty-five, older than many of the people in his basic training, but Mom had been so proud.

Their lives would never be the same after that. If only it were possible to jump into that picture and warn them.

Then his brother would still be alive, and he wouldn't feel so alone in the world, so rudderless without family.

Avery pointed to another photo, one of Stephen in his dress uniform, the red, white and blue of their country's flag forming a backdrop. "This is Stephen?" she asked, touching the photo gently through its glass cover.

"Yes," Isaac said, his voice breaking a little before he coughed and set it right. "My big brother."

Avery turned then and buried herself in Isaac's chest, wrapping her thin arms around his waist. He let her hold him for what seemed like hours. The world slipped away when she was that close to his body, and it took a herculean effort not to react to her touch.

He pulled back, not wanting to overwhelm her.

"It's okay, Isaac. I'm a big girl," she said, looking up at him with a hint of amusement.

"Avery, I… I don't want to push you into anything you aren't ready for. It's been a rough day and you're probably a little shaken up right now."

A tiny hint of annoyance flickered across her features and he hated even the idea that she might think he didn't want her.

"Trust me…if things weren't so volatile, if…if we'd known each other for longer and been on a couple of real dates at least, then this would be different."

She looked away and, though she still had her arms around his torso, tension had tightened her limbs.

"Hey," he said, urging her to face him by gently pulling her chin back until she met his eyes. "I want this. I definitely, definitely want this. But now isn't a good time."

She nodded. "You're right, Isaac. I don't want to go too fast, either." She said the words, but he detected a hint of doubt or disappointment in them—maybe both.

"We really haven't known each other all that long," he said.

Avery giggled, but then her face became serious. "The best weeks of my life."

Isaac started to speak but she put a finger to his lips. "I mean that," she said, and he believed her. "In spite of everything, and it has been a weird whirlwind, I mean it. Before the night we met, I didn't have Foggy, and I didn't have you, and I wouldn't change that for anything."

She rose up on her tiptoes and kissed him. This kiss was different from before—deeper and more intense. Avery opened her mouth and Isaac slipped his tongue gently inside, letting his arms slip farther down her back as he relished the honey flavor of her mouth, stroking along her teeth and the inside of her lips.

In seconds he was back on the edge, wanting her with every cell in his body, lost in the wet heat of her mouth, all the while struggling to maintain some semblance of control.

He lifted her in his arms and carried her to the couch where they continued, hungry for more, but happy all the same just to be able to share kiss after kiss. He was careful with his hands, but couldn't keep himself from sliding them under her shirt, pressing his palms into the warm skin of her back. When she did the same to him, and just before he was certain all bets were off, he pulled away gently, settling her shirt back down as he placed a few more kisses on the tender skin beneath her ear.

Every inch of her body was on fire as Isaac's fingers danced over her flesh, and Avery cursed them both for agreeing not to go any further. At least not yet.

Now that she'd had a tiny sample of what Isaac Meyer could do to her, Avery's appetite was sparked.

He was right, of course, wasn't he? Maybe it was too soon for things to escalate any more, but that didn't mean it was easy to hold back. In fact, it was the hardest damn thing she'd ever done.

How long had it been since she'd been touched like this? How long since she'd last been with a man whose skin felt like lightning when it came in contact with hers?

Never, she thought. This was a first.

No one else had ever made her this desperate for more…of everything. More kisses, more touching, more time together. No one else could set her pulse racing with one look and send it into dangerous territory with a single kiss.

This was all new. This was something *more*.

As Isaac placed a few last kisses on her neck, sending tingles all the way down to her toes, Avery closed her eyes. He pulled away slowly, but immediately she wanted him back against her form, his heated skin soaking through her shirt the way it had been before.

"Ugh, you're torturing me on purpose," she said, her voice husky and full of thinly veiled desire.

"Trust me, I know the feeling," he said, and the gravelly, sexy sound of his words did nothing to calm her nerves.

"Would you like some tea?" he asked, changing the subject for both their sakes.

"I would, yes. Actually, if you don't mind, what I'd really like is to get cleaned up first."

"Anything you want." He gave her a sweet smile before getting up from the couch.

He headed down the hallway and a moment later, Avery heard him fiddling in the bathroom, followed by the sound of bathwater running. She hadn't even thought of that and assumed he'd just grab her some fresh towels and she'd shower. But a bath sounded much better.

Foggy and Jane bounded in from the kitchen.

"Hey, guys," Avery said, glad to see their sweet faces.

Isaac had fed them and they must have been playing together after they'd eaten. She patted the couch next to her and they both jumped up, happy when she covered them in pets, Avery laughing as they licked her face. When they settled down on either side of her, Foggy rested his muzzle in her lap and she scratched behind his ears, smiling when his eyelids lowered in pleasure.

Isaac padded back into the living room and handed her a steaming mug before sitting in the easy chair across from Avery and their dogs.

"I realized something earlier today. One thing we can do to help you out is teach Foggy how to get my attention if I'm near and you feel the symptoms of a panic attack coming on."

She nodded.

"I noticed that when you got too close to Nathan, you started to shake. And even if it wasn't him, even if it was just memories coming on too fast, I think it might help if Foggy had the ability to get me if I happen to be nearby."

"Yeah," she said, rehashing the incident in her mind. "That would be good."

She was quiet for a moment, looking down into her tea, thinking about all that had happened.

Isaac's brows knit. "I'm sorry I didn't get to you

sooner. I wasn't completely sure what was going on until it was too late. I should have been there faster for you."

She took a sip of her tea, letting the smooth liquid warm her as she considered the apology she hadn't needed him to offer.

"It's not your fault at all, Isaac, and you know that. I just lost myself when I saw Connor's little face. He looks so much like his mother, it was like seeing her ghost."

"I can't even imagine, Avery. I'm so sorry you had to go through that."

She released a long sigh, pushing the air out slowly, trying to relieve some of the pressure that had built up inside of her over the course of the day. Isaac was correct; it had been a long one. And it was only the beginning—there would be so many more to go as she walked the road of recovery, able to see only a few feet in front of her, having to trust that the path wouldn't lead her back to where she'd started.

"Can I tell you something that I've never told anyone before? Something I would never say out loud to most people." She had to get this off of her chest for some reason. Maybe, maybe, she hoped, it would help. She knew she didn't deserve to let go of the guilt, but she wanted to see what someone else thought about something that had always puzzled her.

"Of course you can."

She twined her fingers together, making a little steeple as she'd done as a child, thinking about how best to share what had hidden so deep inside her mind for so long.

"I never… I never understood how she could leave him," she said, the words raw inside her throat. "How

Sophie could leave Connor to go off to war, to a place she knew she might not come back from."

Isaac was silent, his expression void of even the slightest hint of judgment. She appreciated that he didn't try to find a solution to the situation, didn't try to make her feel better about it. He just let her say what she needed to say. Few men were like that. Few people were like that. And perhaps the world would be a friendlier place if more could find the patience and the discernment to know when to listen, when to let others release built-up toxins from their hearts without trying to ease the discomfort that resulted.

"I don't think I could have," she said. "And sometimes I can't decide if it was brave or…" She couldn't say the rest, but she knew he understood.

"When I left, I didn't leave anything behind except my brother, and he didn't need me to survive. I had no strings, and I wanted to serve my country, but I also wanted adventure. I wanted to get out of Peach Leaf and see something different than what I had every day of my life up to that point. But Sophie… Sophie had so much here at home."

Isaac let her words settle before speaking. "You were her very best friend, Avery. The two of you had so much history together. Do you think that maybe she did it for you? So you wouldn't have to go alone?"

Tears pooled behind her eyes. She hadn't ever heard anyone put it into such stark terms, in black and white, but maybe he was right.

A sob escaped. "That makes it so awful, doesn't it?"

Isaac got up from the chair and was at her side in an instant, his arms around her shoulders.

"It was her choice to make, Avery. She was a grown

woman, and she made an impossible choice. It doesn't make her bad, and it doesn't make her good. It just is. It was her life and her decision to make, not yours."

He drew her into his arms.

"Don't you think she knew what she was doing, sweetheart? Don't you think she weighed everything out? Just because she was a mother did not mean she had any less ambition than you, any less of a need to serve her country. It's possible she had more of a reason to go. What greater sacrifice could she have given her son than to fight to make his world a better place? To attempt to secure the freedom so many of us take for granted every day? And she obviously trusted that her husband and son would survive if something happened to her."

Everything he said was true, and somehow he was both completely honest, yet gentle at the same time, careful of her tender heart.

"You cannot blame her, and you cannot blame yourself. Neither of you knew what would happen that day when you traded shifts. And, someday, when her son is old enough, he will understand how brave his mother was, and how much she cared about his future, and when he does, you will need to be there for him. You will need to tell him how much you loved Sophie and how much he meant to her."

Avery nodded, wiping tears from her eyes with the palms of her hands. "I would if Nathan would let me. I don't understand why he won't."

Isaac rested his chin against her head. "Give him time," he said. "Give him time to understand that you just want to be there for them. He's mourning her, too, and everyone's grief takes on a different form.

"Okay?"

She closed her eyes, nodding. "Okay."

Sharing that with Isaac had lifted a ton from her shoulders, and she felt like she could breathe again. His presence was healing her, a little at a time, in a way medicine and therapy had not been able to. She knew they were valuable, but being with someone who supported her unconditionally was worth just as much on her journey to recovery. She could see now that isolating herself from community hadn't been the best for her.

Now that she knew it was possible to find light at the other side of all that darkness, she began to hope that she might be able to repair other areas of her life, and maybe even get her job back someday.

Though, now that she considered it, she wasn't sure she wanted to go back to the same job. There was a time when it had felt like the only thing she ever wanted to do, but now that she'd been exposed to something new, she was beginning to think she might want to work with animals. She was a skilled health professional and had given much of herself to making other people better, but being in the company of Foggy and Jane had opened her up to something different, and she had the idea that she might enjoy caring for animals instead. Their presence was so soothing and full of so much joy. They didn't ask for much, just wanted to be treated with respect. It was something she could get used to.

"Now," Isaac said, getting up from the couch. He had to push a few dog limbs out of the way to disentangle himself from the wad. "Your bath is ready, my dear."

He reached out a palm and gave a little bow, making Avery laugh. When she offered him her hand, he helped her up and led her down the hall to the bathroom, making sure she had plenty of fresh towels and anything else she needed before he shut the door, leaving her alone with a tub full of fluffy, inviting suds. On the counter, she noticed, he had set out a T-shirt and sweatpants of his own for her to change into.

Cared for, calm and one hundred percent comfortable in this kind, generous man's home, Avery undressed and slid down into the perfectly warm water, her heart more at ease than it had been since she could remember.

But only a few moments passed before she wanted him back by her side.

She was ready now, to have everything.

"Isaac?" she called.

She heard his footsteps coming closer down the hall and then they stopped just outside the door.

"What is it?"

"I need one more thing," she said, gripping the sides of the tub to lift herself from the warm water.

"Anything. Just say the word." His voice, so near, yet so distant, on the other side of the door, vibrated up her spine.

She bit her lower lip to keep from grinning like a madwoman, to quell the raging desire growing swiftly in the most neglected parts of her body. Drawing in a deep breath, she headed for the door, slowly opening it until she stood completely bare before him. His dark eyes said far more than any words might have as they took in the whole of her form. She'd already given him her heart; now she wanted him to have all of her.

"I need you."

She didn't have to say another word. He gave her the sultriest smile she'd ever witnessed and, within seconds, he'd wrapped his arms around her naked body and carried her, dripping wet, down the hallway to his bedroom, closing the door behind them.

The only light in the room came from the last soft rays of evening sun that slipped in through Isaac's window, but his eyes seemed to be on fire as he laid her gently on the bed, taking a moment to drink in the sight of her once more.

She felt no shyness under his gaze, only raw need as he tugged off his shirt and came closer to the side of the bed, to her. She lifted her torso and wrapped her arms around his waist, hugging him tightly before she let go and slid her fingers up to the waistband of his jeans.

But then he pulled her hands away and lowered himself until he was eye level with her. "Avery, are you sure this is what you want?" he asked, his breath halting over the words, forehead knit with concern. Her insides ached at the knowledge of what she was doing to him, and at how much he respected her boundaries. But that was just it—she wanted no more boundaries between them.

"Absolutely," she said, drawing his mouth to hers as she threaded her fingers through that thick, unruly, dark hair she loved so much. Then his palms were against her cheeks, his thumbs tracing over her face as the kiss deepened, further and further until both of them needed something far more intense.

Isaac rose again and, this time, made no move to stop her undoing his jeans. When they fell to the floor in a heap, leaving only the stark outline of his desire for her against the taut material of his boxer briefs, it was her turn to study him unbridled.

And study him, she did.

He was incredible in every way possible, this man

who loved her, and she wanted him more than anything else in the world.

Resting her hands on his waist, she pulled him down to join her on the bed.

"We can go slow. There's no rush, you know." She heard the words, but they didn't sound too convincing.

"Actually," she said, giggling as she admired the view of him hovering above her, "I am in a rush." His brows rose in confusion, but she went on. "It's taken my whole life to find the perfect guy for me, and now that I have you, I'm totally ready to dive in."

His head leaned back and he laughed, the warm sound affecting her almost as much as the hands that soon covered her breasts. With her, all their clothes and inhibitions now gone, he was wilder and more sensual than any of the rogues and rakes that populated her favorite novels. And it occurred to her suddenly, she was the lucky heroine who got to belong to him, to be the one he placed above all others, the one he fought for and rode off with into the sunset.

"Well, in that case..."

He leaned down to kiss her flesh, moving one hand to stroke the heated center of her, eliciting a moan so primal she wasn't even sure it was she who'd uttered it.

As he drove her to the edge of sanity, she reached out to hold him, drawing his aroused body closer to her own until neither of them could stand to wait any longer, and Isaac paused briefly to get a condom from his bedside table. Their breath came in heavy waves, skin burning with hunger for each other as their mouths met again. And when he finally crashed into her, filling every empty space inside, Avery let go completely and gave him everything she had.

* * *

Hours later, Avery stirred in a fitful sleep, tossing her arms and legs as she struggled against another horrifying nightmare.

In the dream, she and Sophie were together again. Instead of trading shifts, they had gone to visit some of the Afghan women at their normal time. The sun was high in the desert sky as they made their way down the dirt street to the home, and their hearts were lighter than usual. The rays beat down but their skin was protected from the worst of it by the burkas they wore with their uniforms.

The house was quiet as the two women were invited in, welcomed warmly and given tea as usual, but something was different. There was a new woman amidst them, one they hadn't met before who seemed to stare at them with apprehension, and something more. Something like thinly veiled hatred.

Tension buzzed and the air was thick with electricity, as just before a storm. Avery sensed that they shouldn't linger, and she finished her refreshments quickly before suggesting to Sophie that they ask if any of the women needed any medical help and then return quickly to their turf, where they would be relatively safe.

Even as she slept, Avery knew how the dream would end. She knew there would be nothing she could do to stop the bomb from going off while she and Sophie remained in the house. She didn't know why she was with her friend in the dream when she had not been in real life; perhaps on some level it was what she wanted subconsciously, what she wished had happened so that they would both be gone and she wouldn't be home, alone, living with too-heavy guilt in a place where no one understood what she did.

But this time, as she braced herself for the blast, something changed.

When she reached up to touch her face, instead of sand there was moisture, and…something warm. Confusion set in as her eyes fluttered open, and there he was. There was Foggy, his paws near her shoulders as he licked her cheeks with vigor, willing her to wake up and see that she was okay. She wasn't in that desert like she'd been the last time she'd had that nightmare.

Though this time, it didn't take long for her to remember that she was in Isaac's home—that in fact she lay next to him in his own bed. After several hours together the evening before, they'd opened the door and let the dogs pile up at the foot of the king-size bed. Sensing her distress even as she dreamed, Foggy must have crawled to her side.

Coming to, she buried her fingers in the fur just behind Foggy's shoulders and pulled his head close, hugging him for dear life, realizing with elation that he'd woken her up on purpose. He'd saved her from the worst part of the dream. He reminded her what was real.

She put her hands on the sides of his face and planted a giant kiss on his cold, wet nose. "You wonderful little dog," she said, sitting up in bed and reaching around to hug him some more. "You amazing little creature."

Tears began to spill down her cheeks as she understood fully what Foggy had done for her. She held him close for a long time, starting only when she felt Isaac's hand on her shoulder.

"Hey there, handsome," she said, wiping at her eyes with the palms of her hands, as laughter welled up inside.

Isaac sat up and scooted closer to her side of the bed. As she turned to him, her eyes slid over the hard planes of his chest and abs, then back up to his gorgeously stubbled face. His dark hair stuck out all over the place and she wanted to run her fingers through it and mess it up even more.

"Come here," she said again, and Isaac scooted even closer, snuggling her against his chest and burying his sleepy face into her hair.

"Is everything okay? I think I heard you crying but it took me a minute to fully wake up."

"Yes, it's okay," she said, giggling now between little happy sobs. Images filled her mind of him kissing her good-night a few hours before, just after they'd made love for the countless time, bringing a glass of water to place at her bedside table. He'd made sure she had everything she needed to be comfortable in his home before he crawled under the sheets by her side, both of them happily exhausted.

"What happened? Did you have another nightmare?"

She nodded and Isaac's hand landed on her thigh, warm even through the sheets. "But it's all right this time."

Isaac looked confused and she pointed at the dog in her arms.

"It's all right, because this time, Foggy saved me."

Chapter 12

"Avery, I'm so very glad to see you," Dr. Santiago greeted as Avery opened her office door at the Veterans Affairs outpatient clinic the next Thursday, right on time for her one o'clock appointment.

The doctor stood and shook Avery's hand, welcoming her with a broad, sincere smile. "I always look forward to our appointments. Would you like something to drink today? I have the usual Coke and water."

Avery tilted her head and chewed her lip. "I'll have a Coke today, if you don't mind."

Dr. Santiago paused in front of the minifridge in the corner behind her long, oak desk. "Special occasion?" she joked, and Avery smiled.

"No. Just feeling adventurous, I guess."

"Well, by all means. Coke it is." She pulled out a can and handed it across her workspace before sitting down. Avery gripped the ice-cold drink and flipped open the tab to take a sip. It had been ages since she'd had a Coke and she'd forgotten how much she enjoyed the sugary, caramely soda.

"My goodness, this is good," she accidentally said out loud.

Dr. Santiago grinned as Avery took the seat across from her. "I'm so glad you like it. It's good to see you indulging a little."

They had spoken before about Avery's diminished appetite and low body weight, but the doctor had always been kind and gentle, urging her patient to speak about why it was difficult for her to eat, sometimes even having Avery list the things she used to enjoy eating in the hopes of encouraging her hunger to perk back up, so she wasn't surprised at the comment.

"It feels good to enjoy something like this again, even something so insignificant."

"Or maybe not so insignificant," Dr. Santiago suggested. "Sometimes it's the littlest things that give us something to cling to, almost like a breadcrumb to help you find your way back."

Dr. Santiago was tall, with silky black hair and matching eyes, and a deep but soft, soothing voice infused with a native Puerto Rican Spanish accent. She was Avery's favorite therapist, the only one she had been able to commit to seeing on a regular basis. Some of the others had cold, overly bright offices and demeanors that Avery's body actively resisted, making it impossible for her to relax or trust them, but Dr. Santiago had decorated her space in peaceful deep purples and soft greens. The velvety indigo couch Avery now sat on was overstuffed and comfortable, situated directly across from a gorgeous print of the Sangre de Cristo Mountains.

The picture reminded Avery of their first consultation. She'd asked Dr. Santiago if she had ever been to those mountains, and, unlike most of the doctors Avery had visited, this one did not try to avoid the question and redirect her back to the horrors of her own mind. Instead, Dr. Santiago had offered Avery a warm smile and answered, telling of her annual trips there, of the solace she found hiking those foothills with the little terrier that was her constant companion.

Avery considered what the doctor had said about breadcrumbs and trails. "I think I may have found another breadcrumb."

"Oh?"

Avery's lips turned up involuntarily and she hoped she wasn't blushing like a little girl. "I met someone recently…someone very interesting, very different and incredibly sweet. Isaac."

Dr. Santiago leaned forward, and for a moment Avery recalled what it was like to share something exciting with a close girlfriend. She hadn't realized until that moment how much she missed female companionship. Macy was wonderful, but it wasn't often that the two of them were alone without the kids. She should remedy that, Avery thought, and suggest that Macy join her for a drink sometime, out of the house, away from all the everyday stuff. There was a time when going out like that had been a weekly Friday thing, something she looked forward to.

Why had they stopped?

Because of me, Avery thought. Her friends and sister-in-law probably didn't know what to say to get those girls' nights out started up again. Her impulse was to blame them, but Avery knew it was just as much on her end. Maybe they could reach out to her a little more, but she hadn't exactly been outgoing lately. She could stand to make more of an effort, and maybe they would meet her in the middle. Her friends loved her, she knew. They had come by in droves after she'd come home, bringing flowers and magazines and the romance novels she loved, treating her like she might be sick.

And she was. But there was no medicine that could make her wholly better. And she'd thanked them, but eventually pushed them all away, as much afraid of them as they were of her. She realized that now, the same as she realized she needed them.

Maybe they *were* the medicine. Her friends, and Foggy, and Isaac, and her family. She could hold on to them if she wanted to, if she could let herself be that vulnerable, and they would be her borrowed strength until she built enough of her own to stand up again.

"Avery?"

"Hmm?"

"If you want to share, I'd love to hear more about Isaac."

"Oh, yes, Isaac." She let his name linger on her lips, enjoying the soft symmetry of its syllables. "Isaac."

Dr. Santiago smiled.

"He's a certified dog trainer, actually, who also happens to be my brother's neighbor. Oddly enough, even though he lives literally just up the road, I only met him a few weeks ago, and I've been spending almost all of my time with him since." She paused at the memory, thinking of how a bad situation turned so quickly, so unexpectedly, into something good.

"I was having one of my flashback episodes," she

said, looking up to meet Dr. Santiago's eyes. They were concerned but nonjudgmental, full of kindness and understanding, much like those of the man she was describing.

"He found me, or I found him, and he took me home, fed me and took care of me. I was terrified when I realized what had happened, but he was so wonderful with me, so patient and compassionate when I told him what was going on. Then, when I found out that he works with service dogs for veterans with PTSD, it was almost like…like it was meant to be, even though I don't really believe in that nonsense. I can't explain the way I feel around him—it's something completely new to me."

Dr. Santiago nodded, urging Avery to go on.

"He took me to his training facility the next week and introduced me to a dog that he'd been working with. They hadn't found a person for him yet, so Isaac asked if I might be interested in training with the dog—Foggy—and of course I was. I've always loved dogs. We've been working together a little bit every day, and Isaac and I have been on a couple of wonderful dates. This weekend, we're going to the 5K walk/run for the local animal shelter. It'll be a good place for Foggy and I to practice being around a bunch of people and dogs at the same time, plus a lot of other stimulation, though I have no doubt we'll do wonderfully."

"That sounds marvelous, Avery. I'm so very happy for you."

"It is. It is marvelous. I feel so lucky, you know. Sometimes it takes ages for people who need them to get service dogs, yet this one just sort of fell into my lap and I have no idea why."

"Who knows why? But this is a good thing for you,

Avery. I'm giving you full permission to enjoy it. In fact, that's my medical advice for you in this situation. Enjoy it to the fullest."

Avery laughed, but she did let the doctor's words sink in. "I'm just not sure I deserve something so amazing."

"Oh, but you do. I cannot convince you of that—it's something we've talked about previously and it's something you know you'll have to come to embrace on your own—but you very much do deserve good things in life."

Avery nodded, trying hard not to argue with what, on some level she hadn't yet acknowledged, she knew to be the truth.

"Another thing—I've seen this many times—your insurance may or may not have covered a service animal if you had sought one on your own and put in a claim, and in my experience, they can cost twenty-thousand dollars or more. In this field, we are just beginning to understand how valuable these interspecies relationships can be, and we know almost without a doubt that dogs, horses and even other animals can serve as excellent helpers with victims of psychological trauma, but we've only scratched the surface of compiling enough solid research to convince the insurance companies of the numerous benefits."

Avery's eyes widened at the amount. She had never even thought about getting a dog to help with her PTSD. Not until she'd met Isaac. But now, now that she'd met Foggy and spent time with him, she could see his incredible value, and she knew firsthand that it took a long time and a lot of funding to train a service dog. More important, she missed him every second he was away from her, almost as much as she did Isaac. Even then, as the two guys waited for her in the lobby, she had a hard time fathoming her life without either. She needed them. It was a huge sign of weakness, of vulnerability, to need them, she knew. But it was also completely normal. It was human.

"So, in my opinion, based on what you've told me, it sounds like you've stumbled upon a very favorable situation."

Avery beamed. She hadn't known she'd wanted Dr. Santiago's advice, but now that she had it, she felt even better. She knew, and her doctor knew, that she wasn't one to jump headfirst into things that she wasn't 100 percent confident about. It was a leap of faith to choose to trust Isaac, and even though she was still skeptical that any person could be trusted, she knew he was worthy.

"Thank you, Dr. Santiago. That means a lot to me."

"You like him very much, don't you?"

"Yes, very much. In fact, I think I might even be falling in love with him."

"I haven't seen you looking this well or thinking this positively since we met, you know."

"I know."

Sensing that their session was drawing close to the end of its allotted hour, Avery pulled her cell phone out of the pocket of her jeans and slipped her finger across the screen to wake it up. Sure enough, it was almost time for her to go. She usually hated leaving these appointments, knowing that her world would be unsteady until the next one, that she'd miss Dr. Santiago's sanctuary of an office and the woman herself more than was possibly healthy. But today was different. Today, she had time with Isaac and Foggy to look forward to. They were waiting outside the door. For her. And she couldn't wait to see them again and to find out what Isaac had in store for their afternoon.

Their dates were always so much better than just going out to dinner, though they had done plenty of that, as well. So far, Isaac had taken her to pick fresh peaches at the orchards of their town's namesake, which they'd taken home and baked into an incredible cobbler. They'd been boating at the lake, window-shopping downtown, to the dog park and to a movie at the local outdoor drive-in. Each day and night with him was like a new adventure, and even when they just stayed in and hung out together, she was happier than she'd ever been in her life.

She checked the time and put her phone away.

"Okay, for homework—which I already know you don't like—I want you to write down five things that make you happy."

It took concentrated effort for Avery to restrain her reaction to this week's assignment, but she had to laugh at how well the psychiatrist knew her patient.

It wouldn't hurt to be more open. After all, look how much good had happened once she'd chosen to open her heart to Isaac.

"All right, and then what do I do with the list?"

Dr. Santiago took a sip of the peppermint tea she favored. Avery liked the way its subtle, calming scent filled the office. Together, many times, they'd explored Avery's tendency to rush ahead, to try to reach for solutions before she'd really begun to understand a problem—a characteristic that well served her military career, but wasn't always an asset in civilian life.

"For now, just the list, okay?" Dr. Santiago smiled, her eyes filled with warm humor. "Then, we go from there."

Avery nodded, agreeing to another exercise with what small portion of faith she could muster. She had a journal full of these little tasks, half-completed, and would try this one as well, but she'd done enough of them not to get her hopes up. She was fairly certain by now that writing in a journal like a teenage girl, pouring her feelings onto the page, wasn't going to fix her problems. Still, sometimes it helped to get things out of her head and down on paper, and even when it didn't, at least seeing her thoughts in black and white on a physical page often made them clearer.

"I come from a family of Southern farmers, doctor. We don't have time for pain. If you break your arm, you still have to milk the cows."

"I know this well," Dr. Santiago replied, pointing a finger across her desk even as she jotted a few quick notes with the other hand. Avery appreciated that she never took notes during their sessions and each time only spent a few minutes doing so afterwards. Her focused attention when they spoke made an immense impact on how well Avery was able to connect with Dr. Santiago, to open up during their meetings for the sake of her own well-being.

"But you'll recall I've met your brother, Avery, on a day when he had to milk the cows—" she smiled, reaching across the desk to pat Avery's hand "—and I could see instantly that he loves you and wants to help you get to feeling better. Sometimes we have to teach the people around us how to care for us. They don't always know best." She set down her enameled pen and looked up, folding her hands on top of the notepad.

"Isaac is different," Avery said softly, without intending to. But when the doctor nodded, she continued.

"He seems to know what I need, when I need it, without me having to tell him. He is kind and emotionally mature. And—"

She didn't think Dr. Santiago needed to know that just the sight of him made her heart run wild like an off-leash greyhound.

"He sounds wise and supportive, Avery." She paused, blinking. "I think this is a good thing, spending more time with him. Do you agree?"

"I think so," Avery said, hearing the waver in her own words.

Very little ever got past Dr. Santiago.

"But?"

"But—" Avery shifted, suddenly restless despite the couch's soft, inviting cushions "—even though he's wonderful, for some reason, I'm almost as afraid of him as I was of going off to a combat zone, and then of coming home," she admitted. Just saying the words out loud brought a little relief, but not enough.

When Avery stopped speaking, Dr. Santiago was silent for a few seconds. Avery liked that about her. The doctor didn't try to fill quiet with questions, but she also didn't hesitate to ask the often-difficult things that helped Avery get to the bottom of her fears. They had covered much ground together, but the thought of how much more there was to go made Avery feel suddenly fatigued even after the progress she'd made in their hour together.

"Well, let's talk this through, then," Dr. Santiago proposed, apparently ignoring or not overly concerned that their time was up. "What is it that you're afraid might happen?"

Avery considered the gently prodding question. If

she'd learned anything about psychotherapy, it was that mining a heart was exhausting, painful, frustrating work that didn't yield overnight results. In the time that she'd been home, she'd only just scratched the surface of what she knew to be a vast iceberg, the largest portion of which remained hidden underwater. She'd come home thinking everything would be okay, but she quickly realized that although her military training covered extensive wartime coping mechanisms, she didn't know much of anything about returning to normal life.

Medication helped with her anxiety symptoms, at first, but it didn't help her forget the things she'd seen—the darkest corners of human behavior—and there were days she'd do just about anything to empty her mind of all she'd been exposed to. She wanted to believe that people were good, that they did the best they could with what they were given, but she wasn't so sure she bought that theory anymore.

"I guess I'm—"

The words to articulate her emotions wouldn't come, and a knot of frustration began to rise in her throat. Oh, how she hated to cry, especially in front of other people. She'd managed to get through years of providing medical care for battered soldiers without more than a few tears, but once she'd returned, it was as if all of those experiences joined to form a deluge, and there were days she couldn't keep her eyes dry.

"I think I'm afraid that it might be harder to let him all the way into my heart than it would be to shut him out."

Dr. Santiago took another sip of her tea, closing her eyes for a moment, thinking things over the way a friend would.

"What might happen if you show him the darkest parts of you, the places that scare you the most?" she asked, replacing her blue-and-white teacup in its saucer.

"I might—" Avery pulled in a breath as memories slipped past floodgates "—I might love him someday. Maybe I already do. And then I might lose him."

Images of her best friend's face the last time she saw her, of the casual way, on the day Sophie died, that they'd traded shifts so Avery could care for her injured patient. Avery couldn't have predicted or stopped the downward spiral that resulted from a single wrong decision. On some level, she knew that. But it didn't change the fact that Sophie's son would grow up without his mother. It didn't change the fact that every time she ran into Sophie's husband—a circumstance she avoided more and more as much as she could—he would look at Avery and wonder why it was she who'd survived, and not his lovely, sweet wife.

Dr. Santiago must have understood the path Avery's thoughts had taken from the expression on her patient's face. She removed her hands from the teacup and folded them again across the notepad on her desk. Finally, she spoke quietly.

"That's very true," she said. "When we allow others to love us, and when we love them, there is always a price to pay, and paying that price is part of being human. We do it because none of us can be our best selves without others. None of us truly wants to be always alone."

It was Avery's turn to nod.

"But think of it this way, Avery." Dr. Santiago turned her hands, palms up. "If you really enjoy Isaac's company, if he brings you happiness and support, and all of the other wonderful things you've described—don't you think that you deserve those things?"

"No," Avery said, quickly. She didn't need to think about the answer to that question.

"I disagree," Dr. Santiago posed. "I'm sure Isaac has a choice in whom he spends time with. Why would he be spending so much time with you if you weren't also bringing him joy? Do you not deserve to take what he's offered in return?"

Avery didn't respond. Her heart was too full of aches and she was getting tired. They'd gotten to a place they couldn't surpass that day, or maybe ever, and suddenly, she just wanted to go home.

"Let's meet again next week, Avery. You've done so well today, and I know it's very hard on you." Dr. Santiago leaned over on her elbows, her forearms covering the large calendar that covered her desktop. "Listen. I want you to know how brave you are for coming in to see me, for keeping your appointments. The work you're doing here is difficult, but it's important, and you are doing an excellent job."

Avery felt that she was anything but brave. Bravery was what the soldiers she'd cared for had; it was in the sacrifices they'd made to serve their country in an effort to make the world a safer place. It wasn't sitting in a psychiatrist's office, talking about why she couldn't risk spending so much time with Isaac Meyer.

She picked up her shoulder bag and headed for the door.

Chapter 13

The day of the 5K, Isaac stopped by Tommy's house to pick up Avery, pulling another box out of the back of his truck. But this time, it wasn't zucchini.

It was going to be a warm day. Already the sun was hot against his back as he headed toward the porch, Jane at his heels, but he didn't care. All he could see were hours and hours of time with Avery, hours he would fill doing his new favorite thing—making her as happy as humanly possible.

He rang the doorbell and Macy opened it with a big smile for him, getting flour all over his clothes as he stepped into her arms for a hug. "Oops," she said, attempting to wipe it off as Isaac laughed and batted her hands away so she couldn't just make things worse.

"Avery's in her room," she said, "I'll go get her for you. Just head on into the kitchen and help yourself to a muffin."

Isaac stopped midstep. "There aren't any zucchini in them, are there?"

Macy winked at him over her shoulder. "Wouldn't you like to know?"

Armed with what he took to be a warning, he obeyed her anyway and found Tommy munching away on breakfast at the table.

"Isaac!" Tommy said, getting up to shake his hand. "Glad to see you, man." He offered Isaac a cup of coffee and brought one back, black, handing it across the table as he took his seat.

"It's good to see you, too."

"Sounds like you and Avery have become mighty close over the past few weeks," Tommy said, grinning over his World's Okayest Dad mug, which was made even funnier by the fact that Tommy was an inarguably excellent father.

"We have. And I'm glad you mentioned it because I want to talk to you about her."

Concern knitted Tommy's brows and Isaac waved his hand in the air to indicate that everything was okay.

"Nothing's wrong. Nothing at all. I just wanted to let you know that…that I'm in love with her. And that I have every intention of one day asking her to marry me."

Tommy beamed. "That's just wonderful! I'm so happy for both of you, and you absolutely have my blessing."

He looked over Isaac's shoulder and then lowered his voice.

"Just don't tell Macy. She'll go nuts and start planning things left and right before you even have a chance to pop the question. Trust me on that one."

Isaac laughed, happy to have told Avery's brother,

his friend, and relieved that he'd reacted the way he had. "Oh, don't worry. I won't. And I'm not going to ask anytime soon."

He took a sip of his coffee, strong enough to add hair to his chest, just the way he liked it.

"Avery needs time. I want to make sure she's ready when I get to it and, anyway, people would think we were crazy if I asked her after less than a month."

Tommy narrowed his eyes. "Since when do you care what people think of you?"

Isaac grinned. "I don't. But Avery might. We're taking things slow, doing things right, building a solid foundation. We have all the time in the world."

Tommy nodded. "Have you told her how you feel, at least?"

Isaac shook his head. "I'm going to. Just haven't found the right moment yet."

"Well, when you do, I have no doubt you'll be pleased with the outcome." Tommy reached over and punched his friend in the shoulder. "That girl is head over heels, man. Head over heels. And I couldn't be happier that it's with my best friend."

"Morning, boys."

Isaac looked up at the sound of Avery's voice in the doorway, warm as butter. He practically jumped up from the table, eager to be near her, to touch her and to breathe in the sweet scent he'd missed overnight in her absence. They had agreed not to spend every night together, and he couldn't wait for the day when all he'd have to do was roll over in bed each morning and she'd be there, hair golden across her pillow in the morning light. He knew that he wanted to spend the rest of his life with her, and he hoped to God she felt the same.

He'd start to tell her that this morning.

Avery wrapped her arms around him, snuggling in close as he hugged her tight. "Good morning, sweetheart," he said into her hair. "How'd you sleep?"

"Like a baby." She looked up at him and her eyes were clear in the morning light peeking through the kitchen window. "Foggy's been good to me."

Her affection for the dog was evident in her voice, and Isaac thanked the stars that the two had made as good a fit as Hannah had thought they would. He made a note to do something special for Hannah as a thank-you.

"Where is the guy?"

"Oh, he's with the kids. They adore him."

Tommy chimed in. "It was a little tough getting them to understand what it means when his vest is on, but once we got that down, everybody's happy."

"Although they like him best off duty," Avery said, a grin brightening her already lovely face.

She wore a blue tank top that matched her eyes over another white one, and Isaac noted with pleasure that she'd already gained a couple of pounds. Skinny jeans hugged her perfectly curved bottom and he resisted the urge to put his hands all over her.

He always made sure their dates involved food, and even though Avery had called him out on it, she'd started to enjoy eating a little bit more, and they had a blast rediscovering her favorite meals.

"I've got something for you," Isaac said, taking Avery's hand to lead her out of the kitchen.

"See you kids later," Tommy called after them.

"What is it?" she asked, and Isaac laughed. Impatient—just like a kid at Christmas.

"You'll have to wait and see, now, won't you?"

He tugged her down the hallway and sat her down on the couch in the front sitting room, pulling the box he'd brought over to place at her feet. He'd taken a leap of faith on this one, and he hoped she'd like it.

"Open it," he said, and her eyes widened, pretty little crinkles at their corners as she smiled.

She picked up the box and pulled off the giant yellow bow, then made quick work of the soft green paper he'd chosen. Isaac couldn't remember when he'd last been so nervous. It wasn't like he was proposing now, yet the world seemed to hold its breath as he waited to see what she thought.

She pulled out each item, touching them softly, and as she realized what he'd done, her eyes filled with moisture.

"Oh, Isaac."

"I hope this is okay," he said, apprehensive.

On Thursday, after he'd picked her up from her therapy appointment, when Avery was busy with Foggy, he'd noticed a piece of paper on the ground in the room they'd been using at the training facility. Not wanting any of the dogs to get hold of it, he'd picked it up, intending to toss it into the recycling bin out back. But when he picked it up, the paper unfolded, and Isaac had seen what was written on it. It was a list, and he had everything on it memorized by now:

Things That Make Me Happy

Regency romance novels
The Beatles
Blue nail polish

80s movies
Homemade chocolate-chip cookies
Isaac Meyer
Foggy

He watched as she laid each object out on the floor—
five of her very favorite Regency romances, he'd dou-
ble-checked with Macy; every John Hughes film ever
made; a few Beatles box-set albums; every shade of
blue nail polish he could find; and a dozen chocolate-
chip cookies, freshly baked in his kitchen that morning,
using Nana's famous recipe—forming a circle around
her.

When she was finished, she covered her mouth with
a fist, and tears began to slide down her cheeks.

"I didn't mean to invade your privacy, Ave. I found
the list on the ground at the training center, and, well…
I couldn't help myself. I hope it's okay."

"Shut up, Isaac," she said, crawling out of her circle
of happiness and into his lap, covering his face with
kisses as he laughed, thankful he hadn't screwed up.

Finally she stilled, looking into his eyes. "You know,
I don't have any of this stuff. When I left for the military, I pretty much got rid of everything, and when I got
back, I never got around to buying any of the things I
enjoy. I guess I wasn't sure if I would stay."

He brushed hair back from her eyes and kissed her,
long and slow, on her sweet mouth.

"Please do," he said. "Please stay."

"I plan to," she said. "Now that I have you."

He smiled, leaning his forehead against hers.

"Thank you, Isaac," she whispered. "Thank you. For
everything."

* * *

Later that morning, they all piled into two trucks and drove to Peach Leaf Park, where the local animal shelter's 5K fund-raiser was scheduled to take place.

Avery and Isaac unloaded Foggy and Jane, snapping on their harnesses and leashes and Foggy's vest, ready to practice being in public in a place chock-full of every kind of distraction available.

A banner welcomed them as they entered the park, Tommy, Macy and the kids trailing along behind. The air was thick with the smell of delicious food: hot dogs, funnel cake and popcorn, all ready to reward the serious racers after a day's run, Isaac joked.

Avery definitely planned to sample everything, glad that her favorite jeans were close to fitting again, proud of the feminine curves that had begun to make their reappearance. Most women would be horrified to gain five pounds in a few weeks, she mused, but she needed the weight, and Dr. Santiago would be thrilled at her progress. Avery definitely was.

Isaac made everything better, even food.

She made no effort to hide the fact that she was checking him out as they walked. He looked great in a soft, dark green T-shirt that hugged the muscles underneath, and khaki cargo shorts. His unruly hair—hair she'd had plenty of chances to bury her fingers in—just touched his collar under an ancient Peach Leaf Panthers baseball cap.

Her hand felt right at home in his as they walked, a dog on either side, and for the moment, Avery couldn't imagine how her life could be any more perfect, or any different from what it had been a few weeks ago.

She hadn't even known what she wanted until it

landed right in front of her. Now she would do anything to keep it, to keep him.

Isaac. *Her* Isaac.

They strolled around the park for a while, checking out all the booths and making sure Foggy and Jane had plenty of water before they set off to walk the three-plus miles. Isaac told Avery that the race organizers, being animal folks, of course, had opted to start the race by shouting into a megaphone, rather than using the customary air horn or gunshot.

Finally, they gathered at the starting line, waving at Tommy, Macy and the kids, who were going to cheer them on from the sidelines. When the announcer gave the go, Isaac and Avery set off at a quick pace, Foggy and Jane trotting just ahead.

They'd spent a couple of hours that week working with Foggy on Isaac's idea of keeping people at a safe distance from her with the block command, and he showed off his training with honor that day, making sure to keep in front of Avery so that she didn't get too close to anyone, and the crowd, overwhelming at first, lessened its effect on her after a time. She relaxed into her footsteps, keeping a steady pace, enjoying the late spring sunshine on her face, the gentle breeze in her hair and the cool, dewy morning air.

Occasionally, as they walked, Isaac looked over to check on her, and they stopped every once in a while to give the dogs water in a little travel bowl.

The four of them together felt…like family, and Avery let every minute of it soak into her soul, replacing bad memories with good ones. If she spent enough time with Isaac, she knew, the happy would begin to outweigh the sad. It was only a matter of time.

At the finish line, Sylvia and Ben greeted them with fresh water bottles, and they accepted the paw-shaped medals the race officials draped over their necks for completing the distance.

They were headed toward the food booths when Avery thought she heard someone calling her name. Isaac turned as she did and she saw Nathan coming toward them, Connor hurrying to keep pace, his little hand in his father's.

"Avery," Nathan said, breathing hard. He stopped a few feet away and lifted Connor into his arms. "If you've got a minute, I'd love to talk to you. That is—" he glanced from her to Isaac and back again "—if that's okay with you."

She swallowed, her throat tight, and Foggy must have picked up on her nervousness because he stepped forward and sat down between her and Nathan, calmly but with obvious confidence. He didn't even need the block command; he would protect his girl if he needed to without being asked. He would make sure nothing got to her that might cause her to be afraid or upset.

Her heartbeat slowed to normal, knowing her furry companion was there. She lowered a hand and placed it on his neck, letting Foggy know she was okay, and that she appreciated his gesture.

"Yes, that would be all right with me," she said, her voice sounding stronger than she'd anticipated. She looked to Isaac, whose hand had come to rest on her shoulder, reassuring her that he was there for her, as well. Her two guys, there to keep her safe. "I'll be right back, Isaac."

"We'll be right here," he said, taking Foggy's leash as she handed it over. The dog wasn't too happy about having her leave him behind, but he calmly cooperated and followed Isaac and Jane to a nearby drink stand.

She and Nathan walked over to a picnic table and sat down across from each other. Nathan put Connor down next to him and handed his son a fire truck from his backpack.

It must be his favorite toy, Avery thought, as she recalled seeing it the other day.

"Avery," Nathan said, his voice full of emotion. He looked down at the table and she could see that whatever he was about to say was taking a lot of his courage to get out.

"I'm surprised you want to talk to me after the other day," she said.

"I know, and, Avery, I'm so sorry about what happened then. I didn't mean to act like that. I was a real jerk and I wish I could take it back."

"No, Nathan. I'm the one that's sorry. I shouldn't have pushed myself on you like that. It wasn't fair after all you've been through. I was being selfish as hell and I want you to know I didn't mean to bring all that back for you."

He was quiet for a long moment and Avery sensed that he was getting his bearings, that he was trying to hold on to his emotion so it didn't break free and embarrass them both. She wanted to tell him that he would feel better if he just let it go, that it only hurt to keep it inside, as she'd only recently begun to learn, thanks to Isaac's presence and support in her life.

If everyone had their own equivalent of an Isaac and a Foggy, she thought, *the world would be a better place*.

"I miss her so damn much, Avery. Sometimes I can't stand it. Sometimes I think I can't go on because of how much it hurts to do all this without her." He put his face in his hands and glanced over at Connor as if worried that his son might hear, but the child continued to play happily with his truck, lost in his own safe, peaceful world.

"But you have to, don't you, Nathan?" she said firmly, giving Nathan some of the courage she'd gained from Isaac. "You have to keep going for Connor. He needs you. Sophie trusted you to take care of him if something happened to her, and she would want you to be strong." She offered him a weak smile as he swiped his hands over his face and met her eyes.

"Yeah, she would, wouldn't she?" he said, his eyes softening at her memory.

"She was so strong," Avery said. "She was the bravest, best woman I've ever known, and I wish I had her back. I miss my best friend, and I know you miss your wife, but she wouldn't have been too happy if she'd seen the hot messes we've turned out to be."

Nathan laughed, a tight, sharp sound that hinted at the extent of his sorrow.

"I lost a friend," she said, her voice quiet, "but you lost your wife, and I can't even begin to imagine how hard that must be for you."

He closed his eyes.

"But that doesn't give me the right to shut you out, or to keep you from seeing Connor. Sophie would have hated that I've done that for so long."

Shame filled his face, and Avery wanted to tell him that he'd done nothing wrong, that grief was almost impossible to bear sometimes, and other times, it could only barely be tolerated.

He looked over at Connor. "The only reason I've

done so is because it was too hard for me, but seeing you the other day…it brought back too many memories of all the good times the three of us had when she was alive, before you both left. I realized how much I've been shielding him from because of my own pain. And that's not fair. I owe it to my son to be the best father I can be, and I know now that I wasn't doing that."

He looked up at the sky as if deciding whether or not to say more.

"Did you know I don't even have photographs of her in our home? I put them all away when she died." His voice wavered. "I just couldn't bear to look at her, you know?"

His eyes were rimmed with red as he reached over and took Avery's hand.

"That's in the past now. I took them all out the day we saw you in the park, and I've been showing them to Connor every day, so that I can teach him how wonderful his mama was."

Avery felt tears prickle at the back of her eyes.

"And I'm sorry, Avery. I want you to know that I don't blame you for what happened to my wife. She was stubborn, and what she wanted, she got. And she was an amazing woman who wanted to serve her country almost as much as she wanted to be a mom. It was important to her to do her duty, and it was important to her to go with you. She loved you so much, you know. I think she would have followed you anywhere."

They both laughed at the truth of his statement and Avery choked up, wiping away a few drops that had fallen from her eyes.

"I want you to know that you can see Connor anytime you want. You are always welcome in our home, as are Isaac and your dogs." Nathan smiled at Connor. "I'm sure this little guy would love to have them over for a playdate sometime. In the near future, Avery, you hear?"

"Of course." She squeezed his hand. "Thank you, Nathan. I didn't know how much I needed to hear those things until now. I promise I won't be a stranger."

He nodded, and they were both quiet, realizing they had broken frozen ground and could now sow seeds that would become their futures. They could make choices for themselves now, rather than holding on to the grief that had rendered them immobile for so long.

"You know," Avery said, speaking almost as much to herself as she was to Nathan, "when I joined the military, I knew the risks and the danger, and even though there was always a little fear, I felt prepared."

Nathan nodded as his eyes filled, and she continued.

"I knew exactly what I was getting into—" she swallowed "—but I had no idea how to get out. They don't tell you how hard it's going to be to get back to a normal life, if that's ever even possible."

Nathan squeezed her hand. They didn't need to say any more about it.

When Connor grew bored with his fire truck, Nathan reminded him who Avery was, and the two of them chatted for a long time about preschool and when would she please come over and bring her puppies to see him.

Avery's heart was loads lighter when they parted ways and she returned to Isaac's side. He handed her a fresh-squeezed lemonade from a nearby stand and gave her back Foggy's leash.

"Everything okay with Nathan?" Isaac asked, his

brown eyes full of worry as he studied her face for clues about how their visit had gone.

"Better than ever," she said. "We're okay now." She took a sip of the drink, sweetness and tartness teasing her taste buds at the same time.

"So glad to hear it, sweetie."

"We'll have to bring Jane and Foggy by to meet Connor sometime. He's super excited about being around dogs. Nathan works full-time and Connor goes to preschool, so they can't have one of their own right now. It would mean a lot to them if he could play with ours."

"Consider it done," Isaac said, smiling. "He seems like a sweet kid."

"He is, just like his mom was."

"Do you want one someday?" Isaac asked. "Kids, I mean."

Avery looked up at him, surprised. "Isaac Meyer," she teased. "Are you asking me if I'll have your children someday?"

He gave her his sexiest grin, tilting his head so that his dark hair grazed his shoulder, looking for all the world like a rake from one of her favorite books.

"Would that be a problem?" he asked.

"Actually, no," she said, pushing her chin forward to show him she wasn't intimidated by his suggestion of commitment. "And yes, I do want kids. Someday."

Isaac's expression showed her he wasn't satisfied with her answer.

She took another sip of lemonade, drawing it out to bug him.

"My kids?" he asked.

"Yes, idiot," she said, reaching across the table to poke his chest. "Your kids."

They were both being silly, mostly, but now they were dead serious as they caught each other's eye.

It was in that second that Avery knew precisely how she felt about Isaac Meyer—there was no longer any question—and exactly how to articulate it.

The words were on the tip of her tongue when she heard the first blast. Lemonade spilled across the table as she knocked it over in her hurry to get cover. She flew under the picnic table and huddled there, her arms wrapped over her knees, head down as a few more explosions erupted and, once again, the world went black around her.

Chapter 14

Isaac rushed to Avery's side where she crouched under the table, but Foggy made it to her first. He was licking her face between sharp barks, doing his best to get his body as close to hers as possible, but it wasn't helping.

She shook violently, her skin pale and cold like marble, and her hands whipped at him when he tried to touch her. Finally, he was able to get her into his arms, where he held her for several minutes until the rapid heaving of her chest began to subside. He lifted her up and lay her down in the grass underneath the picnic table. Foggy draped himself over her torso, waiting patiently for her to get back to normal.

Isaac knew she kept antianxiety medication at home, but she'd told him she didn't need to bring it with her, that she was okay without it almost all of the time. Now he cursed himself for not insisting that she bring it along, just in case; he wouldn't make that mistake again.

But as he watched, Foggy began to lick her face again, and eventually her eyes lost their glaze, their iciness returning to their calm, ocean-water appearance. She noticed the dog and wrapped her arms around him, pulling him close as he continued to wash her with kisses.

Foggy worked almost as fast as medication, without the unpleasant side effects that sometimes accompanied drugs.

Isaac's heart nearly burst as he watched the dog take care of his person, and a thought hit him like a bullet to the chest.

If only Stephen had waited. If only he'd stuck around for just a few more years until Isaac started this business. If only he hadn't left before Isaac got a chance to save him.

As Avery looked into his eyes, he felt anger flood through him like hot blood, misplaced rage at his inability to keep Stephen from taking his own life, and instead of doing what he should have, instead of comforting her and making sure that she was okay after what she'd perceived as trauma, he took that out on her.

He grasped her forearms and forced her to look at him. Her eyes were full of fear, *of him*. He hated himself for that, but couldn't stop once he'd started. All the things he'd never been able to say, all that he'd never been able to express to his brother, who'd selfishly left him here to take care of their mom, to fend for himself without a father.

"You can't do this to me, Avery. You can't leave me like that. It scares the crud out of me to think I've lost you when you disappear on me that way."

She stared at him, confusion etched into her features now, her eyes huge. "It's okay, Isaac. I'm fine. I just heard the fireworks and got startled, but look, I'm okay." She held out her arms for him to see. "Foggy helped me and my episode lasted only a few minutes. Everything's fine. Really."

"No, Avery. It's not fine," he shouted. He didn't know what was happening to him but he couldn't keep his voice down. "They should know better than to allow fireworks at something like this, where there are animals everywhere anyway, but you can't do that to me— you can't scare me like that. I thought I'd lost you."

His head spun as he fought desperately to make sense of the confusing flood of emotions darting through his brain and heart.

"What's the matter with you, Isaac?" she asked, and he caught the hurt in her voice. He knew he should apologize, but somehow he couldn't form the words.

What *was* the matter with him? This wasn't Stephen. He knew that. At least part of him did, but another part…another part wasn't able to separate the two. He'd loved his brother, yet he'd been unable to save him. No matter how much he'd wanted to, he'd never been able to heal that dark space inside of Stephen. And now… now he wondered if he would ever be able to do that for Avery.

If he cared for her as much as he knew he did, would he always wonder about the possibility of danger, of her PTSD taking over, of the darkness winning? Would he live his life afraid of losing her?

A small voice inside said *yes*. Yes, he would. And as much as it had hurt to lose his brother—losing Avery would somehow be worse. Losing Avery, he knew suddenly, would destroy him.

"I see," she said, her features resigned. She looked… shattered. "Look, Isaac. I laid everything out on the table when we met. You know that I have some pretty big problems—they were never a secret. Because of the way we met, I never even got a chance to decide if I wanted them to be, not that I would have been able to hide them for long. But if you can't handle being around me, if you're going to freak out like this whenever something happens to me, well… I can't. I just can't do this."

She crawled out from under the table as he watched, frozen in place, powerless to stop her. It was too late when he came to his senses, when he finally understood that the reason he'd lashed out was the very reason he absolutely needed her to stay.

"Avery," he called after her as she grabbed Foggy's leash and started jogging away without looking back, leaving him and Jane there in the dirt. "Avery, wait!"

But it wasn't enough. She was gone, and it was his fault.

Avery had no idea where she was headed. She just ran and ran, poor Foggy jogging along beside her.

She finally stopped when she reached the duck pond. She sat on the rock bench to catch her breath and pulled Foggy's portable dish out of her pocket, pouring water from her bottle into the little bowl and setting it down. Foggy lapped it up quickly and she gave him more until he was no longer thirsty.

Tears came, fast and hot, but no matter how many times she went over the scene in her head, she couldn't figure out what had happened to Isaac back there. What on earth had made him so blistering mad at her? He'd been so out of character, yelling at her like that, and it scared her. She hadn't understood him when he'd tried to explain why he was so upset; none of what he'd said had made sense. What was that he'd said about losing her? He wasn't going to lose her. She was right freaking *there*. And she'd given him more of herself than she'd shared with anyone in as long as she could remember.

She shook her head and pulled in deep breaths, going over the previous moments until her temples began to throb. She had no idea how long she sat there like that, staring into the water, right at the same spot that Isaac had first kissed her.

Everything had been so perfect.

What had she done to make it so wrong?

"Avery."

His voice behind her back caused the hair on her neck to stand. She was mad at him, but still her body reacted viscerally to his nearness as he came into view, sitting beside her on the rock as Jane wandered over to stare at the ducks.

A long silence passed before he spoke.

"Avery, please forgive me. I don't know what got into me back there."

"Well, that makes two of us, then," she said, her voice sad and bitter.

They sat in silence until he cleared his throat.

"Just tell me this."

She turned to look at him.

"Are you okay?"

His eyes were full of agony, and she wanted to touch him. But she wasn't sure if that was the right thing to do. He'd been so angry at her for no real reason, and it had challenged her trust in him.

"Yes, I'm okay. Are you?"

"I think so," he said, his voice pleading. "Avery, I'm so very sorry."

"What was that, Isaac? What happened? Why did you blow up like that on me? I hate that you shouted at me that way."

He shut his eyes tight at her words.

"I was taking something out on you that had nothing to do with you."

"I don't think I understand."

"I was the one who found Stephen," he said, barely able to hear his own words. "I was the one who found him after he died, and it nearly killed me. I think a part of me sees you as being fragile, like he was. And if you don't get better, the same thing might happen to you."

She put her hand on his forearm and her touch warmed his skin.

"Oh, Isaac," she said. "I'm not Stephen. I'm not going to hurt myself. I've got so much to stick around for. I've got you and Foggy and my family. I'm not going anywhere. Not if I can help it."

"I'm so sorry I lashed out at you like that, but I can't lose you. I just can't."

"I do worry, though, sometimes. It's just that…well… I worry that I might not ever get completely better. What if I always have these involuntary responses to things, and I'm never all the way back to normal? What if I can't ever hold down a job again? What if I'm a danger to you, or—" she swallowed "—to…to a child?"

"You'll lean on me," he said. "Whatever happens, you and I will handle it together. You won't have to be alone anymore, not if you don't want to."

She thought about what he'd said, wanting desperately to tell him that everything was okay, that they should just forget about it. But she knew that wasn't entirely true. Everything wasn't okay, and if she was going to start a relationship with this man, to maybe start on a path to building a life with him, then she needed everything to be out in the open. She wanted everything this time—no secrets, no holding back. She knew there would always be things to be afraid of. Just like him, she was afraid of losing something precious to her, but somehow she knew they were both ready to take that risk.

If the past few weeks had taught her anything, it was that some things were worth being afraid for. And he was worth it.

"Look, Isaac, I want to forgive you, and I want us to get past this, but if we're going to do that, we have to be honest with one another."

His eyes met hers and the threat of fresh tears choked her next words.

"I need you to know that I'm not your brother. I'm not going to end my life." She offered him a sad smile. "I have too much good to even think about taking that path out. But at the same time, I can't have you treating me like I'm another project. I know you love working with people with PTSD, but somehow you have to find a way to separate me from your work. I refuse to live my life wondering if you're just using me to atone for what you *think* of as your failure to save your brother."

He nodded, slowly, and stayed silent for a long moment.

"You're right about that, Avery. I didn't see it before, but I think I may have thought of you that way at first."

He reached over to grasp her hands, threading their fingers together, sending sparks through her.

"But I don't any longer. I understand that now. In just a short time, you've become everything to me, and I think I worried that I might lose you just as fast. I placed the weight of Stephen's choice on you, and that wasn't fair. I see now that you're your own woman, with your own life to live, and I know now that you're far stronger than Stephen ever was."

She swallowed, working to hold back an onslaught of relieved tears.

"I don't see you as a project—I see you as a partner. Someone I want to share my world with. I think it took this situation for me to truly understand that, and I'm so very sorry that I lashed out at you. I didn't know what to do with this new knowledge, with the realization of how much I care for you, but I do now. I want to continue helping you to train Foggy, but I also want much, much more. I will make you my world, if you let me."

As she looked into his eyes, she knew he meant every single word he said. In just the past few weeks, her life had changed completely, for the better, and Isaac was at the center of those changes.

She knew he couldn't *fix* her, and she didn't need him to. She would do the work herself, and she would be the victor over her own struggles. But he was right—they could be partners. They could share their pain and joy; they could encourage each other through the worst of it and laugh together through the best. She wanted that as much as he did.

"I'm in. But only if I can convince you that you're not going to lose me, Isaac. I promise you that. I'm here for good." She tickled his chin with her fingers, then pulled it so that he would look into her eyes. "Whether you want me or not."

Now was the time they'd both been waiting for. Now was the time to tell him how she felt.

"I do. I do want you." He swallowed, putting his hands on her face. "I love you, Avery Abbott. And I always will."

Her blue eyes filled, spilling over when she closed them. When they opened again, they were overflowing with joy, with peace.

"I love you, too, Isaac Meyer."

As they made their way back to the chaos of booths and families and food, hand in hand, a man dressed in a navy blue polo shirt and slacks—a bit formal for a 5K on a warm spring day—approached and stopped in front of them, holding out a hand.

"Are you Mr. Isaac Meyer?" he asked.

"I am," Isaac said, shaking the man's offered hand. "What can I do for you, sir?"

"Quite a bit, I hope," the man said, giving a little laugh.

Isaac smiled tentatively, uncertain what was so darn funny.

"Mr. Meyer, I'm Fred Palmer," the man said, continuing when Isaac stared back at him with a blank expression. "Fred Palmer," he said again, "of Palmer Motors."

"Oh, yes," Isaac said, the pieces clicking into place. "I didn't recognize you, sir. You look a little different from your TV commercials.

Mr. Palmer laughed again and Isaac decided he liked this guy.

"As well you shouldn't. The wife's had me on a diet the past few months and I've lost about thirty pounds, but they needed to go."

"Well, then, congratulations are in order," Avery chimed in.

Isaac apologized for not introducing them and was quick to remedy that.

"Mr. Palmer," he said, "This is Avery Abbott." He turned to Avery, who stood near his side, holding Foggy's and Jane's leashes, and his heart nearly burst through his chest at the sight of her beautiful face. "My girlfriend."

She beamed at him before he turned back to Mr. Palmer.

"Pleased to meet you, Ms. Abbott," the older gentleman said. "I knew your father—we went to school together at Peach Leaf High, ages ago. And, may I say, thank you for your service."

Avery lowered her chin a little, nodding in gratitude.

He turned back to Isaac.

"Mr. Meyer, let's get right down to business. I have a proposal I'd like to make."

"Of course, sir, I'd love to hear it. What's on your mind?"

A broad smile spread across the man's face, lifting his plump cheeks.

"Well, son, if I do say so myself, my company's doing pretty good, and when that's the case, I like to show my thanks to the community in some way. I wouldn't have the business that I do if it wasn't for the great folks in this town."

"That's very generous of you, Mr. Palmer. I know Peach Leaf owes a lot to you."

The older man waved a hand. "It owes me nothing, son. I was born and raised here and I run a solid company. It's in my power to give back and it's something I enjoy doing, but that's beside the point."

Isaac was beginning to realize where this was going and he couldn't help the excited energy that sprinted up his spine. Mr. Palmer was known for his donations to local causes, and if what he'd heard about the man was even half-true, he could help a lot of people in the near future.

"The point is, son, I've been watching you for a long time, and you're doing some amazing work with vets and rescue dogs, and, well, I've got a soft spot for them—" he glanced in Avery's direction "—for you."

Isaac nodded, his palms sweaty.

"So, here it is. If it's all right with you, I'd like to make a donation, Mr. Meyer."

Isaac stifled a laugh. "Of course it's all right with me."

Avery squeezed his hand.

"In the amount of half a million dollars."

"Holy cow!" Avery bounced up and down with the energy of a happy child and Isaac couldn't help but do the same right along with her before smothering their generous donor with a thousand thank-yous.

"No need to thank me, son," Mr. Palmer said gruffly before moving on, but Isaac caught the shimmer at the corner of the old man's eye.

"I'd like you to use it to sponsor as many veterans as you can, as long as you keep taking and training dogs from the local shelter. You've got a gift for it, Meyer, and I've seen how much you've helped the ones who serve our country—especially my own boy."

Isaac recalled training with Gary Palmer and his Lab, Tex, a few months back. Gary had lost his legs to a mine and was wheelchair bound. Tex had given Gary his smile back, not to mention helping him perform daily tasks with a lot more ease.

"Thank you, again, Mr. Palmer, but Gary and Tex did all the work."

Mr. Palmer chuckled and Isaac nearly choked, overwhelmed at the amount of money the man had just given his organization.

"Truly. I can't thank you enough. You're helping a lot of folks, Mr. Palmer."

"You are, Isaac. You are," Mr. Palmer corrected.

The old man shook Isaac's hand again and bid them good day, promising to be in touch with the details of the donation the following Monday.

As soon as he walked away, Avery threw herself into Isaac's arms and peppered his face with kisses. He twirled her around and around, causing Foggy and Jane to bark at their outburst of glee.

"Oh. My. Goodness," Avery screamed. "Can you believe it? Half a million dollars? Half a million bucks, Isaac. Can you imagine how many people that will help?"

Isaac burst out laughing. "I can, actually," he said. "I'm doing the math in my head right now, and it's… epic."

He stopped spinning and set Avery's feet back on the ground, kissing her nose. She was absolutely beautiful in the afternoon light, sunshine glinting off her golden hair, her blue eyes sparkling with delight. Her happiness, new and precious and hard-earned, was contagious. This joyful Avery was the most magnificent thing he'd ever seen.

He pulled her close so she could see his face.

"But with that much financial backing, I'll need more help, you know?"

"Of course. You'll have to hire more trainers and have people to help you find dogs at the shelter, and—"

"And, I want you," he said.

"Me? What do you mean?"

"I mean, I want you to join me. I'm going to promote Hannah to manager, and I want you to be my new assistant."

Avery's face lit up when she got what he was saying.

"Are you serious?"

"As a heart attack."

"But I have no training. I'm a nurse, not a dog trainer."

"But you have what it takes to make a great one. You're a natural with Fogs and you'll be amazing once you're certified. Besides," Isaac said, grabbing her hand to lead her back to Tommy and Macy, "we have plenty to fund your classes now, don't we?"

"I would say so," she answered, giggling.

"I've had you with me for almost a month now, and it has been, without contest, the best almost-month of my life. I'm not about to let you go now, Avery."

He stopped to kiss her long and hard, right there in the middle of the park. When they caught their breaths, Avery gave him a big smile, her face flushed from sunshine and the sensation of his lips on hers.

"Well, that's good news," she said, "Because I wasn't lying when I told you I'm not planning on going anywhere. And pretty soon, I'm going to need a new job."

"You've got one," Isaac said, pulling her close. "As long as you want."

"How about forever?" she asked, the question holding far more weight than what her words had indicated.

"Forever isn't long enough," he answered.

"Are you happy, Isaac Meyer?"

"The happiest," he said. "Because of you."

Epilogue

July Fourth, one year later

Morning light slipped in through the blinds of Isaac and Avery's bedroom window, spreading golden rays across her blond hair.

He watched her sleep, humbled by the simple rise and fall of her chest as she inhaled and exhaled in perfect rhythm, wondering again where he'd gone so right—how he'd become the lucky man who got to wake up next to such a beautiful, amazing woman each morning.

Isaac leaned over to kiss her forehead, glad when her lips curved to smile at him. Slipping out of bed, he tucked the sheets around her shoulders and roused the dogs from where they slept, tangled together on the window seat.

The three of them went downstairs and Isaac opened

the back door to let Foggy and Jane out, turning on the coffeepot. As it sputtered to life, starting up the strong brew he preferred, he walked into the dining room where he kept a small desk for business when he wasn't at the training facility. Grinning, he pulled out the office chair and sat, reaching into the bottom drawer, all the way to the very back.

He stopped when his fingers touched cool velvet, and pulled out a small box, lifting the lid. It still took his breath away every time he looked at this symbol of his love for her.

The past year of his life had been wonderful beyond words. Avery had passed her dog training certification exam with flying colors, and she and Foggy were an incredible team. Watching the two of them work together to help other veterans and dogs form partnerships brought him more happiness, more fulfillment, than anything he'd ever witnessed before in all the years he'd owned the facility. And to him, she was a greater partner than he ever could have hoped for.

Of course they had their tough days; of course things weren't perfect, but that didn't matter. What mattered, he had come to understand, was that they were together through the ups and downs. She was there for him, truly understood him when the ache of missing Stephen was too much to bear. And he did his very best to be a source of strength for her when she had nightmares and the—thankfully rare, now—panic attacks that still scared her so badly.

Each time he glimpsed the simple, elegant ring, he grew more and more excited about this day—a day he'd anticipated for so long now.

And today—the big day—was no different. He couldn't wait any longer; it was time.

Grabbing a piece of string and snapping shut the lid, Isaac headed back to the kitchen and poured a cup of coffee for himself, leaving it black, then one for Avery, stirring in the ample amount of cream and sugar that his girl liked so much.

He set the cups on the kitchen counter and opened the back door, letting the dogs back in.

"All right, Foggy. You ready for your big job?"

The dog sat and raised his paw, giving Isaac a high five.

"Okay, then," he said. "Good deal. Let's get you all set."

He knelt down, pulled the ring out of his pocket and made a loop through its band with the piece of string, then tied it to Foggy's collar.

"This is it, boy," he said. "Have you got my back?"

Foggy barked.

"Shhh! We don't want to wake Mom just yet, okay?"

Back in the kitchen, he picked up the coffees, padding back upstairs as quietly as he could with two rambunctious dogs in tow.

When he reached the landing, Isaac took a deep breath, not because he had doubts, but because he could hardly contain the joy that threatened to burst out from under his skin.

That is, if she said yes.

He had to remind himself that there were two possible outcomes, though only one was worth dwelling on.

Avery woke to kisses, lots and lots of wet kisses.

"Foggy!" she chided. "I wasn't having a nightmare, boy."

She laughed and opened her eyes.

"What has gotten into you?" She tried to push the dog away, but he wasn't having it. Foggy jumped up onto the bed and lay down, paws on her chest.

"Morning," Isaac said, coming into the room, holding two cups of coffee. He kissed her forehead and put Avery's cup on her nightstand, then walked back to his side of the bed and slid under the covers.

"I think Foggy's trying to tell you something."

Isaac had a funny look on his face—overwhelmed, but happy—as if he anticipated something good, like a little boy on Christmas.

Avery didn't give it a second thought. He always looked like that since she'd moved in, a fact that made her smile every time she thought of it.

She rubbed her eyes and looked at the clock on her bedside table, groaning when she saw the hour.

"You guys are up way too early."

Isaac just grinned and took a sip of his coffee. He set the cup down and snuggled in closer.

"Foggy," he said, "roll over."

"What are you goofs up to?"

Foggy obeyed and flipped over to show off his tummy, making Avery laugh.

"I see you've learned a new trick, boy. Is that what you guys have been doing so early this morning?"

She gave his tummy an obligatory scratch, then rubbed under his chin. Something cold and metallic tapped against her fingers.

"What's this, Foggy?" she asked, tugging it out from the folds of his fur, gasping when it finally dawned on her what she held in her hand. Her pulse drummed at her temples, blocking out all sound.

"Oh, my gosh," she cried, a hand flying to her mouth as tears brimmed at the edges of her lids. "Isaac. It's just beautiful."

She gripped the ring and, with shaking hands, untied the string that attached it to Foggy's collar. Pulling in a breath, her eyes surveyed her surroundings, soaking in everything so she could remember it every day for the rest of her life.

A life she would spend with Isaac, a man she'd grown to love more than she ever thought possible.

He lifted the ring from her palm and got out of the bed, moving to kneel at her side.

"Avery Abbott. Will you marry me?"

She nodded, unable to say anything for a moment as tears rolled down her cheeks. Then, finally, it came— the word that would seal them together forever.

A word she'd said many times over the past year.

To new friends, to a job as a trainer that she absolutely adored, to events and places and things she'd never dreamed she would be able to experience.

And now to the man she loved more than anything else in the world.

"Yes," she said. "Yes, Isaac. I absolutely will marry you."

He slid the ring on her finger, then jumped up from the floor and right into the bed, covering her in kisses, wrapping his arms around her as she laughed, and cried, and laughed some more.

* * * * *

With more than one million books in print, **Pamela Britton** likes to call herself the best-known author nobody's ever heard of. Of course, that changed thanks to a certain licensing agreement with that little racing organization known as NASCAR.

But before the glitz and glamour of NASCAR, Pamela wrote books that were frequently voted the best of the best by the *Detroit Free Press*, Barnes & Noble—two years in a row—and *RT Book Reviews*. She's won numerous awards, including a National Readers' Choice Award and a nomination for the Romance Writers of America Golden Heart® Award.

When not writing books, Pamela is a reporter for a local newspaper. She's also a columnist for the *American Quarter Horse Journal*.

Books by Pamela Britton

Home on the Ranch: Rodeo Legend
Home on the Ranch: Her Cowboy Hero
Home on the Ranch: The Rancher's Surprise

Harlequin Western Romance

Rodeo Legends: Shane

Cowboys in Uniform

Her Rodeo Hero
His Rodeo Sweetheart
The Ranger's Rodeo Rebel
Her Cowboy Lawman
Winning the Rancher's Heart

Visit the Author Profile page
at Harlequin.com for more titles.

HIS RODEO SWEETHEART

Pamela Britton

This one's for Patti Mahany, the best big sister a person could ask for. You make me laugh. You've listened to me cry. You're always there for my daughter, and I appreciate that more than you know.

Chapter 1

There was something about a man in uniform.

Claire Reynolds had seen a lot of them over the years. It had gotten to the point that she hardly even noticed them anymore, but *this* man, she thought as a warm wind blew off the tarmac, this man stood out— and not just because he wore dress blues.

"Ms. Reynolds?" He walked out from beneath the shade of a C-40, although he had to yell to be heard. Behind him, across a strip of asphalt that shimmered from desert heat, the nose of a C-5 cargo plane lifted. The roar of its engines sounded as if a thousand storm clouds hovered overhead.

"You must be Dr. McCall?" she all but yelled back, a hank of her long black hair blowing across her face. She should have pulled it into a ponytail.

The man nodded, his hand lifting to his hat, a black

beret with a gold oak leaf cluster near the pointy tip. Major Ethan McCall. Decorated soldier. Veterinarian for the US Army. She'd been on base before thanks to CPR—Combat Pet Rescue—but she'd never met this man. Was he new?

Beneath his hat, green eyes squinted as he turned to face the back end of the smaller cargo plane, the big bay door yawning open like the back of a semi. In the shade of one of the wings, an aluminum dog crate stood silent. Claire watched as a black nose and part of a snout popped out of one of the holes, then back in again. For some reason, it made Claire smile. She looked up at the man in uniform and found him staring at her.

"Thanks for coming all the way out here." He looked away, and Claire took a moment to gather all her hair in one hand and twist it so that it would stay in place. He was young, much younger than she had expected. And handsome. She hadn't expected that, either. Light brown hair. Strong jaw. Sideburns. A younger version of George Clooney.

"I didn't mind." And she hadn't. She'd needed to get away, even though her troubles had followed her here. As much as she loved her six-year-old son, as much as she wanted to be there for him every step of the way, she'd craved a brief burst of freedom. So she'd made the long drive east and then south to the desert, leaving Adam in the care of her brother and sister-in-law. God help her, she'd wanted to keep on driving.

"Sorry about the uniform." She looked up in time to see something cross behind his eyes. "Funeral detail."

The reason for the heightened security presented itself. She'd been on base enough times to have the routine down by heart. But today there had been an added layer of tension. She did a half turn toward the plane and spotted it then. A casket sat just inside the cargo bay. It caused Claire's heart to stab her rib cage, the same way it did whenever she heard more bad news about her son's health.

"Oh." Of pithy things to say it probably didn't top the list, but there really wasn't much more to verbalize. He probably hadn't heard her anyway. The roar of four jet engines as they reached maximum horsepower made words disappear. When the sound faded somewhat she raised her voice and said, "I better make this quick, then."

He hadn't taken his eyes off the casket, and when he turned back to her, she saw the sadness in them.

"It's his dog." The words emerged from her, unbidden, but when she saw him flinch, she knew it to be true.

Janus. The Belgian Malinois, which a less trained eye might ID as a German shepherd, had belonged to his friend. She had to look away for a moment, her throat closing in mute sympathy because she recognized his type of pain.

"I'm so sorry."

Her security badge caught the breeze and blew against the white shirt she wore. Inside the crate the dog poked his nose through a hole again. She was tempted to present her scent, but there would be time for that later. Instead she took a deep breath and looked Major McCall in the eye.

"Is the family certain they don't want to keep him?"

He shook his head sharply. "He's a great dog. Passed his personality test with flying colors. It's just that the wife has two small kids. She's worried about Janus being too much to handle."

He would be a lot of work. Military dogs were known to be hyper, but they settled down once they realized their job description had changed. From military dog to family pet. It happened all the time.

She inhaled, trying to think of something else to say. "Tell them they can always change their mind."

"They won't."

He shook his head mutely. Inside the kennel Janus whined. You could tell a lot by an animal's cry. There was the feed-me whine and the I-want-out-of-my-crate whine, and the one that always tugged at her heart. The I-miss-my-master whine.

Janus wanted his master.

"Toughest part of the job, listening to their cries." She'd said the words softly, too softly to be heard by him, or so she'd thought. The cargo plane had lifted higher into the clear, blue sky, the sound of its engines slowly fading away, and the wind had caught her words, bringing them to his ears.

"It is, isn't it?" His eyes were so light that the black lashes stood out in stark contrast. From a distance it would look as if they were lined with makeup. Major Ethan McCall was all man. Wide shoulders. Narrow waist. Big hands.

She had to look away because noticing his hands seemed somehow wrong, especially given their conversation.

"I wanted to come do this for Trevor, but after to-morrow…"

She looked up again because something about his

words caught her ear. She tipped her head sideways. "You're getting out?"

He nodded. "Seemed as good a time as any."

She'd met a lot of veterinarians over the years. Army. Marine. Yes, even Navy, but they were always stateside. When he glanced toward the back of the plane again, she knew he hadn't been. He'd been over there. In combat.

"Going into private practice, then?"

He shrugged. "Not sure yet."

She searched for something to say because the sadness in his eyes tore at her heart and reminded her of all she'd lost, too. Funny how you could go through life wrapped up in your own little world, feeling sorry for yourself, only to be smacked in the face by someone else's problems.

"Well, if you find yourself at loose ends, you're always welcome to visit CPR. My family owns a big ranch. You'd be welcome there."

He hadn't heard her. He kept glancing back toward a nearby hangar. The family would be here shortly, she surmised. That was the reason the base commander had stressed the importance of being on time. They wanted Janus off base so the family wouldn't have to see the dog. Less painful to them that way.

"I'll think about it," he added.

So he *had* heard her. "It's a nice drive," she said, even though a part of her warned to just shut up and get the hell out of there. "It might do you good to get out." Damn her need to mother everybody.

She was almost grateful when his gaze shifted back to Janus again. It must have served as a reminder of what they were there to do, because he braced himself.

She saw the physical effects of it when he straightened his shoulders and clenched and unclenched his hands. She knew in an instant that the man whose body he'd accompanied back home had been more than a casual friend. He'd been a brother in arms. A member of his fighting family. Major McCall had been in combat, which meant someone must have pulled some strings to allow him to attend the body. She understood that type of bond all too well. She had two brothers who were military, one of them ex, the other about to be. Her husband, too, had been in the military before...

She took a deep breath. "Maybe we should get Janus loaded."

He nodded, and then turned. The dog's kennel had been placed on casters, making it easy to wheel to her vehicle. She'd been allowed to park near the tarmac, and she'd taken advantage of the shade offered by the massive metal building used to house aircraft. A local car dealership always loaned her a van for free. She chirped the lock, the two of them pausing for a moment near the double back doors.

Janus whined. She glanced at Major McCall just in time to see him swallow. Hard. "You mind if I say goodbye?"

She nodded mutely. He squatted down next to the metal box, cracked the door open.

"Shtopp," she heard him softly mutter the German commands nearly all combat dogs grew up hearing. *"Sitz."*

Inside the kennel, Janus shifted around. She couldn't see much with the metal door blocking her view, but she spotted the black paw that landed over the top of Major

McCall's hand. He turned it until the two were touching palm to pad. It made her want to cry.

"This kind lady is going to find you a new home," she heard him say. "A place where someone won't be trying to kill you every five seconds." She saw him smile bitterly. "Well, aside from maybe a five-or six-year-old kid that might try to saddle you up and ride you around."

That was so close to the truth of what might happen, Claire found herself momentarily smiling, but her smile faded fast because watching Ethan say goodbye to his friend's dog was difficult to watch. Usually a pickup was impersonal, the military staff remote. Not this time. It took every ounce of willpower not to lose it right then and there.

"Take care of yourself, buddy." He reached in and stroked the dog's head. "Trev will be there with you every step of the way."

One last pat on the head before the man closed the kennel door. He didn't look at her as he straightened. "Can you help me lift?"

"Of course."

His hands shook as he reached for an aluminum handle. In a matter of seconds they had the crate inside. Claire stepped back and closed the doors.

"I'll take good care of him."

"I know." He still wouldn't look her in the eye. "The base commander told me about you."

"It's a labor of love."

He met her gaze and she could see it then—how hard he'd fought for control. But he had himself in hand. His eyes might be rimmed with red, but he was a soldier through and through. A combat veteran. A man who'd been trained to keep his cool even when the world fell apart. She knew the type well.

"Thank God for people like you."

She felt close to tears again for some reason. "And thank God for servicemen like you."

They both dropped into silence, Claire wondering what he would do after today and where he would go, warning herself that it wasn't her problem.

"I should get going."

He nodded. "I'll be in touch."

She started to back away, but he held out a hand. She didn't want to clasp it. She really didn't. Stupid, ridiculous thing because there was no reason why she shouldn't, but the moment she touched him she knew she'd been right. It was like a scene from an old-time movie. A slowing down of time. A freeze-frame moment when everything seemed to stand still and all sound faded: *Zoom in camera one. Hero and heroine touch and seem unable to look anywhere but into each other's eyes.*

"Drive carefully."

He let her hand go and smiled. He had dimples. She would have never expected dimples.

"Thanks," she heard herself say, and then she forced herself to take a deep breath as she turned away and headed toward the driver's side door.

Don't look back. Don't look back. Don't look back.

She looked back.

Major McCall still stood there, his hand lifting to his hat as he saluted. She smiled, saluted back, all but wilting into the driver's seat a moment later. She started the engine and slowly backed out, Janus whining one last time. It wasn't until she hit the main road that she pulled over on the shoulder.

She leaned back and closed her eyes, shaken by the touch of his hand.

"What in the world was that?"

Chapter 2

W hat was he doing here?

Ethan McCall looked down at his nearly finished coffee. He'd just driven five hours to pull into a strange town, order breakfast at a place called Ed's Eatery, and then sit and watch traffic pass through the small town of Via Del Caballo, California.

My family owns a big ranch. You'd be welcome there.

He recalled her eyes. They shared the same eye color, only his were nothing like her green eyes. Hers were like the rind of a lime. Bright green. Bottle green. Sun shining through glass and right into her soul green. He'd never seen anything like them before. They'd been filled with kindness, too, and maybe that's why he'd driven to her hometown. That, and the truth was, he had no place else to go.

Out in front a new car pulled into an empty parking

spot, one of the diagonal kind. A small family. Two little kids. Mom laughing at something Dad said. It was such a stark contrast to his view over the past four years—crumbling buildings, half-dressed children, dust-covered cars—that for a moment he simply stared. The mom took the hand of the youngest child, a little girl with cute blond curls that caught the morning sun. Behind them and across the street, someone loaded what looked like grain into the back of their truck. The sign on the store read Via Del Caballo Farm and Feed. Out in front sat a row of livestock feeders. Round. Square. Tall. Feeders of all sizes. When he'd first sat down he'd gazed at them for the longest time, just thinking about the times he'd been in the Middle East, longing for a view like the one he had now.

Hometown, USA.

"Need more coffee?"

He glanced up at the waitress—a teenage girl with dirty blond hair and freckles—and said, "No, thanks."

She smiled and walked away, Ethan would bet she entered her pig in the county fair every year. FFA. Local rancher's daughter. Good kid with no bad habits and a weekend job.

Life in a small town. He'd fought to protect that lifestyle. Had kept going even when the chips were down. And then Trev and Janus had been shot and…

He nearly cracked the handle of his coffee mug. It took him a moment to regulate his breathing again. When he did, he glanced across the street.

And froze.

It was her. Claire Reynolds. The woman he'd come to see. The one he'd convinced himself wouldn't be home. The woman who'd called him on the phone one day—

out of the blue—and asked for his opinion on a dog in her care. Behavioral issues, she'd said. But instead of calling her back he'd slipped behind the wheel of his old truck and found himself heading north and then west.

And there she was.

She'd slipped out of a pickup truck, that long, black hair he remembered so well pulled into a ponytail. She glanced toward the restaurant and he found himself turning away, even shielding his face with a hand, for some reason embarrassed even though he doubted she could see him sitting in the window of the local coffee shop. He'd felt stupid for arriving unannounced. He'd been debating with himself for over an hour whether he should call her now, drop into her place, or just go back home. Except he didn't have a home. Just an empty apartment near the base that he hated with a passion.

She'd moved to the back cab of her truck, helping a little boy down. That must be him. Her kid. The little boy who was sick. After he'd buried Trev, he'd done some calling around to find out more about the woman who now had care of Janus. He'd learned a lot about Claire Reynolds. He knew she'd started the rescue in honor of her deceased husband. They'd had trouble adopting his dog once he'd been discharged. The man had been sick and the dog had been healthy so the military had reassigned the dog—something that happened pretty frequently with wounded warriors— and so they'd lost out on the animal. The whole ordeal had prompted Claire to start Combat Pet Rescue and, when her husband had passed, to help write legislation that mandated combat veterans would have first pick at their dog. She'd thrown herself into the endeavor whole hog—or so he'd been told. And now her son was sick, too. Cancer. Pediatrician had caught it early, but still... Some people had no luck at all.

He watched as she hugged her son, and then straightened. Her hand found the top of his ball cap, rested there for a moment, then gently stroked it, as if she'd forgotten he didn't have any hair. She snatched her hand away.

Some things just weren't fair.

Trev's wife was on her own now, too. At least she didn't have a sick kid.

He found himself standing up before he could stop to think about what he planned to do. The waitress smiled at him as he left, and Ethan nodded before sliding past the family of four and out the glass doors. It was one of those perfect Saturday afternoons. The kind made for sitting on a porch and drinking tea. Blue sky. Probably 70 degrees. The smell of summer hung in the air thanks to a sidewalk planter that held rosemary and lilac.

He headed toward the store. Up and down the street, people went about their Saturday business. It was a picturesque town. Storefront windows. Dark green canvas awnings swooping low over the sidewalks. Boutiques sat next to hair salons that sat next to antiques stores; and in front of it all, cars parked at an angle. He ducked between two of those cars now, pausing for a moment to check traffic. Just his luck to come home after three tours in the Army and get mowed down while jaywalking. The traffic on Main Street was pretty light and he made it across in time to watch Claire and her son enter the store.

"You are not getting the John Deere tractor," he heard her say. She'd disappeared between some shelves and he followed the sound. He spotted her as she made her way down an aisle filled with sprays and ointments and shampoos for animals and at the end of which lay a section of toys.

"But, Mom—"

"Don't 'but, Mom' me. You have more toys than you know what to do with."

Her son had her green eyes. He could tell because he'd stopped in front of a shelf of toys and now faced his direction. "But I don't have *this* toy."

Her ponytail swayed from side to side as she shook her head and reached for his hand. "They all look the same to me." She tugged him toward her. "Come on. I need to talk to Mr. Thomson about that shipment."

And then she faced him and froze. He did, too. Her son smacked into the back of her legs.

"Mo-om."

And it happened again. That same shock of electricity that had hit him the first time he'd seen her, out there on the tarmac, the last place he'd expected to see such a beautiful woman, one with so much sadness in her eyes.

"Hello, Claire."

She had to be mistaken. It couldn't be—

"Dr. McCall?"

He smiled and she knew it really was. A more casually dressed Ethan in jeans and a black T-shirt and a black cowboy hat, but still the man with the green eyes that jolted her to the core. Even now she had to look away and when she did…

Scars.

Her gaze snagged on them like a hangnail. They ran up his arms. Angry red wheals crisscrossed his flesh.

He had a tattoo, too, she noticed now, some type of tribal thing that circled the top of his upper left arm. They were recent, those scars, and for the first time she realized he hadn't just known the soldier who'd died, he'd been in combat with him.

"I thought I'd surprise you."

Their gazes connected again and her stomach gave that familiar lurch, the one that made her feel dizzy and uncertain and maybe even a little scared. What was it about this man? Why did being in his presence elicit such a mix of emotions?

"You surprised me, all right."

She hadn't meant her words to come out sounding so strained, but she could tell he'd picked up on the tension she felt.

"If this is a bad time—"

"No, no." Her eyes caught on Adam, who stared up at the man curiously. Her son might have recently turned six, but he had the mind of an adult, and she couldn't help but notice the curiosity in his gaze.

"Adam, this is Ethan McCall, the veterinarian I was telling you about."

"Were you in combat?"

Leave it to her son to blurt out the first thing that came to mind. He hadn't learned to filter his thoughts, but she could tell Ethan wasn't offended.

"I was." His smile was soft and easy and it made her stomach twirl for a whole different reason. "Now I'm just a civilian."

A civilian who could help her with Thor. She shouldn't forget that. She should be grateful he'd driven all this way—and she was—she just hated the way his mere presence made her feel so out of sorts. He had that effect on her.

"My mom didn't tell me you were a real soldier."

He had wrinkles near the corners of his eyes, the kind that were so deep the skin was lighter where the cracks fanned out. Those lines disappeared as he smiled, as he did now. "Whoa there, partner. Everyone in the armed services is a real soldier."

"I know." Her son glanced up at her as if seeking reassurance. "My dad was in the Army."

"So was I."

Adam's eyes widened, and he probably would have gone on about Marcus if Claire hadn't touched his head as a way to silence him.

"So what brings you to town?" She asked the question even though she knew. Her phone call. She'd dialed his number without thinking. He hadn't called her back. Honestly, a part of her had been relieved.

When he met her gaze she spotted discomfort in his eyes, maybe even uncertainty, something she would never expect to see in a man like Ethan.

"I was thinking I could look in on that dog for you, the one that's giving you trouble. And Janus, if you still have him."

She didn't say anything. It took her a moment to realize he awaited a response. "Sure," she forced herself to say. "Absolutely." *Come on, Claire, inject a little more enthusiasm.* "That'd be great," she said with a big smile. At least she hoped it was big. And not too fake. And that it projected at least a little bit of gratitude because she really was grateful to him for making the trek all the way to her hometown.

She just wished he'd called first.

"You're going to help us with Thor?" They both glanced down at the little boy. "Man, you're brave. He almost bit my mom's hand."

Those green eyes shot to hers. "Is it that bad?"

She shifted from one foot to the other, something close to shame causing her to lick her lips in chagrin. "He's been—" she searched for the word "—a challenge."

"Then I should probably look at him sooner rather than later."

Yes, he probably should, and that was the problem because now that he stood in front of her she wondered what had possessed her to invite him to the ranch.

"You should come out today."

"Adam." Claire had to physically restrain herself from tapping her son with her toe. "I doubt Dr. McCall has time to see Thor today."

He glanced toward the door. "But I do."

"See," Adam said, taking her hand. "Let's go right now. Thor needs help."

She pulled her fingers from her son's grasp. "But I have to check on that order."

"I'll wait," he said.

She straightened. Of course he would wait. He had nothing better to do. Recently out of the Army, on his own, nobody to report to. She, on the other hand, had a million things to do, starting with her errands here in town.

She glanced down at her son, spotted the excitement in his eyes and recognized the reason for insistence. Adam felt sorry for Thor, as so many people felt sorry for her son, something she'd explained to him when he'd been given toys for no reason at all. He'd been the one to goad her into calling Dr. McCall. And here stood the good doctor, and she was grateful, she really was.

"Then I guess I'll be right back," she said, resigned to her fate. She'd just have to catch up on life another day—if she ever caught up.

Chapter 3

What was he doing?

Ethan turned down a Y in the road, following behind Claire's silver pickup, the wheels of his own truck
making a sticking sound as they drove on what looked
to be new pavement.

You're checking up on an old friend's dog.

They were out in the middle of nowhere, mountains ringing a picturesque valley carpeted by grass.
In the distance, at the base of the hills, trees stained
the bottoms a darker shade of green, but the peaceful-
ness around him did nothing to lessen the beating of
his heart. That staccato rhythm was the same type he'd
felt before jumping out of a plane for the first time, or
heading overseas, or facing enemy fire, and damned if
he knew why he was feeling it now.

*Just check in on Janus, take a look at Thor and then
leave.*

And go where? That was the question. That was *always* the question.

They'd traveled the road for at least a half mile, when at last Ethan spotted in the distance a small, square home that sat at the base of a low hill beneath giant oaks. A cute picket fence matched the white house. As they drew nearer, he could see a fence made of rust-colored barbed wire along the back of the property, beneath the line of trees a hundred or so yards away, the fence posts that held it in place stained gray with age. To the left of the house sat a line of kennels, at least a half dozen of them, more than one Belgian Malinois pacing inside, all of them barking up a storm. Well, all except one. He suspected that was Thor, but for now he had eyes only for Janus.

His hands gripped the steering wheel. It'd been tough saying goodbye. Tougher still to see him again. He missed Trev more than he would have thought possible given the short time they'd known each other. Then again, combat will do that to a person: make brothers out of near strangers.

"Welcome," Claire said as she stepped out of her truck.

He'd parked next to her, along the left side of her house, almost in front of the kennels. He got out and stood by the side of the truck, the smell of dirt and oak trees and fresh-cut grass so predominant that for a moment all he did was inhale.

He caught her staring at him curiously. "Nice place."

She had her hand on her son's head again, bending down to say something.

"But I want to watch him with Thor," her son said.

"In a minute," he heard her murmur.

The boy's head bowed. His shoulders slumped. He did everything but kick at a rock, but he did as she asked, muttering something under his breath, something about Hawkman.

His gaze must have reflected his puzzlement because she smiled. "His immune system still isn't up to par." Her smile faded a bit. "He thinks I'm stupid for wanting him to go inside and wash his hands after we've been out and about."

"So he's threatening to have Hawkman come after you?"

The smile turned back on. "He's a friend of the family."

"You have a superhero for a friend?" For the first time since his arrival, he felt like smiling, too. "Wow. I'm impressed."

Something low and soft that he recognized as a laugh filled the air. "Not really. We're friends with Rand Jefferson." She shook her head. "The actor that plays the superhero in the movies. It's a long story."

"Maybe you can tell it to me after I say hello to an old friend."

"Yeah, sure." Her smile seemed to have a short in it because it fizzled. "He's over there."

"I know."

Janus had spotted him. He could tell by the way the dog's eyes had fixated on him, his whole body having gone still, as if he silently tried to telepathically commune with his old friend. He knew what he would say.

Where have you been? What are you doing here? Where's Trevor?

He didn't have an answer for the dog.

"Platz," he ordered sternly as dog after dog jumped

up on the fence of their loafing sheds. Janus just stood there, as if he tried to reassure himself through sight and smell that it really was his master's old friend. Then he shifted his gaze past Ethan, as if hoping to spot Trev.

He nearly stumbled.

I keep looking for him, too.

You deployed with someone. You see them day in and day out. You drink beers with them, you shoot pool with them, you even go on leave together once or twice. And then—*bam*—just not there. He still couldn't believe it. He couldn't imagine how Janus felt.

"How are you?" he asked the dog, flipping up the latch that kept the front gate closed. "Good to see you again, buddy."

The familiar words set the dog's tail in motion. He still glanced behind Ethan again, then he sat down in front of him.

Ethan smiled. This, too, was familiar. When Trevor would bring Janus in for a post-op exam, the dog would walk right up to him and sit down, as if silently saying, "Go on. Get it over with."

"Nah," he said softly, squatting down in front of him. "I don't need to check you for bullet wounds. Not here. Not today."

Not ever again.

His hands had started to shake again. He covered the tremors by burying them in Janus's fur. It wouldn't hurt to check the condition of his injuries, he told himself, parting the fur, finding a diagonal slice that started at the top of his right shoulder blade and ended between his two front legs. A piece of mortar had nearly taken his leg off, but it was healing nicely.

"How does he look?"

Ethan didn't turn, just went on exploring Janus's body as he said, "Good."

He dragged his hand along the dog's side where he found a half-dollar-sized bump. Sniper round. Went clean through. Miracle Janus had lived. Another scar on his other side—this was from an old bomb blast. So many untold stories. So many near misses. Until...

He stood quickly. Janus scooted closer to him, his head tipped back, dark eyes unblinking. He opened his mouth and started to pant, something close to a canine smile lifting the corners of his mouth as their gazes locked.

I missed you, too, he silently telegraphed.

But it was also damn difficult. It brought it all back. The trip home. The funeral afterward. The look on Trevor's wife's face as she'd been handed the flag. She tried to be so strong for her kids, but her hands had trembled as she reached for the talisman, and he'd watched as the weight of her sorrow brought down the roof of her control.

"Ethan?"

"Whatever you're doing, keep on doing it."

Breathe, he told himself. *And again. Don't let Claire see how close you are to crumbling, too.*

"Good. I'm glad. Just as soon as he's healed from his wounds, I've got a home lined up for him."

He had to work to keep his voice even. "He'll do great." He just wished...

"What?"

Clearly she'd read the dissatisfaction in his eyes. "I wish she would have taken him."

"Who?"

"Naomi," he clarified. "Trevor's wife. I wish she would have taken him."

"Me, too."

He should have applied to take Janus home, but that was the problem. He didn't have a "home," a necessary component to being approved for adoption. He might have been able to pull some strings, but to be honest, then what? He had no idea where he was going, or what city he'd end up in, or what he'd end up doing. Before he'd left for Via Del Caballo he'd applied to a number of jobs, most of them working at veterinary clinics, but a few of them doing what he wanted to do—training dogs. Right now, Janus didn't fit into his life. Better to let him go, to let him start over with a family to love him.

"Ready to look at Thor?"

"Sure."

The dog hadn't changed position since his arrival. He still lay huddled against the wall of his shelter. He couldn't even see the dog's eyes, they were buried so deeply into his paws.

"I put him on the end so I could interact with him on my way to and from the kennels." She led him back the way they'd come. "It hasn't helped. He's snapped at me twice. I usually don't neuter them right away, but I'm wondering if it wouldn't help with this dog. To be honest, I'm at my wit's end."

He approached the dog warily, his experience with military working dogs—or MWDs—having taught him that it was often better to approach behind the safety of a fence first, so he once again walked around the corner of the row of kennels. All the dogs had passed a behavioral test, but still, she had a point. Neutering him might help, too. In fact, most MWDs were adopted out already spayed or neutered, but Claire took all dogs in, one of the rare civilian operations in the United States. Clearly, someone had pulled some major strings when setting up her operation, not that he cared. As long as the dogs were well taken care of. Thor looked good, he thought, approaching the kennel. Beneath the shade of a giant oak tree, the dog blended in with a shadow but his coat and his weight told Ethan all he needed to know. His lack of movement told him something, too; he was a dog that clearly didn't want to be disturbed.

"He's obviously eating well."

"He is, but he waits to eat until I'm not around. I've watched him through my kitchen window. He picks at his food, too, I've noticed, eating a little here and a little there."

"Any vomiting or diarrhea?"

"No. I had him checked out by a friend. She did a complete workup. Nothing wrong."

He squatted down next to the dog's run. "Hey, Thor, buddy. How's it going?"

No response. Not an ear twitch. Not a wrinkled nose. Not even a tiny wag of the tail.

"What happened to his partner?"

"KIA."

It was just a phrase—KIA—but it kicked him in the gut. He had to grab at the fence as the familiar anxiety returned, not that Thor noticed. Ethan could still smell the desert if he closed his eyes. Hear the sound of the incoming mortar just before it hit their encampment. Hear the screams…

Stop.

He couldn't change the past. Couldn't change what happened to Trevor any more than he could change the direction of the wind. He took a deep breath, inhaling the scent of oak and pollen-filled air and… Claire.

Mostly, he focused on the smell of Claire; vanilla with maybe just a hint of butterscotch thrown in. Woman were a rarity over there, especially pretty women, women who smelled good. He would focus on her and her kind eyes.

Three, two…

He got ahold of himself, just as he'd taught himself to do, with grim determination. His hands still shook, but he was able to focus on the dog again. "Do you have a whistle?"

"Do I…" He turned in time to spy her look of consternation. "In the house, I think."

"Would you get it for me?"

She turned without another word, and Ethan watched her walk away. The scent of her lingered. Like dessert after Sunday dinner. Like home.

You are home, idiot. Back in the States.

No. Like when he'd grown up with his grandfather, back before he'd died. The best times of his life. And then everything had changed.

And if she knew how messed up you are, she'd stay in her house. To hell with the whistle.

That was the thing; nobody knew how messed up he was. Not even his superior officer. Not even the military shrink. Not even the discharge officer who'd asked him repeatedly if everything was okay.

No. Things weren't okay. And it scared the heck out of him.

She found a whistle with Adam's help, her son insistent that he go outside and watch whatever it was Major McCall was about to do.

"Do you think he'll have him attack someone or something? You know, blow the whistle and tear something to shreds."

Her son might be bald. He might still be recovering from the hell the doctors had put him through to kill the cancer in his blood, but he was still a boy.

"No, Adam. I don't think he's going to do that."

They emerged into the bright, spring sunshine. It'd been a year ago that Adam had been diagnosed. A year ago since her world had fallen apart. Hard to believe time had passed so quickly, but they weren't out of the woods yet. Though the cancer hadn't metastasized, it was still a waiting game. So far the immune depression therapy had worked, but they still had a while to go before they'd be given the all clear—*if* they were given the all clear. Things could change at any moment, which was why she refused to get her hopes up.

"What's wrong with him?" Adam asked Ethan, his baseball cap nearly falling from his head he bounced up on his toes so hard. "Are you going to put him through his paces?"

She had to give him credit; Ethan didn't seem bothered by her son's exuberance. Quite the contrary. He smiled down at him, even tapped the brim of his hat, just as she did, and it was then she noticed it.

His hands shook.

Her eyes shot to his. Was he nervous? Did Thor make him afraid?

"I'm just going to perform a little test." He held out his hand for the whistle.

Yes. No mistaking it. He shook.

"Here." The polished surface caught the light as it swung back and forth.

He snatched the whistle from her so fast she wondered if he knew she'd spotted his quaking limbs. Something about the way he turned away from her, too, as if he were afraid she'd look too closely. Little did he know. The man had held her attention since the moment she'd met him.

He blew the whistle.

Loudly. Shrilly. Unexpectedly. Claire's heart nearly jumped from her chest.

"Ouch." Adam covered his ears. "That was loud."

And Thor didn't move.

Claire stood, frozen, as a dozen little puzzle pieces fell into place. The way the dog ignored her. How he never rushed to greet her when she went outside. How he never came to her when she called his name.

He was deaf. She felt like a fool for never checking something so basic, so in-your-face obvious. Then again, Thor had been given a full physical, and a health clearance following that. He still bore the physical scars of his injuries. She'd just assumed his lack of attention was related to the physiological baggage he carried.

She took a step closer to Ethan and said, "It wasn't just his unresponsiveness that concerned me. There are other…issues, too."

He tucked the whistle in his pocket. "Like what?"

"He seems…detached somehow. He never wags his tail. Barely shows interest in his food. Ignores me for the most part."

He headed toward the entrance to the kennel.

She rushed to catch up to him. "Let me go in with you."

Adam knew to stay behind. He'd been strictly forbidden from dealing with Thor, but that didn't stop him from asking, "Can I go in, too?"

"No," she told her son. "Stay here."

She patted him on the head again, something she seemed to do more and more of late. Reassuring herself that he was still there. At least that was what one of the other moms at the hospital had told her when she'd spotted the gesture.

Ethan had rounded the end of the building. He didn't seem the least bit concerned about Thor's behavior.

Still, she heard herself say, "Be careful," as he slipped inside the "doghouse," as Claire liked to call it, a spacious room with a man-sized door leading to the dog run. Inside, an uneaten bowl of food lay in the corner. It worried her. Every day she hoped the dog would get better. Now she didn't know what to think.

Thank God he made a house call.

Fate, she admitted.

Thor lay just outside the back door, and Ethan moved slowly, his footfalls light. There had been dozens of times when Claire had done the same and she'd always taken care to use a soft voice to announce her arrival. Now she understood why the dog had been startled to the point that he'd tried to bite her. She'd snap at someone, too, if she'd been taken by surprise.

"Hey, Thor," she heard Ethan say. When she joined him, it was in time to see Ethan kneeling by the dog's side, but this time the dog's reaction was different. Normally he cocked an eye, maybe lifted his head in mute greeting, then went back to ignoring the world. This time he opened his eyes, immediately lifted his head, then stood. He moved toward the man who knelt beside him and sniffed, only to be clearly disappointed by his investigation. The dog's head lowered. His shoulders appeared to slump. He lay down at Ethan's feet.

"He's missing his handler," Ethan observed.

His *male* handler, she realized. She was just a poor second in the dog's eyes. Not worth getting to know.

"He was injured pretty severely," she said. "I'm thinking he probably lost consciousness. I would imagine he has no clue what happened to him."

"Yeah, I had a friend send me his file."

He'd done that for her? For the dog? Somehow, that took her by surprise.

He buried his fingers in the dog's fur, held them there for a moment, and if she hadn't been watching him closely, she might have missed the way he inhaled deeply. It was as if the dog's presence reassured him. He ran his fingers through Thor's coat, and she wasn't sure if it was a professional gesture, or a personal one. Another deep breath and then he began to move his hands up and down the dog's body, feeling for the scars now covered by hair, she realized. Another dog that'd been injured by a bomb blast. She'd seen far too many in the past three years. Thor had nearly had his leg taken off. The missing patch of fur right below the knee was the only visible sign of his injuries.

She knelt down next to Thor, too, touching him. Whatever Ethan's problem was, she understood all too well the soothing reassurance of a dog's coat. How many times had she come out and done the same thing, sometimes in the middle of the night, her son completely oblivious to her midnight visits?

"Anything?" she asked.

He shook his head.

Their gazes met and there it was again. The sadness. It lingered in his eyes like a bad stain. "No sign of pain anywhere. That's good." He went back to examining the dog.

She had to inhale deeply, too, but for another reason. What was it with this man, that she found herself studying him just as intently as he examined Thor?

He seemed to have recovered himself now. He cupped the dog's head. Thor looked up at him obediently. "We always do a complete physical before releasing a dog to civilian life, but it's entirely possible the loss came later." He lifted the dog's lips, checking gum color. "Scar tissue can do more damage than the initial injury."

Satisfied with what he saw in the dog's mouth, he examined Thor's ears next.

"So what now?"

"Damn. I wish I were back on base with all my instruments."

"Do you need me to make a call? My brother's wife has a friend who's a vet, and she could bring her truck over."

"No. That's okay." He moved Thor's head so he could peer into the left side ear. "I can't see any obvious obstruction. I'm betting scar tissue."

He held the dog's head again, lifting an index finger and seeing if Thor tracked his progress, similar to what a human doctor would do. His hands had stopped shaking. He had gone into full-on doctor mode.

"Looks good. I was thinking some kind of lingering pain might be causing his lack of appetite, but that's not it. He's unresponsive to pressure test, and his teeth look good, so no abscess in the mouth."

He moved in closer to the dog, sat down next to him,

stroking his head. Thor did something she'd never seen before then; he placed his head in the man's lap. She saw Ethan freeze, and then his expression changed. His face softened as he silently communicated reassurance with his hand. And just like his human counterpart, the dog inhaled deeply and closed his eyes.

Claire wanted to cry.

"What's the matter, buddy?" Ethan said to the dog.

She moved in closer. "Sometimes I wish they could talk."

He stroked Thor's head absently. "Well, if they could, this one would probably tell us he's depressed."

"Is that possible?"

"They're a lot like humans."

"So what do we do?"

"It'll take some time for him to adjust, and to come out of his depression."

"*If* he comes out of it," she added.

He nodded and Claire's heart dropped. If he wasn't in perfect health she couldn't adopt him out to a new family. Well, she could, but it'd be more difficult to place an animal with issues. Nearly impossible, as a matter of fact. There would be interviews and screening and maybe even a trial period. Time. That was what it would take.

"Is he going to need special help?"

She'd forgotten about her son with his nose pressed up against the chain-link fence, but his words tore at her heart. "Special help" was what she called his cancer treatment. She hated the C word, avoided using it at all cost.

"He'll need special training," Ethan said, "to compensate for his lack of hearing. He's used to listening for commands so we have to teach him to look only for nonverbal commands, arm movements. The good news is he already knows most of them. We'll have to teach him some new ones, and teach him to constantly keep his gaze focused on his handler, but retraining him is possible. No more walking up to him unannounced. Make sure he sees you before you touch him. That should stop the biting."

"That's easy," Adam said. "I can do the training, too."

Claire shook her head at her son. "Honey, it's not as easy as that. It'll take a professional. What Dr. McCall is suggesting isn't like teaching a dog to sit and stay. He'll need to learn to listen without hearing. That means he can never be out of his kennel. If he can't hear he won't be able to hear us and learn boundaries. What if he ran into the woods?"

There was nothing but open land between the ranch and the coast. Well, that wasn't precisely true. There were coastal towns, but the point being, if Thor got out, they'd be lucky if they ever found him again.

"I'll help him learn." Adam's soft words pricked at her heart. Alas, her son was in no condition to take on the task of training a dog.

"No." She made sure her word was firm. "We'll have to find someone else to retrain him."

"I know someone." Ethan straightened.

Claire's heart jumped in relief. "Who?"

The wrinkles next to his eyes reappeared. "Me."

Chapter 4

She couldn't have appeared more shocked if he'd announced his intention to drive his car to the moon.

"You?"

He faced her squarely. "I was thinking earlier that I might be able to help you out. At least for a little while, until I decide where I'm going next."

Green eyes that were so beautiful he couldn't stop studying them blinked, then blinked again. She had the world's longest lashes, the tips of them touching the arch above her eyes. Sweeping black brows dropped down low in consternation.

"But you have your own life to get back to."

"What life?" As sad as it sounded, it was true. Why else had he driven a hundred miles to see her? "I'm in between jobs right now, trying to decide which direction I want to go. I've actually been toying with the idea of training dogs, my way of still helping our country. I'd still practice medicine, but I'd like to learn that aspect of military dogs. Finding that type of job might take a little while, though. In the meantime I have a bit of money and plenty of time on my hands. Let me help."

She started to shake her head, that pretty, silky black hair of hers falling over one shoulder, but her son interrupted her midshake.

"He could stay with Uncle Colt."

She whirled around to face the boy. "Adam, no. We couldn't impose on your uncle like that. Besides, your other uncle, Chance, will be coming home soon. He'll need the apartment then."

"But he won't be home for three more months. You said so yourself." The boy's lower lip jutted out, green eyes imploring. "They have that super big place and it's empty."

"Yes, but they won't want a stranger staying there."

"Major McCall isn't a stranger."

"Adam—"

"It's okay." Ethan smiled down at her son. "I can find a place in town."

But the little boy's eyes showed grim determination. "I'll go call Uncle Colt right now."

The boy turned toward the house, calling over his shoulder, "He won't mind."

"Adam!"

She'd been ignored. He saw her mouth open and close a few times. Claire clearly wanted to call to her son again, maybe even run after him. Instead she stood there, something close to embarrassment floating through her eyes.

"I'm sorry."

"What for?" It was hard not to smile in the face of determination like Adam's, but he had a feeling if he showed her his amusement, Claire would feel even worse. "I think he's trying to help."

"You're probably right. Ever since he's been sick he's been worried about me. He says I do too much. That I'm always busy and it's not good for me. He's such a little man but he has grown-up concerns."

Her words had the ability to make him forget his own troubles for a moment. He'd almost broken down earlier. But he'd stopped it—thankfully. And here was her son, fighting for his life. It served as an example that there were worse things in life than dealing with a little anxiety.

A little?

Okay. Some days he would swear he was about to have a heart attack, and as he stared into Claire's kind eyes, he wondered what she would do if she knew the truth—that the man who was at her place to "help" needed help of his own.

A screen door slammed.

"That was quick," she said.

Adam didn't run, but his steps could almost be called a skip. Ethan knew what his uncle's answer had been before Adam even spoke.

"He said to bring him over." His smile could have lit up the inside of a room.

"Adam—"

"He said he thinks it'd be cool to have a dog doctor living on the property."

Claire's mouth opened and closed again. He could tell she wanted to say something, to dash the boy's hopes with words, but she wasn't proof against the excitement in her son's eyes.

"I take it he lives at Misfit Farms?" Ethan asked, having passed a sign along her driveway that pointed to a different road, one labeled with that name.

She nodded.

"I don't mind going over there." He tried to tell her without words that he wasn't about to take advantage of her brother's kindness. He knew she didn't want him to and he would respect that wish. "You can show me around the place."

She must have received the message because some of the concern faded from her eyes. She still searched for something to say, though, something that she could use to finagle her way around her son's high-handedness.

Something wet touched his hand.

He looked down. Thor peered up at him, curiosity in his brown eyes. Ethan glanced at Claire. Her eyes had gone wide.

"He likes you."

No. He probably reminded Thor of his handler, the man who'd been killed in action...*like Trevor.*

"See." Adam's eyes were as wide as his mom's. He pointed. "Thor wants you to stay, too."

Claire stared up at him, then down at the dog, then back at him again.

She looked troubled, and resigned. "Maybe you should go meet my brother."

Thor's nose nudged his palm again.

Maybe he should.

They drove to her brother's place in less than two minutes. Claire tried to ignore the presence of the man in the seat next to her, but it was nearly impossible.

Thor liked him.

For the first time since the dog had arrived she'd seen life in the canine's eyes. What did it mean? Would Ethan be able to get through to the dog, something nobody else had been able to do? She could tell Ethan didn't plan to accept the invitation to stay with her brother, and she appreciated his tactfulness, yet suddenly she wondered…

His hands had shaken.

There had been that look in his eyes, too, the one she'd recognized. She seen the same look in her husband's eyes when he'd come home from the war, and then later, as he'd been admitted to the hospital. The same look in her son's eyes.

Fear.

He fought demons, this man who had suffered through war. It made her want to help him. Marcus had called it her greatest gift—her desire to help. Claire thought of it more as a weakness because she often stretched herself too thin thanks to her inability to say no. It was why she'd gotten into the dog rescue business. Why she'd insisted on nursing her husband herself even though the military had offered hospice care. Why she'd stayed by her father's side, too, even though she had owed the man nothing.

Her tires hummed as she drove over the newly paved road. She couldn't get used to the smoothness, but Natalie, her brother's new wife, had insisted her clients would expect pavement. Still, as she turned left toward Colt's place, she wondered what the cows that still ranged the pastures thought about the strange black strip.

"Wait until you see my uncle's place." Adam leaned forward, as if they would have a hard time hearing him when his voice was just one level above a yell over the sound of the truck's diesel engine. "It's awesome."

Awesome was one word. *Expensive* another. *Amazing* was applicable, too. Her sister-in-law had won a huge jumping event last year, one with an equally huge purse. Natalie must have spent nearly all of it building her new riding facility.

"Wow," Ethan said when they drove between two low-lying hills, and her brother's place came into view.

Wow was right. The big red barn still stood in the same spot as it had in their youth, as did the house directly ahead, but the two-story farmhouse had been given a new coat of white paint. The original barn—the one she and her brothers had hidden from their father in when they were younger—had been converted back to a hayloft. Directly opposite it now, to their left, sat a gorgeous twenty-stall barn that seemed to match the old-fashioned farmhouse somehow. It was two stories, four windows with wooden frames directly above the opening—the apartment her brother Chance would live in one day soon.

That wasn't the only big change.

A covered arena sat behind the barn. A white fence surrounded the whole complex. They had to pass between the pristine posts, her truck's wheels catching the newly installed cattle guard and vibrating the interior.

"That always makes my insides jiggle," Adam said with a giggle.

Hers, too, she admitted, marveling at how green it all was now. Sprinklers. They sprayed every surface that wasn't covered by asphalt, including the square turnout pastures by her brother's old arena to her right. The "outdoor arena" they called it now. There were a few jumps in the middle of it, but the bulk of her sister-in-law's practice fences were in the covered arena. That was because her brother still managed Rodeo Misfits, his specialty act that involved trick riding. They needed the arena for practice. Still, the whole place was like an emerald gem set in the middle of a golden field.

"Does your family compete in riding competitions?"

"You could say that."

"My uncle is a rodeo performer. My aunt jumps horses."

All of which should be self-evident to some degree, Claire thought. Though it was the middle of the week, no less than four people rode in the covered arena, one of them her brother, looking out of place in his Western saddle among all the English riders. His truck and trailer still sat in the same spot, though, the words *RODEO MISFITS* still emblazoned on the sides. At least that hadn't changed.

"This is some place."

"That's the apartment." Adam pointed to the windows above the opening of the barn.

"Adam, we don't even know if Dr. McCall wants to stay with us yet."

Adam all but poked his head between the two front seats. "You do, don't you, Major McCall?"

"It's Dr. McCall," he corrected. "I'm out of the Army now. And I'd love to stay here, but I think we need to talk to your uncle first."

Points in the man's favor for being diplomatic. She had to focus on keeping her gaze straight ahead, though. The urge to look at him, to smile, to reach out to this man in a way that was personal, was nearly overwhelming.

"Uncle Colt said he'd get off his horse when we got here."

He must have called her brother on his cell. Determination, thy name is Adam.

They parked in front of the new barn and it still felt strange to slip out of her truck and hit pavement. Natalie had explained that her wealthy clients didn't like dirt and mud, something that seemed stupid considering they rode horses, but she didn't doubt her sister-in-law for a minute. People who jumped horses tended to be wealthy and drive cars that cost six figures. Prissy people, her brother called them, though he'd become friends with most of them in the past year.

Adam was already on his way through the middle of the barn and the arena on the other side. Prissy people didn't like to get wet, either, which was why they'd erected the covered arena less than twenty yards from the back entrance of the barn.

"This place is amazing," Ethan repeated.

Claire nodded. "I've been afraid to ask how much it all cost."

It even smelled new. New paint. New shavings. New leather. Shiny leather halters straddled brass hooks. She couldn't see any of the horses inside, not at first—the metal grates along the front stopped them from poking their heads out—but as she walked down the center aisle, one sleek animal after another was revealed. Some ate. Some stood. Some peered at her curiously as she walked by.

"Beautiful animals."

"Imports," Claire explained. "Most of them, at least. Although there's a few off-the-track Thoroughbreds and even a quarter horse or two. The majority were bred in Europe."

"I used to see horses when I was in veterinary school, although nothing like this."

He walked next to her along the barn aisle, light shining on his face despite the cowboy hat, thanks to the opening at the other end of the barn. He'd tucked his hands in his jeans. She wondered if his hands shook again and had to fight the urge to turn her head and study him intently. Whether he suffered from anxiety or not, it was none of her business. She appreciated his help, but no more than that.

"You worked on horses in the military?" She glanced at him.

"Cavalry units. Believe it or not, they're still in existence, although they're mostly for parade purposes."

"These horses are strictly for jumping and some of them cost as much as a new house."

"I don't doubt it."

Her sister-in-law received a commission on sales. Between that and her purse earnings she'd been able to build everything around them. It drove Colt nuts. Her brother was very much a man, and the fact that his wife made more money than he did took some adjusting, but they made it work. Her brother had found love and she couldn't be happier for him.

"Mom, Uncle Colt says Major McCall can stay in the apartment above the barn if he wants."

Her brother sat on a horse on the other side of a solid-wood rail, a wide smile on his face, Adam having already accosted him. Not for the first time she noticed how much he'd changed. His gold eyes always seemed lit from within. His black hair was tucked beneath a black cowboy hat—as it always was—but he didn't keep it as closely shaved as he used to. More relaxed, that's what he seemed. And happy. Very, very happy. She doubted their brother, Chance, would recognize him when he came home in a few months.

"I take it you're Major McCall," Colt called out to her guest.

"Ethan," the handsome doctor said—yes, handsome, damn it. It wasn't a crime to notice. "Nice to meet you."

The two shook hands, although her brother had to lean over the rail to do so, not that the horse he rode seemed to mind. Playboy—her sister-in-law's horse—she recognized, the horse's successful reining career having resulted in Colt hitting fewer rodeos and staying closer to home. He still loved his rodeo act, but he loved his new wife more. That was why he'd turned the act over to someone new—Carolina Cruthers—although Claire wasn't quite sure what to make of the standoffish woman.

"My nephew told me you just got out of the military."

"Been out two weeks," Ethan clarified.

"So this is him?" Her sister-in-law rode up next to her husband, a wide smile on her face, blond hair tucked beneath a black-and-gray helmet.

"This is him," Claire echoed, for some reason incredibly self-conscious. Maybe it was because she knew Natalie had noted the doctor's good looks. There was a twinkle in her blue eyes as their gazes connected, and a nonverbal, "No wonder you want him to stick around."

It's not like that, she silently telegraphed.

Okay, so maybe it was. She was human and it'd been a long, long time since she'd been with a man. So long, in fact, that she couldn't even remember that far back.

Scratch that. She remembered. About a year after her husband had died. A quick hookup the weekend of the town rodeo, and a night she'd rather forget, but it served to remind her of yet one more reason why she'd never let her attraction to the man get out of hand. Awkward couplings in the middle of the night weren't her thing.

Not even when the man was as handsome as Ethan.

At least, that was what she told herself.

Chapter 5

"I'm Natalie Reynolds," said a woman on a massive sorrel horse. She held out a hand wearing an odd-looking glove. Half leather, half crochet. "And this is my husband, Colt, since Claire seems too distracted to perform the introductions."

Ethan glanced at Claire in time to see her eyes flick away, seemingly in humiliation, but what did she have to be embarrassed about?

"Nice to meet you." Ethan shook Natalie's hand, her horse snorting in protest at the sudden thrust of his arm. Might be big, but the horse still had the nerves of a Thoroughbred. Couldn't deny it was a beauty, though. The animal looked almost wet its coat glistened so noticeably. When Claire had said her sister-in-law's horses were worth a small fortune, she hadn't been kidding.

"You're the dog doctor, Adam tells me," the woman said.

"MWDs—military working dogs."

She nodded, her eyes the same color as a military ribbon. They projected friendliness, those eyes. "Ever work on horses?"

"Actually, yes." Most people were like Claire. They had no clue that military veterinarians worked on all sorts of different animals. It all depended on the base where they were stationed. He could look at a cat one day, a bird the next, sometimes even cows. All that had changed, however. "I was attached to a cavalry unit once, nonactive, strictly for parade purposes, but it was fun traveling around with them."

That was before. Pre-orders. Off to the Middle East. Life had never been the same since.

"Interesting," Natalie said.

"But I'm not really tied to my veterinary career. My hope is to work for one of the big canine training facilities. I'd like to keep serving my country in a small way and that seems like the best way to do it."

Claire looked impressed, then thoughtful. "That explains why you're so willing to work with Thor."

He forced himself to focus on Claire's words, because that was who'd spoken. He stared into her eyes, observed the different specks of green in them. A distraction technique, one that he hoped would keep his hands from shaking yet again.

"That's part of my master plan, anyway," he admitted.

Focus.

He'd been hoping—damn, how he'd been hoping—a trip to the country might be just what his frazzled nerves needed. He realized too late he'd been kidding himself. Trev's death was still too fresh. The things he'd witnessed still in the forefront of his mind. The help-lessness he'd felt was something he would never forget.

Damn it.

"I think it might actually work out to have him stay here," he heard Natalie say.

"No," he interjected. Natalie drew back a bit and he realized he'd sounded a little terse. "Look, you're re-ally kind to even consider offering me a place to stay." He caught the boy's gaze, forcing a smile. "But I can't accept."

"Actually, you'd be doing us a favor."

It was Claire's brother who'd spoken, the man leaning forward and resting an arm on his saddle's horn, saddle creaking in protest. "One of the owners Natalie rides for has decided to put her horse up for stud. We were just talking about how to handle that." He pointed with his chin at his wife. "We both know a lot about horses, but we're not breeding experts, and the stallion in question is worth a lot of money. We have a friend who's a vet, but she's pregnant and busy, and we have no business risking its health in the breeding shed, and so we need a professional to help us do it right. At least until we can find someone to do it permanently."

Natalie was nodding as she fiddled with her reins. "I was explaining to my husband just yesterday that a lot of big show barns offer stallion service." A strand of blond hair had escaped from beneath the black cap she wore. "It was kind of a long-range plan of ours to do the same, and then my owner called last week and she really doesn't want to have to move her horse…"

"So we were thinking this would work out perfectly," Colt finished. "We'd hire you as a consultant. You could advise us on what equipment to buy and what kind of facility we'll need. And if you're still here after we get it all done, you could be our stallion manager, at least until you decide to move on or we find another full-time veterinarian interested in the job. In between all that, you could work as our barn manager. You know, keep an eye on things when we're gone on the weekends."

"See?" Adam's voice was full of smug satisfaction. "All settled."

Ethan had a feeling the words were something Claire said on a regular basis and that Adam just parroted. Still, their offer was too generous to believe. "You really want me to work here?" He turned and anchored his gaze on Claire's again. She seemed just as surprised as he did.

"Well, maybe." Natalie splayed a hand in his direction. "We realize we only just met you, and this is way sudden. It's sudden for us, too, so worst-case scenario, why don't you stay a night and think about it? Adam tells us you're kind of homeless right now."

He was, but he still couldn't take them up on such a generous offer.

"Look, it's really nice of you to offer, but I wouldn't be comfortable imposing."

"You wouldn't be imposing," Colt said. "You're a brother in arms. Or didn't you know I was in the Army, too? I wouldn't dare let a combat veteran stay in a strange hotel, not when we have a perfectly good place for you to bed down for the night."

"There's an apartment over the barn." Natalie's smile grew. "It's nothing big, but it's new and it's perfect for a single man. Colt and Claire's brother will be living there when he gets discharged in a few months."

"Please?" Adam said, coming up and smiling at him. "It'd be a big help to my mom."

He realized then that the boy didn't want him to stay for selfish reasons. This wasn't about having a cool new adventure learning how to train dogs. This was, and always had been, about making sure his mom didn't have to deal with Thor all on her own. The boy worried about his mother, just as she probably worried about him. They were looking out for each other. He had no idea why that made him feel weird inside, but it did.

He inhaled deeply. He didn't want to do it. There were a million reasons why he shouldn't—his recent anxiety attacks, his horrible dreams, his need to get on with his life, but most of all, his hatred of being a burden on people.

But there was one reason why he *should* do it. Actually two.

He looked into Claire's eyes, and then her son's.

"Okay. I guess I'll stay."

"You shouldn't have made such a big deal about it." Claire stared at her son. Thank God they were back in her own house and Ethan at her brother's place. "The poor man probably felt so guilty about saying no, he didn't think he had a choice."

Her son sat in the same chair he had when she'd broken the news to him about his illness a year ago. He'd lost his hair somewhere in between, but the light from the kitchen window behind him revealed a peach-fuzz scalp. He looked better. Less pale. Maybe a little more flushed than she would like to see, but so much better than at the start of this whole mess.

"Well?" she asked, because he just sat there staring up at her.

"You need help, Mommy."

The kid knew how to work her, that's for sure. All he had to do was call her mommy.

"No, I don't need help. We have plenty of help between Uncle Colt and Aunt Natalie and their friends. And Uncle Chance will be back soon. We're fine."

"Uncle Colt and Aunt Natalie are too busy, and Uncle Chance isn't coming home for three more months." He said three more months as if it were a whole lifetime, and in his world, it probably was. "One more person would be good. You could go to town and things."

Go to town: code words for *stop worrying about me.* He might be six, but her son had the wisdom of someone five times his age. She couldn't help worrying about him, though. The doctors watched Adam like a hawk. Blood samples could be taken locally, but they made the trip to Los Angeles to speak to his oncologist about the results and any adjustments that would need to be made to the myriad of medications they had him on. It served as a constant reminder that her son was in a battle for his life. So, yes, maybe she was a tad overprotective, but that was her job.

"Buddy, we're doing fine, aren't we?" Claire leaned forward in her rickety wooden chair that'd been in her family for generations and had seen better days. Her whole house had seen better days. "I mean, it's not near as crazy as before, right? It's okay."

Before—when he'd been undergoing treatment. Before her life had fallen apart and the center of her world—her son—had nearly died. Not just once, but twice. Midnight trips to the hospital. Long stays while they fought to get his immune system sorted out. Weeks on end of never sleeping in their own beds.

"At least we're home more." She glanced around the kitchen. It was a mess. So were the family room and bedrooms. Adam was still being homeschooled. Until his immune system got back up to normal levels, it was better for him. Honestly, though, she liked him at home. Her life was chaotic. Dogs in the morning, each of whom needed to be taken out and exercised individually, then homeschooling, something she'd thought would be easy but had turned out to be hard, then back to work with the dogs, the office work in the afternoon because her "job" was to place the dogs in her care, and then work at her *other* job: graphic artist. Then it was back to work with Adam, then dinner, then bed, rinse, repeat. Unless there was a doctor's appointment—

"Mom?"

She'd been so lost in thought she hadn't even realized her son had spoken, and whatever it was he'd said must have been pretty important judging by the seriousness in his eyes.

"I'm sorry, bud. What did you say?"

She held back a chuckle when he said, "Jeez, were you even listening?" as a teenager would have said. Too much television.

She didn't bother trying to conceal her guilt. "Nope."

He released an exaggerated sigh that was so much like the old Adam that she smiled.

"I worry about you, Mommy. You're doing too much. There's all that paperwork about Dad. The dogs. Me. I'm not a little boy anymore. I can take care of myself."

The paperwork for Dad. She was part of a lawsuit against the makers of the vaccine that'd made Marcus so sick. Yes, she admitted, Adam was right. That was a lot of work, too. But he was wrong about one thing. He was still a little boy. He might have seen more in this past year—friends dying, his mom's grieving, the harsh realities of life—than most people saw in a lifetime, but he would always be her little man. Always.

"Don't worry about me." She touched his chin. "I'm doing just fine."

"That's what every parent says until they drop dead from a heart attack."

The words were uttered so seriously and so matter-of-factly that she ended up smiling.

"I'm taking care of myself." Okay, so maybe she wasn't. She needed more sleep. Truth be told, she always felt so tired. And she would love some time for herself just as Adam suggested. To know that the dogs were taken care of and Adam looked after so she could escape into town to do a little window-shopping. All things she could hypothetically do right now, except she never did.

"All right." She sighed deeply. "I'll tell you what. When Dr. McCall comes over tomorrow morning I'll let him take care of the dogs for me. You can stay with me and help and I'll run into town for some errands."

Her son's whole face lit up and only in that moment did she truly understand just how much he'd been fretting over her.

"He said to call him Ethan. And that sounds like a deal."

Yes, she admitted, he had said to call him that, but for some reason, it felt better—safer—to add the doctor title in front of his name. He was here temporarily, after all. She wasn't going to become friends with him. Well, okay, she'd be friendly, but that was it.

Yeah. Keep telling yourself that.

Chapter 6

He slept more soundly than he had in months—at least at first. But then, almost as if his subconscious sensed the rising sun, the nightmares began.

Trevor lay on the ground.

Fire.

BOOM.

He'd shot up, and then as his heart settled into his chest, slipped from bed, walking over to the row of windows that overlooked the old hay barn and wondering, not for the first time, what he was going to do. He wanted to train dogs. He knew that, but he didn't want to give up being a vet. He hated being a burden almost as much as he hated the nightmares that haunted him.

Focus.

The word had become his mantra. He had the entire upstairs portion—no little space as Colt's wife had made it sound. The roofline made for shorter walls to his right and left, but dormers had been placed at regular intervals, allowing light to spill in. It was bare. Nothing more than a space that echoed back the sound of his boots against the hardwood floor, but it felt like a mansion compared to his cramped quarters overseas.

He held up his hand, noticed it still trembled and forced himself to concentrate on the view outside. The sun had just started to peek over the horizon to his right. It cast a glow over the pastures and roofs and tops of trees, as if an artist had spilled a bucket of pink paint over one side of the canvas. If ever a place should soothe his nerves, this would be it, and yet he'd still had that terrible nightmare. Still felt the familiar edge of anxiety. Why? He wasn't worried about his new job, if one could call it that, because he recognized charity when he saw it, although in this instance it wasn't directed at him. They were trying to help Claire and her son. Well, okay. He could live with that, and he could play along. He could palpate a uterus with the best of them, and depending on the breed of horse, he could supervise a breeding. Thoroughbreds had to be live covered, meaning the stallion had to breed the mare naturally. Either way—AI or live cover—he could do that kind of work in his sleep.

He just wondered why he didn't get on with his life.

What he needed to do was start figuring out where he wanted to settle down, and which type of work he wanted to do: go to work as a city veterinarian and deal with Fido and his well-meaning but clueless owner? Or train dogs? The wise choice would be to do both, but the odds of doing both jobs well would be slim to nil. He should focus on finding a real job, maybe at a big horse-racing farm. He liked Reynolds Ranch. It would be great to find another place just like it.

Downstairs a horse nickered. He wondered who fed them and at what time. Maybe he could help out, because, damn it, he needed to be busy. His hands refused to stop shaking and he felt the familiar buzz of anxiety deep in the pit of his stomach where he knew it would slowly begin to unfurl as it did every morning until…

He wasn't going to let that happen. Not today, he thought, pulling on an old pair of jeans with a hole in the knee and a green button-down shirt, long-sleeved because he suspected it would be chilly outside. What he needed was work. Hard work. Only that would soothe the demons that haunted his soul.

He shot toward the front door. He had to keep moving. His hand settled on the brass door handle, pushed, but despite the place being new, it liked to stick. He had to rattle it a few times to get it open, and when he did he paused for a moment on the covered landing, inhaling deeply. It was the smell of it all that soothed him like nothing else, he admitted. The air was fresh here, scented by dew and earth and freshly mown grass— the unmistakable smell of small town USA. It acted like a balm.

You can do this.

Colt must have heard him struggle with the door because he didn't seem surprised to see him. "Did I wake you?"

The man stood in the middle of the barn, tossing a flake he'd pulled from a giant feed cart to one of the horses. And what an animal it was. Today the feed doors were open and every single horse had stuffed their head through them, eyeing the human and his cart of hay as if they could somehow will Colt to feed them faster. Each one of those heads was huge and yet beautiful, their coats glistening beneath the fluorescent lights in a way that spoke of excellent care.

"I was already up before these guys started nickering." He went up to the horse Colt was about to feed. "They're beautiful."

Colt used a hand to push the head of a dark bay back inside the feed door, then tossed the hay in afterward. "They should be, considering how much they cost."

Yesterday, Ethan had taken note of the nice-looking animal Colt's wife rode; this morning he realized she had a whole barn full of them.

"Something tells me your wife must be good at what she does." Down the row of stalls a horse began to bang his leg against a stall door. He moved forward. "Here. Let me help."

"One of the best in the world." He turned toward the horse protesting the complete ineptitude of his human caretakers. "Quit it!"

Silence. Colt smiled, shook his head, "Happens every morning." He pointed to the gallon-sized freezer bags housed in the cart, too. "You can give them their grain. Each horse has a packet with their name on it. Just match the packet to the name on the door."

Easy enough. "I take it your wife competes?" It wasn't just grain, he noted, inhaling the sweet scent of oats and molasses. It was grain and some kind of powder, vitamins no doubt, but it was a simple task to open the stall door and pour the baggies in a bright red bucket. In fact, it was just the sort of task he needed. Busywork.

"She just won a big grand prix back East. You should

have seen it." Colt tossed another flake, then moved on to the next horse. "We pull into this big, elite show grounds with my Rodeo Misfits rig. Everyone on the 'circuit'—" he made air quotes with his fingers "—has these fancy buses. We pull up in my old rodeo rig and out comes Natalie and her horse. Of course, everyone knows who she is. They just hadn't seen her in a while, and they sure weren't expecting her to show up in a cattle trailer."

"Did her own rig break down or something?" He stepped back to admire the animal he'd just fed. The horse was huge. His whole opinion of the Reynoldses and their operation shifted. He'd assumed they were a local horse place and Natalie someone who gave lessons, but as they worked their way down the row, what he saw convinced him each one of the animals was world-caliber—not just one or two, but the whole barn.

"Something like that." Colt shrugged. "But these days she can afford what she wants. She's in the process of deciding what she wants to purchase." They'd reached the end of the row, Colt having already fed the other side, and so he turned to face Ethan while the horses quietly munched. "She was in a bad wreck almost two years ago. Nearly died. She was out of the business for a while… Hell, she stopped riding, but then she hooked up with me and all that…changed." He smiled and Ethan could tell Colt looked back on happy memories. "These days she's right back where she left off. Got a waiting list of clients and a bunch of talented horses in the barn, including that stallion over there." He nodded to the other side of the aisle, the black stallion Ethan hadn't fed yet. "We're thinking that guy over there might just win her a gold medal one day soon."

He walked toward the animal in question, a beautiful horse with small ears and a sculpted-looking head. "He's magnificent."

Colt nodded. "And easy to handle. Natalie already called the owner last night and told her our news. Honestly, you couldn't have come along at a better time. My sister needs a break with those dogs and we're about ready to hit the road pretty hard and so your arrival seems like a gift from God, as long as you don't mind a little hard work."

Work? It was the only thing that seemed to calm him down, which was why he didn't understand his inability to focus on the future. He should be out there finding a permanent job, not playing houseguest at a horse farm.

"I'll stick around until you find someone more permanent. It won't take me long to retrain Thor, and I don't want to be a burden."

"You won't be a burden," Colt said as they finished up. "And we'd love to discuss making this permanent. Natalie and I were talking and you've already been a big help, advising us on what equipment to buy last night. In fact, we were hoping you might stick around. There's a real need for a veterinarian in these parts. The closest vet is a friend of ours, but she's all the way in town. We're sure the ranchers out here would appreciate your presence. But, hell, I don't want to scare you with our big plans. Why don't I bring you over to my sister's place? You can get started with Thor."

Permanent? He wasn't ready to make a commitment like that. Not now. Maybe not ever.

His hands started to tingle. He stared down at them for a moment before saying, "Actually, if it's all the same to you, I think I'd rather walk."

* * *

The sound of dogs barking penetrated her consciousness, a little at first. Claire incorporated the sound into a dream where she was being chased by a pack of… Something. She sat up in bed.

Kennels.

The sound came from outside. The dogs were barking.

She crawled out of bed, the sheets clawing at her legs as if they were the paws of her phantom dogs. A quick glance out the window and she saw why they barked. A lonely-looking cowboy walked up the driveway.

Ethan.

She didn't know why her heart quickened. Perhaps it was the remnant of her dream. Then again, her body always seemed to react whenever he was near. She might as well admit that.

"I don't have time for this."

She snatched the curtains closed, before he could see her, before he could spy her standing there in her white cotton nightgown that looked as if it belonged on a woman triple her age. At least, that's what it suddenly seemed like to her.

What was he doing here? And so early. A quick glance at her cell phone made her blanch because it wasn't that early at all. Eight o'clock—and the dogs hadn't been fed yet.

"Crap."

She grabbed the first thing she found—a pair of jeans and a bright orange T-shirt with *San Francisco* across the front. She barely glanced at her reflection in the mirror, just pulled her hair back off her face and shot out her bedroom door. No doubt Adam was sleeping, but she ducked her head in the room to make sure. It'd been a while since she'd felt the familiar fear, the one that robbed her of breath as she crept to his bed and examined her son. *Was he still breathing?*

He was. But his skin was flushed and she knew with a mother's intuition that he was sick. She'd known it last night when he'd gotten irritable just before dinner. And then later when she'd ordered him to bed. She seen it in his glassy eyes and his flushed cheeks, too. Fever.

"Crap," she muttered again. She'd let him sleep, then check his temperature when she came back in from feeding the dogs.

But her feet were heavy when she opened her front door. Not just with fear, but with exhaustion and sadness and a growing sense of frustration.

Would it never end?

Lord, how she longed to be like a normal mother. A mom that had nothing more to worry about than getting her son to school on time and making sure his homework was done. There were days when worrying about Adam made her physically ill.

The sun nearly blinded her when the door swung wide. That's why she didn't see him standing there, not at first, his tall frame outlined by light. He wore a pair of jeans that looked as if they'd seen better days and a dark green shirt that probably matched his eyes. She didn't know. She was too afraid to look into them.

"You look like hell."

Her gaze shot to his. "Thanks."

"Not that you could ever look bad." Her eyes had adjusted enough that she could spot the consternation on his face. "I mean, I've always thought you were pretty."

Despite telling herself that it didn't matter, his words made her cheeks redden.

"You just look, I don't know, tired."

Beneath the brim of his cowboy hat she spotted embarrassment in his eyes. Funny, she felt just as self-conscious all of sudden.

"Long night with Adam," she admitted.

The embarrassment turned immediately to concern. "Is he okay?"

Would he ever be okay? Would their lives ever be able to go back to normal? Would there be a day when she could drop her guard and look to the future without worry or fear?

She took a deep breath. One day at a time.

"He's spiking a fever—I can tell." She slipped out the door and into the morning sunshine because she didn't want Adam to overhear their conversation. "He keeps talking about going into town for ice cream, but it's all just a front. He's getting sick and both of us know it."

"Isn't that dangerous?"

She nodded. "It can be. His immune system still isn't back to normal. Anytime he becomes ill there could be complications. I just have to keep an eye on him."

She shouldn't have taken him into town yesterday, but he'd begged her, and to be honest, she couldn't keep him locked up forever. The doctors had told her to just make sure he didn't come into contact with sick people. She made sure he washed his hands. She avoided restaurants and other places where a lot of people congregated. Still, there was only so much she could do.

"I bet you didn't get any sleep last night."

"I got enough."

The dogs had seen her. Their barking had changed

from a warning to a whine. All except Thor. Once again the dog lay curled up in a ball right outside his loafing shed.

Ethan must have followed her gaze. "I'd like to work with him just as soon as he's finished eating."

"He's probably not hungry."

She kept the dog supplies in a shed she kept latched with a brass snap to keep the critters out of it. Damn raccoons were as clever as a human sometimes, and she would swear they checked that lock every night. Inside the room were barrels of dog food, the high performance kind that cost an arm and a leg and that she had to order from the feed store.

"You can fill bowls while I start scraping."

"How much do you feed?"

"A scoop per dog." She pointed to the white plastic mixing cup. "But if their bowl is already full, I just top it off."

They went to work, and to be honest, it felt good. Being busy took her mind off Adam inside the house and the obsessive need she felt to go back, to check his temperature again, but she couldn't do that. If he was sick, his best bet was rest, not an overanxious mom poking and prodding him every ten minutes.

It didn't take Ethan long to feed. She could hear him talking to the dogs as he went in and out of their kennels. She'd written their names on the outside just for that reason. In case she was suddenly called out of town—like back to Children's Hospital.

Don't think about it.

When he finished he caught up to her. They worked side by side then, Claire trying not to feel self-conscious while standing next to him. His hands weren't shaking this morning, and he seemed far more relaxed. The only time that changed was when they got to Janus. He tensed up then. She could see it in the way his hands gripped the shovel and the way the line of his jaw hardened.

"What are you working on with Thor today?"

She asked the question more as a way of distracting him than any real desire to engage in small talk. She couldn't stop herself from diving in. She hated seeing someone in pain, and Ethan very definitely had a hard time being around his buddy's dog.

He took a deep breath. "Probably keeping his gaze focused on me."

He scratched the dog on the chin one last time before straightening, the two of them finishing up together. When they were done she showed him where to wash up. She had an industrial-sized sink off the back of the shed, one she used to give the dogs their beauty treatments before heading off to a new home, and it was peaceful out back, a thick grove of oak trees just a few feet away. She'd had Colt help her install a gate, one constructed out of old oak so that it blended with the trees behind, and that led to a path where she liked to walk along the nearby creek.

"I'm just going to go check on Adam."

He nodded, but he seemed lost in thought as she quickly slipped away. Adam still slept, and while he didn't feel hot, that didn't reassure her. Her little man tried so hard to be brave.

Ethan was right where she'd left him, or near enough. He rested his arms against a fence post, staring out into the woods. Their gazes met and she saw something in the depths of his eyes that reminded her of the first day they'd met.

"How is he?"

"Still sleeping."

He glanced back toward the kennels. "He's going to hate missing out on my training session with Thor."

She nodded. "Maybe you could do it later?"

She thought he might say no, would bet her best pair of boots that he thought about it, but instead he said, "Why not?" He smiled, but it was brief, like a patch of sunlight that had escaped from between storm clouds. "I don't have anything better to do."

He'd gone back to looking lost again, and sad, and maybe even tense, especially when his gaze hooked on the kennel that belonged to Janus. It prompted her to head toward the gate a few feet away, and to her walking path. Her way of escaping reality, at least for a few minutes. Her balm for the soul because she'd noticed nothing soothed her more than the sweet smell of Mother Nature. Perhaps it would work for Ethan, too.

"Come on. Let's walk."

He seemed surprised by her invite, but she smiled, trying to reassure him without words. They were two peas in a pod. He grieved over the loss of his buddy and she grieved over the loss of her son's childhood.

He seemed to nod, as if somehow reading her mind, then stepped forward.

"He was a good friend, wasn't he?" She asked the question as she opened the gate, stepping aside so he could join her. She had a perfect view of his face and so she saw the corners of his eyes flex, as if he fought to keep from revealing too much.

"The best."

They walked in silence for a moment, Claire feeling her back pocket to ensure she had her cell phone. They had pretty good service out here thanks to a cell tower on the nearby hills. Adam could call her if he needed her. They would be within shouting distance, too, the house visible from her favorite spot through a thick grove of oak trees.

"Did you know him long?"

"Not too long. A few years, but we used to joke that in combat years, it was a lifetime."

Maybe it was her exhaustion, or maybe it was her inability to mind her own business, but for some reason she found herself pushing for answers. "You were there with him, weren't you? When it happened, I mean."

It was just a simple question, one she suspected she already knew the answer to, so she would never have demanded an answer. They'd reached her favorite spot. An old, fallen tree lay alongside the creek, the bark worn away where she and Adam sat all the time. Her footfalls had long since worn a path around it and she followed the path now, urging him to sit next to her as the water gurgled by. Few things seemed to settle a human soul like the sound of running water and the smell of a forest. It was as if something primordial kicked in, a deep-rooted sense of belonging that acted as a balm to the rush of life.

"I was with him," he said as he sat down beside her.

That was all she'd been curious about and so she didn't push him for more. She watched a leaf slide by on the soft current that pushed the creek toward the ocean. She hoped the smell of wet earth and dank vegetation soothed him as it always had her.

"We'd just left base."

She glanced at him quickly because this she hadn't expected. "It's okay. You don't have to talk about it if you don't want to."

He stuck his hands in his pockets and she knew he'd begun to shake again. "No. That's all right. I think maybe I should."

Still, he didn't immediately launch into the tale and for a moment she wondered if he'd changed his mind.

"We were on our way home. We'd made it, both of us, to the end. We were leaving, and when we reached stateside, we were going to open up a training business.

"That morning, Trev left ahead of me to secure our ride. I had some dogs in my care, so I had to wrap a few things up, but I wasn't that far behind."

She could tell the next part would be hard, felt the urge to take his hand in her own, the desire so strong, her empathy so keen, she almost told him to stop, that she didn't want to hear. Instead, she tightened her own hands into fists and simply listened.

"He was gone maybe ten minutes, couldn't have been more than that, when it started. *Boom!* One moment sunshine and sky, the next dirt and broken glass. And then another boom and another. We were under attack."

He rubbed his arms absently and she realized that's where the scars came from, the ones she'd noticed the day he'd arrived. They were covered by the dark green shirt he wore, but he still touched them.

"It doesn't register at first when something like that happens, you know?" He turned and met her gaze and her heart broke into a million pieces at just the look in his eyes. Yes, she'd known he'd lost his friend, but it wasn't until that moment that she realized just how badly it'd affected him. "It felt like a dream. The psychologists say it's a natural reaction to trauma, some sort of mental self-defense. At first I thought it was just a nightmare, that we couldn't really be under attack, and so I just sat there."

She knew all too well that sense of denial. She'd felt the same thing when she'd realized there was no hope for Marcus. That he was going to die. Time and again she'd wake up thinking it was all a bad dream only to roll over and spy the empty bed next to her and realize that Marcus really was in the hospital and that he really wasn't going to come home.

"And suddenly it hits you that it *is* happening and that you have to do something."

His gaze sharpened. "All I could think about was Trevor. And Janus. They were up ahead of me and I knew from experience they'd bear the brunt of the attack."

A part of her didn't want to hear the rest. Another part knew he needed to get it out.

"I jumped out. I don't even remember the explosion next to me, but fragments hit my arms. I just remember the sting of something, but I didn't care. I grabbed my sidearm and took off only when I looked ahead—"

She found herself reaching for his hand and clutching it despite telling herself not to touch him. "It's okay." She squeezed. "You don't have to keep going. I can imagine what you saw." It was her worst fear come to life—being in the wrong place at the wrong time. When Marcus had been overseas she'd prayed every day he'd make it home. She prayed the same thing for her brothers. The irony was that Marcus had made it home, but he'd been terribly ill from the day he stepped stateside.

She'd changed her prayer then. She wanted her brothers to come home healthy and strong.

He'd turned away from her, his face in profile. It was like watching a movie play across his face, one where she could see the actors, but not listen to the lines. She didn't need to hear them, though. She could tell he recalled the scene he'd stumbled upon. Knew he remembered finding his friend's body. That he tried to shut it out, but that he couldn't.

Please, God, keep Chance safe these last few months.

She clutched his hand harder.

"Sometimes I can still smell it. Burnt rubber. Spilled fuel. Gunpowder. And…other things. It was total chaos. But just as suddenly as it started, it stopped. There were medics on scene, but I knew I couldn't help Trev. I needed to let the medics do their thing." She saw his eyes fill with tears, felt his fingers clutch her own. "But I could help Janus, and so I did, yet some days I wonder if I shouldn't have at least tried to help Trev."

She let go of his hand, touched his chin, asking without words for him to turn back to her again. He did so reluctantly, but that was okay. She needed him to hear her words.

"Some memories will always be a part of us. The trick is to learn to let them go. Or to put them in a place where they can no longer hurt us." She could tell he barely heard her. "You need to replace those bad memories with good ones. In time those good memories will outnumber the bad."

He huffed sarcastically. "Good ones?"

She nodded.

"And where do I find those?"

He seemed so lost, so completely adrift in a sea of

fear and sadness and self-rebuke that she did the un-
thinkable. She leaned into him, her lips brushing his
own, whispering the words, "You can start right here,"
kissing him before she could think better of it.

And God help her, it felt right.

Chapter 7

She was his anchor in a storm-tossed sea of memories, Ethan thought. Her lips were soft and warm and all he wanted to do was stay right there, to absorb her heat and her scent and the earthy goodness that was her.

She pulled back. He let her go, but he didn't allow her to pull away entirely. He cupped the back of her head with his hands, rested her forehead against his own and peered into green eyes that seemed both troubled and terrified.

"I'm sorry." She blinked. "That was out of line. I didn't mean to—"

"Shh." His thumb slid forward, the edge of it brushing her lips. So soft. So plump. So tempting. He didn't know what had just happened. He only knew that having her near, holding her like this, peering into her eyes—it all somehow righted his world.

Her eyes closed and she bowed her head. He let her go, inhaling deeply, wondering if this was why he'd driven all those miles. If somehow he'd known she'd be a balm to his soul.

"I should get back. Adam—"

How long had they been sitting there? Five minutes? Ten? He couldn't recall, but he knew she was right. She had a son. A little boy who had battles of his own to wage.

"I'll walk you back."

He grabbed her hand, and as he helped her up, he wondered what she'd do if he tugged her to him. Just as quickly as the idea had come, he let it go. She'd kissed him out of kindness. Even as messed up as he was, he could see that.

"Thank you," he said.

She glanced up sharply. "For what?"

"For listening."

She searched his eyes for something—what, he didn't know. "Anytime."

Once again, he noticed the beauty of her eyes. It wasn't just their color. It was everything in them. Kindness. Strength. And a sweetness of spirit that made him wonder what it would be like to know her—truly know her. He shook his head at such a thought. They were two human beings brought together by tragedy, nothing more.

He had to force his thoughts away from her, and it was hard, but at least he no longer felt like a soldier out on a battlefield, scared, wanting to run, to get away from it all. He could breathe now. It brought everything into focus: The way light dappled the ground in front of them. The sound of the creek as it moved forward.

The smell of dried oak leaves and wild sage. All of it reminded him of happier times. Days from his childhood when he'd gone camping, back when the biggest problem he'd had was how to carry his fishing pole and tackle box and cooler all in one trip so he could beat the other boys to the best spot on the river.

"Did you drive over?" she asked.

They'd reached the gate. "No. I walked."

She nodded. "Do you need a lift back? We could wait until Adam is up."

"No." His gaze caught on her lips, and it shocked him how much he wanted to pull her to him, and how badly he longed to kiss her again, and if they were alone in her house with her son asleep in bed… "I can walk back after I work with Thor."

Her eyes widened a bit and he could tell she'd forgotten about him working with Thor. He wondered for a moment if she wanted him to leave. If maybe she regretted their kiss, but try as he might, he couldn't read her eyes.

"Adam's going to want to watch you."

"You can call me back over once he's up."

"No. I should wake him up now. If he sleeps too long I'll never get him to bed at a decent hour tonight."

"Then I'll wait. He can watch from a window."

"There are leashes and treats in the feed room."

"I know. I saw."

She looked as if she wanted to say something more. He waited, and for the first time, held his breath over something not related to Trevor and the horrors of his past. But whatever it was she wanted to say, she lost her nerve.

"I'll be right back."

* * *

She'd kissed him.

Stupid, stupid, stupid.

It wasn't as if she didn't have enough problems of her own. She didn't need to take on the troubles of a near stranger, too.

"Rise and shine, kiddo." She sat on the edge of Adam's bed. If ever she needed a reminder of all the reasons why she should steer clear of Ethan, this was it, she told herself. Her son's cheeks were still flushed, so much so that she reached out and touched them.

Hot. She drew back her hand as if stung.

"No."

She ran for the thermometer, cursing herself the whole time. She should have been attending to her son, not kissing Ethan.

"Hey, buddy," she said, sitting back down on the edge of the bed and gently shaking him. "I need to take your temperature." She nudged him awake, and he slowly blinked the sleep from his eyes, his cheeks stained red.

His gaze snagged on her own. She saw his eyes move around the room as if trying to reason out if he was awake or if this was a dream. "Don't feel well."

It took every ounce of her willpower to force a smile on her face. Inside, though, she fell apart. Should she call the doctor? They had warned her this might happen. He'd been doing so well, though. She'd been meticulous about keeping him away from sick people and disinfecting his hands whenever he went out.

"Let's take your temperature." First things first. Maybe she was wrong. Maybe she just imagined the heat of his body.

He was so sick, though—fever or no—all he did was

nod his head, and in some ways, that scared her even more. Even before his diagnosis he'd always been her tough kid. The one that had to be practically missing a limb before he slowed down. The whole time they'd been undergoing treatment it'd been the same way. He had been terribly sick once before, but that'd been in the hospital. It'd been a long forty-eight hours while they waited for his temperature to drop. The longest hours of her life, but she'd had a full staff of professionals around her to assuage her fears. This time she'd be on her own.

She trembled as she checked the digital thermometer, but she had herself in control when she went back into Adam's room. If he saw her panic he'd start to fret and if he started to fret she would fall apart.

It's just a little bug, she told herself. *He'll be fine.* "Open up," she told him.

Probably just a cold.

But his immune system wasn't 100 percent. They were optimistic about having cured the leukemia, but that battle had left her son more vulnerable to even a simple cold bug.

Beeeeep.

She didn't want to look. She really didn't, not when she already knew the answer. She forced herself to read the numbers anyway.

One hundred and three.

"Son of a—"

Even as sick as he was, Adam's eyes popped open. "Is it bad?"

Her son, the boy who didn't fear anything, looked terrified now. "Not too high," she lied. "I'm going to give you some medicine, then call the doctor."

"Am I going to the hospital again?"

"No." She forced a smile. "Of course not. Dr. Jones warned me this might happen. He told me to check in with him if it did. You'll be fine."

Would he? Would he really be fine? And if he wasn't, could she face another loss? This past year she'd asked herself that question at least a million times and she always came up with the same answer.

No.

She would not be fine. She would fall apart, and she wasn't certain she could put the pieces back together again.

She glanced outside. Ethan had Thor out. She'd need to tell him. But first, she had to call the doctor.

What was taking so long?

Adam must have been awake, he reasoned. She was probably helping him get dressed. Or getting him breakfast. Or helping him to find a missing shoe. But there were no little boy noises coming from the house. No slammed cabinets and no heavy footsteps. Just near quiet.

He touched Thor's head. The dog looked up at him. He might not be able to hear, but there was nothing wrong with his sight and the dog was already used to looking for hand signals. In just five minutes he was making progress on having Thor keep constant eye contact, something the dog wasn't used to doing since canines relied on their ears just as much as their eyesight and smell. It filled him with a self-satisfaction that he'd made even that little bit of progress in such a short amount of time.

Still nothing from inside the house.

He tugged on the leash. This, too, Thor understood.

The difference would be to teach Thor to keep his eyes on his handler instead of perpetually looking around and being on alert. He needed to undo Thor's training to a certain degree and so he stopped, tapping the dog on the top of the head so he and Thor made eye contact, then praised him and set off again.

Claire.

She had kissed him out of kindness. He wasn't so messed up in the head that he didn't recognize pity when it kissed him, but the fact that he'd broken down in front of her didn't help his self-esteem. It was at an all new low.

The front door slammed. He turned.

"Adam won't be joining you."

Her eyes were rimmed with red—as if she'd recently cried, but gotten herself under control before coming to see him. "What's the matter?"

"He has a fever."

He knew enough about Adam's illness to recognize what a serious issue that was. "Is there anything I can do?"

She shook her head. "I have to go back inside. I'm waiting for a call back from the doctor."

He nodded. She took a few steps back, then waved goodbye. Something in her eyes before she'd turned away made him feel like a jerk for worrying about his own troubles when she clearly had so much more to deal with than he did.

You're alive, buddy. Quit dwelling on the past.

The voice was Trevor's and it caused Ethan's eyes to close. Instantly an image of his friend rose up before him. The smart-ass smile. The cocky grin. The look of impatience when Ethan didn't rush right into something.

That was why they'd gotten along so well. Ethan prided himself on being cautious. Trevor liked to rush right in and get things done.

When he opened his eyes, he found himself facing the kennels, Janus staring back at him.

Trevor would have told him to get off his ass and stop feeling sorry for himself. There were other things he could be doing with his time; like helping Claire, a woman who had clearly reached the end of her rope, yet still had a sweetness of spirit that led her to reach out to others in need.

He would do the same.

He put Thor away, giving the dog a pat on the head before releasing him, then headed toward her front door before he could think better of it and knocked on it. He heard her footsteps, quick and businesslike, before the door swung wide. Claire was just as stressed in appearance as she'd been two minutes earlier.

"What's up?" she asked, glancing past him as if she might glean a clue as to why he suddenly knocked on her door.

"I'm going to cook you breakfast."

Her face registered puzzlement. "But I'm not hungry."

"You will be," he said, sliding past her. He might be many things, messed up in the head being one of them, but he was a hell of a cook.

"But, I might have to leave for the hospital in a few minutes."

"Then I'll finish cooking breakfast, then stay here and keep an eye on the place."

She stood by the door, fingers still on the handle, her green eyes as worn and tired as woman triple her age and his heart broke for her. Even though she had family less than a mile away, he had a feeling she tried to do most of it alone.

"Adam is sick and I'm not sure—"

"Shh." He came forward, pressing a hand against her lips, and for the first time in weeks felt tasked with a purpose. "I'm going to stay."

Chapter 8

It took forever for the doctor to call back. Claire didn't know what stressed her out more: waiting for her phone to ring, or the man who cooked breakfast in her kitchen.

Adam stirred in his bed. She had parked herself next to him, watching, calling herself obsessive at least a million times, but not really caring. Something might change. She might need to be there for him. Bathroom. Drink of water. Medicine. She would always have to be there for him, which was why the man in the kitchen—

"What smells good?"

She glanced at the bed in surprise. Her son's eyes, glassy and red from fever, peered up at her in curiosity.

"It's Ethan. He's cooking us breakfast." And all right. It did smell good. No. It smelled delicious.

Adam's eyes closed.

"Do you want some?"

Adam gave a sleepy nod, one that buoyed Claire's spirits because if he was hungry it couldn't be that bad. At least that was what she told herself as she got up from the chair and headed toward Ethan. She drew up short at what she saw. Ethan stood there, the sleeves of his green shirt rolled up to his elbows, his scars barely visible, an apron of hers tied around his waist, one with the words *Hot Mama* on the front. On the counter next to him sat a pile of pancakes even though she couldn't remember ever buying the mix. And he'd clearly found the package of bacon in her refrigerator because that was the smell wafting through the house and causing her stomach to growl.

"Adam is hungry."

He turned toward her.

She'd kissed him.

Best not to dwell on that, she told herself. "I thought I'd bring him a plate of food."

"I have something just for him."

He bent, opening the oven beneath the stove, and removed a plate. Next he fished a piece of bacon out of the pan, then picked up a smaller, narrower pot, Claire watching as he poured syrup over everything.

"Here you go."

On the plate was a pig, complete with a pig nose and ears, and chocolate chips for nostrils. He'd somehow made it look as if that pig was smiling.

She didn't know why the sight made her heart flip over, but it did.

"Tell him to eat up. That whole 'starve a fever and feed a cold' thing is an old wives' tale. He needs nutrients to help him fight off whatever's attacking him."

And then suddenly she wanted to cry. He cared. He wanted to help. To reassure her.

"Thanks."

He waved his spatula. "You're going to eat, too."

"I will, after Adam."

That must have satisfied him because he nodded once again, then went back to making his bacon. She stared down at the plate and found herself wishing Marcus was still alive with a ferociousness that took her aback. Ethan reminded her of him, she realized. He used to make her breakfast, too.

It took all her effort to slip on a smile, though it felt as false as an infomercial as she gently nudged Adam awake again. "Want some food?"

Her son stared up at her through eyes that were so much like Marcus's that it kicked her in the gut. They might be feverish and red, but those were Marcus's long lashes. Or maybe it was the shape of his eyes or the line of his brows. Something about Adam's face reminded her of her lost husband to the point that she had to clutch the plate to keep from dropping it.

"Come on." She used as chipper a voice as possible. "At least have a few bites."

Though he'd expressed interest in it earlier, she could tell her son wasn't really hungry. She could also tell he didn't want to displease her. It was one thing she'd noticed about him. He always tried to put a brave face on things—for her. It broke her heart.

He slowly shifted until he was sitting up. It was just lack of sleep that made her so shaky. That and the fact that she'd kissed Ethan. Exhaustion had eroded her common sense.

"Do you see what he made you?" she asked with false brightness as she helped him sit up. "It's a pig."

He tried to smile, but it was obvious it took all his effort just to sit up. Whatever it was that attacked his immune system it had managed to physically drain him. When he sat up she didn't even bother to hand him a fork.

"And he must have made it all from scratch." She cut off a bite. "Just have a little bit, then you can go back to sleep."

He obediently opened his mouth and she tried not to fret as she watched him eat. She'd been up half the night running through various scenarios. What she would do if his fever spiked. What she would say to the doctor when he called back. Who she would call if she needed to leave the ranch. Around and around her thoughts had tumbled until, suddenly, it was daybreak and Ethan had been walking up her driveway.

"N'more."

Her fork froze halfway. He'd held up a hand and she hadn't even noticed it. When she glanced at the plate it was to note he'd eaten hardly anything at all.

"Just a little more."

He shook his head, sank down and rolled over on his side, and she just stared, her spirits sinking even further. Days like today it was hard to keep her chin up. She tried to maintain a positive attitude, knew that if Adam saw her lose her cool it would upset him, maybe even cause him to panic, and right now she needed him happy, or as happy as a sick child could be. She refused to distract him with her own mental breakdowns.

But her body quaked as she stood and silently left the room. Her lip quivered. She knew she was on the verge of tears. She stared down at the plate in her hand. The last thing she wanted was for Ethan to see her red-rimmed eyes, because sure as certain she was about to bawl her eyes out.

Dumb, dumb, dumb.

She slipped into her bedroom, swung the door closed behind her and set the plate down on her nightstand. Ironically, though, the tears wouldn't come. It was as if there was so much sorrow inside her that it dammed up her tear ducts to the point nothing could escape. Her stomach roiled, her mind churned, her heart broke for her son—but her eyes refused to let loose.

"You okay?"

She turned sharply, on the verge of telling Ethan to close the door again, but he didn't stand inside the room. He spoke through a crack, one that made her belatedly realize the door hadn't swung closed all the way.

"Fine."

She turned back around, took a deep breath, hoped he didn't hear the way her voice cracked. What a pair they were. Him mourning the loss of his friend. Her morning the loss of her happiness.

"You want to eat?"

Her gaze snagged on Adam's half-eaten food. "In a bit."

She took a deep breath, reminding herself that she would get through this. She would make it through tomorrow, too. And the next day after that. What choice did she have?

Ethan still stood on the other side of the door. "Come here."

She didn't want to. Crazy, really, considering she'd been the one to console him less than an hour before.

She didn't think she could take his kindness, though. She needed to do this on her own—as she always did.

She opened the door and brushed past him. "I'm going to grab something to eat."

The words were a contradiction to what she'd just said, but Claire didn't care. She needed to say something, anything, to escape from him. No, she quickly amended. To escape from the urge to do exactly as he suggested; to sink into his arms and forget for the moment that she was the single mother of a very sick little boy.

"Claire." He called her name and she ignored it, turning toward the kitchen.

He intercepted her halfway there.

"I need to eat."

"No," he said. "You need a hug."

Funny how just a moment ago she couldn't cry to save her life, yet his words roused instant tears in her eyes. "Please don't."

"Don't what?"

She sucked in a breath, trying hard not to crumble because that was all it'd taken—one gentle call of her name, one random act of kindness, one offer of a shoulder to lean upon—for her to lose strength.

"Don't be kind to me because if you touch me I might crumble and if I crumble I don't know if I'll be able to put all the pieces back together again."

He stared down at her with a kindness that melted her self-control. "If you crumble, I promise to help put you back together again."

He tugged her toward him. She tried to resist, but he wouldn't let her, and then the tears were coming. Soft tears because she didn't want Adam to hear. And then the tears turned into sobs. He muffled the sound with his shirt and a part of her worried that she was making a mess on the fabric, probably leaving mascara stains, but he kept on holding her.

A long time later she leaned back, sniffed, a part of her mortified that he'd seen her break down.

"Better?"

She nodded.

"Liar."

She nodded again. He smiled, a tender smile, one that made her whole body go still. Something flickered in his eyes, something that caused a warning to scream through her head.

Step away.

She didn't, God help her, she didn't, and so when he lowered his head toward her own, she didn't move then, either.

"Claire," he said softly.

Whether he closed that final distance or she did, she would never know. All she knew was the heat of his lips against her own and the feel of his body pressed up against her chest was the sweetest slice of heaven she'd had in a long, long time. It started as the softest of kisses, one meant to reassure her and comfort her. But then it changed, and she let it happen because, Lord, it'd been so long.

She'd forgotten about the way a body could tighten and tingle and warm with just a kiss. And so when those lips moved away and nuzzled her jaw and then the side of her neck, his teeth lightly nipping her, she let him do it. She even sighed when he cupped her breast. His other hand parted her shirt even more and she knew what he would do next. God help her, she welcomed his touch, her bra sliding over her sensitive skin until she was exposed to his view, but not for long. Oh, no. His mouth covered her and she thought she might lose it right then and there. How had she managed to forget the way it felt to have a man nip at her? Why hadn't she remembered how good it was, or how exciting, when that same man used his mouth to tease and taunt her? Her body had become a live wire, one that sizzled in his arms.

His hand shifted even lower. The sizzling turned into a burn. When he found her center it was all she could do not to cry out. She wilted. He pulled her to him and she let him carry her away and away and away.

Her knees gave out.

If he hadn't been holding her she would have fallen to the floor. But he held her while she spiraled around and around and around until she slowly, gently returned to Earth.

Her hands clutched his shirt. She hadn't even noticed.

What are you doing?

The words were her first coherent thought. This was neither the time nor the place to be doing something like that. Adam was right on the other side of the door, for goodness' sake.

What kind of parent was she?

She tried to slip away. His arms held her tight, his own head resting against the top of hers.

"It's okay," he said softly.

No. It wasn't okay. She had no business indulging in pleasure, not with her son so sick. She was the worst sort of parent.

"I need to check on Adam."

Chapter 9

He played with fire.

Ethan rested his hands on the counter, staring at the granite surface. She was clearly at the end of her rope. Clearly vulnerable. Clearly in need of an escape, and he'd taken advantage of that fact. He shouldn't have done that.

Outside, the dogs started barking. He glanced up and out the window in time to spy a truck coming down the drive. Colt. Probably wondering what had happened to him. Thank goodness the man hadn't come a few minutes earlier.

He threw back his shoulders. He had no idea where Claire had gone, but he had a feeling she wouldn't want to greet her brother. Not until she composed herself.

The truck came to a stop near the kennels. Ethan headed out the side door.

"There you are," Colt said, a smile on his face. "I was thinking you might have gotten lost."

He forced a welcoming grin. "Nope. Just helping your sister out." His smile collapsed beneath the weight of his guilt for a second. "Adam isn't feeling well."

Colt's smile slipped off his face, too. "What's wrong?"

"He's got a fever. Pretty bad one, I guess." *And I just made your sister cry out in pleasure.* "I just made them breakfast, but Adam didn't eat hardly anything at all."

Colt nodded, heading quickly inside the house. Ethan headed toward the kennels. Fresh air. He needed more of it. Claire had probably heard him talking to her brother. She'd had time to compose herself, no doubt. If he was smart he'd start heading back to his new quarters, but he couldn't just leave her after kissing her like that. They should talk. He should apologize. Hell, he should go get his head examined—for more reasons than one.

Janus eyed him from his kennel. There were times, like now, when he missed his friend with an intensity that hurt. Physically hurt. It made his heart race, the tempo increasing until he found himself setting off in Janus's direction. The dog greeted him at the gate.

"Hey, buddy."

Janus ducked his head as if to say "hey" right back. Ethan scrubbed the dog on the top of the head before straightening again.

"Foos."

The dog instantly moved to Ethan's leg. He set off, waiting until he was in the clearing between the house and the kennels before ordering the dog to run. Janus shot off at a fast clip.

"Sitz."

The dog sat. Hard, and when he turned to face him,

he had what could only be called a canine grin on his face. It brought a smile to Ethan's face.

"Missed this, have you, buddy?"

The dog had begun to pant, the excited kind of pant, eyes firmly fixed on him as he waited for the next command.

"Hier." The dog came at him. *"Blieb."* The dog stopped, and Ethan was suddenly struck by the difference between now and the last time he'd put a dog through his paces. He'd been on another continent. In a war zone. Nothing but desert all around him.

This was better. He took a deep breath and listened to the birds and the gentle rush of water in the nearby creek and the smell of the roses that grew along the edge of the house. This was much, *much* better.

"Impressive." He turned and found Colt watching him. "I've never seen them work before."

"Sitz," he told Janus before turning back to Colt.

"Why do you talk to them in German?" Colt asked. "I've always wondered."

"Because most of the pups come from overseas. They're taught German from a young age. It's just easier to keep using the commands in their native tongue rather than teach them a new language."

Colt nodded. "Makes sense."

Did he know what had happened? Had Claire told him? He didn't think so.

"Is everything okay in there?" Ethan asked.

Colt shrugged. "She's worried."

So she hadn't mentioned anything, not that he thought she really would. "Has she heard back from the doctor?"

"Actually, yes. He said this was all part of the process. We have to build Adam's immunity back up again, and unless he keeps spiking a really high fever, not to worry. So she's in there right now checking his temperature again and I'm sure she'll be obsessing over it all day."

Ethan didn't doubt it. He didn't blame her, either. This was her son. He had a serious illness.

"How bad was the cancer?"

Sadness entered Colt's eyes. "Right now? Not bad. They have it on the run. The problem is we won't know for sure if it's truly gone for a few more months yet. It's a wait-and-see kind of thing."

What a horrible stress to be under. And he'd gone and kissed her as if there was nothing wrong with the world. What a putz.

"Janus." He waited for the dog to look up at him, then motioned for him to run. The dog galloped off. *"Sitz."* He waited for the dog to sit before turning back to Colt. "What can I do to help?"

The man in front of him might wear a cowboy hat. He might seem like a tough as nails cowboy, but Ethan could see the concern in his eyes.

"Just do what you can around here. We could really use the help, what with my wife and I constantly gone and Claire off to the doctors at a moment's notice. I can't tell you how grateful we are that you showed up. It's like a godsend or something."

For the first time all morning Ethan felt less like a jerk, but only just a little. He still shouldn't have kissed her. What was he? In high school or something where he couldn't keep his hormones in check? "Done."

"She likes to think she can do it all herself."

"I've noticed."

"And she'll work herself right into ground."

"I'll make sure that doesn't happen, sir."

The formality of his address clearly caught Colt by surprise, but old habits died hard. "I'd appreciate that." He glanced back at the house. "Maybe you can split your time between here and my ranch. If you're okay with that," he added quickly.

"I've got all the time in the world."

Maybe he really was meant to be here. Maybe, for once, he was in the right place at the right time.

It was the longest two days of Claire's life. She hovered between rushing Adam to the hospital and calling his oncologist every five minutes. When, after a long seventy-two hours later, his fever finally broke, it was all Claire could do not to break down and cry. Again. More shocking was that she didn't want to call her brother with the news that Adam was better. No. The first person she wanted to tell was Ethan.

How bizarre was that?

She glanced out the window, because there he was. Outside. Working Thor. He'd been an incredible help the past few days. He split his time between working at her brother's place and walking down the road to help her with the dogs. He checked in with her every morning and every night, too, keeping his distance, even though all she wanted to do when she opened the door was invite him in and…

No. Not again. She would not be weak ever again.

"Mom. Can I go outside?" Adam stared up at her with wide, green eyes, a blanket wrapped around his shoulders. His Hawkman blanket. Its dark blue color made his skin appear paler than normal. Then again, he had been sick for three days.

"Oh, I don't know, hon. You just got out of bed for the first time an hour ago."

"I know." His green eyes implored. "But I'm better now. No more fever."

No more fever for now. It could come back.

Stop.

She had to quit thinking like that. She needed to focus on the positives in her life. Adam had gotten over an illness, a first for him since they'd stopped treatment of his leukemia. He hadn't been rushed to a hospital. He hadn't spent days in the ER. Still, her baby boy was sick and it broke her heart. Comma-shaped smudges cupped the bottom of his eyes. They made the green stand out even more. He needed color.

He needed sun.

"Okay. For just a bit."

His whoop of joy filled her soul with happiness. She shouldn't be such a spoilsport, she told herself. She needed to let him go have some fun.

"Five minutes," she said, following him to his room where he quickly slipped on a pair of jeans.

He might have been deathly ill yesterday, but you wouldn't know it by the way he moved around, sliding one of his favorite comic book T-shirts over his head. He was out the door before she could tell him to brush his hair.

Let him go. Don't crowd him. He'll be fine.

She might have gone after him but her laptop chimed,

and for a second she forgot about Adam and his illness in her rush to get to her computer in time.

"Chance?" she said, smiling for the first time in days as her brother's face came into view.

"Hey, little sister, how's it going?"

Her brother looked tired, or maybe it was just the feed, or even the military uniform he wore. The pale colors enhanced the green of his eyes, but it made the exhaustion more evident by highlighting the smudges beneath his eyes.

"Better," she said. She'd sent him an email the other day telling him about Adam and how sick he was. She never had any idea when he would see things, but he must have gotten this one relatively quickly. "His fever broke last night."

His green eyes lit up. "That's good news."

His mouth moved before the words arrived. She'd never quite gotten used to the effect—not with her husband, not with Colt and not with Chance.

"It really is. He hasn't gotten over an illness all on his own in over a year. The doctor said it's a good sign."

Dr. Pembra, the oncologist, had called at the crack of dawn, but she hadn't minded. In fact, she appreciated Children's Hospital and their staff more than she could put into words. Between Dr. Pembra and Dr. Jones she knew she had the best team possible.

"And that other matter? Is that still a problem?"

Damn her inability to keep things to herself. She'd been desperate to talk to someone about what had happened with Ethan, and what better way to do it than by pounding her keyboard like some kind of teenage blogger? She must have been really desperate, she thought, but who better than her brother overseas? Although not for long, she reminded herself. He'd be home soon.

"He's still here."

A black eyebrow lifted. The three siblings were all dark. All had fair skin. All had green eyes, although Chance's were more hazel than green. They took after their mother, and not a day went by that she didn't wish she was still alive.

"And is that a good thing or bad?"

The picture froze for a moment and she waited with bated breath to see if they would lose the connection, but in a flash the image caught up with itself.

"Actually, it's been a good thing. He's been a big help while Adam's been sick."

Chance nodded. "Colt tells me he's been a big help over at their place, too."

He'd talked to Colt? "You didn't tell him what I told you, did you?"

Chance smiled, the grin making his eyes light up in a way that seemed so very boyish despite the hell he'd been through overseas. One day some woman would fall for him hard. She just wasn't sure he'd reciprocate the feelings. The military was his life. Always had been and always would be. No ranch life for him.

"No, of course not," he answered. "I wasn't about to spread the news that my naughty little sister had gotten all hot and heavy with a houseguest while my sick nephew slept in his room."

"Oh, jeez." She covered her face with her hands.

She heard Chance laugh. "Hey. Relax. It's not like you had sex. And even if you had, everyone needs to blow off some steam once in a while."

No, but she'd enjoyed Ethan's touch just a little too much for comfort. "I'd rather not talk about it."

The lips moved before the words "Then why'd you tell me?" came through the tiny speaker on her laptop.

"That was a mistake."

"Nah." He shifted back in his seat, crossing his arms. A Gilly suit. That was what Chance called his outfit. "You needed someone to talk to about it."

He was probably right. She hadn't known what to think about her lapse in judgment, but it was clear by the twinkle in Chance's eyes that he thought it was funny. Heck, he might even approve.

"I'm fine about it now," she lied. "And it hasn't happened again."

"Maybe it should."

"And maybe it shouldn't."

Her brother knew her well enough that he knew when to let a matter drop. But just in case, she quickly launched into the latest happenings around the ranch. The last time they'd seen each other had been a month or so after Colt and Natalie had gotten married—a quickie marriage in their own backyard. They'd seen him for a day and she supposed she should be grateful for that.

"Hey, sis," he said as she was about to go get Adam so the two could talk. "Don't forget to take care of yourself."

"I am doing that."

"No," he said. "I don't mean getting rest—I mean living life."

"Chance—"

"I mean it. Time for you to start relaxing and having fun."

He meant she should kiss Ethan again. "I do have fun." Just not that kind of fun.

But he ignored her. "Where's my nephew?"

She thought about pushing the matter, but the truth was she really wanted to escape so she fetched Adam from outside. Still, the next day, as she watched Ethan and Adam from her family room window, she wondered why she'd beaten herself up so badly. So what if they'd kissed? It didn't mean she was an evil person. It meant she was human.

She smiled at the way her son mimicked Ethan's hand movements. It pleased her to see how well Thor was doing at picking up nonverbal commands. The dog had really come out of his shell since Ethan had started to work with him. With any luck she could still adopt the dog out to a willing family.

"Mom. Mom. Ethan says we're going for a ride."

She'd been so deep in her thoughts she hadn't even seen her son break away from Ethan and head for the house. She spun in her seat.

"Were you watching us?" he asked, coming to a stop near the open front door.

"Close the door." She shook her head, wondering when he'd ever learn. "And, yes. Of course I was watching. I don't want you to overexert yourself."

"Mo-om."

She shook her head. "What's this about riding?"

Her son's face filled with excitement, and she had to admit, he looked better. He hadn't been outside very long, but just those few short moments in the sun had done him wonders.

"Ethan said Uncle Colt said we could go riding this weekend. I guess Ethan hasn't ridden in years. Did you know his dad is a cowboy? His parents live in Montana or someplace. They live on a big ranch. No power. No electricity. Just cattle."

No. She hadn't known that about him. She suspected there was a lot she didn't know about the man who'd kissed her so passionately.

Her face heated.

She hoped Adam didn't notice. Her son had the eyes of an eagle, and all she needed was for him to notice her reaction to Ethan. For such a sick little boy, he seemed obsessed with the idea of her dating someone.

"I'm not sure a ride is a good idea."

"Mo-om," he repeated.

"You're just getting over a bad flu bug. I don't think you should exert yourself."

"That's the point, Mom." He stared up at her as if she was an idiot. "The horse does all the work."

Yup. Definitely on the road to recovery. In a lot of ways. He'd been such a little boy when he'd been diagnosed with leukemia. For the first time she saw a glimpse of the young man he would become.

"How about we play it by ear?"

But she should have known she was fighting a losing battle. Her son was persistent, and he remained blissfully unaware of her desire to avoid Ethan. The trouble with that resolve, however, was the shame she felt every time she knew Ethan was outside working or feeding or helping with her dogs. She'd been communicating with him through her brother, and every time she did, her shame only grew. The man had opened up to her, told her of his fears and his anxiety; he'd kissed her after, and she'd kissed him right back. Now all she did was hide in her house and it really was ridiculous.

"Damn it," she muttered. She needed to stop acting like a hermit. As Chance had said, she needed to go out and have fun, not that riding was her idea of fun, but it would be good to get out.

She just wished it wasn't with Ethan.

Chapter 10

She didn't have horses of her own, Ethan learned. The family kept all the livestock at the main ranch. So he waited like a kid on his first day of school. Impatient. Excited. Anxious.

Not the same type of anxiety as before.

He wasn't quite himself yet, not by a long shot. He still had the dreams—those terrible dreams—but staying at Misfit Farms, throwing himself into the care of their animals, and then during this past week even riding for the first time in ages, had helped. He still had the dreams about Trevor, but he doubted he'd ever get over the tragic loss of his friend. And he still had moments where it was all he could do to hang on, but things were better. Day by day. That was how he lived.

And today he'd get to see Claire.

He knew she'd been avoiding him. That was okay.

She would learn that he felt just as bad about their kiss as she likely did. He didn't have a home, a job—well, not a permanent one, anyway—and he still had some serious issues to deal with. He had no business dragging a woman into his mess of a life. No business at all. Especially when that woman had her own problems to deal with.

"Dr. McCall!"

He turned away from the horse he was in the midst of grooming and smiled. If there was one bright spot to his days, it was Adam. The boy had recovered so quickly it seemed almost like a miracle, but as he glanced past him to his mother, he still saw concern in her eyes.

"Well, look at you." He smiled again at the little boy running down the middle of the barn aisle. "No more zombie-pale skin and bags under your eyes."

The boy's feet sent up a cloud of dust as he came to a halt. He had a grin about as wide as the Mississippi. "I haven't had a fever in days."

He said it as if days were a month and it made Ethan shake his head. Nothing like the resilience of youth. Sometimes he wished he was back on his parents' ranch, back before they'd sold out and gone to work for one of the big operations in Montana.

"You still need to take it easy." He would have ruffled the kid's hair except he wore his usual baseball cap, this one with the initials of a popular comic book series, his hair having really grown since he'd first met him. He had way more than peach fuzz now. "You don't want to relapse."

Adam shook his head. "Doctor said I was A-okay. Had a test yesterday and he said my blood looked good."

Claire had walked up behind Adam, her long black

hair reaching past her midriff. She wouldn't look at him, and so he had the perfect opportunity to study her. Still the most beautiful woman he'd ever seen, and not just because of her thick black hair and green eyes. No. It was more that there was a goodness to her, an edge of sadness that haunted her eyes and made her beauty the kind that seemed almost ethereal. Two hundred years ago the great masters would have clamored to paint such an enigmatic face. It was too bad her character had been formed by sadness.

"Is that true? Did he pass a vet check?"

It was a joke. A veterinary term that applied to animals, not little boys, and something he hoped would make her smile because he didn't want to become just another problem to her. He wanted to help. Wanted her to know that whatever may have happened, they would always be friends.

"He did." She met his gaze, and he spotted something like relief. Relief that he hadn't tried to swoop in and kiss her again? Or relief for her son? "Said so far so good."

Her underlying meaning that her son's health might all change. And it might, but he didn't like the way she focused on the negative. Life was too short for that. He'd learned the lesson all too well.

"So you up for a ride?" he asked Ethan.

"Yup."

"Let me go get your horse, then."

Colt had shown him the pony-sized quarter horse that served as Adam's mount. It was the weekend, which meant Colt and Natalie were on the road, this time with some clients. They were all at a horse show. Natalie had joked that Colt looked like a fish out of water at the equestrian events in his cowboy boots and hat, but that secretly he loved all the attention.

"Do you know where his pony is?" Claire asked.

"Colt showed me." He forced himself to hold her gaze. She returned his the same way. It was as if she faced off with him. As if she dared him to mention their kiss. He wouldn't, though. He would act as if it hadn't happened. That was what he silently told her. She seemed to understand, because she looked away and her whole body seemed to relax. Yup. Definitely relieved.

"He told me you keep your own horse in the last stall on the left and that I'm not supposed to help you because you love saddling and grooming all on your own."

Claire whipped around to face him. Someone snorted. Adam, he realized, the child releasing something that could only be called a guffaw. He glanced back at Claire, who had an expression of disbelief mixed with amusement on her face.

"That's what he told you, huh?" she asked. For the first time she smiled, a big grin, one that caught him off guard. "What an ass."

"Excuse me?"

"She hates horses," Adam said with a hooting laugh. "That's why she does dogs."

"Not true," Claire quickly amended. "I like them just fine. They just don't like me."

He stared at her, stunned. He would have thought she'd be as horse crazy as the rest of her family. Come to think of it, though, there were no horses on her property. Just dogs. And no pictures of horses. No horse tack. No cowboy boots. Nothing to indicate she carried the horse-crazy gene.

"Then why did your brother insist I take you for a ride?"

"Because he knows I won't let Adam go on a trail ride without me."

"She's a control freak," Adam said.

"Hey." She frowned down at her son.

"It's true. Even Uncle Colt says so." The boy shook his head at the ridiculousness of it all, as if he were the adult and his mother the child.

"I'm only allowed to ride in the arena if she's not around. If she's here, I can ride outside the arena, but only down the road and back. I can't go out on trails all by myself." He ticked the rules he had to follow off with his fingers. "Well, I can go if Uncle Colt takes me, but she's a stress mess that whole time and it kind of ruins the fun of things, knowing she's back at the ranch pacing back and forth."

"I do not pace."

"You do, too."

"And you make me sound like a freak."

"You are about horses, Mom."

Ethan watched the play of emotions across her face. It fascinated him. No, *she* fascinated him, because he suspected there was more to the story of why she didn't like horses than she let on.

"I just prefer to keep an eye on you," she said to her son.

"And I don't blame her." He tapped the bill of Adam's baseball cap. "Go get your pony."

The kid shot off. That left them alone for the first time since Adam had been sick, and he could tell it instantly made her uncomfortable.

"Don't worry. I'm not going to jump you."

Her gaze shot to his. "Excuse me?"

"You look like a cat in a bathtub."

She tipped her chin up. "That's because I'm about to do something I don't like."

"It's because I kissed you." He had no idea why he pushed the matter, especially when he'd vowed to put the incident behind him. But push her he did, for some reason enjoying the way her face blazed with color and the way her jaw ticked in... Was it annoyance? Or maybe it was embarrassment. He couldn't tell.

"What horse did Colt say I should ride?"

And now she was trying to change the subject.

"I'm assuming the horse in the last stall on the left, like he said."

She nodded and turned in that direction. He stepped in front of her. She glanced up, green eyes wide, and he told himself to leave the matter alone. To reassure her that he wasn't going to try to kiss her again. Tell her that he knew it'd been a mistake, a moment of weakness, for both of them.

Instead he found himself saying, "Don't forget. You were the one who started it when you touched me out by the creek."

And it was all there in her eyes. Dismay. Shame. Anger. Pride. "That won't happen again." She slipped past him without a backward glance.

"No?" he teased, though for the life of him he didn't know why.

Leave her alone, a voice warned. *You're pushing her.*

She swung back around to face him. "No." She lifted her chin. "It won't."

She grumbled under her breath the whole time she saddled up Blue inside the barn, not just because of

Ethan's sudden alpha-male attitude, but because she truly didn't want to ride.

You're doing this for Adam.

That's what she needed to focus on. Her son and the happiness that shone from his eyes whenever he was near a horse. Not the ridiculous man who teased her about something she had deemed a mistake and that she tried desperately to put from her mind.

"You ready?"

She turned to face him. And there she went again, and it really drove her nuts, too. Every time she saw him she couldn't help but think, *oh, my.* She'd had the same thought when she spotted him outside the barn, the horse he'd been grooming like the backdrop of a photo shoot, one with the caption, "Real men wear jeans," or something like that. He wore a black cowboy hat, one that hung low on his forehead, the brim of it curved in such a way that it made the line of his jaw seem more square.

"As ready as I'll ever be." She tried to smile, failed and pretended a sudden interest in Blue's bridle.

"Come on." He smiled. "It's time to quit stalling."

What? She wasn't stalling. She would have told him that very thing except he'd already walked back toward the front of the barn. Outside, her son held the reins to his bay horse, his weight shifting from foot to foot, as if he had to go to the bathroom, but she knew Adam was merely anxious to leave.

"Mo-om."

"Sorry." She hadn't even noticed they were done tacking up. If she had, she would have brought her own horse outside instead of dillydallying inside.

Stalling.

Well, okay. Yes. Stalling.

She tugged Blue forward, temporarily blinded when she joined them. It was one of those days where the sky seemed enhanced by a photo filter, the kind that made everything more vivid: the blue of the sky, the orange of the wild poppies in the field out behind Colt and Natalie's house. The green of the trees off in the distance. Her own small house had been built against one of the low hills that dotted the landscape, but Colt's was out in the open. Her dad claimed that had been done on purpose. His great-grandfather had wanted to be able to keep an eye on his stock at all times and so he'd plopped down a homestead in the middle of nowhere. The home she lived in had been built for the ranch foreman. It was far smaller than Colt's, but that was okay. She didn't need two stories and a huge attic. She much preferred her cozy cottage.

"You going to get on?"

She realized she'd been standing there, staring at Colt's big white ranch house. She shook her head to clear it, and when that didn't work, took a deep breath and faced the saddle.

Here we go.

It'd been so long, but it was impossible to forget how to mount a horse. Once you mastered the skill it was like riding a bike. Her foot slid easily into the leather stirrup. Her hands instantly found the reins. She pulled herself up and over with an ease that was both familiar and troubling.

Troubling?

Yes, troubling, because it brought back memories, none of them good.

"Let's go." Adam's excited voice could be heard across

the plains. He clearly couldn't wait to get out into the open, because he made a beeline to the gate to the right of her brother's house. He had leaned over and worked the metal bar free before she could tell him to wait. She knew what would happen after Adam got through that gate. Sure enough, he pointed his pony toward the hills.

"Adam."

"Be right back."

"You're still not well—"

He galloped off.

"Adam!"

"Let him go."

She turned in her saddle to face him. "He's just getting over a bad flu."

"And he's fine now."

And there, right there, was the problem with ever getting involved with him. He didn't understand. Adam would never be "fine." Not for a lot of years. Though his blood tests showed they were clear of the cancer for now, that was just it. *For now.* There would be monthly monitoring. Then bimonthly. Then every six months. And at any moment—*boom*—they could be back where they started. She would worry about her son's health until the day she died. She wouldn't wish that kind of worry and fear on her worst enemy, much less someone like Ethan with his own cross to bear.

"He's not as strong as he once was."

"He will be if you let him spread his wings a little."

Good Lord, he sounded like her brother, right down to the no-nonsense tone. "It's not that simple."

"No," he surprised her by saying. "It probably isn't, but if there's one thing Trevor's death has taught me it's that bad shit happens."

She almost laughed because she'd learned the lesson early in life. That was what her whole life had been like. One series of bad things after another, and the thought cracked open the door to a memory of watching Marcus during his final days. Of watching him struggle to hang on. He'd been exposed to something over there, a bad batch of vaccine that had wrecked his immune system in the same way cancer did. They tried everything, but nothing had been able to stop the progression of the disease until just a shell of Marcus remained. She'd held his hand, begging him to stay, a part of her wanting him to let go, too, because there was nothing on this Earth worse than watching a loved one die.

Nothing.

Adam whooped, bringing her back from her thoughts. "You look upset."

She moved her horse through the gate she hadn't even realized he held open.

"I just don't like riding much."

He rode one of her other brother's horses, Frosty, an old rope horse that didn't get much use while Chance was in the military. "That surprises me, having grown up on a ranch." He patted Frosty's gray neck when the horse grew antsy about being left behind.

"Why?" she asked, forcing the horrible memories away. Marcus was gone. Remembering those final days did nothing but bring her down, so she took a deep breath, pulling her horse to a stop and waiting for him to close the metal gate held up by matching posts. "Just because a farmer grows corn doesn't mean he likes to eat it."

He smiled briefly as Frosty settled down. "Can't argue that."

She hoped he would leave the matter alone. After he

closed the gate and joined her, they rode along in silence for a moment and the fresh air did her good. This was the here. This was the now. She needed to look toward her future.

"Adam told me your dad ruined riding horses for you."

She glanced up at him and she had to marvel. Last month he'd been far away, on another continent, and now here he sat atop a horse looking as if he'd been riding Frosty his entire life. One day soon her brother Chance would be doing the same thing.

"My son thinks he knows a lot of things, but he really doesn't." She forced herself to stare between her horse's ears. "He likes to think he's all grown-up, too."

"Maybe he is."

"Excuse me?"

"Not really. I mean, I know he's only six, but you should let him have fun more often."

She wasn't certain how they'd gone from her troubled past to her son again so quickly, but she found herself clutching the reins, Blue instantly reacting by tossing his head.

"At least while he's feeling up to it," he added.

She opened her mouth, prepared to tell him he was wrong. That it was her job to protect her son. But when she glanced ahead it was to note that Adam had stopped. He had turned back to face them, waved, and even as far away as he'd run, she could still see his smile. It blazed like the gleam of quartz.

"See," Ethan said. "Look at that smile."

She waved back halfheartedly. Adam turned away and rode off again. She looked at the worn leather of her saddle horn. At her horse's mane. At the reins in her hand, the smell of them both comforting and familiar, and took a deep breath. "What if one day I have to let him go forever?"

Clearly, her memories of Marcus were closer to the surface than she thought.

"You won't."

"You don't know that."

"And you don't, either."

She shook her head, reminded yet again of the differences between them. He'd been marred by tragedy once, and look what it'd done to him. She'd been marred by tragedy her whole life and he had no idea what it'd done to her. No idea at all.

"How did your dad ruin riding for you?"

She wasn't going to tell him, but something about the look in his eyes, something about his words made her straighten in the saddle. "He used to beat the crap out of me if I didn't do it right."

She'd shocked him. That was good. She needed to keep him at a distance, not to feel twinges of desire whenever she looked into his eyes, because she did, damn it. He did something for her. What, she didn't know, but she didn't like it. She'd already let herself slip once. Not again.

"Seriously?"

She nodded. "My brothers and me. Colt got the worst of it. He ran off to the Army to get away from it all. Chance used the military to get away, too. They both tried to shield me from it, but my dad kept pushing and pushing and so one day I did what he asked. I fell off in front of him. From that day forward I refused to ride. He tried to shame me into getting back on and when that didn't work, he hit me, hard. Colt stepped in and then

Chance. They're older and they both protected me and I think my dad knew in that moment that he was out-manned and outnumbered. He never asked me to ride again. It wasn't until Colt came back that I did it again. It wasn't as bad as I thought it would be, but I still don't really like it. Crazy when you think about it, given our family's ties to the rodeo industry."

Too many memories.

"Is that why you're so overprotective? Because of your dad?"

She pulled her horse to a stop. "I am not overprotective."

"I don't mean to offend." He pulled up on Frosty's reins, too, the horse tossing his head. "I just noticed you really keep Adam under your thumb."

"Wouldn't you? The kid has cancer."

"Had."

"What?"

"Colt told me he's in remission, that they think they have the cancer licked."

"They don't know that for sure."

"Nobody knows anything for sure, Claire."

He fixed his eyes on her. It was an unblinking stare. Serious. And she wanted to argue, she really did, but she couldn't think of a single thing to say, because Adam's doctor had said exactly those words last month, and so she looked away. Their big concern was getting his immune system up to par, but even that looked promising. He'd gotten over that flu all on his own, and without a trip to the hospital.

Adam had reached the top of a small hill. He crested it, disappearing down the other side. She was about to call him back when she felt a hand on her thigh. It surprised her so much she turned to face him.

"I think we *both* need to focus on the here and now."

She opened her mouth to comment but he leaned forward and kissed her. Just a soft brush of his lips, because they were on horseback and his horse shifted, and suddenly he had to pull up on the reins, but even that gentle touch had the ability to rob her of breath. When he straightened in the saddle again and she looked into his eyes she knew he felt it, too. There was a connection between them, something almost otherworldly and inexplicable. This man knew her in a way that made no sense, given the short time they'd spent together. It frightened her. It was why she reacted to his touch the way she had the other day. Why, God help her, she didn't want their kiss to end.

"Where did Adam go?" she mumbled to cover her confusion and the fear that suddenly blossomed in her heart.

"Claire."

She kicked Blue into a gallop.

"Claire," he called out again.

But just because she didn't like to ride didn't mean she didn't know how. She was a hell of a rider and she knew it, and so she didn't listen. Blue made it easy with his smooth gaits. So she galloped, faster and faster, running up the small hill, relieved to find Adam on the other side, waiting, green eyes wide.

"Wow, Mom," he said as she pulled to a stop next to him. "You actually *do* know how to ride."

No. She knew how to escape. How to run away from something that scared the crap out of her.

Chapter 11

He'd frightened her off.

She hadn't said a word for the rest of the ride, had somehow managed to keep Adam between the two of them as they traveled toward the line of trees and the base of the foothills. He shouldn't have kissed her, damn it, but he hadn't been able to resist the way she'd looked sitting there, black hair coiled over her shoulder in a ponytail, green eyes haunted by the ghosts of her past. She had been through so much, way more than he had, and she'd somehow held on to her sanity. She had him beat in that department.

They headed back after she took him to what she called the stock pond, but was really a small lake, Adam begging her to go swimming.

"Not today," she told him.

Adam's face fell.

"But we can come back next week."

The kid jerked his head up so quickly Ethan almost laughed. "Seriously?"

"If you want."

"Woo-hoo!"

He rode off, a fist pumping in the air, the other holding the reins. Ethan smiled. He tried to move his horse up next to Claire's to tell her he approved, but she rode off, not that she probably cared for his opinion. Still, he considered it a minor victory. Maybe some of what he'd said earlier had sunk in.

They arrived back at the ranch an hour after they'd left, and he had to admit, Adam looked pretty tuckered out. He helped the boy unsaddle his horse, and by the time he'd finished, Claire was there, observing. She smiled her goodbyes, and Ethan watched her go, wondering why her silence bothered him so much. Their kiss might have been brief, but he'd felt something. She'd felt it, too.

And that's what bothers you.

She refused to acknowledge it.

He didn't see her for the rest of the week, not even when working with Thor. He'd been half-tempted to check in on her, but he gave her space instead. He needed to do some thinking of his own, not just about Claire and where their relationship was headed, but about his own life and how he'd let Trevor's death affect him. Claire had lost so much more than he had over the years: her childhood, her husband, very nearly her son—and yet she still stood strong. Damn, he admired her.

Colt and Natalie kept him busy that week. In addition to moving forward with turning Misfit Farms into a stallion station, he'd held an impromptu vaccination clinic for all the horses in their care. It'd been a huge success, so much so that he'd gotten a call from Natalie's friend, Mariah Johnson, a local vet. She wanted to know if he'd be interested in covering for her while she went out on maternity leave. He hadn't known what to say. He still wanted to train dogs—his work with Thor had emphasized how much he still wanted to do that— but he also liked working at the farm. And right now, the pickings were pretty slim. He'd posted his résumé on a site for veterinarians, but the only places he'd heard back from were big city animal clinics, places he didn't want to go. Being in the country had taught him that much.

His cell phone rang, Ethan so deep in thought he picked it up without even thinking.

"Ethan?" The voice on the other end of the line sounded vaguely familiar, but it took him a moment to bring his thoughts back to Earth, or back to where he sat in his loft above the barn.

"Yes," he answered tentatively.

"It's me," said a soft, Southern drawl.

Recognition dawned, and he sat up in his chair.

"Red?" It had been Trevor's nickname for his wife, and just the sound of it had the ability to kick him in the gut all over again. For the first time in nearly a week his hands started to shake.

"You sound surprised to hear from me."

"Yes. I mean, no, no, of course not. I told you to call me anytime."

"Well, I guess it was time, then."

He heard the smile in her voice, probably forced, because he doubted she could be any more over her husband's death than he was. Despite his words to Claire the other day, it was still hard for him to put one foot in front of the other. The only thing that seemed to help was working with Colt and Natalie's horses. He thanked God for them every day because without them he doubted he would have made it this long without help of the psychological kind. In fact it'd given him an idea, one he wanted to explore at some point in the future when his future was settled.

"How are you?" he asked.

"Hanging in there. You?"

"Same."

He looked out the window of his apartment above the barn, trying to lose himself in the view. It was one of those days, the kind when the sky looked burned to a crisp after being scorched by the sun. Out beyond the big red barn the horses grazed contentedly. Way out where he and Claire had kissed, a lone deer stood, ears flicking, nose sniffing the air.

"It's good to hear your voice," she said softly.

He almost asked how the kids were. Hell, he was godfather to one of them, but he knew they couldn't be good. They'd been as grief-stricken over their father's death as he had. He could only imagine what it was like for Naomi. Of course, she'd coped without Trevor before his death. The onerous life of a military wife. They had to be some of the most resilient women on God's green Earth.

She'd grown quiet and he wondered if she thought about the last time they'd spoken to each other. They'd been at Trevor's grave site. It'd been a cloudy day. More than a few members of their unit had already left but the two of them had still been standing there, wind blowing, rain threatening, both of them staring down at the casket at the bottom of a rectangle-shaped hole.

"You sleeping?" he asked, as inane and stupid a question as he'd ever asked.

No response, not right away at first. "Not very well. It's T.J. He has nightmares."

"Yeah, but he doesn't know—" About the explosion. The way Trevor died. He didn't want to say the words out loud, but she picked up on them nonetheless.

"No. Of course not." She paused as if she shook her head. "He just wants his daddy back."

Ethan's stomach flipped. He couldn't even imagine, but as the silence stretched on once again, he began to sense there was more to her call than he thought.

"Is there something I can do for you?"

She paused and he knew she gathered her thoughts. "Well." She took a deep breath, and he could imagine her standing there in the small kitchen he'd visited once before, back when he and Trevor had been on leave, the children, Samantha and T.J., watching TV in the background, the smell of home-cooked food hovering in the air. "I was wondering if you might know where Janus is?"

And there it was. The question he'd been half expecting. He'd known it might happen, had half hoped it would. It'd been part of the reason why he'd followed Claire to her hometown. He'd wanted to keep tabs on the dog. To be there just in case Red called.

"As a matter of fact I do."

He heard her sigh, knew of her relief based on the way she paused for a moment trying to gather her words the way a child did before asking for a special treat. "I've been thinking about him a lot lately," she finally admitted. "Thinking about what Trevor would want me to do."

He would have wanted the dog to be with his family.

Ethan had tried to tell her that after it'd all happened. He'd tried to convince her Janus would be a great family dog. Trev would have been horrified to know his faithful companion would be sent to strangers. That, too, was why he'd gone to Claire. He'd wanted to reassure himself somehow that the dog would be taken care of. He'd also wanted to reassure Janus, because despite what people might think, canines were as smart as their human counterparts. Janus knew. He'd been next to his master when he'd died. Had tried to crawl over to him even as injured as he'd been. Had licked his hand. The dog knew. He would stake his life on it.

"I think I should take him." He heard her take a deep breath. "I mean, I don't know how I'm going to manage it. Two kids, no husband and a military dog, but it's what he would want."

Ethan felt such relief in that moment that his knuckles hurt from clutching the cell phone so hard. "Do you have a pen?"

"Yeah."

"I'm going to give you directions."

"To where?"

"To Canine Pet Rescue, where Janus is."

"You have the address of the rescue memorized?"

"Of course I do." He smiled. "I live there."

She was *not* a coward.

Claire just felt like one as she rushed around the house like a crazy woman before Ethan came over.

With a woman.

She hadn't heard from him all week and then suddenly he'd called and told her he was bringing someone over. Someone he wanted her to meet and that she wanted to adopt Janus. A female friend. He hadn't even given her time to explain that things didn't work that way. He couldn't just handpick someone to adopt one of her dogs. She had a waiting list. Besides, Janus wasn't ready to be adopted. He still hadn't recovered from his wounds.

You just don't like that he's bringing over a woman.

That didn't matter, she firmly told herself. She just didn't like his high-handedness. It didn't help that her brother and Natalie sang his praises up to heaven and back. He was a huge help, they said. They were trying to convince him to stick around. Natalie claimed half of her clients were in love with him. She'd wanted to bury her head in her hands when she and Adam had gone over for dinner a few days ago.

"They're here."

Adam came tearing out of his back room. She almost told him to slow down, but she didn't.

Let him have more fun.

And she couldn't argue the point because Ethan was right. Adam needed to laugh and smile and be more like other boys. She did keep too close a watch on him. It'd weighed on her to the point that she'd agreed to let Adam ride one of Colt's trick horses, something her son had been dying to do, and not just around the ranch, but at an upcoming rodeo. They would all be attending the rodeo and Adam would be a star attraction. Adam had been in hog heaven all week. He'd probably be at his uncle's ranch right now except he clearly wanted to meet Ethan's friend. He blew by Claire so fast he just about knocked her off her feet. He opened the door just as fast. A gorgeous redhead stood outside.

Wow.

No wonder he wanted to pull some strings. He probably wanted to pull more than that.

She tried to smack the little green monster that reared its ugly head out of her mind, but that she couldn't do. In her light pink shirt and tight jeans the woman was the picture of elegance and chic. Standing next to Ethan in his black T-shirt and jeans, she looked like his perfect match. He wore no cowboy hat today. The wounds on his arms had healed and the T-shirt exposed them. He was the picture of health and fitness, and so was the woman. Claire felt like a homeless person by comparison in her old black capris and long white T-shirt.

"Where have you been?" Adam asked.

She almost groaned. He'd asked about his new friend insistently. Her son had no idea that Ethan walked over at the crack of dawn every morning. She watched him from behind the lace curtains of her bedroom even though she told herself to close the drapes. She just couldn't seem to stop, and it'd taken her until yesterday to admit the bitter truth. He fascinated her. She watched him work with Thor and sometimes Janus, and she knew he had to be a good man. Kind. Thoughtful. Soft with his hands. That much she knew from experience, and it made her cheeks turn so red she hoped like hell Ethan and his "friend" didn't notice.

"What do you mean, where have I been?" He walked inside when Adam stepped aside. His friend followed behind, glancing around the house curiously. "I'm here every morning."

Not much to see, she silently told her.

Their gazes met and Claire expected to see disapproval at the meagerness of her surroundings. Instead she saw kindness and a small, friendly smile, one that lit the woman's blue eyes.

"In the morning," her son repeated. "My mom said you come by during the day, when we're out, because you don't want to bother us."

She did not say that. Well, maybe she'd implied it, but her son's words made her face flame even more. "I just meant you're busy," she quickly amended.

Did he know she watched him in the mornings? Did he feel her stare? Wasn't it weird and slightly stalker-like that she even did that?

She refused to answer her own question. Instead she took a deep breath and prepared herself for looking into his jade-green eyes. When she finally did everything froze inside her because she saw amusement there.

He *did* know.

She wanted the Earth to open up and swallow her whole.

"Naomi, this is Claire, the woman I was telling you about."

Okay, get it together.

She transferred her gaze to the woman, whose friendly smile widened. She came forward, and the hand she held was as slender and fine as a bird's wing.

"So nice to meet you, Claire."

Her name had come out sounding like *Clai-air*. So Southern it made her crave pralines and cream, even though she'd never had them before.

"Nice to meet you."

The hand that shook her own slipped from her gasp. She saw the woman's smile falter a bit, saw something else, too, something both familiar and heartbreaking.

Sadness.

It clung to the woman like an old dress.

It hit her then who she was. Trevor's widow. Janus's old handler. No wonder...

"Mrs.—" Goodness. She'd completely forgotten his best friend's last name. "Ma'am," she quickly amended. "I'm so sorry about your loss."

The woman's eyes sparked in a way that silently tried to reassure her. "Thank you."

"You were married to Trevor?"

They both turned to Adam, who still stood near the door, watching the scene with curiosity in his eyes.

"I was." Naomi smiled at her son. "And you must be Adam."

Her son nodded. "Dr. Ethan told me you have kids."

"I do." She glanced back at Claire. "They're with their grandparents this weekend. I was hoping I can keep what we're doing here a secret. I don't want them disappointed if it doesn't work out."

So she wasn't expecting to just take the dog. The words had the ability to drain the tension from Claire's shoulders. "You want to go see him?"

The woman took a deep breath and Claire realized how hard this would be for her. She'd never had a handler's widow show up for a dog. It was a first for her and something she knew wouldn't be easy.

Adam had lurched forward. He opened the door. Claire watched as Ethan went to Naomi and lightly touched her arm, the silent gesture of support making her look away for a moment. Did he have a thing for his best friend's widow? But the moment she thought it she dismissed it. Ethan wasn't the type to do something like that. He had clearly loved his friend, and that love extended to his friend's widow, nothing more.

It was chilly outside for a midsummer day. The fog

had reached its silky fingers inland, hovering over the hills all day and hanging high overhead. A sheen of moisture clung to the roses along the front of her house even though it was late afternoon, the smell of dank earth and wet leaves filling the air. It was a comforting smell. The smell of her childhood back before her mother had died and everything had gone to hell.

"Nice place," Naomi said.

No. Not really. Some of her sister-in-law's clients had nice homes. Big homes. Her home was small and out in the middle of nowhere but it was all her own. She didn't have a mortgage and she didn't have to worry about neighbors complaining about her dogs, and in the years since she'd taken it over she had made it her own. She'd been the one to plant the roses. Had laid down a cobblestone pathway to the door. She'd even added a sprinkler system that watered twin patches of grass on either side of the stones. Between a widow's pension and her work as a freelance graphic artist, it all came together. The dogs, CPR, that was all a labor of love. A time-consuming labor, but as she watched Trevor's widow walk toward Janus, it reminded her that it was all worth it. She knew immediately which dog had been her husband's because her eyes had settled upon Janus sitting in the middle of his dog run, ears pricked forward. The other dogs paced. Some barked. A few peeked out from their kennels. Well, all but Thor. Janus simply sat there and stared, and Claire knew that Naomi had met the dog many times before.

"Did you want me to bring him out?" she asked.

"Sure."

They all stopped near the corner of the dog runs. Claire headed for the tool shed to grab a leash.

"I'll help," Adam said. Her son ran ahead to open the chain-link door.

"Adam, no—"

Janus didn't hesitate. He burst past her son so fast he nearly knocked him down. He nearly knocked Claire off her feet, too.

"Janus, *hier*," Claire called.

But the dog was on a mission. Claire watched as he made a beeline for Naomi, rearing back when he was a couple feet away, Claire crying out, "No," right as Janus thrust two big paws through the air.

Naomi didn't miss a beat. She opened her arms, welcoming the dog paws on her pretty pink shirt, sinking to the ground at the same time she buried her head in the dog's black fur.

"Janus," she heard Naomi say, but in a voice thick with tears. The dog wiggled free, licking tears off Naomi's face, his tail wagging so hard, it rocked his whole back end and Claire started to smile. Naomi scrubbed her fingers through the dog's fur and Claire realized she still wore her wedding ring, the sight making her throat tighten. Janus had become so excited he made little yelping noises.

"Wow," Adam said.

Claire wiped tears from her face. Yeah, wow. No question that the dog recognized the woman, and that she held a special place in the canine's heart. The mate of his former master, and he loved her the way his master had no doubt loved her.

"I guess Janus has a new home."

"No," Adam said. "Janus is going home."

Chapter 12

A match made in heaven, Ethan thought, watching as Naomi signed her name with a flourish.

"And that's all there is to it," Claire said with a huge smile, one that made it seem she might be on the edge of tears.

"Congratulations," Ethan offered with a grin of his own.

It was a smile Naomi returned, the first smile he'd seen on her face since he'd returned to the States. "The kids are going to be so excited."

"I'm sure they are," Claire agreed. "You can bring them out here when you pick up Janus."

"Are you kidding? I'm going to surprise them."

She probably didn't mean to, but Claire finally glanced in his direction, her smile slipping a notch, and Ethan wondered if he'd pushed her too far the other day. He should have never gotten on her case about her son. He didn't regret kissing her, though. That had been the highlight of his week.

"Did you want to stay for dinner?" Claire asked with what Ethan knew was a polite smile.

"No, no." Naomi shook her head so that her red hair fell behind her shoulders. "I'll be back tomorrow with a proper kennel for Janus." Her eyes slid away from Claire and settled on him. "Walk me out?"

"Sure." He smiled at Claire, observing the way she couldn't quite look him in the eyes. "I'll be right back."

"Wait. Is she leaving?" Adam came rushing out of the family room, where he'd been playing a video game. He didn't have his ball cap on and Ethan noticed his hair had really started to come back in. He looked like a regular kid.

"I am," Naomi answered.

The little boy didn't wait for permission before racing up to his new friend and giving her a hug. Naomi looked up at them awkwardly before patting the boy on his head.

"Thank you for taking Janus," Adam mumbled into her shirt. "He's going to be so much happier back with his family."

Naomi looked close to tears all of a sudden. She leaned down and hugged Adam back. "I think he will be, too."

When she straightened he could tell she was touched by Adam's words. Her smile was warm when she glanced in Claire's direction. "Thanks for taking such great care of my husband's dog."

"You're welcome."

"I'll be back tomorrow."

Ethan held the door as Naomi slipped past. They both stepped out into the dank, evening air. It seemed like hours since they'd gone out to the kennel to see Janus, but it'd been less than two. The sun had begun to sink behind the mountains, and because it was overcast, it was darker than he expected. Clouds still hung overhead, but it wasn't so dark that he couldn't see his friend's face.

"I'll arrange for someone to check his wounds for you."

"That would be great."

"Although he's healing nicely."

She nodded. "He's had excellent care."

"Yes, he has."

Naomi peeked up at him. "She's a nice lady."

Ethan nodded. "Yes, she is."

"With a lot on her plate."

"Yup. Just like someone else I know."

She paused near the edge of the yard, if one wanted to call the tiny patch outside Claire's house a yard. There were no boundaries, just a patch of grass that faded into burned pasture.

"She's strong," Naomi said. "Stronger than me."

"I think you're both pretty remarkable."

"Nah. At least my two kids are healthy."

His smile fell. "Yeah. She's been through a lot."

Naomi glanced back at the house, sadness in her eyes. "I look at her, and what she's been through, and I think, stop feeling sorry for yourself."

"She makes me feel the same way."

"She brings it all into perspective. I miss Trevor so much, but I didn't go through the horrors of watching my kid suffer through chemo and radiation and God knows what else all the while trying to hold my life together. And before that, what she went through with her husband. Claire Reynolds deserves a medal."

She was right, and it made him think that maybe

that was why his anxiety had improved even if the bad dreams hadn't. What did he have to be afraid of compared to what she'd been through? That day when she'd climbed aboard the horse despite the bad memories they evoked. Selfless. That's what it'd been. She lived each day for her son, and for the dogs she rescued, and in honor of the man she'd been married to. He wouldn't be much of a man if he couldn't do the same.

"I don't know that she thinks of herself as heroic," Ethan said. "I think she's just taking it day by day."

"Aren't we all?"

He looked into Naomi's blue eyes, searching her face, for what he didn't know. Approval, maybe.

Approval for what? he wondered.

That he'd done okay. That he hadn't let Trevor down. That she wasn't angry with him or disappointed or that she didn't blame him in some way for her husband's death.

"Ethan?"

He hadn't even realized he stared at the ground or that he'd stuffed his hands in his pockets. His hands had started to shake again, but for a different reason this time. He felt the guilt so much more acutely now that he stood in front of her. When she'd gotten out of the car earlier and he'd seen her for the first time since…

"You okay?"

He sucked in a deep breath of air, forced himself to stand tall and proud as he asked, "Do you blame me?" He pulled his hands from his pocket, though his fingers flexed over and over again into a fist. "For what happened to Trevor?"

Her whole face registered surprise, from the parting of her lips to the widening of her blue eyes. She reached out and grabbed his forearm. "Oh, my Lord,

Ethan, no." She gave his arm a squeeze. "You had no control over that."

He knew that. Deep down inside. He just couldn't seem to stop himself from thinking that way. At night his mind went over it again and again. What if he hadn't delayed those few minutes to check on his canine patients? What if he'd insisted Trevor wait for him? What if he'd been the first one to leave?

"You haven't been blaming yourself, have you?" she asked, her hand tightening even more.

He shrugged. Her hand fell away, but he didn't escape her gaze. "No." Yes. Deep down inside he supposed he did. "Maybe."

She drew up straight. "Would it surprise you to learn that I do, too?"

He saw how seriously she meant the words by the way her gaze held his own. She even nodded before glancing down at the ground.

"Every night as I lie in bed trying to sleep I wonder if he'd still be alive if I hadn't pressured him to get out." A strand of her hair had fallen next to her cheek. He watched as she tucked it back behind her ear. "Did he tell you about our big fight?"

He shook his head. All he'd ever heard from Trevor was what a saint his wife was. How much she meant to him. How much he loved her.

"We got in a big argument the last time he deployed. I said some things. He said some things. We got over it, of course. I made peace with his decision. Told myself that whatever he decided to do when this last tour was up, I'd be okay with it. And then he called me and told me he was coming home and I realized he did remember our argument and I was so excited—"

She shook her head and closed her eyes, and Ethan knew she was on the verge of tears. He moved toward her, pulling her into his arms. "Shh. It's okay."

She wiggled out of his grasp. "No. It's not okay. It's taken me the past few weeks to admit that it wasn't my fault at all. It was the rotten bastards that attacked your base. But the fact is he had a dangerous job, and I knew that, I should never have added to his stress…"

"No."

"Then you need to stop feeling guilty, too. I know I have." She wiped at her eyes with the heel of her hand. "You still have the dreams?"

He'd told her about them at Trevor's funeral. "A little." She tipped her head sideways. "Okay, a lot."

She wiped at her other eye. "What a pair we are." She turned and stared at Janus. The dog peered over at them, unblinkingly, watching her. It was uncanny. He hadn't seen Trevor's wife in months and yet he remembered.

"And that woman in there would be good for you." She pointed to the house. "I can tell."

He didn't comment. What was the point? She'd clearly read his feelings for Claire on his face.

"You're going to need to push her, though."

"You think?"

"She's going to be a tough nut to crack."

That was an understatement.

"Sick kid. Dead husband. Sucky past. It's a wonder she hasn't sworn off the human race entirely."

"I've been thinking lately maybe I should just give her some space. Get my own head screwed on straight before I ask her out on a date or something. Hell. I'm not exactly ready for a relationship, either."

"Yes, you are." She glanced at the house again,

smiled. "Trevor and I used to talk about it all the time. I wanted to introduce you to some of my friends. He told me no. He said you wouldn't be ready to settle down until you left the Army."

"Settle down?" *Whoa, whoa, whoa.* "I like her, but I wouldn't go that far."

"Keep telling yourself that, solider."

He drew back. No. She had it all wrong. He understood Claire. Hell, he didn't deny he was attracted to her. He definitely wanted to date her. When he was ready. When they were *both* ready.

"Naomi, I don't even know which way is up right now. The last thing I need is a woman in my life."

"Trevor would tell you not to let a little thing like that stop you."

Trevor would have loved Claire.

"You're ex-Army. A combat veteran. If you want her, go after her. That's what Trevor would tell you."

"Hoo rah," he muttered under his breath, thinking about the woman inside the house and what she might mean to him.

"Hoo rah," she echoed with a small smile. "So go get her, soldier."

They were out there a long time.

Claire resisted the urge to go to the window and look outside. Whatever they were talking about, it must have been serious, because when Ethan finally came back in, he seemed distracted.

"I'm headed back to my place." He smiled, but it was a weak one.

She used her front door to hold him at bay, the tail-lights of his friend's car fading down the road.

"You going to walk in the dark?"

"It's not all the way dark yet," he said, his gaze moving past her as if searching for Adam. "Besides, I could really use fresh air right now."

She nodded, suddenly as awkward as a duck in a swimming pool. "Then I guess I'll see you later."

"Tomorrow," he quickly amended, half turning and watching Naomi disappear down the road, too.

"Tomorrow?" she echoed stupidly.

He turned back to face her. "When Naomi picks up Janus and then later, at the rodeo."

The rodeo. Heavens to Betsy, she'd completely forgotten about that. Tomorrow night the annual Via Del Caballo Rodeo started. It was Think Pink night, too. Adam would be doing his own version of a rodeo act—riding her sister-in-law's horse without a bridle in front of the audience—while being honored as a cancer survivor even though she'd argued with Colt that he wasn't officially in remission yet.

Don't think like that, she told herself. Ethan was right. She'd turned into a negative Nellie and she needed to stop.

"Are you going to the rodeo tomorrow, then?"

He nodded. "It'll be the first time I've seen your brother perform in front of an audience and I'm looking forward to it."

"You're in for a treat."

"I've watched him practice, and if it's anything like that, it'll be spectacular. A bunch of Natalie's clients from the barn are going, too. They tell me I have to dress up in pink. Don't know that I have the clothes to do that."

"All you'll need is a shirt. No pink jeans."

He smiled. She froze again. Goodness, what was with her?

If she felt this awkward now, what would it be like tomorrow morning, or worse, tomorrow night when she'd be forced to socialize with him? She clutched the handle of her front door. Just the thought of sitting next to him made her whole insides twist like a rope.

"Well, have a nice walk."

Instead of retreating he took a step toward her. "Do you ever think about life after all this? After Adam is all better and you can move on."

The door handle slipped from her grasp. The door started to swing closed but he stopped it with his foot.

"No," she answered with what sounded like a croak. "Not really."

"About what you'll do with all your free time?"

She swallowed. Hard. "I can barely think past the next fifteen minutes, much less months from now. Right now, it's one day at a time. Sometimes one minute at a time. Sometimes even one second at a time."

"You should," he said. And with those cryptic words he turned around and walked away. She stood there, the door still open, wondering what the hell that had all been about, and why she suddenly wanted to run.

Straight into his arms.

No. She had to focus on Adam. Tomorrow night Adam would be around a bunch of people, which meant extra precautions and then later on worrying about him coming down with the flu or a cold or something much worse. She didn't have time to think about her future.

And especially not one that might involve Ethan.

Chapter 13

He'd never been to a rodeo before. In all his years working with animals and all the years growing up on a ranch, he'd never been to one, much to his parents' chagrin. As he stood next to Claire in a dirt lot packed with horse trailers and trucks, the sun shining down on their backs, he wondered why. It smelled like animals and popcorn, two scents that shouldn't mix, but strangely did.

"Can you believe I get to ride in grand entry this year?"

"I know." Ethan smiled down at Adam, who stood between him and his mom. They were watching Colt groom a good-looking dark bay horse named Playboy. "That's great."

Claire didn't seem so enthusiastic, or so Ethan thought. Then again, she'd been doing a good job of pretty much ignoring him the whole time he'd been at the rodeo grounds. He wondered if she was upset about Janus leaving this morning, but that didn't make sense. She'd been genuinely happy to help Naomi load up the dog, or so it'd seemed. After Naomi had left, however, she'd made it clear she was too busy to talk to him. She'd disappeared inside the house so fast you'd have thought a tornado was coming. He just didn't understand.

Her brother must have noticed the pinched look on his sister's face because he said, "Relax. He'll be fine."

"He better be." She nervously fidgeted with a strand of her black hair. "If anything happens, I'll kill you."

Of course, she had a right to be a little more tense than normal. Adam wouldn't be riding in grand entry like a normal kid. No. He'd be riding without a bridle as part of the opening act. They were spotlighting his recovery from cancer. He'd practiced back at the ranch, and that had gone terrifically, but Claire had gotten sick every time she'd had to watch—or so Colt had claimed.

Her brother paused in the midst of brushing the horse's back. "Nothing will happen." He went back to brushing, puffs of dust temporarily filling the air. "You've seen Playboy perform without a bridle a million times. You know how safe it is."

"He's never carried my son before."

Natalie came around the edge of the trailer then, and ironically, she carried Playboy's bridle, her blue eyes settling on Claire. "He has when we practiced at home." She smiled at her sister-in-law. "Believe me, he'll be fine."

Ethan had been told the horse Adam rode was a champion reining horse that she'd bought to help her overcome a serious riding injury. He knew Colt and

Natalie trusted the horse implicitly and so there was no reason to fear. He almost told Claire to relax, too, but he had a feeling that would earn him a glare. He didn't want to be on her bad side. He had plans for Claire later that night, not that she knew anything about it. He caught Colt's gaze right then, the two of them exchanging glances. When he'd told Claire's brother he wanted to take his sister out on a date, Colt had simply said four words: *Leave it to me.*

Operation Claire on a Date had been born.

"How much longer?" Claire asked, shifting from foot to foot. Ethan worried she'd pull that strand of hair out of her head.

"Show starts at one," Colt said. He tugged his cell phone out of his back pocket. "That's in a half hour."

"I'm just not sure standing out in this sun is a good idea."

Sun? What sun?

"Mom. I'm fine."

Ethan had parked behind the rodeo grounds, next to where Colt had parked his giant rig, beneath the shade of a giant oak tree.

"That's what you say now, but then I'll get you home and you'll be burnt to a crisp."

Adam might be a young kid, but he could look like an adult at times and his glare clearly told his mom to take a hike. Ethan almost laughed.

"You ready there, partner?" said another woman, Colt's lead trick rider, a woman who'd recently taken the place of a longtime family friend as head of the Galloping Girlz. Carolina was her name. She had blond hair and eyes the color of a new swimming pool and Ethan sensed she had troubles of her own to bear.

"You bet I am." Adam already wore his pink shirt, Ethan noticed, as did he. So did everybody, although the trick riders were in pink spandex outfits. Claire, too, had dressed for the occasion, and the color suited her ivory complexion and black hair. She was beautiful standing there watching her son. It amazed him, though, to see how both the crowd and the competitors supported cancer awareness. Even the hardened bull riders wore the color. Plus, Claire had been wrong. They did make pink jeans and the current Miss Via Del Caballo rodeo queen wore them—that and pink chaps.

"All righty, then," Colt said. "We're going to let you warm up a little in the practice pen. Ride around just like you did at home. When we're ready to go into the main arena, I'll drop his bridle."

Adam crammed his straw cowboy hat down on his head as if he were about to get on a saddle bronc. "This is going to be so cool."

He heard Claire release something that sounded like a hiss and he couldn't help himself. He placed a hand on her shoulder, but it was as if he'd shot her with a cattle prod. She ducked away so fast his hand was left hanging in the air.

"You scared me," she said, turning to face him, hand on her chest.

Had he? Somehow he doubted it. That had been the move of a woman who didn't want to be touched. Who'd put up a barrier between them. No Trespassing. Plus, her complexion was fair enough that he spotted the blush spreading across her cheeks like spilled paint.

"Sorry."

She had refocused her gaze on her son, but she nodded her acknowledgment of his apology. Maybe he should tell her brother to call the whole thing off. What stopped him, however, was the absolute certainty that she needed to get out for a little bit. He might only be taking her to dinner, but it would do her good to let her hair down and socialize with someone other than her own son. Clearly Adam felt the same way. The boy shot him a look that practically begged him to do something about his mother. Ethan almost smiled again.

"All right, let's head on over," Carolina said. "Gonna be center stage today, huh, Adam?" The woman tapped the top of Adam's cowboy hat.

"If my mom doesn't freak out and die of a heart attack first," they all heard him mutter.

Okay, that blew the lid off the smile he'd been holding back. He even chuckled a little before saying, "If she does, I'll take care of her."

Claire glanced over at him, then immediately looked away, and that did it. First this morning and now this. He crossed to her side, brushed her arm with his hand. At least she didn't jerk away this time. Still he saw her tense.

"He'll be fine."

She crossed her arms in front of herself and said, "I know."

"Colt would never let something happen to him."

"I know," she repeated.

"Climb aboard," Natalie said.

"Time to go practice," Colt added, motioning Adam over to Playboy's side. "And remember, when you're out there, listen to Carolina. She's in charge now."

They helped Adam mount up, the smile on the kid's face big enough to spot from space. He all but bounced in the saddle as they moved as a group toward the practice arena out behind where everyone had parked.

A grizzled old cowboy nodded as they walked by. "Colt."

"Hey, Hank."

Ethan had learned Colt was something of a celebrity in the cowboy world, but if he hadn't already known, he would have figured it out by the time they made it to the practice arena. The whole way there he'd been greeted by males and females alike. Ethan knew Colt traveled all over the US performing. His horse was trained to rear and dance and take a bow, all without Colt touching him. Natalie had explained he was booked years in advance, and although he'd cut his performance schedule back since he'd married her, Adam had told him he always made time to perform in front of his hometown crowd.

"You look like you're ready to puke."

They stood by the rail of the warm-up arena; Colt and Natalie stood a little ways away, Claire leaning against the rail as though she needed it for support.

"I'm just tired."

That sounded like a canned excuse, but he didn't push the matter. She'd slipped on thick sunglasses once they'd left the shade of the tree. It was impossible to see her eyes and he found himself wishing he could. She'd been so distant today. More so than ever before. He'd been hoping his question last night might shake her up a bit, but he was beginning to think it'd upset her more than anything else.

"Adam is a heck of a rider." He watched as the kid loped the horse around the pen. The rest of the Galloping Girlz all egged him on. The boy had ridden more this week than he had in a long while and it showed. His pale skin had been bronzed by the sun. His eyes were brighter, too. He looked like a normal, healthy kid in his pink shirt, jeans and cowboy boots. More important, he'd been smiling nonstop since he'd climbed aboard Playboy.

"It's in his genes."

He hadn't expected her to answer, had half thought she'd continue with the silent treatment, and so when she spoke, he found himself thinking maybe things were all right between them after all.

"He told me he wants to be a rodeo rider when he grows up," Ethan said.

"He's been saying that since he was old enough to talk."

"But you refuse to think that far ahead."

Now, why'd he go and push her button? He should be trying to keep the peace, especially in light of the plans he had for later. But he couldn't seem to stop himself.

She went back to watching her son. "I told you last night. One day at a time."

Yes, she had. He'd thought about those words all evening. It was part of why he'd been so determined to take her out this morning. He wanted to fill at least one day with happiness and laughter. She deserved that.

"I guess that's all we can do."

He kept quiet for the rest of Adam's practice session. All too soon they were headed toward the main arena, Ethan following at a distance. Carolina would be carrying the American flag while she stood atop her horse, but the rest of the girls would perform with Colt later on. Still, they all walked over together.

They were nestled against the base of some small

hills. The rodeo committee had built grandstands into the slope of the hillside to give spectators a better view of the arena below. Cattle trucks were parked outside, as were horse trailers of every shape and size, some old, some new, some state-of-the art like Colt's. A whole mass of people milled around outside the arena, most of them on horseback, a few trying to make their way through the crowd on foot. Even with as much experience as he'd had around animals it seemed insane to push their way through the hind ends of so many animals, but push through they did until they were at the gate.

"There you are," said a woman with a clipboard when she saw Colt. "We're just about ready to start."

"That's what I figured," Colt said, turning to his nephew. "You know the drill, right?"

"Yup."

"Just the same, I'm going to go over it again. Once the gals carrying the sponsor flags line up in the middle, Carolina here is going to present the American flag while someone sings the national anthem. Once that's finished you'll go in. Just one lap around. That's all. When you're done, you need to go right to the center and stand next to Carolina."

"Yes, sir."

"Then you can lead the crowd out."

"Here comes my flags," said the lady with the clipboard, staring at a group on horseback, each one carrying the flag of a rodeo sponsor. "You'll need to move out of the way."

Ethan almost asked Claire if she wanted to go up to the grandstands, but it was clear she didn't want to move. She had eyes only for her son as they all stepped aside to make way for the horseback riders.

"All right, all right, all right," the announcer said in a Matthew McConaughey voice. "Are you all ready for a rodeo?"

The crowd cheered, the gate swung open and the sponsorship flag team entered at a full run.

"Ladies and gentlemen, welcome to the 51st Annual Via Del Caballo Rodeo."

The audience cheered again, the announcer pausing for a moment to ask the audience to stand as they saluted Old Glory. A young girl walked to the middle of the arena, microphone in hand.

"Have fun," Carolina said, and stood on top of her horse, something that never ceased to fill Ethan with awe, and then entered the arena as the girl started to sing. It was a beautiful performance. Carolina loped along, but her speed built in intensity as the song progressed until as the last glorious verse was sung, she ran at a breakneck speed, blond hair streaming, flag crackling in the wind, arena dust churning.

"Beautiful," Ethan said to Claire, putting his hat back on his head after it was all over. She barely nodded.

"Before we get started with our grand entry, we wanted to remind everyone that today we're dedicating this rodeo to those who're fighting the biggest battle of their life." Ethan looked down at Claire. There wasn't a lick of emotion on her face. "Folks, we know cancer affects one out of two people, and we know most of you know someone who's lost a family member to this horrible disease, so today we thought we'd do something different. Today we thought we'd celebrate the life of a six-year-old boy who's not only surviving, but so far beating cancer."

"You ready?" Colt said.

Adam merely nodded.

Colt moved to the front of Playboy and dropped the bridle. The horse lifted its head, clearly aware that he was about to perform because it seemed he waited for the gate to open. The moment it did, Adam surprised them all by hollering, "Yee ha!" and pounding his heels against Playboy's sides.

"Adam," Claire screamed.

Her son was gone. Playboy pinned his ears and ran as if a legion of hellhounds was at his heels.

"Damn that kid," Colt said.

"He's going to kill himself." Claire sounded ready to faint.

"He'll be okay," Ethan said, placing a hand on her shoulder, because Adam didn't look in danger at all. Playboy kept to the rail, Adam like a flea on his back, the horse's mane and tail streaming.

"Ladies and gentlemen," the announcer said. "Meet Adam O'Brian, nephew to rodeo legend Colt Reynolds and a little boy who's a cancer survivor."

The crowd went wild. Claire covered her mouth with her hand. Adam waved. And when the audience realized Adam rode without a bridle, another round of cries and yells filled the air. Adam just smiled and ran. Just as they'd practiced, Playboy rounded the last corner and headed to the middle. He came to a sliding stop in front of the girls carrying the flags. And there was such a look of pride on Adam's face, such a look of happiness, Ethan felt his throat thicken. He glanced down at

Claire. She stared at her son, her hands slowly dropping away, eyes only for the little boy that stood center stage.

"That was perfect," Natalie said.

"Little bugger's going to get an earful when he gets out of there," Colt said. "That was *not* how we practiced it."

"No." Claire half turned. "Natalie's right. That was perfect."

She faced her son again, smiled, turned back to clap, and it was in that exact moment, outside the Via Del Caballo rodeo arena, that Ethan realized he was falling in love.

Chapter 14

Ethan had been right. One look at Adam's face and Claire knew riding Playboy had been better medicine than a million rounds of injections. As he stood waving and smiling to the crowd, she caught her first glimpse of Adam again. The old Adam. Her son before cancer had taken over their lives.

She had to inhale back her tears. Wouldn't do for her son to see her crying.

A hand had settled on her shoulder. She wanted to shrug it off. Every time Ethan touched her she was reminded of their time in her house, the time she'd lost control.

"He did great."

She nodded and gently eased away from his touch. He didn't try to touch her again, but that was okay. That was how it should be.

She barely heard the rodeo announcers invite everyone into the arena after they introduced Adam. A part of her watched the rodeo queens ride by one by one, their horses galloping hell-bent for leather, their smiles and waves as bright as their crowns. It was as if the Earth had been flipped on its side and everything knocked askew.

"Good job, buddy!" Colt called when it was all said and done.

Adam got to lead everyone out of the arena, a look of pride on his face. He had eyes only for her, she noticed, tears filling her eyes again. Thank God for the sunglasses.

"How'd I do?" he asked her.

"You did great," she said as Colt slipped the bridle back on Playboy's head.

"I'm not sure I liked how you jacked your heels into my horse's sides," Natalie gently scolded.

"I know." Adam had the grace to look abashed. "But I knew you'd never let me run like that with my mom around."

No. She wouldn't. She'd have told him it was too dangerous. That he wasn't ready for the exertion. That he might fall. A million different excuses would have been offered, all under the guise of keeping him safe. But Ethan was right. It was time to let go. Time to move on. Her son wanted that, and because he wanted it, she would learn to live with it, too.

"You were amazing," she heard Ethan say.

She inhaled because there was pride in his voice, too. Pride and approval and joy. For her son.

So what if he loves Adam, she told herself. Because there was that in his voice, too. He cared for her son.

She saw it in his eyes when she gained the courage to look up at him.

"Thanks, Ethan," her son said, smiling back.

They all headed toward the parking area, Claire making sure she kept her distance from Ethan. She'd seen him glance at her in puzzlement earlier, and again now as she made sure to keep Playboy between the two of them. He probably thought she was mad at him about his question last night, but that wasn't it at all. When he'd touched her earlier, it had jolted her, to the core. It was that way every time he touched her. Time and distance hadn't done anything to make that stop. If anything, it'd made her crave him more.

Stupid physical attraction.

That was all it was, she firmly told herself. The man did it for her and she had no idea why. Well, aside from the fact that he was good-looking. And kind. And smart. And sweet. And good to her son.

Stop it.

"Did you see my slide stop, Mom?"

"I did."

"That was a *blast*."

"That wasn't in the game plan, either," her brother said.

"I know." Adam's smile was full of pride. "But we pulled it off okay."

"You sure did," Natalie said with a glance at her husband. Colt wouldn't perform until later, toward the middle of the rodeo, when he and the Galloping Girlz would do some impressing of their own.

"Can I do it again?" Adam asked Colt.

"Only if your mom says it's okay."

"Mom?" Adam said, peering back at her from atop Playboy.

"Let me think about it."

That seemed to appease her son. He went back to talking to Colt and Natalie and Carolina and the other Galloping Girlz, she and Ethan trailing behind. She tried not to be aware of him as they crossed between cowboys swinging ropes and horses tied to the rail. He fit right in with his pink-and-white-checkered shirt and off-white cowboy hat. More than one cowgirl had eyed him up and down as he walked past. Those ladies would go completely gaga if they knew he was a veterinarian. That he loved dogs. That he was good with kids. That he knew how to kiss…

What is with *you?*

It was *him*, she admitted. Ethan and his kind words and his sweet touch and the way she'd tossed and turned all night thinking about the way he kissed and how good it felt to have him hold her. Just the thought made her tingle and squirm and flush as she fought off the memory of the touch of his hands.

"I think when we're all done here tonight we should go out and celebrate." It was Colt who spoke the words, and something about the tone caught her attention. "Natalie and I were thinking we could take you to dinner and then ice cream, Adam."

"Cool!"

"We're all going, right?" Claire asked warily.

"Actually, Natalie and I would like to spend time with our nephew all on our own, if that's okay with you. We were even thinking of doing a sleepover." His smile was pure cheese. "You know, like we used to do in the old days."

"Yay!" Adam said with fist to the air.

The sly look Colt shot Ethan made Claire think this wasn't just uncle-nephew bonding time. In fact, she would bet this was all planned. He might try to hide his self-satisfaction behind an innocent smile, but she saw right through him.

"I don't know," she hedged.

"Please, Mom?" Adam pulled on Playboy's reins. They all stopped. "It's been so long since I've been able to spend the night at Uncle Colt's."

Shame on you for using my son like this, she told Colt with her eyes, not that he could see them behind her sunglasses, but he knew what she was thinking.

Colt just smiled. "Let him go. He'll be fine."

You'll be fine. That was what he really meant.

"Please," Adam added again.

She didn't want to, she really didn't, but with everyone staring at her... "Okay, fine."

"Terrific," Colt said. "Ethan, you can take my sister to dinner on your way home."

Pfft. As if she hadn't seen that coming.

"I'd be delighted."

And that, too. She should be furious. She'd spent hours last night convincing herself to keep on staying away from Ethan because despite the way he'd helped her with Adam, she still refused to think about him romantically. Yeah, she desired him. No doubt about that, but it was just physical. Mentally she wasn't ready for him or any other man. She was used to being on her own. Life was comfortable that way. She didn't need the stress of a new relationship.

Even though you want him, taunted a little voice.

Physical, she reminded herself. She would let Colt

think he'd gotten one over on her. She'd smile at Ethan and act as if she planned to go home with him, but in fact, they were at her hometown rodeo and she could find her own way home. Ethan wouldn't know what happened until it was too late.

It would be better that way.

She'd ditched him.

Ethan could have cheerfully choked her. He'd looked for her for half an hour before receiving her text.

Caught a ride with a friend. See you later.

"I'll see her later, all right," he muttered, turning down the road that led to her house. Enough of this. They needed to hash out their feelings for each other. He needed to tell her what he'd realized earlier in the evening.

I'm falling in love with you.

He didn't know if she was ready to hear the words or not. Hell, he didn't know if he was ready to say them or if any of this was even real. They'd only met a few weeks ago. It seemed crazy to think he could go from fighting in the Middle East to falling in love with a woman in so short a time, yet there it was.

Her truck was still parked out in front. That was a relief. He'd been worried she'd leave on the off chance he might stop by. It surprised him that she hadn't. Then again, maybe this was part of her plan.

See you later.

Had it been an invitation?

When she swung her front door open he knew that it hadn't.

"What are you doing here?"

Okay. So she really *had* ditched him. She really didn't want to see him. Fine. "We need to talk."

He might not be able to buy her dinner, but he could get to the bottom of her cold shoulder.

"About what?"

He took off his cowboy hat, holding it in front of him like a shield. "About why you had a hard time saying two words to me all day? And why you just ditched me. Are you mad at me or something?"

"No." She lifted her chin, her black hair falling over her white T-shirt. She'd changed out of pink and she looked super sexy in a sleeveless tank top loose around her waist but low enough that he had a hard time keeping his gaze on her face. She still wore the jeans, but he suddenly found himself wishing he could peel them off.

"Then what was the problem?"

She shrugged. "I was nervous about my son riding."

Bull. He almost said that very thing except he suddenly noticed that she fidgeted with the door handle. She twisted it back and forth and back and forth. It even slipped from her grasp with a loud *snick*. She gave him a faux smile and went back to twisting it again.

It dawned on him then with a certainty that drove him to take a step closer. He knew what bothered her, and it had nothing to do with fear for her son. Her problem was with *him*.

"Adam was in good hands." He took another step closer.

Her voice sounded raspy as she said, "Adam has been sick."

Another step. Her eyes flicked left and then right, as if she sought to escape. "But he's not sick anymore."

"Technically, he is because he's still not officially in remission."

"Shush."

"Excuse me?" But she held her ground. He saw it then, the spark of excitement in her eyes. She might pretend indifference, but she was far from that.

"We've been over this a million times before."

"I know, so there's nothing left to say."

"I know that," he said, stepping inside her home before she could close the door on him, and tossing his hat onto the coatrack that stood by the door. "And I agree with you. We shouldn't talk."

"What do you mean?"

"We should do something else."

"Ethan—"

"Are you going to deny you have feelings for me?"

She lifted her chin. "How I feel is irrelevant."

"No, it's not."

He clasped her face between his palms. She tried to pull back, but not very hard. Oh, no. Her eyes invited him closer.

"Shh," he said again, and then he kissed her.

She'd gone completely still, but that was okay because it gave him time to caress those silky soft lips with his own, to sip the taste of her: honey and vanilla. That was what she tasted like. He wasn't content to lightly taste her, though. He wanted all of her and so he tipped his head a bit, increased the pressure, all the while still cupping her jaw with his hands.

She collapsed.

That was how it felt. Her body melted into his, and he found himself dropping his hands to her waist, propping her up. Her mouth opened beneath his, and then

her tongue touched his own and it nearly killed him.
The smell of her. The taste of her. The way she brushed
up against him. The tips of her breasts pressed against
his chest and he wanted to bend down and taste each
one of them, but he didn't.

He broke off the kiss, tipped his head back. "Lord,"
he heard himself say. "You're going to kill me."

She breathed hard, too. He could feel those breasts
touch him and then retreat, touch him and then retreat,
the sensation both erotic and frustrating. As if sensing
the direction of his thoughts she shifted in his arms. He
thought she might move away, gave her every opportunity to do so, but she didn't.

"What are you doing to me?" She rested her head
against his chest.

"Kissing you," he answered.

*Fantasizing about you. Thinking about what it'd be
like to do so much more than merely kiss you. Wanting to touch you in places that would make you groan
again.* But he didn't say that.

"No." She reared back to look at him. "It's so much
more than that."

She felt it, too, then, he realized. She felt the emotions building between them. It wasn't just sexual attraction.

"Claire," he said, cupping her jaw again, and she
didn't move away. No, she tipped her head so that she
pressed her cheek into his palm, like a contented cat. He
grew brave then, bent to kiss her again. She watched his
head lower. He saw her pupils dilate in anticipation, but
she didn't move away. When their lips connected, she
kissed him back and he knew what he wanted then. It
wasn't just to be with her. He wanted to be one with her.

To love her. To bring her joy and pleasure and happiness as she'd never known before. It was a need as fierce as the one he'd felt to fight for his country.

"Where's your bedroom?"

She pointed behind them. Her cheeks were flushed. Her eyes were soft and she was the sexiest damn thing he'd ever seen.

"Let's go."

Chapter 15

What was she doing?

You're going to have sex.

The answer was as clear and as simple and as firm as that. She was going to go to bed with Ethan McCall and she wasn't going to regret it. She was going to revel in what it felt like to be touched by a man once again because, damn it all, it'd been far too long.

"Do you have protection?" he asked, stopping by the side of her bed.

"No." She'd had no need of birth control, not when she didn't plan on sleeping with anyone. "Do you?"

He shook his head.

She didn't want to get pregnant, although as she did the mental math she figured she should be okay. Still, that wasn't the point. It mattered.

She just didn't care.

Her whole body tingled. Not just the center of her. Everything, everywhere, all over. She wanted him and the release that would come from being with him and damn the consequences.

"I guess I should ask if I need to be worried about you."

He shook his head. "I've been overseas for months, and I don't make a habit of using my leave to chase down women. It's been a long time for me, too."

The confession, coming as it did from such a handsome man, should have surprised her. Somehow it didn't. He didn't seem the type to mess around. He seemed the type to want to care first.

"Then I guess I'm not worried."

"Good," he said, his hand reaching out and sliding under her shirt. She didn't wear a bra. Had he known that? If he didn't he knew it now because her nipples contracted the moment his fingers brushed her belly. The tingling turned into ripples of pleasure, and she closed her eyes as she allowed him to touch her, all of her, her shirt sliding off her shoulders with her barely noticing.

"I've been wanting to kiss you like this for days."

She felt the brush of his breath, knew what he was about to do and arched into him in anticipation because the ripples had intensified. Something soft yet sharp captured the tip of her and she moaned.

"Just like this," he said, circling her with his tongue.

Somehow she found herself backed up against the bed although she had no idea if he'd guided her there or if she'd moved. He kept kissing her, though, and it made her grow weak at the knees to the point that she sank onto the bed. He didn't follow her down. He simply stared at her and the look in his eyes made her feel so sexy and so wanted that she didn't hesitate to unsnap her jeans, and then lower the zipper. Her underwear followed the pants. He did the same, first pulling his shirt out of the waistband of his jeans, then unbuttoning his pink shirt. She'd never seen him so naked before and she realized then how fit a body he had. The wounds on his arms had long since healed, but they did nothing to detract from the physical splendor that was Ethan.

He drew his jeans down next, kneeling to pull them over his feet, which had been stripped of their boots at some point although she didn't recall him taking them off.

"Slip on over," he said softly.

It was the moment of truth. They were both naked, and once she moved he would be on the bed with her. This wonderful, glorious man would make love to her. It would be only the second time she'd been with a man since Marcus.

Don't think about that.

He slid down next to her, on his belly, his shoulders so wide and so big she found herself reaching out and touching them. He touched her, too, her face, swiping a lock of hair off her cheek.

"So beautiful," he said.

No, she wasn't. Her nose was too big and her mouth too wide. She hated how little her breasts were and she felt as if she had monster thighs.

He didn't appear to notice. No. He looked into her eyes, not at her body.

"So very, very beautiful," he said.

He talked about her soul. It melted her heart in a way that made her eyes warm with tears. That was the last thought she had before the ripples of pleasure took over again, and desire replaced thought because he leaned toward her and kissed her. She opened her mouth to him immediately and it all became a jumble. His hand on her thigh. Her tongue brushing his lips. His fingers trailing a path to her center. She didn't want him to wait, but he took his time. His mouth moved off her own, soft lips brushing her neck and then her collarbone, his hand cupping her and causing her to cry out in pleasure. He worked her like a master craftsman, her body clay in his hands as he molded her and touched her and turned her desire into a frenzy.

"Ethan."

He must have heard the frustration in her voice because he moved. She felt his knee nudge her and she didn't hesitate as she welcomed him home.

"Oh, sweet heaven," she thought she heard him mutter.

He filled her perfectly and she thought she might die of pleasure right there and then, but he refused to hurry. She tried to edge him on, lifted her hips, pressed him down into her, and yet he took her gently and slowly and she wanted to cry all over again at how perfect it all felt.

Her soft sighs turned into moans and her moans into cries of pleasure. Her hips matched his slow rhythm and it was as if they'd been together before. He knew exactly how to move and when to slow down and when to speed up and as she drew closer and closer to her breaking point, he knew when to let her go.

"Claire," he cried out.

She followed the sound of his voice, landing on the sweet side of pleasure, her cry of release so loud she knew she should feel shame. No, she silently amended as she slowly drifted back into the reality of his arms, not shame. Wonder. And delight. And something else she couldn't identify, a something that caused a sharp jolt of fear, but she thrust that something back down before it could take over her thoughts. What she wanted right now was to hold Ethan. To sleep for a while held in a man's arms. She'd missed that for so long.

"Here," he said, shifting so that she could move to the side and he could hold her tight.

"Thank you."

Is that what you say to men these days? she wondered. What was the protocol after you'd just had mind-blowing sex with someone you'd met less than two months ago? She didn't know, and at that moment, she didn't care. Her lids grew heavy and she didn't want to fight the sleep that tried to claim her. For once in her life she didn't want to fight at all. She was tired of doing battle. She wanted to rest and to be held and to feel as if she hadn't a care in the world.

So she slept.

And Ethan held her. He doubted she felt him kiss the top of her head. Knew she had no idea that he drew back a bit and stared into her face, studying her, memorizing her.

What am I going to do with you? he silently asked. *You're going to fight this. I know you are.*

But he was a soldier, a warrior. Someone who didn't fear combat, even when the war about to be waged was simply a battle to win a woman's heart.

She dreamed she was at the ocean and Marcus, no, Ethan was there with her. They were frolicking in the ocean and water lapped at her calves.

She awoke with a start.

Ethan still held her. His toes were twitching as he slept, his legs entwined with hers so that she felt the movement on the back of her leg. It was daylight outside.

Adam.

She had no idea when he'd be home this morning. In the old days, back when she'd had "date night" with Marcus and Chance had been out on leave her brother wouldn't bring him back without calling first. But it'd been a while since she and Adam had been apart and she wondered if he'd miss her and what he'd say if he knew Ethan had spent the night.

That she couldn't deal with right now. Right now she needed to get up and get dressed. But first shower. Definitely shower.

She moved slowly, for some reason not wanting to awaken Ethan. No. That wasn't true. She didn't want to talk right now. She needed time to absorb what had just happened, to figure out where it left her and what it might mean. He'd been such a tender and gentle lover. At one point she'd found herself crying at the beauty of it all, but looming in the back of her mind, always there in the after moments, were thoughts about the morning and what would happen then.

Somehow she managed to extricate herself without him noticing. She scurried to the bathroom, listening for signs that he'd awoken as she waited for the water to warm. She caught a glimpse of herself in the mirror, fingered her swollen lips, tried to straighten her wild hair, checked to make sure there were no marks on the side of her neck where the scruff of his chin had rubbed her raw, or so it had seemed. She saw no evidence of their lovemaking.

So she showered to help clear her mind. She emerged from it feeling grateful that if Adam arrived home now, she would be reasonably presentable. Of course, there was the matter of the sleeping man in her bed.

She attempted to rectify that problem the moment she pulled on clothes. Goodness knew why, but she tiptoed to the bedside, about to shake him awake when she paused to simply stare. He appeared to be dreaming, and not a good dream, either, based on the way he twitched and flicked his head from side to side. She watched, wondering if she should wake him. Clearly that was what he suffered from, because his movements became more jerky and more frantic until she couldn't stop herself.

"Ethan."

Green eyes popped open. They instantly found hers, his face going from frightened to puzzled to understanding.

"Damn." He quickly sat up, and then shifted so he sat on the side of the bed. "Thanks."

"Are you okay?"

He rested his elbows on his knees, rubbed his temple. "Nightmare."

"Figured as much."

"What time is it?"

"Seven." He nodded and she wondered if he had bad dreams on a regular basis. "I was going to wake you up anyway. I'm not sure what time Adam will be back."

He scrubbed the sleep out of his eyes and she found that gesture adorable. "Yeah. Good. I should probably get a move on."

He started to stand and she retreated like a frightened cat. He froze for a moment and she realized he'd noticed, but didn't say anything.

She turned away, murmuring, "I'll make breakfast." Something about the terror she'd glimpsed in his eyes tore at her heart. He wasn't over his time in the Middle East. Not by a long shot. "There's a fresh towel in the bathroom. Feel free to use my shampoo and whatever else you want."

She called the words out over her shoulder because she didn't want to see him standing there naked. It seemed so silly to be suddenly shy around him, not after all they'd done, but it was different this morning. Last night had been magical. Today, reality.

Which leaves you exactly where? she asked herself.

She didn't know. Didn't want to think about it. Breakfast first. Then maybe she'd be able to think clearer.

He entered the kitchen as she was sliding fried eggs onto plates. The toast was already done and the smell of bacon filled the air. Once upon a time he'd cooked for her. Funny. That seemed like a lifetime ago.

"I could get used to this," he said as he took a seat. And he looked better. More himself. Less shaky. He still had his five-o'clock shadow and she was struck by the notion once again of just how much he looked like a younger version of George Clooney with his salt-and-pepper hair.

"Mom!"

She froze. Ethan didn't. He just took the plate and sat down at the table.

"Mo-om."

"In here," she called back.

Adam arrived at the doorway to the kitchen, looking

adorable and a little boyish with a crooked smile on his face that melted her heart. To her utter shock, he didn't bat an eye when he spotted Ethan sitting at the table, just said, "I'm hungry. What's to eat?"

She froze with her own plate in her hand. "I, um…"

Ethan caught her gaze, smiled. "I just made fried eggs."

"Yum." He went to the kitchen table and sat down. "Uncle Colt only had cereal at his place. I was hungry for real food. Natalie offered to make it for me, but she only does the scrambled eggs and I don't like that."

She almost laughed. It was as if Ethan wasn't even there. No. That wasn't right. Her son smiled in the man's direction. "Hey, Ethan."

"Mornin', Adam."

"Can I have a fried egg, Mom?"

"Sure." She handed her son her own plate. "I'll make another."

"Cool."

And that was that. No funny looks. No curious comments. No awkward questions.

The knot in her stomach eased a bit.

Of course he might think Ethan had arrived early in the morning, as he often did. Her son probably had no idea he'd spent the night. That made more sense than anything else. She'd been worried over nothing.

Her son munched on a strip of bacon. "The rodeo was awesome. Colt said I can do it again at another rodeo if I want."

She didn't know what to say other than, "Oh. Well, yeah. I guess."

"Gonna ride Playboy again later today." Her son looked up. "If that's okay with you."

There it was again, the familiar urge to tell him no, to

hand him the excuse that he was too weak or not ready or unable to handle the physical exertion. It was hard, but she somehow managed to say, "That sounds fine."

She was rewarded with a smile that made her throat tighten.

"Why don't we all go riding?" Ethan said.

"Yeah." Adam gobbled down another bite, then said, "Can we, Mom?"

Claire looked up. She shot Ethan a look that clearly expressed her opinion of the idea, and it wasn't favorable. Ethan just smiled, and oddly, she suddenly wanted to smile, too. Wretch.

"After we feed the dogs and work Thor," Ethan said.

"Cool. I'll go text Uncle Colt."

He was off like a shot, and Claire was surprised to realize he'd finished his breakfast. He left silence behind, but it was comfortable and Claire didn't mind because she was able to finish her own breakfast, Ethan watching her take every bite. It was both erotic and annoying to feel his gaze upon her, but she did her best not to let him see.

"You don't have to go with us if you don't want to," he said when she finished.

"No." She set her dishes in the sink. "I can tolerate riding one more time."

He nodded, smiled. "Good. Why don't you meet me in an hour or so? That'll give me time to finish my chores for your brother, too."

"Sounds good."

"I was actually wanting to take Thor on a ride, if that's okay, to test him. See if he's ready for the big outdoors. I figure if he runs I have a better shot at catching him on a horse."

"You probably would."

"So you're okay with that?"

"Of course."

"Good." He got up, and before she could say another word, pinned her to the counter with his arms on either side. "I'll see you later, then."

The ripples struck with a force that left her breathless. "Later," she echoed.

She thought he would kiss her, but he didn't. Instead he brushed his lips against her neck. Just a light touch but it was enough to make her knees weak.

He left her standing there, wilting against the countertop. She heard him leave the house, saw him head toward the kennels out of her kitchen window. She felt herself move then. She didn't recall making the decision to watch him, but she did, smiling at the way Thor spotted him the minute he stepped outside, and the way the dog got up and headed toward the entrance. A minute later they both emerged, Thor's tail wagging, a canine grin on his face.

The dog worshipped Ethan. It was so obvious. Equally obvious was Ethan's affection for Thor. He reached down, scrubbed a hand through his fur, playfully grabbed an ear. Thor loved it. She watched the two and just smiled.

She could love Ethan.

The thought landed like a brick. She staggered back from the counter.

"Mom. What's wrong?"

She turned away from the window, wiped a tear from her eyes she hadn't even known had fallen. "Nothing, kiddo."

"Did Ethan leave?"

"He's outside working with Thor, but he said to meet him in about an hour."

"I'm going outside to help him, then."

"Sure."

But her son stared at her funny. "I like him, Mom."

She wasn't going to say anything, just nod, but instead she heard herself say, "I like him, too, honey."

And it scared the hell out of her.

Chapter 16

His cell phone rang the moment he entered his apartment above the barn. It startled him because he'd forgotten he had the thing with him.

"Dr. Ethan McCall?" asked a voice after he answered.

"Affirmative," Ethan answered, the response automatic after all his years in the military.

"This is Lance Kittrick."

It took him a moment to place the name, and when he did, he jerked upright. "Mr. Kittrick, it's an honor."

The man was a legend in the world of combat dogs. One of the few known breeders of Belgian Malinois in the States. His training facility in Montana was world-renowned, too—police officers, military personnel and private contractors were regular customers. He'd applied there on a whim even though he knew they kept a veterinarian on retainer already, but he'd thought maybe he could get his foot in the door, to do what he really wanted to do, which was get into the business of breeding and training military dogs. He could learn from the best while still practicing medicine, move in with his parents if he had to.

"Actually, the honor's all mine, Major."

"Not major anymore, sir. It's just Dr. McCall."

"Well, Dr. McCall, we were glad to receive your résumé."

He'd sent out a bunch when he'd arrived at the ranch, back before he'd realized how much living at Misfit Farms suited him. And now with Claire in his life…

"Yes, sir. About that. My situation has changed. I'm working for a farm and I'm not going to lie, I'd like to stay here."

For as long as Claire would have him. With any luck, she felt the same way, too.

"Really?" said Mr. Kittrick. "That's too bad. Your résumé came at the perfect time. Our staff veterinarian has decided he'd like to retire and so we're starting to put out feelers for a new one. With your military experience and connections, you'd be a perfect addition to our outfit."

He wouldn't be human if he didn't feel a twinge of regret. What were the odds that he'd be offered his dream job at this point in his life? When he'd first gotten back home he'd have jumped at the chance; now all he did was hold on to the phone tighter. It was a dream job, but he couldn't take it. It would mean leaving Claire…

"When would you be looking to hire someone?"

"Soon, and before you say no again, why don't I fly you out here so you can look over the place? I think you'd be pleased with what we've got. Plus, your cover letter said you wanted to learn how to train."

"Yes, sir. I know the basics, but I've never done it professionally."

"Well, son, that's our specialty, as I'm sure you know." The man paused to let his words sink in. "Look, I'm not going to lie. When I got your résumé I put it aside, thinking if something came up we'd give you a call. I had no idea our doc was thinking of retiring. He'd mentioned it but I didn't think he meant right away. Took me by surprise last week when he sat me down and broke the news, but then I thought about your résumé. You're my first call."

He took a deep breath, glanced out the window, at Misfit Farms and the horses in the pasture and the way the sun made the mountains in the distance look like something an artist would paint.

"Can I get back to you?"

"Sure, sure," Mr. Kittrick said. "Why don't you think about it for a couple days? I'll hold off making any more phone calls until I hear back from you."

He released the breath. "I'd appreciate that, sir."

When he hung up he realized his hands were shaking again, but for a different reason this time. Come to think of it, he hadn't felt anxious in over a week. He had Claire to thank for that. She'd shown him the true meaning of bravery in the face of adversity. Yes, he'd lost his best friend, but like Claire, he would stand strong.

He couldn't leave her.

Still, when Claire showed up with Adam and Thor in tow, his mind was a million miles away. What would it hurt if he flew out there and took a look? There was nothing wrong with a long-distance relationship. It would mean making adjustments, but if anyone could handle the strain of an out-of-state boyfriend, it would be Claire. She'd been a military wife.

"Thor, hey," he said, greeting the dog. Not that the animal could hear him but he was pretty certain Thor could read the expression on his face and maybe even his mouth. "Ready?"

"I hope he doesn't run away," Claire said.

"He won't."

"Let's go!" Adam shouted, running to the pasture where his horse was kept.

"He's been like this all morning."

Ethan nodded, motioning for Thor to sit. "He likes riding."

"He likes swimming even better and that's what he plans to do once he gets to the stock pond."

Did he tell her? Or should he keep the news to himself? He honestly didn't know.

"I'll go get your horse," he offered.

"No. It's okay. You've got Thor. I can get Blue myself."

He didn't argue. Plus, keeping busy gave him time to think. Thor followed him to his horse's side. He worried about how the dog would react with the horse, but Thor hung back as Ethan went to work brushing and saddling. When he emerged from the barn a few moments later he was happy to see Thor following. The dog never took his eyes off him.

"Where'd you put your swim trunks?" he was just in time to hear Claire ask Adam.

"In here." Adam pointed to saddlebags he must have found in the tack room.

"You ready?" she asked Ethan next.

"Let's go."

Claire mounted up and so did Ethan, and when he was on board, he motioned for Thor to heel. The dog didn't hesitate.

"That's a good sign."

Ethan nodded. Thor would be okay. He cued his horse to move forward. Adam rode up alongside him and he was like a different kid, Ethan noticed. The boy he'd been when Ethan had arrived had still been recovering from cancer treatment. This boy was alive and well and full of youthful enthusiasm.

"Thor sure is behaving," the boy observed.

"He is."

Who would work with the dog if he left?

"What's wrong?" Claire asked, riding up to him.

How had she so easily gleaned that the thought of leaving Thor, of leaving them all, had him distracted? He inhaled deeply, trying to clear his thoughts. The familiar scent of leather and horse should be a comfort to him, but it wasn't. It was both a comfort and a curse because it was yet another reminder of what he would miss if he left. No more horseback rides with Claire.

"Ethan?"

Adam seemed oblivious. The boy was already halfway to the gate.

"I had a phone call just before you arrived."

She sat up straighter in the saddle. "What kind of call?"

He clucked his horse forward so they were side by side. "From a potential employer. In Montana."

Her face actually twitched as if she'd been hit. "You're leaving?"

"Just for a few days." It wasn't until that moment

that he realized he wanted to go and at least check out the place. "I'll be there and back before you know it."

"Come on, you guys." They both turned to Adam, who waited by the gate. He waved them forward. "We don't got all day."

Claire clucked her horse forward, and he knew she wasn't happy, but he really couldn't blame her. The whole scope of their relationship had changed last night and here he was less than twenty-four hours later talking about leaving.

"It's just a quick trip."

She nodded, but she wouldn't look at him. "So you're considering the job, then?"

"No. Well, maybe. I don't know."

"And what about your commitment to my brother and his wife?"

He glanced at Thor to ensure the dog was still with him. He was. "That was always just a temporary thing."

"So you've never planned on sticking around?"

"It's not like I'm saying yes to the job."

"But you're considering it."

He felt as if he was back on the front lines, afraid of making a wrong step and potentially blowing everything up. "I think it's smart to keep my options open."

"So you *are* considering it?"

Okay. This conversation was going nowhere fast. He wished he could change the subject, except he knew he'd never get away with that.

"Claire, I can't keep mooching off your brother."

She pulled her horse up. "You're not mooching. Just the other day he was saying what a big help you are around here. Not only that, but you've made it clear you're happy here, that you were considering staying."

He stopped, too, making sure Thor did the same. The dog instantly sat near his horse's shoulder. "I'm a veterinarian, not a stable boy."

"And you'll be doing veterinarian work once you start Misfit Farm's breeding program."

"That's just looking through a microscope and palpating mares, and dealing with a single stallion. Honestly, a vet tech could do that."

"And what about that offer from Mariah Johnson? She was hoping you could cover for her while she's out on maternity leave."

"That's months away. She has plenty of time to find someone else."

"So you really are leaving, then."

"I don't know!" He hadn't meant to say the words so loud, but a quick glance at Adam revealed the kid's eyes were wide. He stood by the gate, watching the adults, a frown quickly replacing his smile.

"You've done the long-distance relationship thing before, Claire. I didn't think it'd be a big deal if I proposed the same idea now."

She glanced at Ethan, too, and he had to strain to hear her when she said, "Is that what we're in? A relationship?"

He didn't like the way she said the words, nor the look on her face. It wasn't that she was angry, it was more that she seemed hurt, so much so that she softened his own voice. "Of course it is."

He saw her hands tighten on the reins. She stared straight ahead and suddenly all he wanted to do was pull her into his arms, except he couldn't.

"I was young when I first met Marcus. Too young. I honestly think part of my attraction to him was that he could take me away from all this." She motioned with her hand toward the farm. "But now I'm older and I like my life and I love where I live. I could never leave this ranch."

"I'm not asking you to."

"And I don't know that I'm willing to be in a relationship with someone who lives halfway across the country. I would want more."

Adam must have sensed the need for the two adults to have some privacy because he left the gate open and started to ride on. Ethan was surprised Claire didn't call him back, but maybe she didn't notice. She stared down at her saddle and she seemed so sad all of a sudden that he shifted his weight and placed a hand on her thigh.

"It's just a scouting mission. I may not even like the place."

"And if you do? What then?"

"We'll talk about it."

She lifted her head, watched her son ride off, and Ethan could see the play of emotions on her face. She took a deep breath and he saw the sadness deepen and in that moment he wanted to pull the words back, to unsay what he'd said, to ease her pain, except he couldn't.

"You know, when I first met you I didn't want to like you." Her thumb absently toyed with her reins. "I was attracted to you right from the get-go. Getting involved with you scared the hell out of me."

"I know."

"But you want to know what scares me more?" She turned and pinned him with a stare. "The thought of you leaving."

"Claire—"

"No." She lifted a hand. "Let me finish. I care for

you, Ethan. After last night, I'm no longer in denial. I'm not the type to jump into bed with someone without it meaning something afterward. And you're right. I was a military wife once before, but I met and married Marcus while he was in the States. It happened fast." She smiled wryly. "I'm starting to think that's a habit of mine. I don't fall slow and easy. I fall hard."

What was she saying?

"But I'm older and wiser now. I know what I want, and a long-distance relationship isn't it."

He knew what she tried to tell him then. If he stayed she would commit to him 100 percent. And if he didn't…

"It wouldn't be like I was in the military," he felt the need to point out. "I'd be able to fly back and forth on a regular basis. You'd be able to come and see me."

"And who would take care of my place?"

He glanced at the house to their left. "Your brother."

She shook her head. "I've had enough of that. My brother probably has, too. No, Ethan. A long-distance relationship won't work for me. Not anymore. I'm too old for that. Too set in my ways. It's me or…"

Nothing.

She didn't need to say the word. He understood. But he wasn't going to argue. It might all be a moot point. He just wanted to go look. To meet a man who was a legend in the military dog world. And if something happened and he ended up wanting to take the job, he would have to change her mind.

He just wasn't certain he could.

Chapter 17

He left two days later. Ethan didn't know it, but she watched him drive away. She'd taken Thor out, had walked the dog far away so that he couldn't see them standing there, watching from the line of trees.

"He'll be back," she told Thor, who whined. He knew his master was leaving. She didn't know how he knew. It wasn't as if he could hear the sound of Ethan's car. Or that he even knew what car Ethan drove since he walked over most of the time. Yet somehow the dog knew his favorite human had left.

She walked back the long way around. And even though it was a weekday, Misfit Farms was a hive of activity. Natalie had an assistant trainer working for her now, a former student who'd gone on to success in the hunter/jumper world, and Laney waved hello when she spotted her walking past.

"Hey, Claire," she called, pulling up the horse she schooled next to the rail in the covered arena. "You're up early."

She waved back. "Needed some fresh air."

"Claire," someone called to her right. She turned to see Natalie standing at the entrance to the barn. Colt was there, too, the couple waving her over. "We were just talking about you," Natalie added.

Uh-oh. That boded ill. Colt had a sixth sense when it came to her emotions. There'd been so many times when they'd been growing up when their dad had been cruel to her in some small way and Colt had come home just knowing.

"Do you have a second?" Colt asked.

"Sure," she said with a glance down at Thor. The dog's big ears were aimed at Natalie, as if he tried to hear her words, and when he couldn't he glanced up at her. "Come," she mouthed, motioning with her hand for him to heel.

Her brother and Natalie had an office overlooking the covered arena. She entered the Western-themed room and marveled at how much had changed in the space of a year. They had pictures of Laney, the teen with a passion for horses, on the wall. She'd grown six inches since Natalie had started working with her, making her the perfect big equitation rider, which Natalie claimed was a gift from the gods. There was win photo after win photo on the wall, all mixed in with pictures of Colt and Natalie riding.

"Sit down."

The feeling that something serious was about to be said only intensified. She took a seat on the leather couch that hugged the same wall as the one the door was set into. They leaned against the edge of the oak desk that took up the other wall.

"Will I need a stiff drink?" she asked.

Natalie and Colt exchanged glances. Those gazes held for a moment and she watched as the look on Natalie's face softened in a way she'd never seen before. And even though they were both in profile, she clearly saw the gleam of excitement in their eyes. It was Natalie who turned toward her and said softly, gently, "We're pregnant."

And Claire just sat there, dumbfounded, the word repeating over and over in her head. "Pregnant?" she repeated.

Natalie nodded.

"Oh, my goodness, are you serious?"

Colt nodded this time, and Claire couldn't breathe. No. That wasn't true. She could breathe. It was just her throat was thick with tears. Happy tears, she told herself, and she was happy. Thrilled.

"That's great, you guys." She wiped at her eyes. "I'm so happy for you."

Natalie and Colt exchanged glances.

"We wanted to wait to catch you alone," Natalie said. "So you could tell Adam in your own way. We weren't sure how he would take the news."

"Are you kidding? He'll be thrilled." And the tears kept coming. In fact, she had to work to regulate her breathing because all of a sudden, she felt like sobbing. "That's amazing news."

"Then why are you crying?" Colt asked.

She thought about playing dumb, but she'd never been anything but honest with her brother and sister-in-law. "I don't know."

And then she did bawl. She bawled like a baby, which was horrible because they'd just shared some fantastic news and she felt as if she'd just lost her best friend and she had no idea why.

"Claire," her brother said gently. She hadn't even noticed when he'd moved to stand in front of her. "What is it, sis? Is it Adam? Did a blood test reveal some bad news?"

She shook her head, so blinded by her tears she had to keep wiping at her eyes. "No." And the word had come out sounding like a wail and she was mortified because she had never, not once in all the years, sounded so pitiful. Not when Marcus had come back from the Middle East sick. Not when she'd realized he was going to die. Not even when Adam had been diagnosed with cancer.

What was wrong with her?

"Maybe you two should have a moment alone."

"No, stay," she said, grabbing Natalie's hand as she tried to pass. Her sister-in-law's face was a mask of concern and it was humiliating, because this wasn't about Claire. This should be about her brother and his wife.

"I'm thrilled for you," she said. "I really am. I can't wait to be an aunt." She hoped they saw how sincerely she meant the words, because she knew there was a time when Colt didn't even want children. The fact that he was expecting his first child, and that he clearly brimmed with pride over the whole thing, was a sign of how much he loved his wife and what a beautiful marriage they had.

"We know you're happy for us," Natalie said gently.

Claire scrubbed at her eyes again. "It's just been one of those days."

"Is it because Ethan left?" Colt asked. "Is that why you're crying?"

"No," she said quickly, emphatically. "This has nothing to do with that."

"Did you fall in love with him?" Natalie asked.

"No. Of course not." How could she fall in love with a man in a matter of weeks? "It's not like that."

Her brother and his wife exchanged glances again, and it was Colt who said, "Are you sure?"

"Well, I mean I'm sad that he's gone. But he'll be back."

But she knew how much he wanted to train dogs. It was a big deal that he'd been invited east to meet Lance Kittrick. Even she knew who the man was. She wouldn't blame him if he *did* want to leave and take a job with him. She was just sad, was all, sad that he'd be moving on.

Because you've fallen for him.

No, she firmly told herself. She cared for him deeply, but love? No.

"What will you do if he wants the job?" Natalie asked.

"What do you mean what will I do?" She had better control of herself now. The tears had faded, thank God. "Nothing. He needs to make his own choices."

Choices that wouldn't involve her. That was what made her sad. She'd thought they were headed someplace with their relationship, but then the very first time he'd been offered an opportunity to leave, he'd jumped at it. It hurt, damn it. She wouldn't lie to herself.

"Congratulations," she said, getting up and hugging Natalie. Hard. "Really. I can't wait to hold my new niece or nephew." She hugged her brother next, only he didn't let her go.

"I love you, sis," she heard him say.

She got weepy again. "I know."

"I'm here if you need me."

"I know. Thanks." But she didn't need any man. She'd just forgotten that, but she remembered it now. It was something she would not forget, not ever again.

He drove home slowly.

Home.

Funny how that was what he called Misfit Farms in his head. Was it home? He couldn't deny that as he pulled into the main drive he felt his heart accelerate. He wanted to see Claire, to share with her the details of his trip, to tell her how much of a thrill it'd been to meet Lance Kittrick and to tour his state-of-the-art ranch.

He drove straight to her place. She wasn't home, though, her van missing from the driveway. Thor was glad to see him. He could hear the dog's cries from Claire's front yard and their reunion a few seconds later solidified in Ethan's head that he wanted to adopt the dog. He'd been meaning to talk to Claire about it for a few weeks now, had meant to tell her about it on the day of that disastrous trail ride. But she'd clammed up on him after he'd broken the news about his potential job offer and the timing hadn't felt right. He would rectify that situation the moment he saw her, he vowed, bending down and scratching Thor's thick, black head. He'd missed the dog. Missed this place.

Missed Claire.

He wasn't going to take the job. He wanted to. Lord,

how he wanted to, but his absence from the ranch had made him realize just how much he loved the place.

"What do you think, boy? You think I should stick around?"

Thor tried to lick his face. He smiled and scratched his head. He hung out for a little while longer; put Thor through his paces. He half hoped Claire would show up, and when she didn't, he reluctantly put Thor away. He thought maybe she might be over at her brother's, but she wasn't there, either.

"She went to go pick up another dog," Colt explained the next morning when Ethan arrived to help him feed. "She won't be back until tomorrow."

Was it his imagination, or was the look on Colt's face one of disappointment? It'd dawned a chilly morning thanks to coastal fog that had reached its smudgy gray fingers inland, but the cold in the barn aisle was echoed in Colt's eyes.

"Really?" he asked curiously. "I'm surprised she didn't mention it to me."

"Why would she, when she wasn't even sure you were coming back?"

Ethan almost flinched at the sharpness of Colt's words. "Is that what she said?"

"No," Colt admitted.

Clearly, that was what everyone thought. "I'm not going to move to Montana."

Some of the animosity faded. "You're not."

"I thought about it, but in the end California has something Montana doesn't."

"What's that?"

"Your sister."

Colt's face went completely still, but then he smiled

a bit, a wry kind of smile but also one tinged by approval. "I'm glad to hear that."

"I care too much for your sister to leave."

"Good, because I'm pretty sure she's halfway in love with you."

Ethan tipped his head because he couldn't have heard him right. "What?"

"She won't admit it. Cried like a baby right there in the office that day you left."

"She did?"

Colt nodded. "Told us she was 'just emotional,' which I know she was." And then Colt's smile took on the intensity of headlights. "My wife is pregnant."

Ethan didn't even hesitate. He moved forward, held out his hand. "Wow, man. That's awesome."

"Yes, it is." Colt's swiped a hand through his dark hair. "We weren't really trying, either, so it's a little surreal."

"You're going to be a great dad."

Colt's smile lost some of its luster. "I just hope I can be half the parent my sister is."

"Adam's a great kid."

"She would do anything to protect him."

"I know."

"She deserves to be happy."

"She's the reason I came back to California."

"Just make sure she knows that."

Chapter 18

It was a good trip, Claire told herself repeatedly as she drove through Via Del Caballo's darkened streets. She'd picked up another dog to re-home and she'd dropped off a dog to a new family. That was the best part of her job and the reason she'd pulled every string she knew to become one of the rare kennels in the United States approved to re-home MWDs.

Marcus would be proud.

She tried not to think about Marcus and the shame she felt at having slept with Ethan. That was why she'd been such an emotional wreck the other day. She'd slept with a man and she'd had feelings afterward, serious feelings, and she didn't know what to do about that.

Colt had told her Ethan was back. Of course, she'd known that. He'd texted her and called. She'd ignored him. Colt had also told her Ethan had said he didn't want the job back in Montana, something she was pretty sure Ethan wanted to tell her himself. She hadn't given him the chance. She should have been relieved. Happy. Thrilled. Instead she felt scared, anxious and upset.

"Mom, I'm tired," Adam muttered sleepily as they passed between the electronic gates.

That was the other bit of good news. While they'd been down south, they'd seen his oncologist. Adam had had another blood test and scans, and the results had been good. Zero cancer cells. Normal white blood cell levels. No growths. No evidence of disease, the doctor had said.

Remission.

It was within their reach. Oh, he would still need to see his oncologist on a regular basis, but those visits would get further and further apart until he wouldn't have to go at all. Eventually. A long time in his future.

The future.

She didn't want to think about that, or the fact that Ethan was back at the ranch, and that she would have to talk to him and tell him—

What?

She felt her eyes begin to fill with tears all over again, and it made her mad because she had nothing, absolutely nothing to cry about and yet that was all she'd been doing since he'd left for Montana. Lord, she still couldn't believe she'd turned into a blubbering fool when Colt had told her they were expecting a child. She'd completely humiliated herself, and she felt horribly guilty because the news should have been a joyous occasion and instead she'd acted like a crazy woman.

Somehow she got Adam into bed without waking him. It meant carrying him to his room and forcing him into his jammies before tucking him beneath the sheets, the new dog she'd brought home having to wait in the back of the van. Since it was night outside and cool, she didn't worry. Instead she took a moment to observe Adam's sweet, innocent face illuminated by the night-light in the corner of his Hawkman-themed bedroom.

Remission.

His blood work was news that should make her cry, except it didn't. She hadn't even told Colt or Chance yet.

With a kiss on the forehead she headed back outside. The new dog greeted her with a canine smile and a wag of his tail.

"Come here, Fido."

That was really the dog's name. A joke on the part of the breeder, no doubt, but it didn't make her smile. Not tonight.

She went to work, switching on the kennel lights, making sure the new dog had water. Watching, once she turned Fido loose in Janus's old kennel, to make sure he got along with the other dogs. When she was done, she went up to the animal.

"I hope you enjoy your new digs." She patted the dog's head. "We'll have you in an even-better home in no time."

She'd re-homed a lot of dogs in recent weeks. It was a crazy process. Online applications, background checks, references. The dogs, too, needed to be prepped. Health check. Spayed or neutered if that wasn't done already. Travel arrangements. She could have had the whole place emptied out if she wasn't so picky about matching the right human with the right dog. Sometimes she had a person come back two or three times before she

agreed to the adoption. Sometimes it was just once—
like Naomi.

Naomi.

The woman had sent her a video of her kids' reaction when Janus had arrived. It'd made her bawl like a
baby all over again. If she didn't know better she would
swear she was pregnant, but she knew for a fact she
didn't have to worry about that.

The dogs grew restless, but that was to be expected
given they'd just been introduced to a new roommate.
One of them started to bark. Then another.

"Lass das sein," scolded a voice.

Silence. She could hear his footfalls then, turned and
sure enough, there he was.

Ethan.

"Hey," she all but croaked.

"You're back," he said.

"What are you doing here?" She didn't mean to be
rude, but he was the last person she'd expected to see
this time of night.

"I saw the headlights on the road."

Had he? She didn't think that was possible, but she
wasn't going to argue.

"It's late," she said, hoping he would take the hint.

"Why haven't you returned my texts or my calls?"

She lifted her chin. "What was there to say? Whatever your decision, it was yours to make, not mine."

"I'm not leaving."

"I know. Colt told me."

He appeared puzzled. "Then why didn't you want
to talk to me?"

This was the conversation she'd been hoping to have

tomorrow. The one that she'd known would be hard. The reason she'd been crying, she finally admitted.

"Because I didn't want to tell you that, go or stay, California or Montana, it wouldn't matter in the end." She took a deep breath. "I can't do this, Ethan. I can't…" She searched for the right words, the words she'd been hoping she'd have a whole night to find before facing him. "I can't be in a relationship."

"Why the hell not?"

Great. And now he was angry, only that wasn't the look in his eyes. No. He seemed determined.

"I don't want to hurt…" *Me. I don't want to be terrified of losing you. I can't face another loss.* "Adam," she said instead. "He's still so fragile healthwise. I need to focus on him."

It was a bunch of bunk. He'd be fine. At last she had started to believe that, and if she didn't miss her guess, Ethan thought so, too.

"You're a coward."

She jerked upright. "I am not."

"All this time I thought you were so brave, but in the end, you can't face the truth."

"What truth?"

"You're afraid of falling in love."

"No, I'm not."

"You are. I can see it in your eyes."

"Okay, fine. Maybe I am."

He took a step toward her. She told herself not to retreat. She needed to stay strong. This was for the best. "It's going to be okay," he said, resting his hands on his shoulder. "You're not going to lose me."

"I'm not afraid of that."

Aren't you? Isn't that exactly what's wrong?

"Then why are you pushing me away?"

"Because it won't work out," she finally admitted. "Because my life is too crazy." Lord, it felt good to say the words out loud. "Because we hardly know each other. Because I have a son who has a tender heart and he'll fall in love with you, too, and when it all falls apart, he'll be hurt in the process."

"No," he said with a shake of his head. "It won't fall apart. Have some faith."

"Faith." She huffed in derision. "I had faith my husband would get better, and look where that got me."

He drew back, clearly surprised by the venom in her voice, but it felt good to let that out, too.

"I had faith that nothing else bad would happen, but look at Adam."

"He's getting better."

She ignored his words. "And before that. I had faith that my dad would change. That he would stop beating the crap out of me and my brothers, but he never changed. Even at the bitter end he was just as cold-hearted and mean as he always was. You know what he said to me just before he died?" She swallowed back a lump of emotion in her throat. "He said maybe if I'd taken better care of my husband he wouldn't have died."

It was as if she'd struck him. "That's horrible."

"But you know what, there's a part of me that wonders if he was right."

"No, Claire, don't think that way." He tried to pull her into his arms again.

She stepped away, and damn it all, the tears were back. "He insisted Colt take care of him. He didn't want me to do it because I'd done such a lousy job nursing my husband."

"He was sick in the head. He had to be."

"I know that. Just as I know I did everything in my power to help Marcus. I loved that man with every fiber of my being and I'll never love another man like that again."

That hurt him. She could see it in his eyes and she wouldn't be human if his pain didn't cause her pain, too. Still, she lifted her chin as the truth finally came out.

"I'm sorry, Ethan, but that's the truth."

"Is that so?"

She nodded.

"Then I guess there's nothing left to say."

"I guess not."

Still, he didn't leave. They stood there in silence, crickets chirping in the distance, one of the dogs crunching on food, the smell of sage filling the air. These were the things she noticed when she broke Ethan McCall's heart—because that was exactly what she'd done, and if she were honest with herself, it broke a piece of her own heart, too.

"I hope you find happiness, Claire. I hope Adam is all right."

"He will be." Because by the grace of God, she wouldn't lose another thing she loved. Not ever again.

"I'm sure you're right." He moved forward, and she could see that his hands shook and she knew she was responsible for that and it dug at her heart and made her want to vomit, but it was for the best. What she did was for both of them. He would see that in time.

"Goodbye, Claire."

He kissed her cheek. That was all he did before he turned and walked out of her life.

Chapter 19

It was for the best.

The words were her mantra when the next day dawned. For the best, even though it felt like a divorce. He'd asked for Thor. She'd given him the dog without a qualm, but since he didn't plan on driving out to Montana, he'd arranged for shipping. Thus the dog would be in her care for a few more days.

It was Adam who cried when he heard Thor was leaving. Or maybe he cried over the loss of Ethan. He'd been floored by the news that his friend would be gone, and then had been so recalcitrant that it'd been hard to get to the bottom of his moodiness. She, however, had nothing to cry about. She was the one who'd ended it, and thank goodness, too. Look at how Adam had reacted. What if they'd been living together, or worse, married, and it'd all fallen apart?

And would you have married him?

It was the voice, the ever-present voice that had asked the question, the one she always ignored. She did exactly that once again.

"Do you think he thinks about us?"

There was no need to ask who Adam was talking about. They'd just been discussing Thor and the fact that he was due to be shipped out tomorrow. Mariah would be over later today to do a health certificate. Until then they were in the middle of cleaning dog kennels, the only bummer about being well again, Adam claimed: chores.

"I think he's too busy to give us much thought."

She received updates through Colt. Her brother and Ethan had remained friends and so she knew he'd already had his stuff shipped out from his storage unit, something he'd never done while living in Via Del Caballo, which just went to show that he'd never really been serious about living on the ranch. She'd heard he loved working with the dogs. That his new boss was a dream. That he was happy to be back in the same state as his parents.

He had a sister. She hadn't even known that. Funny how you could be intimate with someone and yet not even know the basic facts about their life.

"What do I do with the food Thor didn't eat?"

She'd been so engrossed in her thoughts she hadn't even noticed that Adam had moved on to the next kennel. That he stood in the outdoor run, a shovel in his hand.

Food? "What food?"

"The food in his bowl."

She just about dropped the shovel she'd been holding. Instead she rested it against the wall of the kennel she'd been cleaning, and then headed to Thor's enclosure.

"Doesn't look like he ate any of it," her son observed.

No. It didn't. She bent to examine the bowl. No ants. Sometimes they swarmed the food to the point that the dogs wouldn't touch it. It wasn't super warm out that day, either. Sunny, yes, but cool enough that heat shouldn't have affected his appetite. She moved to the doorway of Thor's dog run. The canine had assumed a position she recognized from before. Sad. Depressed. Not happy.

"Shit."

"Mom!"

She waved her son's complaint away. Okay. So not a big deal. Thor was upset. Ethan had left. Thor probably thought he was gone forever, like his last master. There was just one little niggling fear. He'd coughed a little yesterday. Not a lot, and he'd quickly stopped, but it was just enough...

"What's wrong with him?" Adam asked.

"I don't know, but I'm glad Mariah is coming later today."

Unfortunately, Mariah was as puzzled as she was. "His lungs sound fine. Are you sure you heard him cough? It wasn't a gag on food or something?"

"I'm sure."

Mariah frowned, her red hair so curly she looked like something out of a Disney movie. "Well, I don't think he's got fluid in them if you were thinking canine distemper, but there's no way to know for sure unless I x-ray him. Did you feed him anything different?"

She knelt down by the dog, her mass of red hair pulled back into a ponytail, her belly big enough it was a wonder she could get up and down.

"Nope. Same food as always."

Mariah nodded, pulling out her stethoscope. "Any

chance a raccoon might have gotten into it? Or maybe vermin? They can leave feces behind that can put an animal off the taste."

Claire just shot her a look before saying, "Mariah. Really. When have I ever not taken care of the food that I feed my animals?"

"Just asking," she said, moving the stethoscope. "Never hurts."

No, it didn't, but she was grasping at straws. When she finished moving the stethoscope around, Mariah stood, and Claire could tell it wasn't easy for her.

"Lord, I feel like I swallowed a swimming pool."

Claire eyed her friend. "Not to be mean, but you look like you swallowed an ocean."

"And I'm only six months pregnant," she all but wailed. "Every other woman I've ever known didn't even look pregnant at six months, but me, no, I'm as big as a whale."

"A cute whale," she placated.

"Thanks."

She waited for her friend's prognosis, but it took her a moment between bending back and placing her hands on her hips and moaning in complaint.

"Well?" she prompted.

"I have no idea."

"Really?"

Mariah had the grace to appear abashed. "Everything sounds great. Good gut noises. His lungs are clear. Heart rate normal. I see no reason why he'd be off his feed."

"They why isn't he eating?"

"He's probably missing Ethan."

"You think he's pining?"

"Maybe. It's possible he ate something bad. Or that he's choking from scarfing down too much food. Or that he's caught some kind of bug. Unfortunately, that requires blood work and that I can't do out here. I mean, I can draw it, but you might as well just bring him in. That way I can x-ray him if need be."

That was *not* the news Claire wanted to hear. Usually she could diagnose her own animals. Only in extreme circumstances did she have to bring an animal into a clinic. That it was Thor that suffered right now made it even harder to stomach. What would she tell Ethan?

"When should I bring him in?"

"Today, if possible." Mariah stretched again. "Bring him in after I finish my farm calls. Should be around four."

She hated to wait that long, but she knew Mariah was the best in the business.

A few hours later, however, X-rays didn't reveal anything. No obstructions. No swollen organs. No crazy growths.

"I don't know what to tell you," Mariah said as they stood in front of her laptop peering at the X-rays. "He must be drinking, because his electrolytes are still good. And the markers on his blood panel all look normal."

"He's pining for Ethan."

"It's totally possible, but it's also possible that he has something going on inside that we just can't see. Not yet at least. Give him a few more days."

She wasn't happy with the news. "So no health certificate, then?"

"Not yet. Not until he's eating normally. I can't risk that he might be coming down with something."

Just as she feared. That meant having to call Ethan

and to explain the situation, something she didn't want to do, but that she knew was a necessity as a responsible kennel owner.

But as it turned out, she didn't have to call Ethan. Colt offered to do it, and she was just coward enough to take him up on the offer. But when her brother called her back a short while later, she wasn't so happy with his news.

"He's flying out."

"But he doesn't need to."

"I don't think he cares," said her brother. "He's doing it anyway."

He couldn't get there fast enough. When Colt had called and told him the news he hadn't hesitated. He'd hung up, called airlines and paid the astronomical price to get there the next day. Thor needed him, and his new boss understood.

Still, it felt like a week later though, in fact, it was less than twenty-four hours when he pulled to a stop next to Claire's van. She wasn't in her house. She was out in the kennel with Thor and his heart stopped when he saw the dog lying outside. Surely he'd seen him drive up. Granted, he wouldn't recognize his rental car, but when he stepped out of the vehicle, he would know.

The dog didn't move.

His heart dropped. His eyes fell upon Claire next. She tried to smile. Even from a distance he spotted the attempt, and it killed him to see her there, clearly upset, clearly wanting to ease his fears, unable to do so.

"Mariah looked at him yesterday," she said, the moment he entered the kennel, and it was all he could do not to go to her and put his arms around her. She didn't want him. Fine. He could keep his distance. "She said just to wait and see, and she's the best veterinarian I know, so I trust her."

"Yeah, but she doesn't know Thor like I do."

He had her on that point and she knew it because she didn't protest when he knelt down next to his dog. Thor hardly lifted his head.

"Hey, buddy."

Only when he touched him did he perk up. He looked into Thor's eyes and saw the recognition dawn. His black tail began to thump, but there was no effusive greeting, no open mouth smile, no pricked ears. Thor just stared and in that gaze he caught a look...

His heart stopped.

It was a nearly human plea for help. "He's sick."

"I know, but he doesn't have a fever, and his blood work came back fine. Mariah ruled out a virus and she said his white cell count looked fine so she's not thinking cancer. He's just...listless."

He instantly went to work, opening Thor's mouth. Gum color good. No extra saliva indicating his stomach might hurt. No abscessed teeth.

"Do you have a thermometer?"

"He doesn't have a fever."

"Not yet, but I'm betting he will sooner or later."

Green eyes held his gaze and he marveled at their beauty. It might have been only a few days, but it was as if he'd never seen her before. Black hair. Soft red lips. Honey and vanilla.

Claire.

"I'll go get it."

He nodded, though his hands had started to shake, but it wasn't because of anxiety. It was being around

Claire, he suddenly realized. She was it. His soul mate. And he just then realized it.

"It's okay," he told Thor, although he spoke more to himself than to the dog. He would fix Thor up, and then head back to Montana because that's what she wanted.

"Here," she said, handing him a plastic tube that contained a canine thermometer. She helped to hold the dog while he checked to see if he had a fever. When he read the digital readout, he thought he'd misread it.

One hundred and four degrees.

Shit.

"What does it say?"

He showed her the thermometer. "Shit," she echoed his thoughts.

"I'm going to need access to an X-ray and an ultrasound. Whatever's causing his infection might show up now on a scan."

"Mariah told me to bring him back today. Let's just go."

"Where's Adam?" he asked as he scooped Thor up, the big dog heavy in his arms, but he didn't care.

"At Colt's."

Good, one less thing to worry about. He glanced down at Thor. The fact that the dog didn't struggle was another indicator of just how sick he was. He didn't feel well enough to move and so he instantly relaxed in his arms.

That was the moment Ethan felt the first twinge of panic.

He'll be okay.

He tried to convince himself. Usually he was the optimist. He really had meant it when he'd told Claire to stop fearing the worst, but that was before she'd sent him away, so he was running a little low on optimism right now, and Thor only added to the mix.

They arrived at the clinic in record time, mostly because Claire drove like a crazy woman. She'd had him call to warn her friend they were on their way, so when they pulled up to the back door of a single-story wood building, it instantly opened, and a woman with a mass of red hair greeted him.

"You must be Dr. McCall."

He recognized the woman's voice from the phone. "And you must be Dr. Johnson."

"I am." She was so pregnant her lab coat didn't cover her bump. "I'd say it was a pleasure. But it's not a pleasure to meet under these circumstances." She waddled to the back of the van.

"No. It's not."

They worked in tandem, though Ethan did all the lifting. He liked that they seemed to read each other's minds when it came to diagnosing the dog. Together they went through the necessary steps to figure out what was wrong.

They came up empty.

"It's not cancer," Mariah said after looking at his blood work for the tenth time. Claire just stood back and watched and it occurred to him that she had a lot of experience with that. How many times had she done the same thing, first for her husband and then for her son?

"At least I don't see anything to indicate that," Mariah added.

He'd scanned the same test results and came up with the same answer. No cancer indicators. Not a virus. Definitely an infection of some sort, they just couldn't find it. Short of opening him up and doing exploratory surgery there was nothing they could do. They would have to wait to see if the infection that clearly wreaked havoc on his body would eventually show itself. Could be a tiny stone in his kidneys, or a foreign body, or a staph infection. Lord knew what it could be, just that Thor was sick and growing more ill by the moment.

"We can keep him in the back," Mariah told him.

They'd given Thor a sedative, not that he needed it. It just made things easier when dealing with X-rays and scans.

"I'm sorry," Claire said once they settled Thor into an oversize crate.

"What are you sorry for?" he asked, stepping back.

"This happened on my watch."

"And you noticed he was off before whatever this is manifested itself into a fever."

"Actually, it was Adam who noticed he hadn't finished his food."

"And you didn't just dismiss it as an upset stomach."

Lord, it was hard not to pull her into his arms. He wanted to console her so badly it was a physical ache. Any doubt that he wasn't in love with her had disappeared the moment he'd spotted her kneeling by his dog's side. If anything, time away had made him love her all the more. She just didn't love him, though. Would never love him. The words still stung to the point that he had to look away.

"Did you need me to stay?" she asked.

"No," he said sharply. Too sharply. He looked up, spotted the hurt in her eyes. "I'm sorry. Just worried about Thor."

"I understand."

Yes, she did. If anyone understood what it was like to fear for something you loved, she did.

"I've got it from here. You can get back to Adam."

"Actually, Colt is watching Adam and he'll be just fine there. I don't want to leave, either."

"It may be hours before we know anything. At this point it's just a waiting game."

"I'm good at waiting."

He would bet that was true, too, and it broke his heart all over again.

"I just don't understand," he heard her say. "He's been doing so well. I've been taking him for walks out behind Colt's property and he loves it. His favorite game is to play hide-and-seek in the weeds."

He could picture Thor doing that. Could imagine him crouching down behind—

He jerked upright. "Wait. You've been walking him where?"

"Out behind Colt's property. We follow the creek, and then I turn back and we walk across the big pasture."

"Son of a—"

"What?"

"There are foxtails out in that pasture. I saw them that day I walked with you."

"I know, but they're everywhere, and animals usually sneeze like crazy when that happens."

"Sometimes. Sometimes not. And it's not something we've checked for."

He saw recognition dawn. "Then we probably should."

They found Mariah in the back room washing blood off her hand.

"I hate small animals," Mariah said, showing them

a dog bite. Or maybe a cat bite. "What's up? You two look anxious. Thor okay?"

"Foxtail," was all Ethan said.

She lifted a brow. "I checked him for that when he came in."

"In his throat or in his nose?"

"Just his nose." She shook her head. "To tell you the truth I ruled it out pretty quickly because he wasn't sneezing or coughing or gagging."

"Yeah, but I've seen shrapnel get stuck in some pretty crazy places. No symptoms other than they get sick as the foreign body becomes infected, kind of like what we're dealing with now." He turned to Claire. "Colt said on the phone he coughed a little the other day."

"He did." And her spirits sank. "When we were out on that walk."

He turned back to Mariah. "Do you have an esoph-agoscope?"

"Of course."

"Mind if I use it?"

"No. Of course not."

Mariah bandaged her finger—compliments of a cat, she explained—while her assistant, a girl named Alyssa, helped them set up. It didn't take long, but it did mean putting Thor under general anesthesia, which meant waiting for the muscle relaxant they'd given him to wear off. As the minutes ticked by and Ethan had to wait, he became more and more convinced of his diagnosis. It all fit. The brief coughing spasm. Foxtails, especially the small ones, could act like darts. They could lodge themselves into the wall of an esophagus like a thumb-tack. It would hurt to swallow, which would put Thor off his food. Depending on where it was lodged, he wouldn't cough anymore, either, just be in pain. Then the infection would set in…

"It'll be okay." Claire touched his arm. "He's in good hands between you and Mariah."

It was just a dog, he reminded himself, but caring for that dog, trying to fix him up—it brought it all back. His time in the field. Watching dog after dog fight for their life. The chaos and madness and sadness of practicing medicine on animals that were soldiers, most of them wounded in the field. No wonder he didn't want to go back into practice. He didn't like the memories that came along with doing what he used to do. Much easier to focus on breeding dogs. And training dogs. That way he didn't have to remember, or be reminded.

Claire moved. He barely noticed. She tried to slip her arms beneath his own. He didn't want her to touch him. It was hell to want her and know that she didn't want him back.

She had told him she could never love another man the way she had loved Marcus. Her words still cut with the sting of a razor. But somehow she wiggled her way through, and he couldn't stop from holding her back. It felt good. So damn good. She was his anchor. The one thing on Earth that kept him sane. The cement that kept his feet on the ground. The one thing that could always soothe his anxious mind.

"We should be good to—" Mariah drew up short when she spotted Claire in his arms.

He pushed her away, and it was one of the hardest things he'd ever had to do. "Let's do it."

Chapter 20

He'd pushed her away.

Claire told herself that she deserved it. She was the one who'd broken things off with him. Who'd hurt him. Who continued to hurt him because it was clear he still had feelings for her. She just hoped they could still be friends.

He's way more than a friend.

She shut the door on the thought. She knew what she felt for him, and it wasn't love. It couldn't be love. She didn't have the heart to love someone again.

"Ready?" she heard Mariah ask.

Somehow they'd prepped Thor without her noticing. The dog lay sprawled on a stainless steel table, prone, the IV still attached to his leg. She forced herself to focus. She wanted to help, although between Mariah and Ethan and no less than two veterinary technicians, she felt like a third wheel. No. A fifth wheel.

"Here we go," Ethan said, inserting the scope down Thor's throat. The video screen filled with an image that looked like the inside of a giant, pink worm. The opening was wide at first and then narrower and narrower until all that she could see was the pink and the white. He fished the probe down slowly, and Claire knew both he and Mariah were scanning the digital screen for signs of anything out of place. As it turned out, they needn't have worried because the brushy tip of a foxtail was obvious even to her.

"Look at that," Mariah said in relief.

Ethan just nodded. "The wound is infected, too. Been bleeding into his stomach."

"No wonder he isn't interested in eating," Mariah said. "He's had a stomach full of yuck. Not to mention, that has to hurt."

"Can you pull it out?" Claire asked.

"I'm going to try." Ethan straightened. "Unless you'd like to do it," he said to Mariah.

Mariah leaned back, patting her belly. "Are you kidding? I don't think I could get close enough to the table to do a good enough job."

That wasn't true, but it was clear Mariah had complete confidence in Ethan. And why wouldn't she? He'd been a veterinarian on the front lines. Emergency situations were nothing new to him. She could tell by the way he handled himself.

"Okay, let's do it, then."

"You'll need to get hold of it by the bottom," Mariah said, a frown on her face as she watched. "Those things are notorious for coming out in pieces."

"I know."

He moved the probe this way and that by twisting

it around. He got the thing a little closer to the base of the foxtail, the resolution on the screen refreshing and instantly changing so that the image was sharper.

"That's amazing." She'd never watched a vet use a probe before and she was fascinated by Ethan's expertise. In a matter of minutes he had the thing where he wanted, squeezed on something on his end, the tiny ends closing, Ethan pulling back…

Out it popped.

There were audible sighs all around. Claire resisted the urge to shout. If Ethan hadn't been able to remove the thing it would have meant surgery and that added a layer of risk that a sick dog didn't need.

"Thank goodness," Mariah said with a wide smile.

He placed the seed pod in his hand. Such an innocuous weed, yet so deadly.

"I'm sorry," she said again.

"What are you sorry for?" Mariah asked.

"I was the one taking him on walks." To think about Ethan. To try to understand why she felt so empty inside. "I heard him cough. I should have kept a closer eye on him."

Mariah moved to her side. "You had no way of knowing what happened. Most dogs inhale these things through their nose. It's crazy that it went down his throat, but it's good. Much easier to fix." She patted her on the back. "You are not to blame."

"We'll need to monitor him," Ethan said. "I don't like how infected the area looked."

"We can keep him overnight," Mariah said.

"I would appreciate that."

"I'll call Colt and ask if you can stay there again," Claire offered.

"No. That's okay. I can stay in a hotel."

She had no reason to feel hurt, no reason at all, but she did. "You don't have to do that."

No. But he would, because breaking up with her had hurt and she could see the lingering evidence of that hurt in his eyes.

"Well, okay," Mariah said, clearly sensing the tension in the air. "I'll have my receptionist make some calls for you, then. There's a few hotels nearby."

He held her gaze for a split second longer, and in his eyes she spotted anger and sadness and a plea for something. Then he tore his gaze away and looked at Mariah. "I'd appreciate that."

She found herself backing away from him.

"Do you mind bringing Thor out of anesthesia?" Mariah asked. "I have a patient to see in the front."

"I don't mind at all."

"I think I'm going to leave."

They both turned to look at her, Mariah's expression turning to one of concern. "Are you okay?"

"Fine," she said with a mouth so dry it was like swallowing the Southern California desert.

"You look a little sick," Mariah observed.

"I'm fine," she repeated. "Just going to head on out of here so I'm not in the way."

And so I can't see the sadness in Ethan's eyes. Sadness and regret. Love and understanding. Desire and regret. And she felt it, too.

She turned away from her friend so quickly she almost slipped on the tile floor. She ran toward the back door without another word. When she burst outside, she sucked in a breath because she couldn't breathe all of a sudden.

You're losing it, said that little voice.

No. She wasn't losing it. She was just admitting the truth. It wasn't that she *didn't* love Ethan. It was that she did. Dear Lord. She loved him. And he was so disappointed in her. She could see it in his eyes. And he didn't want anything more to do with her and it was all her fault. She'd pushed him away.

Because you're a coward.

She tipped forward, resting her hands on her knees. No. She was afraid. A coward would jump in a car and drive away and never look back, never admit how much the thought of loving him scared her because it meant opening herself up to the risk of loss. Again. She didn't think she'd survive another heartbreak.

You can't think like that.

It was Ethan's voice that she heard in her head, his words so soft and gentle that she squeezed her eyes shut.

"Claire?"

She stood quickly, the change in altitude causing her vision to blur and for her to sway. He stepped forward and caught her before she fell.

"Claire, what's the matter? Was it the procedure? You looked ready to pass out in there."

She stood there for a moment, her throat swollen, unsure what to say, a part of her wanting to push him away, another part of her wanting to collapse in his arms.

"Claire?" he said, and she saw it then. He didn't hate her. He still loved her. A lot.

She had to take a deep breath, had to steel her heart as she looked into his eyes.

"I love you," she whispered.

She felt him stiffen, but she rushed on. "I love you and I told you to go away and I'm such an idiot, because it took me until right now, right this very second, to recognize the truth."

His eyes were steady as they searched hers, but he didn't say anything, just held her gently.

"And I'm scared."

Only then did he move, and it was so he could rest a palm against the side of her face, the gesture so familiar from their night of lovemaking and so dear that she felt tears come to her eyes.

"You don't have to be scared," he said softly.

"But what if I lose you?"

There it was. Her worst fear. The one that kept her from telling him to stay and from falling into his arms.

His other hand lifted. "You might." He cupped her face. "And I might lose you, too."

She shook her head.

"No. Don't shake your head. I might lose you, Claire. Neither one of us knows how much time we have."

"Ethan."

"And so, in a way, I'm just as scared as you are."

She blinked. "You are?"

He nodded, green eyes filled with tenderness and something else. "Terrified. But I'm tired of being afraid, Claire. When I came back from the Middle East my hands shook for weeks. I couldn't sleep at night. I had nightmares." He looked down. "I still have nightmares," he confessed, but then his gaze connected with hers again. "But you helped me to see that no matter what happens, no matter how much we lose, it's worth it to fight."

She forced herself to breathe. "I did?"

He leaned his head down close to hers. "You're the bravest woman I know, Claire."

"No, I'm not."

"Then let me be there for you," he said. "Let me carry the weight of your worries."

His words took her breath away.

"I love you," he said, rocking her, holding her, trying to reassure her. "Leaving you was the hardest thing I've ever had to do in my life. It was like dying myself. Don't make me live without you, Claire, because that's something to fear. That's a life I don't want to lead."

"Oh, Ethan."

He leaned back again. "I love you, Claire Reynolds. I have no idea what tomorrow will bring—nobody does—but I know I don't want to face it without you by my side."

She started to cry. He wiped the tears away.

"I don't want to, either," she confessed.

He started to smile. "Good."

She started to smile, too, because she was tired of fighting her feelings for him. She'd been fighting them since the first moment she'd seen him standing there on the tarmac, sadness stamped into his face. Fighting them when she'd watched him work with the dogs, so kind to them and gentle. Fighting them when he took care of her. Fighting them as she watched him work with her son.

"I love you," he said again.

"I love you, too," she said.

"Marry me?" he asked.

She closed her eyes, warm tears falling. She gave up then. She would give him her fears, just as he asked, and her heart. She reached up on tiptoe and kissed him, and it was funny, because it was as if his love poured into her soul. That love washed the fear and sorrow and sadness of the past away. A moment later, when she looked into his eyes, even more tears fell. It was *her* turn for happiness. *Her* turn for a marriage that lasted a lifetime—that was the promise in his eyes.

And for once, she believed.

Epilogue

"Mom! Mom! Mom! Wake up! It's happening."

Claire sat up so fast, she clocked her elbow against the lamp sitting on her nightstand. "Ouch," she cried, blindly grasping for the thing before it crashed to the floor.

"Hurry," Adam added, the crack of light that stretched from the bedroom door seeming to slice the room in half.

"I'm coming, I'm coming," she murmured sleepily, glancing at the clock. Two o'clock in the morning. Of course it would have to be at 2 a.m. Wasn't that when every pregnant mother gave birth? She glanced at the spot where Ethan had lain next to her earlier that evening. He'd been called out to a farm and actually he was the one that insisted babies—even the furry kind—always seemed to know when nobody was around.

"Who called?" she yelled to her son, but he was already gone, probably off to get dressed. How had she not heard the house phone?

You're exhausted.

Planning a wedding. Organizing a baby shower. Traveling between her place and Ethan's. They didn't want to live together. Not until they were married. It'd surprised her how old-fashioned Ethan turned out to be when it came right down to it. He even refused to live at Colt and Natalie's place, insisting he get a place of his own. So they sneaked around behind Adam's back, keeping their visits short, although tonight's visit had been preempted with Ethan leaving before Adam came home from spending time with his aunt and uncle. It was hell, but she'd set a date around Christmastime. Chance would be out of the Army by then. She'd have her whole family around her, including Natalie and Colt's new baby.

Speaking of that…

She hurriedly pulled on her clothes. No time to doll herself up, at least not according to Adam, who practically bounced on his toes.

"Took you long enough."

She ignored him, even though inside she smiled at his impatience. There was little doubt her son was on the mend. His blood tests continued to show no signs of cancer, so much so that they were told not to come back to the doctor for another six months. By the time she and Ethan were married she hoped to receive the gift of her son's official remission. Adam's doctor seemed to think that was more than probable. And one thing she'd learned during this whole ordeal—doctors didn't say things like that unless they were pretty darn sure.

"Have you heard from Ethan?" She started her van,

glancing over at the row of kennels. Thor's was empty. The former combat dog had become Ethan's constant companion. Ethan took him everywhere, even when he was called out at night.

"That's who called."

So he was already at the hospital. Good.

They arrived in record time, although not fast enough for Adam, who raced through the clinic's back door. She raced, too, if she were honest with herself, because now that the time was finally here she couldn't wait to see what the stork would bring them.

"Is she okay?" Adam asked when he spotted Ethan standing by a room off to the side of the main examination area.

"It's all looking good." He caught her eyes and his smile did the same thing to her that it always did. It made her insides warm and her spirits lift in a way that always seemed to make her feel less troubled, less anxious—and loved. "I think she's going to be okay."

Claire moved up next to him, peering into the room that was lined with kennels, one at the end containing a female Belgian Malinois that panted as if she'd run a mile.

Thor's babies were about to be born.

As if sensing his impending fatherhood, Thor stood in the middle of the room, a low-pitched whine barely audible above the drone of the electronic equipment in the exam room.

"So no C-section?"

Ethan wrapped an arm around her, drawing her close, a smile on his face as he stared down at her. "I don't think so. I did an ultrasound when I noticed she was dilated and I actually think she's going to be okay.

All that worry for nothing, although I'm glad we kept her here just in case."

They'd been worried that as a maiden bitch she might have trouble delivering. It was common to Belgian Malinois, being more slight of frame than their German shepherd cousins.

"Well, I'm glad you looked in on her before going home."

He nodded. "Going to be a long night."

"But you're used to it."

He was the hardest-working man she'd ever met. Once he'd made the choice to go back into veterinary work he'd thrown himself into it whole hog. Mariah couldn't stop singing his praises. Together they'd increased their client base by 50 percent—in just a few months. They were already talking about bringing on another veterinarian. Ethan even had someone in mind, a friend of his from the Army.

"I'm used to it, but it'll make for a long day tomorrow."

She nodded in sympathy, only to jump when the back door burst open, a pregnant Natalie sailing through the door. Her sister-in-law was one of those women who didn't look pregnant, not yet at least, unlike Mariah, who'd given birth to a healthy baby boy a few weeks ago. It was why Mariah had brought Ethan on board, although she'd long since asked to make it permanent. Ethan had accepted and so the Via Del Caballo Veterinary Hospital had a new partner.

"Well?"

"I can't believe you came down here," Claire said.

"Are you kidding? I wasn't going to miss this. That's my bitch in there."

The words sounded so funny they all laughed. Natalie had purchased the female Belgian based on Ethan's recommendation. She wanted a dog to help protect the ranch and the precious number of high-dollar horses they cared for, but she didn't want to take a dog from Claire's program, and since Ethan wanted a breed, a plan had been born. Four months later that plan was about to happen.

"Well?" Colt asked, bursting in next.

"Nothing yet," Ethan said.

Her brother wore his usual denim shirt and black cowboy hat. He caught her gaze and shot his gaze heavenward before saying, "You'd have thought we were on the way to the birth of Jesus."

"I can't wait to see what my baby's babies look like," Natalie said.

"You say that now, but wait until you have to take care of them all," Colt said.

"How could you not love taking care of puppies? Besides, they'll be at Claire's until they're big enough to come home."

She clearly had him there, and Claire had to smile. If she and Ethan shared half the love her brother shared with his wife, they'd be the luckiest people on Earth.

As if sensing her thoughts, Ethan's gaze caught her own, his eyes softening, and there it was again, the feeling of peace and happiness and contentment.

"Something's happening," Adam said.

They'd talked about banning him from the birthing room, but it wasn't as if her son hadn't seen cows born in the pasture, and so her six-year-old stared transfixed as Lady went to work. Ethan moved in close. Natalie moved to the head of her dog, soothing her. She'd owned the dog for four months, but it was clear they were already bonded.

"It's a boy!" Ethan announced.

"Whoo-hoo," Adam said. "My own Thor."

As if he could hear his name, the father of the puppies whined again. Claire smiled and patted his head. Soon Natalie would be giving birth. Then it would be their turn. With any luck, she and Ethan would have a child of their own next year.

As if sensing the direction of her thoughts, Ethan met her gaze again, a puppy cuddled in his arms. She didn't know why, but the sight of her big handsome military hero holding that tiny bundle of fur made her heart flip over backward. He smiled. She did, too, her eyes misting up as she watched her family huddle around the dog, even Colt assisting at one point. Nine puppies later, Lady was all done, mom and puppies resting quietly while brother, sister, wife, fiancé and son looked on.

"That'll be you soon," Colt said to Natalie.

"Good Lord, I hope not. If I give birth to nine babies someone will need to shoot me."

They all chuckled. Claire felt a hand on her back. She looked into Ethan's eyes. She knew he was thinking the same thing she was. One day they would be pregnant. One day Adam would have a brother or a sister. One day their family would be complete. It might not happen next year. It might not happen for a while, but Claire was okay with that. They had their whole life ahead of them.

"I love you," he silently mouthed.

She smiled, lifted her head, kissed him as a way of answering back.

Adam snuggled up next to them. Her hand fell on his

shoulder and in that moment, that exact second, Claire knew the dark days were behind her. It was as if God gave her a glimpse into the future, a moment of clarity in which she somehow knew that it would all work out. Adam would be cured. Ethan would love her forever. And if there were bumps in the road, their love would carry them through.

And it always did.

* * * * *

WE HOPE YOU ENJOYED
THIS BOOK FROM

HARLEQUIN

SPECIAL
EDITION

Believe in love. Overcome obstacles. Find happiness.

Relate to finding comfort and strength in the
support of loved ones and enjoy the journey
no matter what life throws your way.

6 NEW BOOKS AVAILABLE EVERY MONTH!

"Don't look at me like that, April."

She raised her gaze to his. "Like what?"

His fingers tightened in her hair and her mouth ran dry.
She swallowed. Moistened her lips.

She wasn't sure if she moved first. Or if it was him.

But then his mouth was on hers and like everything
else about him, she felt engulfed by an inferno. Or maybe
the burning was coming from inside her.

There was no way to know.

No reason to care.

Her hands slid up the granite chest, behind his neck,
where his skin felt even hotter beneath her fingertips, and
slipped through his thick hair, which was not hot, but
instead felt cool and unexpectedly silky.

His arm around her tightened, his hand pressing her
closer while his kiss deepened. Consuming. Exhilarating.

Her head was whirling, sounds roaring.

It was only a kiss.

But she was melting.

She was flying.

And then she realized the sounds weren't just inside her head.

Someone was laying on a horn.

She jerked back, her gaze skittering over Jed's as they both turned to peer through the curtain of white light shining over them.

"Mind getting at least one of these vehicles out of the way?" The shout was male and obviously amused.

"Oh for cryin'—" She exhaled. "That's my uncle Matthew," she told Jed, pushing him away. "And I'm sorry to say, but we are probably never going to live this down."

Don't miss
A Promise to Keep *by Allison Leigh,*
available March 2020 wherever
Harlequin Special Edition books and ebooks are sold.

Harlequin.com

IF YOU ENJOYED THIS BOOK
WE THINK YOU WILL ALSO LOVE

LOVE INSPIRED

INSPIRATIONAL ROMANCE

Uplifting stories of faith, forgiveness and hope.

Fall in love with stories where faith helps
guide you through life's challenges, and discover
the promise of a new beginning.

6 NEW BOOKS AVAILABLE EVERY MONTH!

SPECIAL EXCERPT FROM

LOVE INSPIRED
INSPIRATIONAL ROMANCE

Can the new teacher in this Amish community help the family next door without losing her heart?

Read on for a sneak preview of
The Amish Teacher's Dilemma *by Patricia Davids,*
available in March 2020 from Love Inspired.

Clang, clang, clang.

The hammering outside her new schoolhouse grew louder. Eva Coblentz moved to the window to locate the source of the clatter. Across the road she saw a man pounding on an ancient-looking piece of machinery with steel wheels and a scoop-like nose on the front end.

When he had the sheet of metal shaped to fit the front of the machine, he stood back to assess his work. He knelt and hammered on the shovel-like nose three more times. Satisfied, he gathered up his tools and started in her direction.

She stepped back from the window. Was he coming to the school? Why? Had he noticed her gawking? Perhaps he only wanted to welcome the new teacher, although his lack of a beard said he wasn't married.

She glanced around the room. Should she meet him by the door? That seemed too eager. Her eyes settled on the large desk at the front of the classroom. She should look as if she was ready for the school year to start. A professional attitude would put off any suggestion that she was interested in meeting single men.

LIEXP0220

Eva hurried to the desk, pulled out the chair and sat down as the outside door opened. The chair tipped over backward, sending her flailing. Her head hit the wall with a painful thud as she slid to the floor. Stunned, she slowly opened her eyes to see the man leaning over the desk.

He had the most beautiful gray eyes she'd ever beheld. They were rimmed with thick, dark lashes in stark contrast to the mop of curly, dark red hair springing out from beneath his straw hat. Tiny sparks of light whirled around him.

"I'm Willis Gingrich. Local blacksmith." He squatted beside her. "Can you tell me your name?"

The warmth and strength of his hand on her skin sent a sizzle of awareness along her nerve endings. "I'm Eva Coblentz. I am the new teacher and I'm fine now."

Don't miss
The Amish Teacher's Dilemma
by USA TODAY *bestselling author Patricia Davids,*
available March 2020 wherever
Love Inspired books and ebooks are sold.

LoveInspired.com

HARLEQUIN

Heartfelt or suspenseful, inspiring or passionate, Harlequin has your happily-ever-after.

With new books published every month, you are sure to find the satisfying escape you know you deserve.

HNEWS2020